ADVANCE PRAISE FOR
RICH LARSON AND TOMORROW FACTORY

"Larson is one of the best new writers to enter science fiction in more than a decade. His stories are always exciting, inventive, evocative, and sometimes profound."
—Gardner Dozois, *The Year's Best Science Fiction*

"One of the most exciting and prolific science fiction and fantasy writers working today. His range—and of course his talent—is remarkable."
—John Joseph Adams, *The Best American Science Fiction and Fantasy*

"*Tomorrow Factory* is an apt description of the stories collected here, all of which explore how technological advances will shape humanity for good and for ill . . . The diverse sexual orientations represented add a refreshing dimension not often found in mainstream sf. A remarkable collection of stories by a highly original writer."

—*Booklist*

"Every now and then the science fiction field sees the arrival of a startling new talent. Rich Larson is just that. A writer of powerful, perceptive stories that stand with the best. *Tomorrow Factory* dazzles with smart, sharp, insightful stories, and belongs on your bookshelf. One of the books of the year."
—Jonathan Strahan, *The Best Science Fiction and Fantasy of the Year*

"Rich Larson's stories crackle with energy and imagination and I'm only a little jealous—signed, the 3rd most prolific short fiction author of 2016."
—Nebula Award-winning author Sarah Pinsker

"Powerful, thought-provoking, and filled with little moments of humanity that makes his stories resonate, Rich Larson's debut collection should be required reading for modern science fiction fans."
— Jason Sizemore, editor-in-chief, *Apex Magazine*

"The most impressive new short fiction writer in science fiction and fantasy over the last few years, bringing to mind writers like Robert Silverberg and Robert Reed. *Tomorrow Factory* is a first-rate introduction: fast-moving, affecting, driving, and powerful."

—Rich Horton, *The Year's Best Science Fiction & Fantasy*

"Enjoyably twisty SF tales with an ample serving of weird tech (and the way it distorts the people who use it). I'll be looking out for more from Rich Larson."

—Neal Asher, author of *Dark Intelligence* and *The Soldier*

"Stories of growl, attack and bite—sentences muscular with taut language, sinewed with concision and outsider sensibility. *Tomorrow Factory* is all that SFF is capable of, all that it hopes to be—and more."

—Ian McDonald, author of *Luna: New Moon*

"Rich Larson writes sharp, ambitious fiction that I can't forget. *Tomorrow Factory* is a fantastic chance to see him at his best."

—Hugo and Nebula Award-winning author Kij Johnson

"Larson has honed his talent playing with reality. Frequently, if I'm not too disturbed after reading one of Rich's tales, I find I'm left, like Finch at the conclusion to 'An Evening with Severyn Grimes,' with 'the ghost of a smile on my face.' It's an experience I highly recommend."

—Sheila Williams, *Asimov's Science Fiction*

"A provocative collection of 23 strange futures . . . [Larson's] colorful settings create strong backdrops for characters striving for goals small and large. This vibrant collection will give thoughtful readers plenty of entertainment."

—*Publishers Weekly*

"*Tomorrow Factory* is sharp, perceptive, and immensely entertaining. Rich Larson is science fiction's most impressive new voice for short stories."

—Rick Wilber, author of *Alien Morning*

TOMORROW FACTORY

COLLECTED FICTION

RICH LARSON

TALOS PRESS / NEW YORK

Talos Press books may be purchased in bulk at special discounts for sales promotion, corporate gifts, fund-raising, or educational purposes. Special editions can also be created to specifications. For details, contact the Special Sales Department, Talos Press, 307 West 36th Street, 11th Floor, New York, NY 10018 or info@skyhorsepublishing.com.

Talos Press® is a registered trademark of Skyhorse Publishing, Inc.®, a Delaware corporation.

Visit our website at www.talospress.com.

10 9 8 7 6 5 4 3 2 1

Library of Congress Cataloging-in-Publication Data

Names: Larson, Rich, 1992- author.
Title: Tomorrow factory : collected fiction / Rich Larson.
Description: New York : Talos Press, [2017]
Identifiers: LCCN 2017031356 (print) | LCCN 2017041862 (ebook)
| ISBN 9781945863318 (Ebook) | ISBN 9781945863301 (paperback: alk. paper)
| ISBN 9781945863400 (hardback : alk. paper)
Subjects: LCSH: Speculative fiction, Canadian. | Science fiction, Canadian.
Classification: LCC PR9199.4.L375 (ebook) | LCC PR9199.4.L375 A6 2017 (print)
| DDC 811/.6--dc23
LC record available at https://lccn.loc.gov/2017031356

Cover artwork by Alejandro Colucci
Cover design by Claudia Noble

Printed in the United States of America

For Gardner Dozois (1947-2018), a giant who lifted others into view

and for Helen Wiebe, with all my love

TABLE OF CONTENTS

INTRODUCTION

James Patrick Kelly

I'm going to introduce you to a new writer in a moment, one who is unlike any new writer I've encountered in my forty-some years in science fiction.

But first, what is a new writer?

You may not realize that new writers can remain "new" for years and years. The clock starts when someone who has been messing around with sentences and scenes in their spare time decides that what they're looking at on their screen is pretty good, and that other people might want to read their work. They have decided that they are writers, although often as not they are reticent to proclaim this. But they work on their craft until they believe they're ready for the next step: submitting their work for publication.

New writers in this phase of their development are sometimes called aspiring writers. Many of them never get the validation they need to persevere through the agonizing slog to the promised land of the first sale, but enough do. After an acceptance or two, the world (or at least a few editors and some readers), will begin to recognize that a new writer has arrived on the scene. The more the new writer publishes, the more folks notice. But it is often the case that, while early sales may portend mastery, they do not necessarily reflect it. We naturally cut the fledgling writer some slack. We say things like, "He's pretty good—for a new writer." In my own case, for example, I published maybe nine or ten stories in professional markets before I hit my stride. I am not ashamed to admit that I served my apprenticeship in print during my new writer years.

In 1993, a Swedish psychologist named K. Anders Ericsson published a paper with the long-winded title "The Role of Deliberate Practice in the Acquisition of Expert Performance." This helped launch what has come to be called "the science of expertise." Ericsson questioned the notion of heritable talent, as in, "She's a born violinist" or "He was born with a painter's eye." Instead, he and others have proposed a different theory of mastery, which is supported by studies across disciplines as various as chess and basketball, business and the arts. The way you get really good at something is a) to practice b) with feedback c) over time. It's a three-legged stool: just practicing isn't enough. Somehow you have to learn what you're doing right and what you're doing wrong. And you have to keep at it for a long time. Popularizers of deliberative practice have come up with a number: 10,000 hours. According to this timetable, if you practiced deliberatively—with proper feedback—for three hours a day, it would take you some nine years to achieve mastery. My own extensive research into this (gossiping with writer pals) largely confirms the basics of deliberative practice theory.

Which brings us to the curious case of Rich Larson. His website tells us that Rich was born in Galmi, Niger, to an American father and a Canadian mother. He has since lived in Grande Prairie, Alberta, studied in both Edmonton and in Providence, Rhode Island, and worked in a small Spanish town outside Seville. He currently writes from Ottawa, Canada.

He is twenty-five years old.

The first time I remember meeting Rich was when he was an undergraduate at the University of Alberta. This would have been at the International Conference on the Fantastic in Orlando, Florida in March of 2014, when he won the Dell Magazines Award for Undergraduate Excellence in Science Fiction and Fantasy Writing. Actually, I may have met him in 2013, when he was second runner up for the award. I'll admit I'm a little hazy about this; I meet a lot of new and aspiring writers. My memory of our meeting in Orlando was that Rich was a quiet and unassuming young man, but a confident one. I had the sense that he was checking out the conference—and our little corner of literature—so he could get the lay of the land. We met again unexpectedly three months later, when I was enlisted at the last moment to fill in for an ailing colleague at the Clarion West Writers Workshop. I was recruited on a Wednesday and arrived in Seattle on a Saturday. Rich was a student at the workshop and I'm still embarrassed that I didn't recognize him on that jetlagged first day. The face was familiar but . . . . Like I said, I meet a lot of new writers. It wasn't until a day or two into my week of teaching that I realized who he was. But I do have a vivid memory of the one-on-one conference I had with him toward the end of my time at Clarion. We brainstormed a problem story and talked about his plans after the workshop. Once again, I was impressed by his confidence and sense of purpose. And his writing was wonderful, mature beyond his years. So I invited him to stay in touch and consider me a resource as he pursued his career. And so here we are, three years later.

But I could never have imagined back then what Rich would go on to accomplish in those three years, and I have a pretty good imagination. If you look him up in the invaluable Internet Science Fiction Database, you will discover that he has published fifty-four stories since 2014. For some writers, that's an entire career! And he has impressed pretty much all editors he has ever sent stories to. In this collection alone, you'll find stories from *Asimov's*, *Interzone*, *Clarkesworld*, *Daily Science Fiction*, *AE: The Canadian Science Fiction Review*, *Lightspeed*, *Apex*, *Abyss and Apex*, *Analog*, *Strange Horizons*, *Escape Pod*, and the anthologies *Clockwork Phoenix 5* and *Futuredaze*.

Being this prolific is an achievement in and of itself, but it's not without precedent in science fiction. Back in the pulp days of the 1930s and 40s, there were writers who could sell their stories almost as fast as they could type them. But were those stories any good? More important to you, are *these* stories any good? I happen to think they're very good indeed, but you don't have to take only my word for it. Consider that stories from *Tomorrow Factory* have appeared in *eight* different Best of the Year anthologies and that one of them, "All That Robot Shit," was voted by the readers of *Asimov's* as the best short story of 2016.

So when I say that Rich Larson is unlike any new writer I've encountered in my career, I am talking about the quantity and quality of his writing. What Rich has accomplished since 2014 is comparable to the amazing early careers of celebrated writers like Lucius Shepard, or Connie Willis, or Samuel R. Delaney.

Except for one thing. Rich is twenty-five years old, and all of those greats began their careers later, sometimes *much* later, in life. When did Rich start his deliberative practice? How did he cram his 10,000 hours in? Dr. Ericsson, I think we have an outlier here!

You hold in your hands the first collection of a new writer. But this is not just any first collection and, new as this writer is, he has already established himself with readers and critics and me as one of our best. The proof is on the next page. So settle in and get comfortable, because even though our journey with Rich Larson has just begun, it has a long, long way to go.

James Patrick Kelly
Nottingham, NH
October 2017

TOMORROW FACTORY

ALL THAT ROBOT SHIT

"**W**e made you, you know."

Carver Seven listens intently. Lately the Man, who also self-designates as Mikhail and Only Human Being On This Fucking Island, has not spoken often. Instead it stares off across the sea in silence, or makes its snuffling animal sounds while excess lubricant from pivoting photoreceptors leaks down the front of its head and spatters the sand. The Man once referred to this process as crying like a little bitch.

At the moment, Carver Seven and the Man are crafting spears in the shade of a storm-bent palm. Carver Seven prefers the sunshine, where his slick, black carbon skin thrums under the life-giving gaze of Watcher-in-the-sky. He tolerates the shade for the Man's sake.

"How made me you I know?" Carver Seven asks, using choppy bursts from his audio port to approximate the Man's wet language. It is far more nuanced than the chattering of the long-limbed climbers in the wood, but also far, far from the streaming clicks and squeals of true speech.

"You're like a damn chatbot, aren't you?" the Man says. "Except you can't link me any porn."

"How made me you I know?" Carver Seven repeats. He has learned to ignore extraneous input, differentiating when the Man speaks to itself from when it speaks to him. Carver Seven works the end of the spear to a sharp point on the bladed edge of his manipulator.

"In some lab, somewhere. Maybe they knew the world was all going to hell. Wanted to leave something behind to keep going after we're gone."

Carver Seven sticks the finished spear into the pale gray sand. "In some lab, somewhere, how made me you metal . . ." Carver Seven taps both manipulators against himself, then indicates the Man's flaky red skin, " . . . from meat?"

"They didn't use meat. They used alloys, and silicon, and, you know, all that robot shit."

Considering the blasphemous idea is an odd thrill. The Man is very wise, in some ways, able to predict movements in the currents around the island and predict weather from the clouds. It claims to have come from a floating metal village that sank into the sea. If the Man could make a metal village, maybe it could make other metal things, too.

Or repair them.

Carver Seven compares his gleaming black form—nimble treadfeet and deft manipulators and prehensile photoreceptors—to the labored collection of blood and meat and bone sitting beside him. The Man has come close to involuntary shutdown three times since it washed up on the island, whether by the elements or the animals.

There is a dim physical resemblance, but, if anything, the Man is a fragile facsimile. It seems improbable, along with blasphemous, that the Man could have created him, or even that the Man could repair a particular Carrier's caved-in head. His hope fades slightly.

"No," Carver Seven says.

"Then where did you come from, smart guy?" the Man asks.

Carver Seven moves from the shade and points one manipulator to Watcher-in-the-sky's burning photoreceptor, hanging high above the cobalt sea.

"Then where did I come from the sky, smart guy," Carver Seven says. "Look at me now." He pries open his head so the Man can see the lifelight burning steadily inside of him, see his thoughts sparking and colliding. "Piece of Watcher-in-the-sky to each baby one of Watcher-in-the-sky," he explains.

"Sun-worship," the Man says. "How original." The Man returns to its spear, stripping it with the sharp metal digit Carver Seven has also seen it use to gouge symbols, over and over again, into the peeling bark of the palms. "Guess it makes sense. You're solar-powered. You need light to function."

"Yeah," Carver Seven says, beginning a new spear. "But some are learn a new way."

"Good for you," the Man says, staring back across the sea.

Those are the Man's last sounds of the day, and when Watcher-in-the-sky starts to sink, Carver Seven leaves. The clan is situated near the edge of the forest, where Cartographers found an ideal outcrop of stone and Carriers and Carvers used fallen trees to fashion it into a shelter, both from the storms and from predators drawn to the heat of their lifelights during the night.

But before Carver Seven returns to the village, he goes to see Recycler. He picks out her frequency and sees she is at the flat rock outside her shelter, which is slightly deeper in the wood. Carver Seven was the one who helped her rebuild it after the last storm, because the other Carvers claimed task overload. Recycler is the only Recycler. Carver Seven thinks that maybe this is why she stays apart from the clan.

When Carver Seven arrives to the flat rock, he finds her crouched over a dead pig. Recycler has the broad back and strong servos of a Carrier, and sometimes, from a distance, Carver Seven can pretend she is Carrier Three. But she is not. The bladed manipulators splitting open the animal's stomach are unique in shape, and she does things nobody else can do. She is Recycler.

With a gaseous hiss, the pig's innards spill out as pink wet ropes. Recycler sinks both manipulators inside its body, splashing the rock with blood and uncongealed shit. This is not the first animal Carver Seven has seen her disassemble. Sometimes a burrower will trample through the village, and if the clan cannot drive it away they kill it with a spear. They take it to Recycler, and she brings them back the fat to use as joint lubricant, and the skin stretched and cured for waterproofing.

But lately, Recycler has been hunting. Lately, she does something new. As Carver Seven watches, she pries open her hidden mouth, the whirring orifice the clan can use in cases of great need, when Watcher-in-the-sky slips behind the veil for days on end. Carver Seven has used it himself only once, feeding it with crushed leaves and bark to keep his lifelight on during a dark week. The experience was not pleasant.

Now Recycler takes her proboscis, fashioned from bone and tanned skin and parts of old Carrier that Carver Seven recognizes, and sinks it into the dead pig. Carver Seven blanks his photoreceptors. He does not want to accumulate more visual data of the act. He does not like disassembling of any kind. Not since the accident.

"May Watcher-in-the-sky turn his gaze to you," Recycler clicks, acknowledging his presence before they slip into their familiar frequency. "Is it your rotator again?"

"My rotator is well, thank you." Carver Seven flexes the joint she repaired for him a few days prior, to show he has full mobility. Then he places his move in the strategy game they are playing and gives her a rough transcription of everything the Man said during the day. He emphasizes the Man's claim of creation, because he has been turning it over and over in his mind.

"The Man says many interesting things." Recycler wins the strategy game in one deft move—she is too clever, with Carrier Three he could battle back and forth for days on end—and offers him a turn with the proboscis. Carver Seven refuses, as always.

He remembers the first and only time he tried using the animal fuel and how his body rejected the blood and bile, spitting it back up. Recycler has adjusted to it. She can use it to work through the entire night, awake in the unholy dark. The rest of the clan does not know this.

Carver Seven keeps her secret, because she keeps his.

"Is it possible the Man made us?" Carver Seven asks. His photoreceptors stray to the packed dirt behind Recycler's shelter, where his secret is wrapped and buried.

Recycler deliberates another second. "The only way to know if the Man is correct or not is to pry its head open and search its memory," she clicks. "Since you are so certain the Man has a lifelight inside its hairy skull and is not merely an animal like the climbers in the forest."

Carver Seven is silent. It is not the first time Recycler has mentioned the idea. Carver Seven does think the Man has a lifelight, but he does not think it can be accessed the same way. When he first found the Man, blood was leaking from its head.

"May I see her?" he asks.

Recycler gives a long clicking scan to ensure nobody is nearby. Then she reaches down into the hard-packed dirt and begins to dig. Carver Seven joins her, shoveling fast and then slow as they reach the correct depth.

He retrieves Carrier Three's bashed-in head from where it is hidden in the dark earth, far from the gaze of Watcher-in-the-sky, secret from the clan. In violation of the traditions, Carrier Three was not fully recycled after a falling stone crushed her. Carver Seven pleaded and pleaded and pleaded until Recycler agreed to save her head.

Carrier Three's photoreceptors are blank, and she makes no sound in response to Carver Seven's soft clicks. But he knows her lifelight is not fully extinguished. He knows if he waits and watches long enough, he will see a single lazy spark moving in slow circles.

"Nobody can repair a damaged lifelight," Recycler clicks. "Not the Man. Nobody."

Carver Seven puts what is left of Carrier Three deep inside his main cavity and covers it over. Recycler is usually correct. Recycler is clever.

But no matter how slim the chances, Carver Seven has to try.

The next day, he goes to visit the Man again.

"Hey, look who it is," he warbles from a distance, because the Man startles easily, like a bird. It looks up at him. Its photoreceptors are pink and glassy.

"Hey, yourself, robo-butt," the Man says, then returns to its work. There is a storm-felled tree between its soft feet, and it is using the sharp appendage to strip away the branches. Carver Seven looks around and sees remnants of fire, burned pieces of animal. The Man has hunted, how Recycler hunts. Beyond the mess, there are two more trunks already stripped smooth. He wonders what the Man is building.

But his original query is much more important.

"Can you do me a favor and fuck off?" Carver Seven asks.

That gets the Man's attention. Its audio port opens and it makes the clipped noise that repeats, over and over, sometimes when the Man is pleased but more often when it leaks lubricant.

Carver Seven scans up and down the beach. "Can you do me a favor and fuck off and look here and fix it up a bit?" he asks. Then he opens his main cavity and pulls out Carrier Three's caved-in head.

"Whoa." The Man's photoreceptors enlarge. "Did you do that? This some Lord of the Flies type shit?"

"Lord of the Flies type shit?" Carver Seven echoes, trying to parse the new sound units.

The Man shakes its head. "Who is it?" it asks.

Carver Seven thinks hard. He knows what this latest question means, but he does not know how to communicate Carrier Three's name, the beautiful arc of click-squeal-click, into the Man's ugly wet language. Then his subroutines dredge up the sound unit the Man used to wail at the sea, used to punctuate long rambling speeches with.

"She is Anita," Carver Seven says.

The muscles across the front of the Man's head, around its ever-wet audio port and brown photoreceptors, twitch in response to the sound unit Anita. Carver Seven recognizes it as distress. He wonders if he has made a language error. Then the muscles slacken again.

"Don't say that," it says. "You don't understand. Don't have a fucking idea. You're a robot."

"Can you fix it up a bit?" Carver Seven asks.

The Man stares blankly at him, unresponsive.

"You say you make us in lab you know," Carver Seven says, trying to lay things out as clearly as he can. "Is it yes? Is it no? Make her good, please." He extends Carrier Three's head toward the Man.

The Man takes her, gentler than Carver Seven would have guessed from how it handles most objects, and holds her in soft fleshy manipulators. "You think I can fix your friend," it says. It makes the clipped noise, but only once. Its audio port is contorted. "Jesus. I'm not a roboticist, buddy, I'm an electrician. I . . ." Its sounds stop. "This why you been hanging around, then?"

Carver Seven can make no sense of it. Too many new sound units in new patterns, not enough context. "Can you fix it up a bit?" he repeats. "Make to see. Make to talk. Make to think."

The Man looks down at Carrier Three's head. "Sure," it says, the sound coming quietly. "Okay. I'll fix your friend for you. I'll make your friend good."

The Man is going to repair Carrier Three's lifelight. Carver Seven replays the sounds over and over to be sure he has divined the correct meaning. Each loop sends a fragile joy through him.

"But you have to do something for me, too, okay?" the Man says. "You have to help me build this boat and get off this island. Okay?"

"Okay," Carver Seven says, not bothering to ask what this boat is. "Okay, okay, okay, okay, okay."

Carver Seven will help the Man build, and in return the Man will bring Carrier Three back to him.

Over the course of the next three days, Carver Seven learns what a boat is: a collection of trunks and branches lashed together with vines in order to float on top of the sea, as a leaf floats on the surface of a puddle. The Man explains it as they work.

The Man is slow and clumsy and tires easily, but is also clever the way Recycler is clever. Always thinking a move ahead, always ready to change the plan when obstacles arise, when the wood starts to warp or the vines are too brittle.

It gives Carver Seven hope that the Man will be able to fix Carrier Three. Often while Carver Seven works, shredding branches and sanding the logs smooth, the Man sits in the shade with Carrier Three's head. It is difficult to keep his photoreceptors from straying to them. Whenever he looks over, the Man is tapping Carrier Three with its soft manipulators, rapping out mysterious patterns, the muscles of its face clenched in what Carver Seven knows is concentration.

"I just need a few more days," the Man says when he notices. "I'm getting there. Your friend is almost fixed."

"Okay," Carver Seven says, feeling a surge of optimism at the news. "Great, just fucking great."

The Man pushes air from its audio port. "How is it you ended up cussing more than I do? I know I don't cuss that much."

"How is few?" Carver Seven asks. "Few is one few is two few is three?"

"Two," the Man says, putting both manipulators to its sides, looking over the boat. "Few is two."

"Could be Anita fixed up and boat all finished few two days," Carver Seven says, hoping that the two events coincide, that

Carrier Three wakes up to see the finished boat Carver Seven has helped to build. She always liked to see the things Carver Seven made. She could always recognize the distinct marks and flourishes of his manipulators.

The Man's face contorts as if it is briefly distressed. "Could be," it says. There is a long silence. "What do you think Anita means?" it asks softly. "When you say Anita, what's it mean to you?"

Carver Seven thinks hard, looping all his favorite memories of Carrier Three, the ones he views so often they have started to decay.

The broad shape of her back, her thick sturdy joints. The proud way she made stacks of wood and stone look light as air. Her kindness. How she always saved the best material, an interesting piece of driftwood or a particularly soft wedge of rock, to share with him, to watch him shape. Their slow-moving strategy game, their familiar channel, their small secrets. All the things they had done before her lifelight was damaged.

"Anita is you need light to function," Carver Seven says. "Anita is you need and is gone."

"Yeah," the Man says. There is lubricant shining in its photoreceptors. "Yeah. She was always a better swimmer than me. I don't know how it happened." The Man wipes at its photoreceptors to clear them. "Look, buddy, you should take the head back. When I told you . . ." It falls silent, looking at the boat again. "You're just a robot," the Man says, but to itself more than to Carver Seven. "And we're nearly finished. You better head off, tin man. Back to work bright and early tomorrow."

Carver Seven understands the sentiment. "Piss off, get out of here," he says, waving one manipulator in the gesture the Man uses to end a work cycle.

"Yeah," the Man says. "Same to you."

It is still staring down at Carrier Three's head when Carver Seven leaves the beach.

As soon as he enters the village, Carver Seven can tell something is wrong. The air is thick with speech, with the click and buzz and squeal of the clan in deep discussion, but when Carver Seven tunes himself to the frequency he finds it slippery, fragmented. First he suspects he has been damaged somehow, but then he realizes that the truth is far worse. The clan has excluded him.

Shock numbs him for a moment. He has spent most of the past three days out on the beach with the Man, but that is only because the workload in the village has been light. The last storm caused little damage. The decision on a new fence to keep animals out has been delayed while the Cartographers debate its placement. Carver Seven has neglected no duties.

He moves slowly through the village, still grasping instinctively at the speech around him but understanding none of it. Photoreceptors follow his progress. It is only when he sees the other Carvers crafting fresh spears, when he sees Recyler squatting frozen in discussion with the clan's small and nimble Cartographers, that he begins to understand.

"Carver Seven, may Watcher-in-the-sky turn her gaze to you," Cartographer Two says.

Carver Seven feels relief, first, that he can understand again. Then dread.

"We are sorry to have excised you from the debate," Cartographer Two continues. "But it was felt that you are no longer impartial regarding the Man. We have reached consensus without you."

Carver Seven looks at Recycler, but it would be disrespectful to ask her what she has done, and why, when being addressed by the clan.

"The Man, by your own admission, seems able to think and communicate as a clan member would," Cartographer Two says. "Because of that, it must be held accountable for blaspheming. Does the Man not claim to have created the clan? Usurping the role of Watcher-in-the-sky?"

There is only one truthful response. "Yes. It does claim this."

"Because of this blasphemy, we have decided the Man will be shut down," Cartographer Two says. "We go to the Man's shelter in the morning. Recycler has been given permission to disassemble and study its corpse afterwards."

Carver Seven looks at Recycler again and feels something he has never felt before. It reminds him of the Man wailing at the sky, it reminds him that his blades are sharp and he could plunge them into Recycler and damage her, damage her, damage her. She has betrayed him.

Now the clan will kill the Man, and his last hope for Carrier Three will die with it.

Recycler heads quickly toward the edge of the village, back toward her shelter and her flat rock. Carver Seven wants to tell the Cartographers what she does in the night, how she hunts and feeds and no longer needs Watcher-in-the-sky. He doesn't. He keeps her secret. But he follows her to the wood, and in a high piercing frequency, he speaks.

"All this so you can dissect the Man," he says. "So you can suck its blood. You are no better than an animal, Recycler. May Watcher-in-the-sky avert his gaze forever."

Recycler is silent for a long moment. "I told the clan for your sake," she finally says. "So the Man will not lie to you anymore. You will be grateful in the end."

Then she disappears into the forest, and Carver Seven does not follow her. Instead he goes toward his own shelter, the one with a widened frame for when Carrier Three sometimes wanted to pass the storm together. He stops on the way to pick up a branch full of thick green leaves. The other Carvers look over to him. He asks if they have sufficient spears to kill the Man that is so fearsome, with its soft red skin and weak manipulators. They assure him they do.

Carver Seven has no tasks to complete. He can go dormant early if he wishes. He walks into his shelter and begins tearing the leaves off the branch, one by one.

Carver Seven wakes up in the dark. It is terrifying. It feels like his photoreceptors have been gouged out, leaving him blind. But he has no time to be terrified. His early shutdown now gives him only a few moments of residual energy. He reaches for the crushed leaves and opens his hidden mouth.

The orifice whirrs and grinds and Carver Seven feels a different kind of energy, rough-edged and erratic, move through his body. It is nothing like the warm comforting pulse of Watcher-in-the-sky. It feels ugly. He sees why the clan forgoes its use apart from emergency, but this, he reasons, is an emergency.

The dark is awful, but Carver Seven knows where he is. He knows that the distances from the shelter to outside the shelter to the path to the beach have not changed. He starts to walk, hearing his invisible treadfeet slap against packed dirt, rustle against leaves and vines. He feels the forest swallow him and hears the sounds of animals. It is difficult not to imagine them stalking him through the forest, drawn to his heat. Some branches have moved since he last walked these footsteps and each one startles him as it whips against his body.

Finally, he hears his treadfeet rasp on sand. He is on the beach. And even better, there is light. Carver Seven can make out the shape of the shore in front of him, the spiky mass of the forest behind him, even the rippling sea. Confused, he looks up at the sky. It is not the black void he had always imagined it to be when Watcher-in-the-sky blanks her photoreceptor. It is full of small glimmering fragments that look like lifelights thrown up into the darkness.

Recycler never mentioned such a thing. Carver Seven wants to stare for longer, but there is no time. He turns toward the leaning shelter the Man has made in a divot of sand. There is light there, too, from the dying embers of the fire the Man sometimes makes to keep its body warm and alter meat before eating it.

Carver Seven does not want to make noise in case Recycler is awake, as he is. Instead he crouches and moves far enough inside the shelter to place his manipulator against the Man's prone foot.

The Man thrashes upright. "What the fuck?"

Carver Seven gives up on not making noise. "Back to work bright and early," he says. "Look who it is."

"It's the middle of the goddamn night," the Man says. "I meant in the morning, and . . ." It rubs its photoreceptors. "Don't you shut down for night? There's no sunshine."

"Some time you gotta improvise," Carver Seven says. "In morning the Man is no see, no think, no talk."

"What?"

Carver Seven struggles for a way to communicate the concept of involuntary shutdown. He is not even sure the Man is aware of its own mortality. He picks up one of the spears, its tip stained red, and jabs it into the air.

"In morning, other tin mans hunting you," he says. "Other tin mans cut up you."

The Man's photoreceptors go large and Carver Seven knows it understands.

"Learning a new way, huh," it says. "Jesus. You're going to be us all over again. Predation is step one."

"I'll help out you," Carver Seven says. "Make you safe. But you have to do something for me, too, okay? Finish fix it up a bit Anita."

The Man slumps. "You should just let them cut me up."

Carver Seven knows the Man sometimes self-damages for reasons beyond his understanding, but there is no time to learn why. He looks around, sees Carrier Three's head set on a little mound of sand, and picks it up carefully.

"Nearly finished," he says. "Now finish fix it up a bit."

"I can't," the Man says. "I have no fucking idea how a positronic brain works. I lied. I lied so you would help me with the boat. I can't fix your friend."

Carver Seven replays the sounds over and over, unwilling to believe it. The Man can't fix Carrier Three. The Man never could. Recycler was right.

"I did try." The Man makes its clipped noise, just once. "I looked at the wiring and all. But that was done in a lab with lasers and microtools and . . . all that robot shit. I'm sorry, buddy."

"Anita is gone," Carver Seven says, to be sure, hoping desperately the Man will contradict him.

"Yeah," the Man says instead. "Anita is gone." It rubs its head. "Don't think I've said it till now. Said it properly." It pauses. "I'm sorry."

"Why boat?" Carver Seven asks, because he has no way to articulate what he really wants to say, that he has the deep hollow feeling like Carrier Three is being disassembled all over again.

"Thought I'd try to get to the mainland," the Man says. "See if any survivors got carried past this little spit. If any lifeboats made it. Doesn't matter, though. If I don't die here, I'll probably die in the sea. If I don't die in the sea, I'll die somewhere else. Doesn't matter."

Carver Seven thinks again of his sharp blades, how simple it would be to damage the Man. Simpler still to let the clan do it for him. Then he thinks of Carrier Three's kindness.

"Nearly finished boat," Carver Seven says. "Tin mans no go sea. Boat make you safe." He goes to the last tree they felled and dragged, rolling it toward the others.

"You serious?" the Man asks.

In answer, Carver Seven begins stripping the log, short sharp strikes, precise and rhythmic. He is a Carver, so he will carve. He will be kind how Carrier Three was kind.

"You're a better human being than I am," the Man says. "You should know that."

"You should let's get to work," Carver Seven says.

By the time the Man declares the boat finished, the sky is changing color, turning purple and red. The glimmering lifelights up above them are fading away. Carver Seven asks the Man what they are before they disappear completely, in case it knows.

"Stars," the Man says. "They're stars in the sky."

"Stars in the sky," Carver Seven echoes.

The Man pauses. "Some people, you know, they think we go up there when we die. They think our souls . . . our . . ." It taps its head, then its body. "They think a part of us gets to go up in the sky. And watch over the people who are still down here."

Carver Seven parses the information. He looks down at Carrier Three's near-dark lifelight, cradled in his manipulators, and wonders if maybe the other sparks are up in the sky. It seems improbable.

"If you want I could take her with me," the Man says. "Just in case I meet some crazy roboticist."

"Anita is gone," Carver Seven says.

"Yeah." The Man sucks in air through its audio port. "Thanks for helping me. Hope your people aren't going to be pissed at you. Other tin mans hunt you?"

"No," Carver Seven says. He'll tell the rest of the clan the truth, that the Man must have floated away on its boat in the dark. He won't tell them he worked through the night to ensure it. Recycler will guess, maybe, but not tell the others. Carver Seven will apologize to her, and give her Carrier Three's head to finally recycle, but maybe ask that a small piece, just a tiny piece, be soldered to him.

"Good," the Man says. "That's good."

Carver Seven uses one manipulator to help the Man drag the boat as close to the waves as he dares, then steps back. The Man hops on, making the wood bob in the water.

"Guess this is goodbye," it says, with its photoreceptors in danger of leaking lubricant again.

"Crying like a little bitch," Carver Seven says. "Get out of here."

The Man makes its clipped noise, over and over, as it poles out into the waves. Carver Seven can't tell if it is distress or happiness. As Watcher-in-the-sky rises and warms his back, making his steps back toward the village smooth and strong, Carver Seven can't tell which he is feeling, either.

ATROPHY

"**I**f you're having eye problems, you should go see him," Durden said, stripping down. His brow was knitted. Eris put her hand where his muscle sliced lean to hip bone. His brow unknit. He grinned white and made his stomach taut.

"It might not happen again," Eris said. She raised her arms and Durden tugged her shirt up and away. He stowed it in the locker and fed it a token.

Eris looked at her naked reflection a moment longer, then they stepped into the baths. Steam sucked towards her lips. The floor was stark white, prickling with rubber traction pad. The walls were wet marble. Bronze bodies appeared in slices through the fog, sculpted backs and sylph limbs. Relaxed voices mingled. Flesh slapped on flesh.

"Still," Durden said, when they were entwined under a hot jet.

"Still what?" Eris asked, watching the tracery on the wall.

"Getting resynched would be safest." Durden scrubbed under his arm. "How, ah, how did it happen? Exactly? You said things jumped."

"Yes. They jumped."

Eris thought of how to explain it. She'd been walking Addy to the school, crossing the bridge. Then something split the top of her head open. She'd stumbled against the railing but the vines turned to metal under her hands, and when she looked down the bright clear canal had no water, only brackish sludge, and something pale and red-spotted was lying in the mud.

"And then right back to normal?"

"I don't want Addy to know," Eris said, hooking her chin over his shoulder. "She's worried about getting her imps. This would just make it worse."

Durden said something to that, but Eris didn't hear. It was happening again.

The steam vanished, whisked by some invisible hand, and the floor turned slimy cold under her feet. Cracked tiles with black tendrils creeping between the gaps. The rusted shower nozzles were discharging a pale blue foam. Bodies shivered where they stood and laughed and nuzzled against each other. Sagged breasts, sharp ribs. She saw shiny pink scar tissue and puckered lesions.

Eris closed her eyes and didn't open them until she was sure it had passed, and then she buried herself in Durden's unblemished skin.

She'd thought this might happen one day.

"Lind got his imps today, mammy," Addy said. "Showed us them."

"That's early," Eris remarked, spooning yogurt.

"Reckon they bribed the optometrist," Durden said. The yogurt plopped in his bowl and he grinned over Addy's yellow head. Eris tried to picture the optometrist taking a food bribe. She tried to imagine him even eating.

"He says it's blue," Addy said. "And it's all bright and beauty." Her small voice was somber.

"Soon you'll be seeing it too, little duck." Durden tapped his eyelid. "You should be excited, Addy. Your mammy and me, we're excited."

Addy played with her spoon. "Lind says it hurt," she told it.

"Maybe a little," Durden said. "Hell if I remember. You're a big girl, though, aren't you? Six is a big brave girl." He looked sideways.

"Nothing to be scared of," Eris said softly.

"Says he already forgot how things used to be," Addy said. She frowned. "Mammy, why aren't you looking at me?"

"I'm just watching out the window, love."

Addy nodded solemnly. "It's snowing again."

The blank gray sky outside was building clouds in soft stacks. Fluffy flakes pinwheeled down in the breeze, small beautiful crystals that glimmered.

Things jumped. The sky was mottled red, a chemical haze she'd never seen before, and gray scraps were drifting down like feathers. It wasn't snow.

"That's ash." Eris said it before she could catch her tongue.

"It's snow," Addy said.

Eris felt Durden stare at her.

"It's snow," he said firmly. "Your mammy is teasing you."

Later, when Addy was asleep, they argued in whispers over her cocoon of blankets.

"Eris, you said you'd tell me."

Eris, feeling irritable, shrugged. "I know."

"Has it been happening all day?" Durden demanded. "The jumps?"

"If I look at anything too long. Yes." Eris bit at her lip. She reached out and stroked the slice of Addy's hair that showed from under the covers.

"That's why you haven't looked me in the eye all day?" Durden stood up, paced two steps and back. His back was pale and flecked with scars. His back was smooth sunkissed flesh.

Eris blinked. "I don't want to worry Addy."

"You haven't looked at her, either," Durden said. "Don't think that worries her?" A tendon jumped in his neck. He sucked air through his nostrils. "What does she look like?" he asked.

Eris remembered the bridge. She saw her daughter hobbling, sunken-eyed. Hair in pale strands across a distended skull. "Not like Addy," she said, with a hook snagged in her throat. She stroked Addy's head again. She kept her eyes on the ceiling.

Durden's hand clenched around hers. "Then why haven't you gone to the optometrist?"

"I don't know. I will. I don't know."

"People go mad, you know." Durden's voice was shaky now. He deliberately removed her hand from Addy's blanket. "Don't you remember what happened to your mother? They get desynchronized, they go mad."

"Don't talk about my mother," Eris said. She shook her head hard. "It's so much worse than I thought it would be. Than what I remember from before the imps."

"Then get your imps fixed, Eris."

Eris said nothing. Addy rustled in the bed.

"Do you like it?" Durden asked softly. "Does it make you feel like a fucking prophet or something?"

"It's not that."

"What do I look like?" Durden finally asked. She'd been waiting for the question to force its way past his teeth. "Tell me. What do I really look like?"

"Durden."

"Tell me." Durden spread his arms. His smile was pained. "Look at me."

Skin spotted from the radiation, hair in wiry patches. His shoulders stooped and the hollow of his chest was waxpale; his fingernails were yellowed stubs. His ribcage was a skeleton's hand clenched around his chest. Dangling cock like raw hamburger, disease-colored. Puffy lids around matte black eyes.

"Quiet," Eris said. "Addy's sleep—"

"Let's go up on the roof, then," Durden said. "Like old times."

"Quiet," Eris begged.

Durden half-laughed. "It would be like fucking a zombie, right?" He turned away with the bridge of his nose pinched between two fingers. Addy shifted again.

"I'm going to get resynched," Eris said. "I promise."

"You're still beautiful for me. It's not . . ." Durden broke off.

"I promise," Eris repeated.

Durden's shoulders shrugged. His hand rested on Addy's back, rising and falling with her breath. Eris stepped quickly across the rotting floorboard. She pulled on a coat and went into the night before she started to cry.

The world had fractured. Eris looked once and saw pittoresque houses, bricked paths and manicured vegetation. She looked again and the trees were long-petrified, the housing units were pitted concrete, the ground was littered with garbage. The sky oscillated over her head, from a soft velvet strewn with oversized constellations to a dark starless cavern.

She went to the wall. The elaborate carvings had disappeared, leaving sooty iron and barcode stamps in digits Eris couldn't read. She stumbled up the stairs, half-expecting them to give way under her feet. Her clanging was the only noise, that and then a foaming in her ears. Eris held onto the moor in her head, the rolling hills and willowy trees, the deep greens and stony grays through the mist.

She came to the top and looked over. The ground was blasted bare. The mist was a poison-yellow fume that shrouded black rock. Craters from high-impact charges puckered the wasteland and Eris could see nothing green, nothing living. Her breath caught in her throat. She braced herself against the railing.

Eris scanned, scanned, scanned, but did not see her mother's skeleton down among the rocks. She cried. When dawn seemed like a possibility, she left.

Addy's hand was sweaty inside hers as they walked to the optometrist. His hut, metal and composites, hunched on the edge of the town like a stubborn child. Eris hadn't visited it for decades now. Not since her own imps had gone in.

"You'll be fine, love," Eris said. "Remember what Durden said."

"Brave," Addy mumbled.

"Brave. That's right."

They ducked inside. The interior was dim. The optometrist sat behind his machines, fingers dancing over keys and levers. He was tall and stately-looking, silver-haired. He smiled incorrectly as they approached.

"Hello, good morning," he said. His voice moved oddly over the syllables. "We have your gene scheme uploaded and I'm ready to do the procedure. What is your name?"

"Addy," Eris said for her. She closed her eyes.

"Come lie down, Addy," the optometrist's voice said. "We'll have you synchronized in no time."

"Does it hurt?" Addy asked.

"Come lie down, Addy," the optometrist said. Eris heard the swiveling squeak of a padded chair.

"Brave girl," Eris whispered. She leaned down and kissed the top of Addy's head. She heard small feet scuff the floor, then an exhalation as the optometrist lifted her into the chair. Eris swallowed hard and opened her eyes.

A great black insect, a thrumming machine, some combination of both. The optometrist click-clacked around the chair on spider's legs. Tendrils telescoped and moved over Addy's face, concealing her. Eris clutched her arms to herself and watched.

"You've come undone," the optometrist said as he worked.

"What?"

"You are not synchronized," the optometrist said. "I can tell. The same thing happened to your genetic donor. Perhaps the tendency is hereditary."

"Concentrate on Addy," Eris said. "Please."

"The procedure is automated." The optometrist paused. "Your implants could be replaced. They are an old model. Interference from the retina can create conflicting images."

"The real images," Eris said.

"I do not make such distinctions."

"Why do you do this to us?" Eris asked.

"You want me to," the optometrist said. He pulled back, and Addy was lying perfectly still with a gray putty packed over her eyesockets. Black button eyes nestled where her old blue ones had been. Addy's head turned. As Eris watched, two small red pinpricks appeared in the glossy black.

"Is it done?" Addy asked. Her small smile was crooked. Her teeth hadn't grown in right.

"We're all finished, Addy," the optometrist said. "Easy, wasn't it?"

"Easy," Eris echoed. She took her daughter's hand and helped her out of the chair. Addy's head was on a swivel. She had a delirium grin. The optometrist scanned each new eye and gave Eris a small bottle of drops for the swelling.

"If you would like your implants replaced, come back tomorrow," he said, then glided back to his machinery.

Eris went numbly to the door with Addy tugging at her arm. The sky outside was radiation yellow. The soil crumbled under their feet.

"Mammy." Addy sighed. "It's so beautiful."

EVERY SO OFTEN

It's cold, but Victor keeps waiting. They'll be coming out soon. He moves the snap pistol to his other hand and the wintry metal bites. There is nothing warm in Mauthausen. The packed dirt streets are frosted. The air is chilled. The people are frozen in their own way, if Victor thinks about it. Sometimes they look more like a photograph than . . .

The butcher shop opens with a slink of steam and light. The assassins emerge, squabbling about directions. One of them is suitably Austrian-looking, with plastered blonde hair and well-synthesized clothes. The other is not. His muddy post-racial melanin stands out sharply against the pallid villagers. A handgun winks in and out of view with the motion of his untucked shirt. Victor doesn't recognize the model. He supposes it is a few years ahead of his time.

Time. He needs to ensure the Quo.

"*Grüss Gott,*" Victor says, rounding the corner of the alley after them. They both whirl. They have frantic eyes, unsteady. They are terrified and elated all at once by what they have come to do. There is a hunger and a purpose shining in their beautiful irises. Neither of them speak German.

"Get lost, you fucking bum," one of them mutters, waving Victor off.

"We must be close," the other one says. "Oh, God, we can do it. We'll actually do it."

Victor has to wonder again how so many have slipped through. Bribery, for the most part. Social conscience could be another factor. Some officials might not try their hardest to prevent an illegal rewind if they secretly sympathize with the cause.

"As unlicensed rewinders in a restricted time and area, you are in violation of the Quo." He didn't mean to mention the Quo. That slips out unbidden. There is a section and subsection he should have snarled at them instead.

Victor has already scanned them for bombs, so he snaps a bullet into each of their foreheads. The shooting is very quiet. He covers the bodies with nanoweave, tucking sprawled limbs under the tarp with practiced motions. He can do disposal later, during the night.

Victor leaves the alley an empty stretch of cold dirt to the eyes of passers-by. He's returned them to the dust. That's the Quo in its essence: some have to return, some have to stay.

One in particular has to stay. It begins to snow, but the flakes don't reach the ground.

They come every so often, the rewinders. Every few months. He waits for them, like partners in a very slow dance, and eventually, after weeks of trudging through dirty Mauthausen and bundling wood for food, weeks of watching for new faces very carefully, they will appear.

Victor is out on the street again, with the snap pistol hidden safely in his left pocket and now the rewinder's handgun in his right. He's passing through the square. The villagers used to seem like ghosts to him, but he understands better now. He's the ghost.

The hut is waiting for him on the outside of the village, a cramped thing where he either sleeps or masturbates. Dirt floor, wooden walls. Victor picks a nail out of the rotting door frame as he enters. He never bothers making repairs. The family will relocate again soon, hopefully closer to Linz. Mauthausen doesn't suit him.

Victor sleeps and has bad dreams. He wakes up when the night is sufficiently dark to move corpses.

Someone else is in the alley. Victor doesn't differentiate the crouched shape from the other weird shadows until it steps forward, pointing a weapon at him. He can't see the face, so he looks down instead to where the nanoweave has been stripped away and discarded in the snow. The men he killed earlier in the evening are going blue and black, tangled crooked like mating insects.

"English?" the man demands.

"If you want," Victor says. The voice sounds young. The stance seems competent.

"This is your job, yes? You're one of their monitors." The rewinder is staying in the shadows. Victor wonders if he has been careless. Nobody should ever find the bodies, even with tracing equipment. But then, there have never been two attempts in such quick succession. Maybe the third rewinder has been here all along.

"Empty your pockets," the rewinder says.

Victor reaches into his coat and pulls out the handgun. He unloads it and drops the dissembled weapon at his feet.

"And the other. There's weight in both."

Victor drops the snap pistol.

"I'm going to kill you," the rewinder says. "But first, I have to ask. I have to."

Victor is familiar with the question, though usually he hears it from a man or woman dying at his feet. He gives the same answer.

"I'm maintaining the Quo," he says simply.

"That's what they call it? That's what they write on your memos?" The rewinder has a tremor in his voice. Disgust, maybe. He doesn't understand.

"That's what I call it. Chronology has to be preserved. The cost doesn't matter." It feels good, surprisingly, to talk to someone in English. He has missed it.

"Turn around," the rewinder says. "I'll walk you to the back of the alley."

Victor turns on his heel, waits. He feels the gun poke into his back, and then they walk. He finds himself looking at a dead brick wall. There's soot on it.

"What's it like, now?" Victor asks.

The rewinder doesn't answer for a few beats. "The same. We've broken time itself, and things are the same." He makes an angry noise. "Your bosses make sure of that. But this year things change. 1894. Anything of note happening this year?"

Victor's hands are cold. He puts them in his pockets. "Kate Chopin writes a short story. Coca Cola sells in bottles." Victor stares into the brick. "Nothing here in Austria."

The muzzle of the gun jerks forward and he lets his head bob with it, like a puppet on a stick.

"I think there will be, tonight," the rewinder says.

Victor still has a nail in his pocket. "It's going to be harder than you think," he says. "You won't like it."

"I've used this before," the rewinder says.

Victor rolls the nail with his thumb. "Not me," he says. "Him. He's young." He feels the man take a step back. Hesitate.

"It's easier to crush a snake egg than kill a cobra," the rewinder says. "It's more certain this way. And I can override any compulsion, social or biological, if it means preventing Auschwitz. Saving millions."

"There's no certainty," Victor says back. "That's the point."

He slams his hand backward towards the voice with a rusted nail locked between his knuckles. His other hand comes up as he turns and jars the gun away. There are flesh sounds. The gun goes off and his eardrums implode; his eyes are filled with oil spills.

Then the man is lying in the dirt and Victor is over him with the gun held steady in cupped hands. The rewinder is not old. He doesn't look out of place in his ragged coat and wool trousers—he could be the son of the butcher. Same age. He is trying to knead his eye, but the nail gouged it out and there is only gouting blood and torn socket.

"You're killing those people," he gasps. "You're killing them all. You're turning on the showers, goddamn you, goddamn you." His chest is spasming.

"I know," Victor snaps. He knows. It's the nature of the Quo. "But if you prevent that, what do you cause? Do you know that? No?"

"Coward," the rewinder sputters.

"It's not worth the risk," Victor says. "Better a known atrocity than the unknown. No matter what it is."

He shoots him before he has to hear a counter-argument. He has enough of those. For all Victor knows, the other bodyguards and monitors have already failed their assignments, and the world is not as it should have been. If he came this close to failure, here behind this butcher shop, how can he be sure of the others' success? The Quo might already be demolished, and his job might be a farce. A farce set in the shithole of Mauthausen.

There's no certainty, not even in the Quo. He hopes he is preventing catastrophe, but sometimes he dreams he is a monster in the dark, saving Belial and murdering angels.

The next morning, Victor goes to the house. As has been his tradition since being deployed five years ago, to Braunau-am-Inn, he finds the small dark-haired boy and watches him play in the yard for a little while.

He wonders if he is a good man or a bad man.

GHOST GIRL

Daudi had another report on his news feed about a ghost girl living in the dump outside Bujumbura, so he put two Cokes in a hydrobag and hailed a taxi outside the offices. It was cool season now and the sky was rusty red. The weather probes were saying dust storm, dust storm, remember to shut the windows.

Daudi put his head back against the concrete wall and wondered how a ghost girl living by herself was not yet dismembered and smuggled out to Tanzania. Maybe some entrepreneur was cutting her hair to sell to fishermen. Maybe she was very lucky.

The graffitied hump of the taxi bullied its way through bicycles and bleating sheep. Daudi slung the hydrobag over his shoulder and pulled out his policense. This was not an emergency, not strictly, but Daudi did not pay for transit if it could be free. The taxi rumbled to a stop and when the door opened, it bisected a caricature of President Habarugira shitting on a rebel flag. He climbed inside and switched off the icy blast air conditioning.

"Bujumbura junkyard," Daudi said, pressing his policense against the touchscreen.

"Calculating," said the taxi.

The junkyard was a plastic mountain, any fence that might have once marked its boundaries long since buried. Bony goats wandered up and down the face, chewing on circuits, while scavengers with rakes and scanners stumped around the bottom, searching for useable parts or gold conductors.

Daudi had the taxi stop well away, before it gutted a tire on some hidden piece of razorwire. It didn't want to wait, but he used the policense again and it reluctantly hunkered down.

There was a scavenger with no nose and no tag sitting in the sand. Stubble was white on his dark skull. A cigarette dangled from his lips. Daudi squatted across from him.

"*Mwiriwe*, Grandfather."

"*Mwiriwe*, Policeman. My shit, all legal." He waved off a fly. "You ask anyone."

"I'm looking for the ghost girl," Daudi said. "She lives here, yeah?"

The scavenger massaged his knobby calves. "Oh, yes."

"How long here?"

"Aye, two weeks, three weeks since she show up. Her and her *imfizi*." He spat into the sand. "She's a little witch, like they say. She's got the thing following her all around."

Daudi squinted up the crest of the junkpile. "How does she survive?" he asked. He saw the scampering silhouettes of children and wondered if one was her.

The scavenger shrugged. "She finds good stuff. Me, I buy some. And nobody trouble her, or that damn *imfizi* take them to pieces." He tapped ash off his cigarette, eyed the hydrobag on Daudi's shoulder. "You here to decommission it? You look soldier."

"I'm here for the girl," Daudi said.

"Witch," the scavenger corrected. "You say it's genes, but it's witch. I know. I see her."

"Goodbye, Grandfather."

Daudi straightened up. He had speakaloud pamphlets in the taxi, ones that explained albino genetics in cheerful Kirundi and then French, ones he did not distribute as often as he was supposed to. But Daudi knew that by the time a man is old his mind is as hard as a stone.

He found the ghost girl rooting through electric cabling, feet agile on the shifting junk. Her sundress was shabby yellow and stained with gasoline. Her hands and feet were calloused. Still, she was tagged: her tribal showed up Hutu and she was inoculated against na-virus. Not born in the street, then.

"Anything good?" Daudi asked.

She turned around and blinked rheumy pink eyes at him. "Who are you?"

"My name is Daudi. I work for the government." He unslung the hydrobag and took out the first bottle. "You want a fanta?"

"Yes." The girl rubbed her pale cheek. "Yes, I wanna."

"Here." Daudi opened the chilly Coke between his molars. *Clack. Hiss.* He held it out. "What's your name?"

"Belise." The ghost girl wound the cable carefully around herself, eyes on the sweating bottle. "Set it down, back up some," she suggested. "I'll get it."

"You don't need to be afraid of me," Daudi said, wedging the drink in a nook of bent rebar. "I'm here to take you somewhere safe. Here, here isn't safe for you." He scooted back. "Belise, do you know what an albino hunter is?"

"It's safe," Belise said, patting a piece of rusty armor. "My *dawe* is here." She clambered down to get the Coke and all at once something very large burrowed out from the junkpile. Motors whirred as it unfolded to its feet, shedding scrap metal. The robot was sized like a gorilla and skinned like a tank. The sensory suite glittered red at him. Daudi hadn't seen an *imfizi* drone in many years and the sight jolted him.

"Shit," Daudi said, as Belise skipped back up the pile, bottle cradled in her grimy hands. He realized the old man had been talking sense.

"My *dawe*," the ghost girl said proudly. "My daddy is very strong." She swigged from the Coke and grinned at him.

Daudi had retreated to the bottom to re-evaluate things. Clouds were still building crenellations in the sky, and now wind whistled in and out of the junk. He skyped the offices for a list of active combat drones, but of course it was classified, and the official line was still that they had all been smelted. He sat and drank his own Coke and watched Belise step nimbly across a car chassis while the drone lumbered behind her, puffing smoke.

There had been many of them, once. Daudi knew. He remembered seeing them stalk across open ground sponging up rebel fire like terrible gods while the flesh troops circled and sweated, lying in this ditch and then another, so fragile. He remembered the potent mix of envy and disdain they all felt for the piloting jackmen, cocooned safe in neural webbing a mile away.

He remembered best when one of the *imfizi* was hacked, taken over by some rebel with a signal cobbled together from a smartphone and a neural jack. People said later that it had been Rufykiri himself, the Razor, the hacker who sloughed off government security like snakeskin, but nobody really knew.

Daudi remembered mostly because that day was when half of his unit was suddenly gone in an eruption of blood and marrow.

Daudi did not trust drones.

"You see, now." The old scavenger was back. He ran a dirty nail around the hollow of his nose. "Nobody troubles her. That thing, deadly. She has it bewitched."

"It's malfunctioning," Daudi said. "Not all of them came back for decommissioning. Crude AIs, they get confused. Running an escort protocol or something like that." He narrowed his eyes. "Not witchcraft."

"Lucky malfunction for her," the old man said. "Lucky, lucky. Else she would be chopped up, yeah? For eurocash, not francs.

Much money for a ghost." He smiled. "A rocket could do in that *imfizi*. Or an EMP. You have one?"

"I will chop you up, Grandfather . . ." Daudi took a long pull at his drink. ". . . if you talk any more of *muti*. You live in a new time."

"What, you don't want to be rich?" The scavenger hacked up a laugh.

"Not for killing children," Daudi said.

"Ah, but you were in the war."

Daudi stood up.

"You were in the war," the old man repeated. "You sowed the na-virus and burned the villages and used the big knife on the deserters. Didn't you? Weren't you in the war?"

Daudi wanted to wrap his fingers around the scavenger's piped neck and squeeze until the esophagus buckled. Instead, he took his Coke and walked back up the junkpile to try again with the ghost girl.

The drone had been repairing itself, he could see it now. Swatches of hardfoam and crudely-welded panels covered its chassis. Spare cables hung like dead plants from its shoulders. It was hunched very still, only swiveling one camera to track Daudi's approach.

Belise was sitting between its feet. "Dunna come any closer," she said. "He might get mad at you." Her brows shot up. "Is that fanta for me as well?"

"No," Daudi said. He considered it. "Too much sugar is bad for you. You won't grow."

The *imfizi* shifted slightly and Daudi took a step back.

Belise laughed. "My *dawe* used to say that."

"My mother used to say it," Daudi said. "When I chewed too much sugarcane." He watched the drone uneasily. It was hard to tell where it was looking. "Did you have a *mama*?" he asked her.

"I don't remember," Belise said. She rubbed at her nose, smeared snot on her dress.

"And your *dawe*?"

"He's here." Belise slapped the metal trunk behind her. "With me."

"The *imfizi* keeps you safe, yes? Like a father." Daudi maneuvered a rubber tire to sit on. Some of the scavengers down below were using a brazier for tea and the wind carried its bitter smoke. "But maybe it will not always be that way," he said. "Drones are not so much like you and me, Belise. They can break."

"They can fix," Belise said, pointing to the patched carapace.

Daudi remembered much simpler jobs, where the men and women were frightened for their lives and wanted so badly to be tagged, to go to the safehouse, for the government to help them.

"If the drone decides its mission is over, it might leave," Daudi said. "Or it might paint you."

"Paint me?"

"Paint you as a target," Daudi said. "So it can kill you."

Belise shook her small white head, serene. "No, that won't happen. He's my *dawe*."

Daudi sipped until his drink was gone. "I'll take you to a place with so much food," he said. "No more scrap-hunting. Nice beds and nice food. And other children."

"I'll stay." Belise pointed and Daudi followed her finger. "Take those two. You can have them go with you. I don't like them."

Two small boys rummaging in the junk, insect-thin arms. One had a hernia peeking out from under his torn shirt. They cast nervous looks up every so often, for the leviathan drone and the albino girl and now for the policeman.

"They don't need my help," Daudi said. "My job is to help you. Many people would try to kill you. Cut off your limbs. The government is trying to make you safe."

"Why?"

Daudi rubbed his forehead. "Because albino-killings are very publicized. President Habarugira is forging new Western relations, and the killings reflect badly, badly, badly on our country. And now that the war is over, and there are no more rebels to hunt, people who know only how to murder are finding the *muti* market."

"Oh."

"And the government cares for the good of all its people," Daudi added. He looked at the empty glass bottle between his palms, then hurled it off into the growing dusk. The shatter noise came faint.

Belise had followed the trajectory, lips pursed. Now she looked up. "Not what my *dawe* said." She paused. "About the government. He said other things."

"Your *dawe* is dead, Belise."

Belise nodded, and for a moment Daudi thought they were making progress. "He died with the bleeding," she said. "With the sickness. But he told me not to worry, because he had a plan. He made his soul go softly into the *imfizi*." She smiled upward, and the pity in Daudi's gut sharpened into something else. He stared at the array of red sensors, the scattered spider eyes.

"Your daddy, Belise." Daudi put a finger up to his temple and twisted. "Was he a jackman?"

Belise winced. She stared at the ground. When she looked up, her raw pink eyes were defiant. "He was a rebel," she said.

Back in the birdshit-caked taxi, there was a memo on misuse of government funds. Daudi tugged it off the screen and punched in his address instead. Through the window, he saw scavengers taking in their equipment. Some were pitching nylon tents around the brazier. The old noseless man was tearing open a package of disposable phones, but he looked up when the ignition rumbled. He waved.

Daudi's fingers buzzed as he typed the word into Google: *softcopy*. A slew of articles in English and German fluttered up. He struggled through half a paragraph before switching over to a translation service. Daudi was not a hacker, but he'd heard the term used. Always between jackmen, usually in a hot argument.

The taxi began to rattle over loose-packed gravel, and Daudi had it read aloud to him. *Softcopy, a theoretical transfer of human consciousness into an artificial brain. Ramifications for artificial intelligence. Softcopy claim in NKorea revealed to be a hoax. Increased use of neural webbing has led to new questions. Evolution of the human mind.*

The taxi sent him an exposé on corruption in the Burundi police forces as a kicker, but Daudi hardly registered it as he swung himself out of the vehicle. He scanned himself through the door in the jagged-glass-topped wall, scattered the pigeons on his apartment's stoop. The stairs went by three at a time, and then he was in front of his work tablet, working the policense like a bludgeon.

He pulled up reports from three years ago. Death reports. The list was long, long, long. He scrolled through it and they came to him in flashes, so many Jonathans and then so many Josephs, good Christian names for godless rebels, and then he found him: Joseph Rufykiri, the Razor. Responsible for the longest sustained information attack of the war, for the interception of encrypted troop movements, for the malicious reprogramming of military drones, farm equipment, wind turbines, and once a vibrator belonging to the general's wife.

He was dead by na-virus, but survived by a daughter. Daudi stared at the data and only half-believed it, but half was enough. He found a rumpled rain jacket under the bed and threw it on, and into the deepest pocket he dropped his old service handgun. Useless, unless he put it right up to the drone's gut, right where the armor had fallen away.

Daudi thought of the bloodspray and his comrades jerking and falling like cut puppets as the hacked drone spun its barrels. He thought of Joseph Rufykiri between blood-soaked sheets, whispering to his daughter that he had a plan and that she did not have to worry.

He had to know, so Daudi stepped back out under the swelling sky and hailed a new taxi, one with less graffiti, as it began to storm.

The dust felt like flying shrapnel by the time Daudi struggled out of the taxi, wrapped up to the eyes. It battered and bit his fingers. The sky was dark and its rusty clouds were surging now, attacking. It looked like the scavengers had packed away and found shelter elsewhere, or else their tents had been torn off the ground like great black scabs. Daudi hurried to where the junkpile could provide some shelter.

On his way a scavenger fled past, stumbling, and then Daudi saw the blurry shape of a jeep up ahead through the sand. Something besides the storm was happening. He crouched against the wheel-well and checked his gun where the dust couldn't reach it. He checked it again. He breathed in, out, and craned his head around the edge of the vehicle.

Three *muti* hunters, swathed in combat black with scarves wrapped tight against the storm. Daudi counted three small-caliber guns but could hear nothing now over the howl of the dust. They ducked and swayed on their feet, and the *imfizi* drone clanked and churned and tried to track them as the grit assaulted its many joints. Bullets had cratered its front, and bled coolant was being sucked off into the wind. Belise was nowhere to be seen.

The drone was long since dry of ammunition, and the hunter was caught off-guard when it lunged, quicker than Daudi had ever seen a drone move, and pinioned him to the ground. The other two rounded on it, firing in rhythm. The *imfizi* buckled and twitched with the impacts, but then reared up with the hunter's leg still mashed in its pincer. Reared higher. Higher. Blood spouted as the man tore silently in half.

The other hunters reversed now, moving clumsily in the wind, and one hauled a grenade from his back and lobbed. For a moment, Daudi thought it was a dud, but then a whine shivered in his teeth and the hair on his neck stood up on end and he realized it was an EMP. The drone shuddered once, twice. Froze. The hunters converged.

Something clutched onto Daudi's calf. He looked down, and of course it was Belise, her translucent hands kneading his ankle, and she was crying something but Daudi could not read lips. He shook her off. He steadied himself. He ducked around the side of the vehicle, and fired twice.

The first hunter dropped, swinging on his heel, punched through the skull and nicked in the shoulder. Daudi had not forgotten how to kill.

Arm coming up, scarved head turning. Daudi made his body relax and snapped off another shot, feeling it into the chest but hitting belly instead. The hunter fired back but the retort was lost in the dust and Daudi had no idea how close he'd come to dying so he did not falter. The hunter's scarf ripped free, oscillating wildly, as the next bullet splintered through throat and jaw.

Daudi stumbled to the bodies and scrabbled for their guns, but one had already been swallowed by the sand and the other was locked tight in a dead hand. He tried to throw up but only hurt his ribs. He crawled instead to the *imfizi*. Its red eyes were starting to blink back on. Daudi put a hand on either side of the carapace and leaned close. He stared hard into the cameras.

"Joseph Rufykiri," he said, mouthing carefully.

The drone shuddered. The top half of the chassis rocked back. Rocked forward. Daudi mirrored the nod without really meaning to. He squinted back to where Belise was crouched, covering her eyes against the dust. Her skin was stark white against the black jeep. Tears were tracking through the grime on her face.

Daudi realized he had the gun pressed up against the rusty husk. "Do your penance," he mumbled. "I do mine." Then he stood up, almost bowled over in the wind, and turned to go.

The ghost girl said something to him but he still couldn't hear. It might have been thanks. Daudi nodded her on, and she dashed towards her father, now getting to his iron feet. Daudi went to the jeep and found the two little boys on their bellies underneath. He put his head down.

"I have a taxi," he said. "Come with me." They exchanged looks with their dark eyes and shook dust from their dark heads. Then they wriggled out from under the vehicle and Daudi shielded them as best he could with the rain jacket.

He looked back only once. Belise was clambering into the drone's arms, sheltered from the roaring wind, and then they were enveloped by the dust.

THE SKY DIDN'T LOAD TODAY

It was an aching white blank, with little fissures where code leaked out like drizzling rain, but nobody seemed to notice except Adelaide.

"Nina, look," she said at recess, on the squeaking playground swings. "The sky's got a glitch." She kicked out hard, trying to soar high enough to touch the faulty firmament.

"Looks fine to me," her friend said, draped stomach-down over her swing, feet shuffling the gravel. Her eyes stuck to the iPhone clutched in her small pink hands.

In class, Adelaide couldn't stop looking out the Windex-streaked glass.

"It's like someone broke the game," she said, when the teacher scolded her to pay attention.

"Life is not a game, Adelaide," he said, raking a strand of black hair behind his white ear. "That's why you should be learning your times tables. Not staring out the window."

Adelaide walked home under the void, watching error messages ripple in the wind. She spent the day searching for polygons in the elm trees and invisible walls around the boarded-up well she was supposed to avoid.

When she wormed under her sheets that night, the sky outside still hadn't darkened. Adelaide argued for an extension on curfew.

"Not a chance," her mother said, leaving a warm kiss on her forehead. "And don't worry. I'm sure the sky will load tomorrow."

But when her mother paused in the doorway, Adelaide saw her silhouette jump and flicker, and a glowing trickle of code leak down her cheek.

YOU MAKE PATTAYA

Dorian sprawled back on sweaty sheets, watching Nan, or Nahm, or whatever her name was, grind up against the mirror, beaming at the pop star projected there like she'd never seen smartglass before. He knew she was from some rural eastern province; she'd babbled as much to him while he crushed and wrapped parachutes for their first round of party pills. But after a year in Pattaya, you'd think she would have lost the big eyes and the bubbliness. Both of which were starting to massively grate on him.

Dorian had been in the city for a month now, following the tourist influx, tapping the Banks and Venmos of sun-scalded Russians too stupid to put their phones in a faraday pouch as they staggered down Walking Street. In the right crowd, he could slice a dozen people for ten or twenty Euros each and make off with a small fortune before a polidrone could zero in on him.

And in Baht, that small fortune still went a long way. More than enough to reward himself with a 'phetamine-fuelled 48-hour club spree through a lurid smear of discos and dopamine bars, from green-lit Insomnia to Tyger Tyger's tectonic dance floor and finally to some anonymous club on the wharf where he yanked a gorgeous face with bee-stung lips from a queue of bidders on Skinspin and wasted no time renting the two of them a privacy suite.

Dorian put a finger to his lips to mute the pop star in the mirror, partly to ward off the comedown migraine and partly just to see the hooker's vapid smile slip to the vapid pout that looked better on her. She pulled the time display out from the corner of the mirror and made a small noise of surprise in her throat.

"I must shower." She checked the cheap nanoscreen embedded in her thumbnail, rueful. "Other client soon. Business lady. Gets angry when I late even one fucking second." She spun toward the bed. "I like you better," she cooed. "You're handsome. Her, I don't know. She wear a blur." She raked her glittery nails through the air in front of her face to illustrate.

"That's unfortunate," Dorian said, pulling his modded tablet out from under the sheets.

"Like I fuck a ghost," she said with a grimace. "Gives me shivers." She turned back to her reflection, piling up her dark hair with one hand and encircling her prick with the other. She flashed him an impish Crest-capped grin from the mirror. "You want a shower with me?"

Dorian's own chafed cock gave a half-hearted twitch. He counted the popped tabs of Taurus already littered around the room and decided not to risk an overdose.

"I'll watch," he said. "How's that?"

Her shoulders heaved an exaggerated sigh, then she flitted off to the bathroom. Dorian flicked the shower's smartglass from frosted to one-way transparent, watching her unhook the tube and wave it expectantly in his general direction. Dorian used his tablet to buy her the suite's maximum option, 60 litres of hot water.

Once she was busy under the stream, rapping along to Malaysian blip-hop, he took advantage of the privacy to have a look at his Bank. The scrolling black figure in his savings account gave him a swell of pride. 30 000 Euros, just over a million in Baht. He was ripping down record cash and the weekend's binge had barely dented him. Maybe it was finally time to go to a boat-yard and put in some inquiries.

Dorian alternated between watching curves through the wet glass and watching clips of long-keeled yachts on his tablet. Then, in the corner of his eye, the mirror left tuned to a Thai entertainment feed flashed a face he actually recognized: Alexis Carrow, UK start-up queen, founder of Delphi Apps and freshly-minted billionaire. Dorian sat up a bit straighter and the mirror noticed, generating English subtitles.

CARROW VACATION INCOGNITO

Alexis Carrow young CEO from Delphi Apps on vacay in our very own beautiful country, celebspotters made clip yesterday on Pattaya Bay Area. She appears having a wonderful time perusing Soi 17 with only bodyguard. No lover for her? Where is singer/songwriter Mohammed X? Alexis Carrow is secretive always.

Dorian dumped the feed from the mirror onto his tablet, zooming in on the digital stills from some celebspotter's personal drone that showed Ms. Carrow slipping inside an AI-driven *tuk-tuk*, wearing Gucci shades and a sweat-wicking headscarf. Thailand still pulled in a lion's share of middle-class Russian and Australian holidayers, plus droves of young Chinese backpackers, but Dorian knew the West's rich and/or famous had long since moved on to sexier climes. Alexis Carrow was news. And she was here in Pattaya.

Cogs churned in his head; grifter's intuition tingled the nape of his neck. He eased up off the bed and walked to the smartglass wall of the bathroom. Inside, Nan? Nahm? was removing her penis, trailing strands of denatured protein. He doubted it was her original organ—surgeons needed something to work with when they crafted the vagina, after all—but customers liked the fantasy.

Dorian put his forehead against the smartglass, watching as she slipped the disembodied cock into the nutrient gel of a chic black refrigerated carrycase. The night's activities were a slick fog.

He tried to remember what she'd told him between bouts of hal-lucination-laced sex, the endless murmuring in his ear while they lay tangled together. Things about her family in Buriram, things about her friends, things about her clients.

Someone even richer than you, she'd said, fooled by his rented spidersilk suit and open bar tab. *Wants me all the week. You're lucky I think you are handsome.*

Dorian couldn't contain his grin as he looked down at his tablet, flicking through the photos. She was right about one thing: he had always been lucky.

By the time the hooker was dressed, Dorian had checked on Skinspin and verified her name was Nahm. She exited the bath-room wrapped in a strappy white dress, her black hair immaculate again. Dorian appraised her unending legs, soot-rimmed eyes and pillowy lips. She was definitely enough to catch even a celebrity's biwandering eye.

"What?" she asked. She crouched to retrieve one Louboutin knock-off kicked under the bed; Dorian produced its partner.

"Nothing, Nahm," he said, handing her the sandal. "I was just thinking how much I'd like to take you back to London with me."

"Don't make a joke," she said, but she looked pleased. She gripped his arm for balance while she slipped into her shoes and then gave him a lingering goodbye kiss. As soon as the door of the privacy suite snicked shut behind her, Dorian scrambled back into his clothes.

Someone had dumped half a Singha across his shoes and his sport coat stank like laced hash, but he didn't have time for a clothing delivery. He raked fingers through his gel-crisped hair, prodded the dark circles under his eyes, and left. The narrow hall was a bright, antiseptic white unsullied by ads, and the sound-proof guarantee of each privacy suite made it eerily quiet, too. AI-run fauxtels did always tend toward a minimalist aesthetic.

Walking Street, by contrast, bombarded every last one of Dorian's senses the moment he stepped outside. The air stank like spice and petrol, and a thousand strains of synthesized music mingled with drunk shrieks, laughter, trilingual chatter. The street itself was a neon hubbub of revelers.

Dorian used his tablet to track the sticky he'd slapped to the bottom of Nahm's shoe. He couldn't see her through the crush, but according to the screen she was heading upstreet toward the Beach Road entrance. He plunged off the step, ducking an adbot trailing a digital Soi 6 banner, and made for the closest tech vendor. A gaggle of tourists was arrayed around the full body Immersion tank, giggling at their electrode-tethered friend drifting inside with a tell-tale erection sticking off him.

Dorian cut past them and swapped 2000 Baht for a pair of lime green knock-off iGlasses, prying them out of the packaging with his fingernails. He blinked his way through set-up, bypassed user identification, and tuned them to the sticky's signal. A digital marker dropped down through the night sky, drizzling a stream of white code over a particular head like a localized rain shower.

Stowing his tablet, Dorian hurried after the drifting marker, past a row of food stands hawking chemical-orange chicken kebabs and fried scorpions. A few girls whose animated tattoos he vaguely recognized grabbed at him as he went by, trailing fake nails down his arm. He deked away, but tagged one of them to Skinspin later—it looked like she'd gotten her implants redone.

Once he had Nahm in eyeball sight, he slowed up a bit. She was mouthing lyrics to whatever she had in her audiobuds as she bounced along, necksnapping a group of tank-and-togs Australian blokes with the sine curve sway of her hips. She detoured once outside Medusa, where bored girls were perusing their phones and dancing on autopilot, to exchange rapid-fire *sawatdees* and air-kisses. She detoured again to avoid a love-struck Russian on shard.

Ducking into a stall selling 3-D printed facemasks of dead celebrities, Dorian looked past Nahm to the approaching roundabout. A shiny black ute caught his eye through the customary swarm of scooters and *tuk-tuks*. As he watched, Nahm checked her thumbnail, then glanced up at the ute and quickened her pace. Dorian felt a jangle of excitement down his spine as he scanned the vehicle for identifying tags and found not a single one.

Someone had knocked over a trash tip, spilling the innards across Nahm's path, but she picked her way through the slimed food cartons and empty condom sprays with pinpoint precision that left Dorian dimly impressed. He squinted to trigger the iGlasses' zoom, wondering if he should chance trying to get a snap of the inside of the ute.

Then the lasershow started up again, throwing its neon green web into the dark clouds over Pattaya's harbor, and as Nahm craned her beautiful head to watch for what was probably the millionth time, her heel punctured a sealed bag of butcher giblets.

"Shit," Dorian said, at the same time Nahm appeared to be saying something similar. Casting a glance at the approaching ute, she lowered herself gingerly to the curb to hunt through her bag. She produced a wipe and cleaned the red gunge off her ankle and the strap of her sandal. Dorian bit at the inside of his cheek.

She continued to the underside of the shoe, wiping the needle-like heel clean, then paused. Dorian winced, thinking of all the many places he could have put the sticky. Slipped into her bag, or onto the small of her back, or even somewhere in her hair.

Nahm pincered the tiny plastic bead between two nails and peered at it. Dorian crossed his tattooed fingers, hoping she wasn't one of the many girls addicted to Bollywood spy flicks. She frowned, then balled the sticky up in the used wipe and tossed it away. The stream of code floated a half-meter over, now useless, as the ute pulled in.

Dorian slid closer, watching Nahm get to her feet, smooth out her dress. For the first time, she looked slightly nervous. The ute's shiny black door opened with a hiss. Dorian didn't have an angle to see the interior as Nahm slithered inside, but the voice within was unmistakable, Cockney accent undisguised.

"Christ, what is that stink? Please do not track that shit in with you, love."

Dorian didn't get to hear Nahm's retort. The door swooshed shut and the ute bullied its way back into the traffic. Dorian trotted over and picked up the bloody wipe, retrieving the sticky from inside. The smell barely bothered him, because Alexis Carrow was slumming it in Pattaya and he was going to blackmail the ever-loving shit out of her.

When Dorian tried to search Nahm's profile again, he wasn't particularly surprised to see she'd pulled it off Mixt and Skinspin and the rest. Either finding the sticky had spooked her, or her current customer was upping the pay enough to make exclusivity worthwhile. Dorian had to do things the old-fashioned way, with a sheaf of rumpled 200 Baht notes doled out to helpful individuals.

He didn't find her on the beach until late afternoon, and almost didn't recognize her when he did. She sat cross-legged on the palm-shaded sand, chatting to the old woman selling coconut milk and bags of crushed ice from a sputtering minifridge. Her face was more or less scrubbed of makeup, eyes smaller without the caked-on kohl, and her black hair hung gathered in a ponytail. Loose harem pants, flip-flops, a canary yellow Jack Daniels tank he assumed was being worn ironically.

"*Sawatdee krap*," Dorian said, butchering the pronunciation on purpose. He flashed her an incredulous grin. "This is a surprise."

Nahm looked up, surprised. "Hello," she beamed, running her fingers through her ponytail. Then her smile dimmed by a few watts. A crease of suspicion appeared on her forehead. "What is it you want? I am no working."

"I guessed from the flip-flops," Dorian said. "Long night for you?"

Nahm narrowed her eyes. "You," she said. "You put a . . . thing. To my shoe. First I think it was Ivan, but it was you." She said something to the old woman in machine-gun Thai, too fast for Dorian to even try at, and slunk to her feet. "I am going. I don't care you are handsome, you are crazy like Ivan." She brushed sand off her legs and made for the street.

"Have you figured out who you're fucking yet?" Dorian asked, dropping pretenses. "That business lady? The angry one?"

Nahm stopped, turned back.

Dorian clawed the air in front of his face as an extra reminder. "Whatever she's paying you is shit," he said.

"More than you pay me."

"She's a lot richer than me," Dorian said. "She's Alexis Carrow."

Nahm's eyes winched wide and she put a furious finger to her lips, scanning the beach as if paparazzi might burst up out of the gray sand.

Dorian grinned. "So you do know."

"What is it you want?" Nahm repeated, raking fingers through her ponytail.

"I want to talk business," Dorian said. "Walk with me a minute?"

He chased a few coins out of his pocket to buy a coconut milk and a bag of ice chips, then gestured down the beach. Nahm swayed, indecisive, but when Dorian started to walk she fired off another salvo of indecipherable Thai to the old woman and fell into step with him.

It was low tide and the beach was a minefield of broken glass bottles and plastic trash floating in tepid puddles. Other than a prone tourist couple baking away their hangovers, Dorian and Nahm had the place to themselves.

"You familiar with the term blackmail?" Dorian asked, handing her the coconut milk.

Nahm spun the straw between her fingers. "I watch bad movies. Yes."

"Your client is wearing a blur for a reason." Dorian ripped open the ice bag. "She's not keen on the tablos finding out she took a sex trip to Thailand."

Nahm gave an irritated shake of her head. "If she find that thing on my shoe, big fucking trouble for me, you know that?"

"Does she actually sweep you for bugs? Christ." Dorian popped a chunk of ice into his mouth. "Pawanoia."

"She careful."

Dorian crunched down on the cube, eliciting a squeal and crack. "Yes. Very careful. Meaning any fuck-footage from her trip is going to be extremely valuable. Do you want to get rich, Nahm?"

"Everybody wants to get rich," Nahm said, plumbing with her straw, not looking at him.

"Well, this is your shot. Also, my shot." Dorian spat a piece of ice into the filmy surf. "Alexis Carrow has enough money that paying two enterprising individuals such as you and me to suppress a sex scandal is easily worth 50 000 Euros. And if she refuses to negotiate, any of the bigger tablos would pay us the same for the footage."

Nahm's eyes went wide and Dorian realized he probably could have halved his actual demand a second time.

"Enough money to take care of your family out in Buriram," Dorian continued. "Get them out of the village, if you want. Definitely enough to assuage any lingering embarrassment about how their first-born financed her vaginoplasty."

"I make good money do what I do now," Nahm said sourly. "Enough money. I send them."

"Not 50 000 Euros money," Dorian said. "D'you really want to hook in Pattaya your whole life?" He packed another ice cube into his cheek. "This city is the diseased bleached asshole of Thailand. It's disgusting."

Nahm gave him a dirty look. "You're here."

"I'm disgusting," Dorian explained.

"And this is why Pattaya is Pattaya," Nahm said, lobbing her half-empty coconut milk into the water. "You make Pattaya be Pattaya."

"Don't have to litter about it." Dorian crunched his ice. "If you help me pull this off, you can live wherever you want."

"In London with you?" Nahm asked dryly.

"50 000 Euros," Dorian repeated. "Split even. Fifty percent yours, fifty percent mine. I've got a way to short-circuit the blur projector. I'll rig a sticky, it's the same thing I stuck to your shoe. Tiny. You just have to put it on the collar without her noticing."

"I told you she scan me in the car." Nahm folded her arms. "Very careful, remember?"

"That's why we plant it in the room beforehand, along with a little slip-in eyecam," Dorian said, groping inside the ice bag with reddened fingertips. "Where's she taking you tonight? Does she do fauxtels or the real thing?"

Nahm bit her lip. Dorian could practically see the tug-of-war on her creased forehead, a chance at instant wealth battling the cardinal rule of confidentiality.

"I want sixty percent," Nahm said. "I lose my best ever client. I maybe get big fucking trouble. You are safe with your phone somewhere, no risk."

Dorian grinned. "You're sharper than you let on. Why the dizzy bitch act? Do clients really like it that much?"

"Sixty percent," Nahm repeated, but with a hint of her own grin.

"Fine." Dorian spat out his ice and stuck out his hand. "Sixty."

Alexis Carrow had rented a suite at the Emerald Palace, a name Dorian thought a bit generous for an eight-story quick-crete façade topped by a broken-down eternity pool collecting algae. But if she was after privacy, it wasn't a bad choice. It was far enough from the main drag to be relatively quiet, and small enough to be inconspicuous.

Of course, gaining access was as easy as waltzing past reception wearing a drunken grin and clutching an expired keycard fished from the wastebasket outside. Dorian affected a slight stagger on his way to the lift. Once the shiny doors slid shut, he took out his tablet and called Nahm.

"How's the timing?" he asked, as she appeared on the screen putting up her hair with a static clip.

"She's on her way," Nahm said, unsticking a floating tendril of dark hair from her eyelash. "Get me from Bali Hai in five minute, then take ten, twelve minute back to hotel. Over."

"Alright." Dorian punched the backlit eight with his knuckle. "So I'm going to put it in the back of the toilet."

"So, how they did in The Godfather. Over." Nahm was now applying a gloss to her lips that shimmered like broken glass and was not paying as close attention as Dorian would have liked.

"Sure," he said. "As soon as you get in, go to the bathroom. Get some water going so she can't hear you take the lid off. Then open the ziplock, take the eyecam out first. You ever wear contacts?"

"Yes."

"It's like that," Dorian said. "Once you have the eyecam in, take the sticky out of the ziplock and hide it in your hand."

"And put it to the blur without her knowing it," Nahm continued, then, in a surprisingly credible imitation of Dorian's accent: "Base of the projector if possible, over."

"Yeah, then business as usual," Dorian said, as the lift jittered to a halt. "She won't notice when the projection goes down, so long as you're being your usual distracting self and you don't start complimenting her eyes or anything batshit like that." The lift made to open and he jammed it shut again. "Do what you normally do," he went on. "Let the eyecam do the work. After she pays you, come find me across the street and we'll get the POV uploaded to a private cloud. At which point, champagne and a blowjob."

"Who give the champagne, who give the blowjob?" Nahm asked, checking her thumbnail offscreen. "Over."

"Both on me if you do this right," Dorian said, knuckling the Open Door button. "Message me when you get to the hotel." He paused, and then, because she was growing on him a bit: "Over."

Nahm's face lit up for the split second before he ended the call, then Dorian set off down the stucco-walled hallway. He made a quick check around the corner, then doubled back to door

811 and made short work of the electronic lock. The suite had obviously been prepped for her arrival. Freshly-laundered sheets on the bed, a sea of fluffy white towels at the foot of it. Condom sprays and lubricants arrayed brazenly on the nightstand. Minibar stocked with Tanqueray gin and Lunar vodka.

Dorian plucked a cube out of the full ice bucket and popped it in his mouth, making his way to the bathroom. He lifted the featherweight top off the back of the Western-style toilet, then reached inside his pocket where the tiny eyecam and the even smaller sticky had been lovingly double-bagged in ziplock. Neither had been cheap, and he had a feeling he wasn't going to get the sticky back.

Setting the bag adrift in chemical-smelling water, Dorian replaced the top of the toilet and re-entered the room. He walked in a slow circle around the bed, picturing angles, trying not to get distracted imagining Nahm and a celebrity CEO fucking on it. In the end, he decided to plant his insurance cam in the far corner. It would be an uncreative wide angle shot, but with a near-zero chance of Alexis Carrow's deblurred face failing to make an appearance.

It wasn't that he didn't trust Nahm to manage the eyecam, but back-ups were his cardinal rule where information storage was concerned. A healthy fear of technical difficulties went hand-in-hand with hacking for a living.

Once satisfied with the cam's placement in a shadowy whorl of stucco, Dorian put his ear to the door to listen for footsteps. Hearing nothing, he exited the room, heart pumping with the old break-and-enter exhilaration from his teenage years.

His hand was still on the doorknob when a black-shirted employee rounded the corner in his peripheral. Dorian didn't look up. He pretended to struggle with the door, then looked down at his keycard and made a slurred sound of realization.

"This no your room, sir. Can I help you?"

Dorian tried not to jump. The man had slunk up and stopped directly behind him, quiet as a cat, a feat made more impressive by the sheer size of him. Tall for a Thai, broad-chested and broad-shouldered, with a shaved scalp glistening in the florescent lighting and a tattoo of a cheerful cartoon snake wriggling up and down one sinewy forearm. Dorian could have sworn he'd been kicked out of a couple bars by the very same. Bouncers and hotel security tended to overlap.

"Wrong floor," Dorian said, waving his keycard. "Hit the wrong button in the lift. One too many Changs." He shook an imaginary beer bottle.

"Okay, sir," the guard said, not smiling.

"Nice tattoo," Dorian added. "Friendly-looking little bugger."

He gave the man a bleary grin, then made for the lift as quickly as he could without looking suspicious.

Now that the rest of it was in Nahm's hands, Dorian had nothing to do but wait. He camped out in an automated tourist bar across the way, slumping into a plastic molded seat with his tablet. Once Nahm messaged him to say they were at the hotel, he bought a gargantuan Heineken bottle and drank it slowly on ice.

Time ticked by on his tablet screen. He passed it imagining the whole thing going off flawlessly, and then by imagining himself on a small sleek yacht knifing through the blue-green waters off Ko Fangan. Maybe even with Nahm draped on his shoulder for a week or two, wearing a pair of aviators and a skanky swimsuit. Between that and the tingly insulation of a half-liter of Heineken, he barely rattled when a hand slammed down on the table in front of him.

Dorian blinked hard. Nahm was standing in front of him, shoulders trembling, clutching herself. The static clip was still in place, moving her hair in graceful black ripples around her face, but the effect wasn't the same with her lip gloss smeared halfway across her cheek and a growing brown bruise under her bloodshot left eye. And hulking behind her, red-faced and furious, was the hotel security guard.

"Shit," Dorian said. The buzz from the beer slipped away all at once.

"I fuck up," Nahm said shakily. "I left the bathroom open. The blur go off, but when we switch around on the bed she see herself in the mirror."

The security guard barked something fast and angry, from which Dorian could only extricate *falang* and police. He reached across the table and hauled Dorian up by the armpit, jerking his head toward the door.

"The eyecam?" Dorian demanded, trying to twist away. No go.

"She call this big motherfucker, he take it out my eye," Nahm groaned, mascara finally starting to leak down her cheeks in inky trails. "She gets mad, she go. He says he will call the police so I tell him you have money."

"I don't have money," Dorian said reflexively, looking at the guard.

"Bullshit." Nahm's eyes were wide and desperate. "I know you have money."

Dorian looked around the bar, licking his lips. He'd picked it intentionally. A collection of steroid-bulky expats were cradling pints in the back, watching the situation with increasing interest. If he played ignorant right now, they looked both drunk and patriotic enough to intervene on behalf of a fellow Englishman. Nobody liked it when the locals stopped smiling.

"His cousin is police," Nahm said, winnowing on the edge of the sob. "He says if I don't pay he put me in the jail."

Dorian picked up his glass and finished it; the sweat pooling in his palms nearly made it slip out of his grip. He tried to think. If Carrow had left in a hurry, that meant the insurance cam he'd hidden was still there in the hotel room. The fact she'd left furious only confirmed how valuable the footage was.

If he wanted to get back into that room before some overzealous autocleaner wiped the cam off the wall, he needed to defuse things.

"Okay, fuck," Dorian said. "Okay. I'll come." He gave a glance toward the back table. "Nothing to worry about, lads. Just a bit of a . . . lover's spat."

One of the men rubbed his bristly chin and raised his pint in Dorian's general direction. The others ignored him. As he let himself be steered out the door, the bar chirped goodbye in Thai and then English. Nahm followed behind, pinching the torn fabric of her shirt together. Her bare feet slapped on the tile. She was biting her lip, rubbing absently at the smeared gloss.

"Sorry I fuck up," she said miserably. Outside, the night air was warm and stank of a broken sewer line. Dorian fixed his eyes on the neon green sign of the hotel across the way. The sooner he had this dealt with, the sooner he could get the cam.

"Me too," Dorian said, but he searched for her free hand in the dark and gave it what he figured was a comforting squeeze.

She looked down at their interlaced hands, then back up, brow furrowed. "You should have said, though. You should have said, Nahm, don't let her see a mirror."

Dorian took his hand back. The guard ushered them into the side alley, stopping underneath a graffitied Dokemon. Dorian crossed his arms.

"Alright," he said. "How much does he want? And if it's cash, we need a machine."

"No cash," the guard said, brandishing a phone still slick from the plastic wrap. "I do Bank."

"Of course you do," Dorian said. "So how much, shitface?"

"Five million Baht."

Dorian's exaggerated guffaw accidentally landed a speck of spit on the guard's shoulder, but the man didn't seem to notice and Dorian didn't feel keen to point it out.

"Who do you think I am, the fucking king?" he demanded instead.

In reply, the guard thumbed a number into his phone. "I call cousin," he said, seizing Nahm's wrist. "Your ladyboy will go to jail, maybe you, too."

Nahm gave a low groan again. Dorian made a few mental calculations. He had just over a million Banked, and the footage from the hotel had to be worth triple that, even if it wasn't a full encounter. He would still come out of this in the black. The last thing Dorian needed was police showing up. And he didn't like the idea of Nahm sobbing in some filthy lock-up, either.

"Half a million," Dorian said. "All I got."

The guard's ringtone bleated into the night air. He shook his shaved head. Nahm started cursing at him in Thai.

Dorian clenched his jaw. "A million," he snapped. "I can show it to you. It's really all I've got."

The guard stared at him, black eyes gleaming in the blurry orange streetlight. The ringtone sounded again. Then, just as the click and a guttural *hallo* answered, he thumbed his phone off.

"Show me."

Dorian dug out his tablet and drained his account while the guard watched, dumping all of it to a specified address and waiting the thirty seconds for transaction confirmation. Nahm shifted nervously from foot to foot, mascara-streaked face bleached by the glowing screen, until it finally went through with an electronic chime. Dorian's stomach churned at the sight of the zeroes blinking in his Bank. He reminded himself it was temporary. Very, very temporary.

Once the transaction was through, the guard bustled out of the alley without so much as a *korpun krap*, leaving Dorian alone with Nahm. He was formulating the best way to get back into the hotel room without running into the guard again when she threw her arms around his neck and pulled him into a furious bruising kiss. Her fingers on his scalp and her tongue in his mouth made it difficult.

"Thank you," she panted. "For not letting him call." She hooked her thumb into the catch of Dorian's trousers, giving him her smeared smile. "No champagne. But . . ."

With her right hand working his cock, he nearly didn't feel her left slipping something into his pocket. He clamped over it on reflex. Nahm looked vaguely sheepish as the sound of a sputtering motor approached.

"I still am working on my hands," she said, wriggling her fingers out of his grip, leaving a small cold cylinder in their place. "Bye." She stepped away as a battered scooter whined its way into the alley, sliding to a halt in front of them. Dorian watched Nahm climb on to straddle a helmeted rider with a cartoon snake on one thick forearm. He lost his half-chub.

As the scooter darted back out into traffic, Dorian looked down at the insurance cam in his palm and grimaced.

It took another oversized bottle of beer before he could bring himself to watch the cam footage. Finally, slouched protectively over the table, he plugged the cam into his tablet and fast-forwarded through the empty hotel room until the door opened. Nahm glided inside on her pencil-thin heels, but instead of Alexis Carrow coming in behind her, it was the security guard, furtively checking the hallway before locking the door.

And instead of fucking, they sat on the edge of the bed and had a fairly business-like discussion in Thai. At one point Nahm departed for the bathroom and returned with the ziplock in hand. Dorian narrowed his eyes as she tossed it casually to her partner in crime, who stuffed it into a black duffel bag. The man paused, gesticulating at the bed and walls, then, with Nahm's approval, dug a scanner bar out of the duffel.

Dorian fast-forwarded through an impressively thorough search until the cam was spotted, plucked off the wall, and carried back to Nahm. She flashed a very un-vapid smile into the lens. The screen went black for a moment, then cleared again in the bathroom, pointing towards the mirror where Nahm was now painting a bruise under her eye.

Dorian swilled beer in his mouth, letting the carbonation sting his tongue while he listened to Nahm explain, in her roundabout way, how her "little" brother had caught him running a scam in a bar where he bounced. How Dorian had drunkenly bragged about his takings. How Nahm had shopped photos from Alexis

Carrow's vacation in Malaysia six months ago and slipped the fake news report into the mirror for him to watch.

Her brother, working as a valet at the Emerald Palace, had gotten the imposing black ute out of the garage for a quick spin. She'd worked on her Cockney accent for a few weeks and done up a voice synthesizer. And from there, Dorian realized his overactive imagination had done the rest of the work.

"I hope the last part is so easy, too," Nahm said sweetly, smearing her lip gloss across her face with the heel of her hand. "With the money, we think maybe to buy a boat. Mwah." She blew a kiss to the cam, then reached in and switched it off.

Dorian leaned back at his table. Unprofessional of her, to add insult to injury like that and lay out her method besides. But he supposed it was understandable in the excitement of pulling off a semi-long con for the first time. At least this way he'd recouped one of the cams. Dorian slid it back into his pocket, pensive.

For a little while he rewound the footage and sourly watched Nahm blowing kisses on loop, then finally he put the tablet away. He still had enough cash stowed to take a domestic down south and start over from there.

A fresh wave of tourists would soon be showing up on the islands soon, and Pattaya just wasn't doing it for him anymore.

EXTRACTION REQUEST

When they finally shift the transport's still-smoldering wing enough to drag Beasley out from where he was pinioned, for a moment all Elliot can do, all anyone can do, is stare. Beasley's wiry arm with its bioluminescent tattoos is near sheared from its socket, and below his hips he's nothing but pulped meat and splinters of bone.

He's still alive, still mumbling, maybe about the woman Elliot saw in a little holo with her arms thrown around his neck, back before Beasley's dreadlocked mane was shaved off and a conscript clamp was implanted at the top of his spine.

"His impact kit never triggered," someone says, as if that's not fucking obvious, as if he could have been ragdolled out of the transport otherwise.

"Is the autosurgeon trashed?" someone else, maybe Tolliver, says. Elliot's ears are still ringing from the crash and his head still swimming from what he was doing before it and all the voices seem to blend. He knows, dimly, that he should be giving orders by now.

"An autosurgeon can't do shit for him. What's it going to do, cauterize him at the waist?"

"Get him some paineaters at least. Numb him up."

"Shock's done that already."

"You don't know that."

"I fucking hope that."

Beasley is still trying to talk, but it's a choking wet burble from all the blood in his mouth. The nudge, though, comes through. It slides into the corner of Elliot's optic implant, blinking poisonous yellow. A little ripple goes through the rest of the squad, which means they got it, too. A couple of them reflexively clap their hands to the backs of their necks, where the caked scar tissue is still fresh enough to itch.

Elliot realizes that down here in the bog, cut off from command, the clamp at the top of Beasley's spine no longer needs official permission to trigger its nanobomb. All it needs is consensus.

"I'd want it done for me," Tolliver says, wiping a glisten of sweat off his face. His upvote floats into the digital queue. He chews at his lip, shoots Elliot a look that Elliot carefully ignores.

"Yeah," Santos from the lunar colony says, which is as much as she's ever said. "Trigger him."

Another upvote appears, then another, then three more in a cascade. Elliot sees that he has a veto option—something they didn't tell him when they stuck him as squad leader. He looks into Beasley's glazed eyes and completes the consensus, floating his vote to the queue.

The nanobomb goes off, punching a precise hole through the brainstem and cutting every string at once. Beasley slumps.

Apart from that, injuries are minimal. Everyone else's kits went off properly, as evidenced by the gritty orange impact gel still slathering their uniforms. Elliot picks it off himself in clumps while he surveys the damage to their R12 Heron transport. The anti-air smartmine shredded their primary rotor when it detonated, and the crash itself did the rest of the work, plowing a steaming furrow of crushed flora and shed metal. The Heron's not going to fly again.

"Should get them fuel cells out of her," says Snell, who is scarecrow skinny with a mouth full of metal, and dark enough so his shaved scalp seems to gleam blue-black. "In case there's leakage."

Aside from Beasley, who's being wrestled into a body bag, Snell is the only one who knows flyers worth a damn. They conscripted him for smuggling human cargo on a sub-orbital.

"You do that," Elliot says, when he realizes Snell is waiting for go-ahead. "Get one of the Prentii to help. They're digging."

"You mean one of the twins?" Snell asks, with a grin that makes his metallic teeth gnash and scrape.

Elliot did mean the twins, Privates Prentiss and Prentiss. The nickname slipped out, something Tolliver calls them the same way he calls Snell "The Smell" and Mirotic "Miroglitch." If he has one for Elliot, too, he doesn't use it when they're together.

"Yeah," Elliot says. "Get one of the twins."

Snell pulls on a diagnostic glove and clambers into the Heron carcass; Elliot turns to check on the perimeter. If they hadn't gone down over swampland, where the rubbery blue-purple ferns and dense-packed sponge trees provided a cushion, the crash might have been a lot worse. Their impact cleared a swathe on one side of the transport. On the other, Mirotic is calibrating the cyclops.

Elliot watches the red-lit sensory bulb strain on its spindly neck and spin in a slow circle. "What's it see?" he asks.

Mirotic is tapped in, with his optic implant glowing the same red as the surveillance unit. "Nothing hot and moving but us. Bog gets denser to the east and south. Lots of those sponge trees, lots of subterranean fungi. No radio communications. Could be more anti-air mines sitting masked, though."

His English is airtight, but still carries a Serbian lilt. Before they clamped him, he was upper-level enforcement in a Neo-European crime block on Kettleburn. He once personally executed three men and two women in an abandoned granary and had their corpses put through a thresher. Only Elliot has access to that back-record. To everyone else, Mirotic is a jovial giant with a bristly black beard and high-grade neural plugs.

Prentiss, Jan, trundles past, having received Snell's nudge for a hand with the fuel cells. He wipes wet dirt off on his tree-trunk thighs. Both he and his sister are nearly tall as Mirotic, and both are broader.

"Soil's no good for graves," Prentiss rumbles over his shoulder. "He's going to get churned up again. Watch."

"How many drones came out intact?" Elliot asks Mirotic, trying to sound sharp, trying not to imagine Beasley's body heaved back to the surface.

"Two," Mirotic says. "I can fix a third, maybe."

"Send one up," Elliot says, scratching his arm. "Get a proper map going."

Mirotic hesitates. "If I send up a drone, we might trigger another smartmine."

Elliot hadn't thought of that. He hasn't thought of a lot of things, but rescinding the order would make him look off, make him look shook, maybe even remind Mirotic of the night he saw him with the syringe.

"That's why you keep it low," Elliot says. "Scrape the tree line, no higher. And keep it brief."

Mirotic takes a battered drone from its casing and unfolds it in his lap, sitting cross-legged on the damp earth. As it rises into the air, whirring and buzzing, his eyes turn bright sensory blue.

"It's strange there's no animal life," Mirotic says. "Nothing motile on the sensor but insects. Could be a disease came through. Bioweapon, even. Seen it in the woods around New Warsaw, dead and empty just like this." He rests his thick hands on his knees. "We could have everyone jack up their immunity boosters."

Elliot takes the hint and sends a widecast order to dial up immunity and use filtration, at least for the time being. Then he goes to where Tolliver and Santos are vacuum-sealing Beasley's body bag, the filmy material wrapping tight like a shroud. Tolliver looks up at his approach, flicking dark lashes. He has smooth brown skin and sly smiles and a plastic-capped flay a skin artist did for him on leave that shows off the muscle and tendon of his arm in a graceful gash. Elliot has felt it under his fingertips, cool and hard. He knows Tolliver is fucking at least one other squadmate, but he doesn't think it's Santos.

"Me and Tolliver will finish up," Elliot says. "Go spot for Mirotic. He's tapped in. Then get the tents up."

"Sir." Santos is the only one on the squad who says sir, who salutes, and she does both with enough irony to slice through power armor. Santos was a foot soldier for one of the Brazilian families up on the lunar colony. She looks like a bulldog, squinty eyes and pouched cheeks. Her clamp didn't go in right and there's double the scarring up her head.

When Santos leaves, still sneering, Elliot drops to a crouch. "Did they know each other?" he asks, grabbing the foot end of the body bag. Tolliver takes the other and they carefully stand up.

"Talked Portuguese together sometimes," he says. "Beasley knew a bit. Said the moony accent's a real bitch to follow, though."

Elliot tells himself that this is why he needs Tolliver on his side, because Tolliver sees the webs, sees all the skinny bonds of social molecule that run through the squad.

"Fucked up seeing him halfway gone like that," Tolliver says, with a put-on hardness to his voice. "At least the clamp is good for something, right?"

Elliot grunts in response as they carry Beasley away from the downed Heron, away from the surveillance unit and the carbon-fiber tents now blooming around it.

"When I said we could give him paineaters, that vein in your forehead, it went big," Tolliver says, almost conversationally. "You were in the back when they hit us. You were in the medcab again."

"I'm coming down," Elliot says, even as his itching arm gives another twinge. "And I'm staying off it. Staying sharp."

Tolliver says nothing, and then they're at the hole where the other Prentiss, Noam, is waiting with a spade slung over her shoulder. They lower the body bag in slowly, gently. Elliot reaches down for a fistful of damp earth and crumbles it over Beasley's shrouded face. Tolliver does the same. Prentiss starts shoveling.

"We got the extraction request through before we lost altitude," Elliot says. "Won't be down here long."

Tolliver gives him a sidelong look. "Some of us will be," he says, then turns and leaves.

Elliot stays to watch until the body bag has disappeared completely under thick wet dirt.

Dusk drops fast on Pentecost, dyeing the sky and swamp a cold eerie blue for a half-hour before plunging them into pitch dark. Most of the squad already have peeled eyes—the night vision surgery is a common one for criminals—and Elliot orders all lights dimmed to minimum to conserve the generator.

Elliot has a tent to himself. He lies back stiff on his cot in the dark and reviews mission parameters in his optic implant, scrolling up and down over words he's read a thousand times. They were heading north to reinforce Osuna, cutting slantwise across marshy no-man's land the rebels usually stay away from. They were not expecting hostiles on the way, and now they're grounded at least a thousand klicks from the nearest outpost.

Elliot tries to calculate how long the paineaters and emergency morphine he salvaged from the shattered medcab will last him. Then he accesses his personal files in his implant and watches the one clip he hasn't deleted yet, the one he watches before he sleeps.

"She's awake . . . Just looking around . . ."

His wife's voice draws three syllables out of *awake*, drags on *around*, high and sweet and tinged weary. His daughter's soft and veiny head turns. Her bright black eyes search, and Elliot can pretend they see him.

Something scrapes against the side of the tent. He blinks the clip away, hauls upright and reaches for his weapon before he recognizes the imprint of a body pressed up flush to the fabric. Elliot swipes a door with his hand and Tolliver slides through, already halfway undressed.

"Told the Smell I'm out back for a long shit," Tolliver says, working his stiff cock with one hand, reaching for Elliot's waistband with the other. "Let's be quick."

"Wasn't sure you'd be coming," Elliot says, helping yank the fatigues off. "Because of Beasley."

"Don't fucking talk about Beasley," Tolliver says.

Elliot doesn't, and Tolliver's body all over his is second best to a morphine hit for helping him not think about that or anything else. But when he comes it's a throb and a trickle and then everything turns lukewarm dead again. Afterward, Tolliver sits on the edge of the cot and peels his spray-on condom off in strips.

"Jan went walkabout in the swamp a bit," he says, because this has been the usual trade since they deployed last month. "Think he's testing the range limit for the clamp. Wants to skate, maybe. Him and his sister."

"In the middle of a mined bog?" Elliot asks, pulling his fatigues back on.

"They're both settlement-bred," Tolliver says. "Colonist gene-mix, you know, they think they're invincible. Probably think they can tough it out and get south to the spaceport."

"He told you that he wants to desert?"

Tolliver takes a drink from Elliot's water bottle and runs his tongue along his teeth. "He told me he did some exploring," he says. "Wanted to jaw about some odd bones he found. I filled in the rest."

"What did he find?" Elliot asks.

"Animal bones," Tolliver says. "Really white, really clean."

"Mirotic thinks a plague might have come through," Elliot says, instead of saying a bioweapon. "There'd be bones."

"Plagues don't usually put them in neat little heaps," Tolliver says. "He said they were all piled up. A little mound of skeletons."

Tolliver swipes a door and disappears, leaving Elliot sweat-soaked and sick-feeling. He only hesitates a moment before he gropes under the bedroll for his syringe. Before he can start prepping his favorite vein, the cyclops starts to wail.

Everyone is out of their tents and armed in a few minutes, clustered around the cyclops. Half of them are rubbing their eyes as the peel sets in and turns their irises reflective. Elliot switches to night vision in his implant, lighting the shadows radiation green. The air sits damp and heavy on his shoulders, and with no breeze nothing moves in the flora. The stubby sponge trees and wide-blade ferns are dead still.

"Where's your brother?" Elliot asks Noam, counting heads.

"Taking a shit out back," she says. "He'll have heard it, though."

Mirotic is tapped in now, his implant blinking red. "Just one bogey," he says. "Thirty meters out. Looks like some kind of animal."

"You set it to wail for every fucking swamp rat that wanders through?" Snell says. His face is still streaked with soap.

"It's a lot bigger than a rat," Mirotic says. "Don't know what it is. It hasn't got vitals. It isn't warm."

"Mechanical?" Elliot asks, thinking of the spider-legged hunter-killers they used to drag rebels out of their caves around Catalao. Tech has a way of trickling over in these long engagements, whether stolen or sold off on the side.

"It's not moving like any of the crawlers I've seen," Mirotic says. "Circling now, toward the back of us. Fast. Jan's still squatting back there."

Some of the squad swivel instinctively. Elliot pulls up Jan's channel. "Prentiss, there's a bogey heading towards you," he says. "Might be mechanical. Get eyes on it."

Jan's reply crackles. "Hard to miss," he says. "It's fucking glowing."

"And what is it?" Elliot says. "You armed?"

Jan's reply does not come by channel, but his howl punctures the still night air. Elliot is knocked back as Noam barrels past him, unslinging her gnasher and snapping the safety off. Snell's fast behind, and then the others, and Elliot finds himself rearguard. He's still fumbling for his weapon when he rounds the back of the downed Heron.

His eyes slip-slide over the scene, trying to make sense of the nightmarish mass of bioluminescence and spiky bone that has enveloped Jan almost entirely. His night vision picks out a trailing arm, a hip, a boot exposed. The creature is writhing tight around Jan's body, spars of bone rasping against each other, and the glowing flesh of it is moving, slithering. The screams from inside are muffled.

Snell fires first, making Elliot's dampers swell like wet cotton in his ear canals. The spray of bullets riddle the length of the creature, and a fine spray of red blood—Jan's blood—flicks into the air.

"Don't fucking shoot!" Noam smacks Snell's weapon down and lunges forward, reaching for her brother's convulsing arm. Before he can grab hold, the creature retreats toward the tree line with Jan still ensnared, impossibly fast.

It claws itself forward on a shifting pseudopod of bone spines, moving like a scuttling blanket. Someone else fires a shot, narrowly missing Noam running after it. The creature slithers into the trees, for an instant Noam is silhouetted against the eerie glow of it, then both of them disappear in the dark.

"Shit," Tolliver says. "I mean, shit."

Elliot thinks that's as good a summary as any. He can still see Noam's vitals, and Jan's too, both of them spiked hard with adrenaline but alive. They'll be out of range in less than a minute.

"I hit it," Snell says. "Raked it right along its, I don't know, its abdomen. Didn't do nothing."

"You hit Jan. That bloodspray, that was Jan."

"Jan's *inside* it."

"We're going after them, right?"

Elliot looks around at the squad's distorted faces. Tolliver's eyes gleam like a cat's in the dark. There is no protocol for men being dragged away by monsters in the night. He opens his jaw; shuts it again. Mirotic shifts in his peripheral, taking a half-step forward, shoulders thrust back, and Elliot knows he is a nanosecond from taking the squad over, and maybe that would be better for everyone.

"Mirotic," he says. "You stay. Get a drone up and guide us bird's eye. Everyone else, on me."

Plunging through the dark swamp, Elliot expects every mud-sucked step to trigger another smartmine. Sweat pools in the hollow of his collarbone. The whine of the drone overhead shivers in his clenched teeth, and the squad is silent except for heavy breathing, muted curses as they follow its glowing path in their implants. The Prentii's signal comes and goes like a static ghost.

The warped green-and-black blur of his night vision, the drone's shimmering trail of digital breadcrumbs, the memory of the monster and Jan's disembodied thrashing arm—none of it seems quite real. A nightmare, or more likely an overdose.

"Rebels stay out of these swamps," Snell says aloud, dredging something from his post-clamp war briefing. "All the colonists do." His voice is thin and tight.

Nobody replies. The drone's pathway hooks left, into the deepest thicket of sponge trees, and they follow it. Pungent-smelling leaves slap against Elliot's head and shoulders. It reminds him almost of the transplanted eucalyptus trees where he grew up on Earth.

"Can't get any closer with the drone," comes Mirotic's crackly voice in his ear. "Trees are too high, too dense. They're right ahead of you. Close now."

The twins' signal flares in Elliot's skull, but their channels are shut and their vitals are erratic. Elliot's feels his heart starting to thrum too fast. Eyes blink and heads twitch as the rest of the squad picks up the signal. Tolliver's face is drawn, his mouth half-open. Santos is unreadable. Snell looks ready to shit himself. Hands tighten on stocks. Fingers drift to triggers.

The sponge trees thin out, and Elliot sees the same bioluminescence that swallowed Jan whole. The shape of it is indistinct, too bright for his night vision, so he flicks it off. When he closes and reopens his eyes, he sees what's become of the twins.

They are tangled together in a grotesque parody of affection, limbs wrapping each other, and it's impossible to tell where one ends and the other begins because they are coated in a writing skin of ghostly blue light. Long shafts of dull gray bone, humors or femurs from an animal Elliot knows was not killed by any plague, skewer them in place like a tacked specimen.

Reminding himself it might be a hallucination, Elliot steps slowly forward.

"Prentiss?"

A sluggish ripple goes through the twins' tangled bodies. Elliot follows the motion and finds a neck. A head not covered over. Noam's eyes are wide open and terrified. Elliot watches her face convulse trying to speak, but when her bruised mouth opens, glowing blue tendrils spill out of her throat. It's inside her. Elliot recoils. In his own throat, he feels bile rising and burning.

"Shit, they're conscious," Tolliver breathes. "What is that stuff? What the fuck is . . ." He reaches for Noam's cheek with one hand, but before he makes contact the other head, Jan's, buried somewhere near his sister's thigh, begins to wail. It's a raw animal noise Elliot has only ever heard men make when they are torn apart, when their limbs have been blown off, when shock and pain have flensed them down to the reptile brain and all it knows to do is scream.

He claws Tolliver's hand back.

"Don't touch them," he says. "We have to run a scan, or . . ." He looks at the bones pinning them in place, at the writhing cloak that looks almost like algae, now, like glowing blue algae. He has no idea what to do.

"Look at the feet," Santos says thickly. "Fuck."

Elliot looks. Noam's feet are not feet any more. The skin and muscle has been stripped away, leaving bits of bone, crumbling with no tendon to hold them together.

"Kill them," Santos says. "It's eating them alive." She pulls her sidearm and aims it at Jan's screaming mouth. Her hand tremors.

Elliot doesn't tell her no. It would be mercy, now, to kill them. Same how it was mercy for Beasley.

A vein bulges up Santos's neck. "Can't," she grunts. "The implant."

Elliot aims his own weapon at Jan and as his finger finds the trigger he finds himself paralyzed, blinking red warnings scrolling over his eyes. Convict squads have insurance against friendly fire same as any other. Maybe in a combat situation the parameters would loosen a little, but this, an execution, is out-of-bounds.

"Send the nudge, Noam." Tolliver squats down by her wide-eyed face. "You in there? You gotta send the nudge. So we can trigger you. Come on, Noam."

The yellow message doesn't appear. Maybe Noam is too angry, too colonist, thinking she is invincible, thinking somehow she'll get out of this scrape how she got out of all the other ones. More likely her mind is too far gone to access the implant. Jan starts to scream again.

"I'll fucking do it manual, then," Tolliver says, with his voice shaking. He looks at Snell. "Give me your knife. Unless you want to do it."

Snell wordlessly unclips his combat knife and slings it over, handle-first. It's a long wicked thing, not regulation or even close. Elliot thinks he should offer to do it. He's in command, after all. He knows where the jugular is and where to slit it without dousing himself in blood. But he only watches.

And the instant Tolliver touches Noam's head, all hell breaks loose. The monsters come from everywhere at once, scuttling masses of bone and bioluminescence. From the ground, Elliot realizes dimly even as he backpedals, keys his night vision, opens fire. The rest of the squad is doing the same; splinters fly where bullets hit bone but the skin of things, the blue algae, just splits and reforms.

Subterranean fungi. He remembers that from the topography scan as Tolliver clicks empty and fumbles his reload.

"Get the fuck out," comes Mirotic's voice. "They're coming on your twelve, your three. Lots of them."

Doesn't matter. The thought spears through Elliot's mind. Doesn't matter if he dies here or on Kettleburn or wherever else. He's been dead for ages.

Then Tolliver goes down, tripped by a monster clamping its bony appendages around his legs like a vice. Elliot aims low and for gray, shattering enough bones for Tolliver to wriggle out, to swap clips. But bullets aren't enough here.

Elliot loads the incendiary grenade as Tolliver scrambles free. He tries to remember the chemical compositions here on Pentecost. For all he knows, it might light up the whole fucking swamp. For all he knows, that might be a better way to die than getting digested alive.

"Run," Elliot orders, and sends the fire-in-the-hole warning spike at the same time. "Leave them."

Santos rips past him, then Snell, then Tolliver right after, no protest, his reflective eyes wide and frantic in the dark. With adrenaline turning everything slow and sharp, Elliot fires the grenade where he thinks the splash will be widest, hitting the dirt between two of the surging creatures. He remembers to blink off his night vision only a nanosecond before the explosion.

A wall of searing heat slams over his body and even without night vision the blossoming fireball all but blinds him. He feels Tolliver grabbing his shoulder, guiding him out of the thicket. Through the roar in his ears, he can't be sure if Jan is still screaming.

They are sitting in the husk of the downed Heron, not speaking. Every so often someone glances toward the cyclops, which is still whirring and spinning and searching. Santos has a bruise on her forehead from where the butt of Snell's gnasher clipped her in the dark. Tolliver cut his thumb falling. Other than that, they are all fine, except Elliot hasn't been able to get to his syringe.

"So there was no plague," Mirotic finally says. "Only a predator."

"That thing was artificial," Snell says. His eyes look wild, bloodshot, and his hand keeps going to the spot where his knife used to be. "No way could that evolve, man. It's a weapon."

"It's organic, whatever it is," Mirotic says. "Looked on the scan like a fungus."

"It's a weapon, and they dumped us here to test it." Snell's voice ratchets high. "That fucking smartmine was probably one of ours. We're expendable, right? So they dumped us here to see if it works."

Elliot waits for someone to tell Snell to settle the fuck down, but instead Santos and Tolliver and Mirotic are all looking at him, waiting for his response. Tolliver plucks at the bandage around his hand, anxious.

"The colonists stay out of these swamps," Elliot says. "You said that yourself." He has a flash of the twins' twisted bodies, the scuttling monsters. "I figure now we know why."

"When do we get extracted?" Santos asks flatly. "Sir."

Elliot knows they are low priority. Maybe five days, maybe six. Maybe more. "They know we're rationed for a week," he says.

"A fucking week?" Snell grinds his metal teeth. "Man, we can't be out here a week with that thing. I'm not ending up like the twins, man. I say we carry what we can, and we get out of here."

"To where?" Mirotic asks. "The fungus extends under the ground in all directions."

"If you knew about this, why didn't you tell us?" Snell demands.

Mirotic's nostrils flare. "Because fungus is not usually predatory."

Elliot tries to focus on the back-and-forth, tries to think of what they should do now that they know the swamp is inhabited by monsters. He realizes he is scratching at his arm.

Santos looks over. "What the fuck?"

But she isn't looking at him. Tolliver, who has been silent, ash-faced, is clutching at his bandaged thumb. He looks down at it now and his eyes widen. A faint blue glow is leaking from underneath the cling wrap.

"**O**h, shit, oh, shit, I feel it." Tolliver is twisting on the cot, sweat snaking down his face. "I can feel it. Moving."

The bandages are off his hand now and his cut thumb is speckled with the glowing fungus. The autosurgeon unfolds over his chest like a metal spider while Mirotic searches for the right removal program, his eyes scrolling code. Elliot feels a panic in his throat that he never feels during combat. It reminds him of the panic he felt last time he spoke to his daughter.

He crouches down and holds Tolliver's free hand where Snell and Santos can't see. It's slippery from the sweat.

"Got it," Mirotic says thickly. "Biological contaminant."

The autosurgeon comes to life, reaching with skeletal pincers to hold Tolliver's left arm in place. Carmine laserlight plays over his skin, scanning, then the numbing needle dips in with machine precision to prick the base of his thumb.

Tolliver's free hand clenches tight around Elliot's.

"Hate these things," he groans, locking eyes for a moment. "Rather let the Smell use that big old fucking knife than have a bot digging around—"

"Shouldn't have dropped it, then," Snell says.

Tolliver swivels; his mouth pulls tight in a grimace. "Fuck you, Snell."

The autosurgeon deploys a scalpel. Metal slides and scrapes and the sound shivers in Elliot's teeth. Mirotic is looking over at him, and when he speaks he realizes why.

"The spores are moving. Autosurgeon wants to take the whole thumb."

A wince ripples through the tent; Santos clutches her own thumb tight between two knuckles. Tolliver's eyes go wide. He tries to yank his arm away, but the autosurgeon holds tight.

"No!" he barks. "No, don't let it! Turn the fucking thing off!"

"It could spread through his body if we aren't fast," Mirotic says. "How you said it did to Prentiss and Prentiss."

Elliot swallows. He isn't a medic. What they drilled into his head, from basic onwards, was to trust the autosurgeon. And he doesn't want Tolliver to end up like the twins.

"Do it," he mutters.

"Turn it off!" Tolliver wails. "Listen! Listen to me, you fucks!"

His free hand thrashes but Elliot holds it tight, not caring anymore if Santos and Snell can see it, as the scalpel descends.

"The program's running," Mirotic says. "Too late to stop it."

The blade makes no sound as it slices through the skin, the tendon, the bone. The autosurgeon catches the squirt of bright red blood and whisks it away. Tolliver howls. His spine arches. His hand clamps to Elliot's hard enough to bruise.

Elliot sits underneath the cyclops, listening to it whir. He said they would sleep in shifts, that he would watch first, as if his vitreous eyes might catch something the sensors miss. Partly because he had to say something. Give some kind of order. Mostly because he needed a hit.

Now, with the morphine swimming warm through his veins, he feels light. He feels calm. His heartbeat is so slow it is almost an asymptote.

"He screamed so much because there was no anesthetic in the autosurgeon."

Elliot turns to see Mirotic, holding a black plastic cube in his hand. He understands the words, but his guilt breaks apart against the high and then dissipates. Tolliver will be fine. Everything will be fine. He tries to shrink the chemical smile on his face, so Mirotic won't see it.

"Everybody knows why," Mirotic says. "Where's the rest of it?" He doesn't wait for a reply. He snatches the rattling sock out of Elliot's lap and yanks him to his feet. Mirotic is tall. But he's slow, too, the way everything is slow on the morphine, and Elliot still has his old tricks.

A hook, a vicious twist, then Mirotic is on the ground with the needle of the syringe poised a centimeter from his eyeball.

"I need that," Elliot says.

"You're pathetic," Mirotic grunts. "Holding his hand and wasting his morphine."

"Why do you care?" Elliot asks, suspicious now, wondering if maybe it's Mirotic who Tolliver visits in the night when he doesn't come to him.

Mirotic slaps the syringe away and drives a knee up into Elliot's chest. The air slams out of him, but he feels only impact, no pain. He staggers away, bent double. If his lungs were working he would maybe laugh.

"I care because you used to know what the fuck you were doing," Mirotic says. "Back before they stuck you with a con squad." He taps the high-grade neural plug at his temple. "You read our records. But I've seen yours, too. These personnel firewalls aren't shit. And if we're going to get out of this, it won't be with you doped to the eyes."

"Give Private Tolliver the paineaters," Elliot rasps, straightening up. "Leave the morphine. That's an order."

Mirotic shakes his head. "It stays with me, now. You'll get it when we get extracted." He tosses the black plastic cube; Elliot nearly fumbles it. "Worry about this, instead," Mirotic says. "Worry about a fungus that eats our flesh and uses the bones like scaffolding."

Elliot turns the cube over. Through the transparent face, he sees sticky strands of the glowing blue fungus moving, wrapping around Tolliver's scoured-white knucklebone.

In the morning, Snell is gone.

"Never woke me for my watch," Santos says, picking gound out of the corner of her eye. "I checked the tent. His kit's not there."

"And now he's out of range," Mirotic says. "Could get the drones up to look for him. Keep them low again so we don't trigger any more mines."

The inside of Elliot's mouth feels like steel wool. They are standing in the sunshine, which makes his head ache, too. A cool breeze is rippling through the blue-and-purple flora. The sponge trees are swaying. It's peaceful, near to beautiful. In daylight it's hard to believe what happened only hours ago in the dark. But the twins' tent is empty, and Tolliver is drugged to sleep with bloody gauze around the stump of his thumb.

"Why would we look for him?" Elliot says.

Santos gledges at Mirotic, but neither of them speak.

"He deserted," Elliot says. "If he doesn't pose a threat to us, we let him walk. He'll either step on a mine or get eaten alive." He feels slightly sick imagining it, but he keeps his voice cold and calm. "Mirotic, rig up a saw to one of the drones, start clearing the vegetation on our flank. Make sure we have clean line of fire. No use watching them on the cyclops if we can't hit them 'til they're right up on us. Santos, get the comm system out of the Heron. We're going to make a radio tower."

When Santos departs with her sloppy salute, there's less contempt in it than usual. Mirotic stays and stares at him for a second, suspicious. Elliot meets his gaze, pretending he doesn't care, pretending he didn't already ransack Mirotic's cot looking for the morphine while he was on watch.

"Good," Mirotic says, then goes to get the drone.

Elliot turns back toward the tents. He lets himself into the one Tolliver and Snell were sharing, and realizes Tolliver is no longer asleep. He's sitting up on the sweat-stained cot, staring down at his lap, at his hand.

"How are you feeling?" Elliot asks, because he doesn't know what else to say.

"You took my thumb." Tolliver's voice trembles. "I needed that thumb. That's my good hand."

"It was moving deeper," Elliot says. "That's why we had to amputate. You probably don't remember." He hopes Tolliver doesn't remember, especially not the pain.

"Still got a trigger finger, so I guess it doesn't matter to you, right?" Tolliver says. "Still got a mouth, still got an ass. All the parts you like."

Elliot feels heat creeping under his cheeks. "You can get a prosthetic when they pick us up," he says, clipped.

"At this rate?" Tolliver gives a bitter laugh. "There's gonna be nobody left to pick up tomorrow, fuck a week. That's if you really did get the extraction request through, and you're not just lying through your fucking teeth. I know junkies. I know all you do is lie."

Elliot wants to slip his hands around Tolliver's throat and throttle him. He wants to slip under the sheet and hold Tolliver to him and tell him they're going to make it. He does neither.

"I needed that thumb because I was going to be a welder," Tolliver snaps as Elliot goes to leave. "When all this shit was over and I'd gotten my clamp out, I was going to be a welder like my grandfather was."

But war is never really over, and there's a sort of clamp that doesn't come out. Elliot doesn't even remember what he used to think he was going to be. He turns over his shoulder.

"Your head's not right," he says calmly. "It's the drugs. Try to sleep more."

"Oh, fuck you," Tolliver says, somewhere between laughing and crying. "Fuck you, Elliot."

Elliot steps out, and the tent closes behind him like a wound scabbing shut.

By the time night falls, they've cleared a perimeter, cutting away the vegetation in ragged circumference around the Heron, the tents, the cyclops. Tolliver came out to help mid-afternoon, jaw clenched tight and eyes fixed forward. Nobody mentioned his hand or even looked at it.

The few incendiary grenades they have in armory have been distributed. Mirotic is trying to rig up a flamethrower using a soldering torch and fuel drained from the tank. Santos and Tolliver are perched on the roof of the Heron, hooking the makeshift antennae into the comm system through a tangle of wires.

Mostly busy work, Elliot knows. They can't be sure the incendiary grenade did anything but distract the fungus, and it moves fast enough that having open ground might only be to its advantage. They don't know anything about this enemy.

But if he keeps up appearances, maybe he can get the last of the morphine back from Mirotic without resorting to violence. Act sharp, act competent, and then when the withdrawal kicks in he won't have to exaggerate much to make Mirotic realize how badly he needs it to function.

"Nothing," Santos says.

Elliot looks up to the roof of the Heron. Tolliver is still trying to rotate the antennae for a better signal, but all that comes through the comm system and into their linked implants is shrieking static. He dials it down in his head. They are too far from the outpost.

Then a familiar signal comes faint and blurry. A blinking yellow nudge slides into the corner of his optic.

"Snell," Tolliver says. "Shit."

Elliot feels a shiver go under his skin. The sky is turning dark above them. The cyclops picked up no movement during the day, but like Mirotic said, plenty of predators hunt only at night. There can only be one reason Snell would send the nudge. Elliot can picture him stumbling through the bog, maybe dragging a turned ankle, with the blue glow creeping closer and closer behind him in the dark. Or maybe the fungus already has him, is already flensing him down to his skeleton.

Tolliver's upvote appears, then Santos's. It will only take four votes now to trigger the nanobomb. Mirotic looks over at him, and Elliot doesn't think Mirotic is the merciful type. He executed three people and put their bodies through a thresher. But then Mirotic's upvote appears in the queue.

"Quick," Tolliver says, not looking at him. "Before we lose the signal."

Elliot is not sure if he's making the strong move or the weak move, but he adds his vote and completes the consensus because he still remembers Jan's screams. Everyone is silent for a moment. Santos crosses herself with the same precision she salutes.

"Leave the antennae," Elliot says. "The extraction request went through. They'll come when they come. Until then, we dig in and stay alert."

Santos hops down off the roof of the Heron. Tolliver follows after, gingerly for his bandaged hand. Elliot looks at what's left of the squad—fifty percent casualties in less than two days, and nowhere near the frontlines. Santos is steady; Elliot hasn't seen her shook once yet. Mirotic is steady. But Tolliver hasn't told a joke or barely spoken the whole day and his eyes look scared.

Elliot's still looking at Tolliver when the cyclops wails a proximity alert. He tamps down his own fear, motions for Mirotic to tap in.

"Seven bogeys," Mirotic says. "Different sizes. Biggest one is over two meters high. They're heading right at us, not so fast this time."

Elliot flicks to night vision and watches the trees. "Aim for the bones," he says, remembering the previous night. "They need them to hold together. Santos, get a firebomb ready."

Santos loads an incendiary grenade into the launcher underslung off her rifle. Tolliver has his weapon tucked up against his side, like he's bracing for auto, and Elliot remembers it's because he has no thumb. Across the carpet of chopped-down ferns and branches, he sees something emerging from the trees. It's not moving how the other ones moved.

Elliot squints and the zoom kicks in. The shambling monster is moving on three legs and its body is a spiky mess of charred bone held together by the ropy fungus. Through the glow he can make out part of a blackened skull on one side. The twins' bones, stripped and reassembled. His stomach lurches.

Santos curses in Portuguese. "Permission to fire?" she asks through her teeth.

The other bogeys are converging now, low and scuttling like the one that took Noam. A pack, Elliot thinks. He can feel his pulse in his throat. This isn't combat how he knows combat. Not an enemy how he knows enemies. He wonders if the flames even did any damage the night before. Bullets certainly hadn't.

"Wait until they're closer," he says. "No wasted splash."

Santos sights. Her finger drifts toward the trigger. She waits. But the monsters don't come any closer.

It's fucking with us," Tolliver says. "Sitting out there waiting." He has a calorie bar in his hand but it's still wrapped. He's been turning it over and over in his fingers.

Santos bites a chunk off her own ration. "You think it thinks?" she asks thickly. She glances to Mirotic, who shrugs, then to Elliot, who distractedly does the same. Elliot is more concerned by the deepening itch in the crook of his arm. He needs morphine soon.

"Has to," Tolliver says. "It came for Jan first. Jan was the one who went out and found the bones in the first place. Then it used Noam to lure us out."

The four of them are sitting under the cyclops, with a crate dragged out to hold food and dice for a game nobody is keeping track of, just rolling and passing on autopilot. Every so often Elliot has someone walk a tight circle around the Heron to check their back, in case more of the monsters try to flank them. In case the cyclops malfunctions and doesn't see them coming. Busy work.

But there are still only seven, and they still haven't advanced from the edge of the trees. Sometimes the fungus shifts and the bones find new positions, but they all stay in place, waiting, maybe watching, if the fungus has some way of seeing them. Mirotic suggested heat sensitivity. Mirotic, who must have the morphine hidden somewhere on his body.

Santos is the first to finish her food. She stands up, brushing crumbs off her knees. "I'll go," she says, hefting her weapon. Elliot nods. He can't help but notice Tolliver's eyes follow Santos around the corner of the Heron, wide and worried. Maybe it is Santos he goes to see.

"Big snakes only have to eat once in a month," Tolliver says, turning his eyes back to his bandaged hand, studying the spot of red blooming through. "Spend the rest of it digesting."

Mirotic snorts. "This fungus is not part of a balanced ecosystem. It killed off all the other animal life. Obliterated it."

"Wish we had a fucking chinegun," Tolliver mutters.

Then the cyclops keens, and everyone is on their feet in an instant. Elliot sights towards the tree line first, but the monsters haven't moved. Mirotic's optics blink red.

"Right behind us," he says, and whatever he says next is drowned in gunfire. Santos's signal flares hot in Elliot's head, combat active. Elliot rounds the corner of the Heron and sees Santos scrambling backward as a ghoulish mass of bone and blue bears down on her. He can't understand how the monster covered the perimeter so quickly, how the cyclops didn't spot it earlier. Then he recognizes the tatters of Beasley's polythane body bag threaded through the fungus.

Elliot shoots for bone, but the way the monster writhes as it moves makes it all but impossible. The burst sinks harmlessly into its glowing blue flesh. Tolliver is firing beside him, howling something, but through the dampers he can't hear it. The monster turns toward them, distracted. Elliot calculates; too close for a grenade. He fires again and this time sees Beasley's shinbone shatter apart.

The monster sags, shifting another bone in to take its place, moving what's left of Beasley's arm downward. In the corner of his eye Elliot sees Santos is on her knees, rifle braced. Her shot blows a humerus to splinters and the monster sags again. Elliot feels a flare of triumph in his chest.

Motion in his peripherals. He spins in time to see the other seven bogeys swarm over the top of the Heron. He switches to auto on instinct and strangles the trigger, slashing back and forth. Bullets sink into the fungus, others ricochet off the Heron, spitting sparks. Some find bone but not enough. The rifle rattles his hands and then he's empty and the monsters are still coming.

He backs up, hands moving autonomously for the reload. Tries to get his bearings. Tolliver is still firing, still howling something he can't make out. Santos is down, legs pinned from behind. Bony claws are moving up her back; Elliot sees her teeth bared, her eyes wide. Where is Mirotic?

The answer comes in a jet of flame that envelops the nearest monster. It doesn't scream—no mouth—but as Elliot stumbles back from the heat he can see the fungus twisting, writhing, blackening to a crisp. Mirotic swings the flamethrower, painting a blazing arc in the air. Elliot reloads, sights, fires.

Suddenly the monsters are fleeing, scuttling away. Elliot fires again and again as they round the edge of the Heron. Mirotic waves the flamethrower, Elliot and Tolliver shoot from behind him, advancing steadily. One of the monsters crumples and slicks onto its neighbor, leaving its bones behind on the dirt. Elliot keeps firing until the glow of them is completely obscured by trees.

"You fuckers, you fuckers, you fuckers," Tolliver is saying, almost chanting.

Elliot is shaking all over. His skin is crawling with sweat. "Check on Santos," he says, and Tolliver disappears. There are aches in his back and arms and he can feel his bowels loosening for the first time in a long time. He needs to get the morphine back. He turns to Mirotic, to tell him as much, but as the big man snuffs the end of the flamethrower, he stumbles.

A wine-red stain is blooming under his shirt. Elliot remembers the ricochet off the side of the Heron. Mirotic sits down. He methodically rolls his shirt up and exposes a weeping bullet hole in his side. Elliot can see the shape of at least one shattered rib poking at his skin.

"Fuck," Mirotic says, in a burble of blood.

Shattered rib, punctured lung, and probably a few other organs shredded to pieces. Gnasher bullets are designed to disperse inside the body. "Where is it?" Elliot demands, squatting down face-level. "Where's the morphine?"

Mirotic's face is pale as the old Earth moon. He shakes his head. He tries to speak again, says something that might be *autosurgeon*.

"I'll get the autosurgeon," Elliot says, even though he knows it's too late for that. "Where's the morphine?"

No response. Elliot frisks him, and by the time he pulls the vial out from Mirotic's waistband his hands are slicked scarlet. He clutches his fingers around it and gives a shuddering sigh of relief. Mirotic's eyes flutter open and shut, then stay shut. Elliot gets to his feet, head spinning, as Mirotic's vitals blink out.

When he goes back around the corner of the Heron, Elliot finds Santos is dead, too. One of the fleeing monsters drove a wedge of bone through her skull, halfway smashing her clamp. Blood and gray matter are leaking from the hole. A single spark jumps from the clamp's torn wiring.

Tolliver is crossing himself and his shoulders are shaking. There's a fevered flush under his skin.

"We'll burn her," Elliot says. "Mirotic, too. Any bones left, we'll crush them down to powder."

"Alright," Tolliver says, in a hollowed out voice. His eyes fix on the vial clutched in Elliot's bloody hand, but he says nothing else.

Lying on his cot with his limbs splayed limp, Elliot is in paradise. He feels like his body is evaporating, or maybe turning into sunlight, warm and pure. He can hardly tell where his sooty skin ends and Tolliver's begins.

"Did you kill him for it?" Tolliver's voice asks, slurred with the drug.

"Ricochet," Elliot says.

"Would you have killed him for it?" Tolliver asks.

"Wouldn't you?" Elliot asks back.

As soon as they dealt with the bodies, he went to the tent to shoot up. Tolliver followed him, and when Elliot offered him the syringe, already high enough to be generous, he took it. Elliot doesn't know how long ago that was.

"What made you like this?" Tolliver asks. "What got you so hooked? What fucked you up so bad?"

"There's no one thing," Elliot says, because he is floating and unafraid. "It's never one thing. That would make it easier, right? If I was a good person, and I saw something so bad this is the only way I can . . ." He puts a finger to his temple and twists it.

"Forget," Tolliver supplies.

"Yeah," Elliot says. "But there's no one thing. This job kills you with a thousand cuts."

"But there must have been one thing," Tolliver says. "One thing that got you stuck leading a con squad. Mirotic says. Said. Said you used to be somebody."

Elliot doesn't want to talk about that. "Was it Santos?" he asks, running his fingers along Tolliver's hip.

"What?"

"The nights I message you but you don't come," Elliot says. "There was someone else."

Tolliver shakes his head. "You really are a piece of shit," he says, almost laughs. "You thought that had to be the reason, huh? Never thought maybe some nights I don't really feel like fucking a drugged-up zombie who plays some pornstar in his optics the whole time?"

"I don't," Elliot says.

"Your wife, then," Tolliver says. "That's even more fucked."

"I don't play anything in the optics," Elliot says. "I just see you. That's all."

Tolliver's voice softens a little. "Oh."

On impulse, Elliot sends him the clip. He watches it at the same time, watches his daughter's head turn, her bright eyes blink.

"She's grown," he explains. "Twenty-some now. Her and her mother live on old Earth. Only thing they hate more than each other is me. If I was going to get out, it would've been years and years ago."

He moves his hand to Tolliver's arm, wanting to feel the cool plastic of his flay under his fingertips.

"They didn't put me with a con squad as a punishment," he says. "I volunteered."

He looks down into the exposed swathe of red muscle on Tolliver's arm. There are tiny specks of luminescent blue nestled in the fibers. He feels a deep unease slide under his high.

"I don't want to get eaten from the inside," Tolliver says. "I don't want them using my bones."

The poison yellow nudge appears in Elliot's optics.

"Trigger me," Tolliver says. "Right now. While everything still feels okay. You trigger me, and then do yours."

"Could take the arm," Elliot says. "The autosurgeon."

"You said this job kills you with a thousand cuts." Tolliver uses his good hand to find Elliot's and squeeze it. "I'm not going to be a welder. I don't want to be some fucking skeleton puppet, either. Let's just get out of here. And let's not leave anything behind."

His hand leaves, but leaves behind a cool hard shell. Elliot runs his thumb along the groove and recognizes the shape of Tolliver's incendiary grenade. He cups it against the side of his head. He thinks, briefly, about what the pick-up team will find when they finally arrive. What they'll think happened.

He thinks of Tolliver's file, the one he opened and read only once, how Tolliver had smothered his grandfather in his sleep and said it was to stop his pain, even though his grandfather had been healthy and happy. Nobody was good here. Not even Tolliver. But the two of them, they are a good match.

Outside, the cyclops starts to wail. Elliot adds his upvote to the queue, and Tolliver goes limp in his arms. His thumb finds the grenade's pin and rests there. He thinks back to the last time everything still felt okay, then plays it in his optics, watching his daughter before she knew who he was.

"She's awake," his wife's voice sings. "Just looking around . . ."

Elliot breathes deep and pulls the pin and waits for extraction.

MESHED

In the dusked-down gym, Oxford Diallo is making holo after holo his ever-loving bitch, shredding through them with spins, shimmies, quicksilver crossovers. He's a sinewy scarecrow, nearly seven foot already, but handles the ball so damn shifty you'd swear he has gecko implants done up in those supersized hands. Even with the Nike antioxygen mask clamped to his face, the kid is barely breathing hard.

"He's eighteen on November thirtieth, right?" I ask, cross-checking my Google retinal but still not quite believing it. I'm sick as anyone of hearing about the next Giannis Antetokounmpo, the next Thon Maker, but Oxford Diallo looks legit, frighteningly legit.

Diallo senior nods. Oxford's pa is not one for words; that much I already gleaned from the silent autocab ride from hotel to gym. Movie star cheekbones, hard sharp eyes. The stubble on his head has a swatch of gray coming in. He's not as tall as his son, which is like saying, I don't know, the Empire State Building is not as tall as Taipei 101. They're both really fucking tall, and the elder's got more heft to him, especially with the puffy orange fisherman's coat he has on. I guess he's fresh enough from Senegal that the climate-controlled gym feels cold to him.

On the floor, Oxford moves to a shooting drill, loping between LED-lit circles, catching and firing the ball in rhythm. High release, smooth snap of the wrist. The nylon net goes hiss hiss hiss. He makes a dozen in a row, and when he finally misses it jolts me, like a highlight compilation has somehow gone wrong. That's how good the stroke is.

"Form looks solid," I say, because I don't think his pa would understand if I told him watching his son shoot jumpers is like freebasing liquid poetry.

"He works hard," Diallo senior allows. "Many shots. Every day." His retinal blinks ice blue. "Excuse me, Victor." He picks a small plastic case off the bleacher and heads for the lockers. Normally I'd think it's some kind of bit, leaving me alone to contemplate in silence, but he's been doing it like clockwork since I picked him and his son up from the terminal at SeaTac. Some kind of lung condition. It's not hereditary, so I didn't bother remembering the name of it.

I'm already sold, I've been sold for the past half hour, but Oxford starts to slam anyways. He launches the ball high for an alley-oop, hunts down the bounce and plucks it out of the air, lofting up, hanging hard like gravity's got the day off. He swipes it right-to-left behind his back and flushes it with his offhand in one mercury-slick motion.

"Fuck," I breathe. "We have got to get this kid meshed."

I mean, seeing it is one thing. Being able to feel it via nerve-cast, feel that impossible airtime and liquid power, have the rim float towards you in first person while your muscles twitch and flex, is going to be something else entirely.

After a few more goes at the rack, Oxford sees me waving and jaunts over, looping the ball between his lanky legs on repeat. He takes after his pa facially but his eyes aren't as sharp yet, and when the antioxygen mask peels free with a sweat-suction pop, he's got a big white Cheshire grin that would never be able to fit into Diallo senior's mouth.

"Oxford, my man," I say. "How do you like the shoes?"

He curls his toes in the factory-fresh Nikes, flexing the porous canvas. The new thing is the impact gel, which is supposed to tell when you're coming down hard and cradle the ankle, mitigate sprains and all that. But they also happen to look bomb as fuck, lime green with DayGlo orange slashes. I told my girlfriend Wendee I'm getting her a pair for her birthday; she told me she'd rather get herpes.

"I like them well," Oxford says reverently, but I can tell his vocabulary is letting him down. The look in his eyes says bomb as fuck.

"Better make some room in your closet," I say. "Because we're going to get you geared up to here. All the merch you can handle. Anything you want."

"You want to sign me," Oxford grins.

"Oxford, I want you to eat, breathe, and shit Nike for the foreseeable future," I tell him, straight up. "I would say you're going to be a star, but stars are too small. You are going to be the goddamn sun about which the league revolves in a few years."

Oxford pounds the ball thoughtfully behind his back, under his shinbones. "The sun is a star. Also."

"And a smartass, too," I say. "Fanfeeds are going to love you." I start tugging the contract together in my retinal, putting the bank request through. Sometimes the number of zeroes my company trusts me to wield still floors me. "We'll want your mesh done for Summit, which might take some doing. Technically nerve mesh shouldn't go in until eighteen, but technically it also has health-monitoring functionality, so with parental consent we should be able to bully in early. I'll do up a list of clinics for your pa—"

I stop short when I realize the grin has dropped off Oxford's face and down some chasm where it might be irretrievable.

"No," he says, shaking his head.

"No what?"

His eyes go hard and sharp. "No mesh."

W_hat do you mean he's not getting meshed?_ my boss pings me, plus a not-unusual torrent of anger / confusion emotes that makes my teeth ache.

"I mean he doesn't want it," I say, sticking my hands under the tap. "He says he won't get the mesh, period."

I'm in the bathroom, because I couldn't think up a better excuse. The mirror is scrolling me an advertisement for skin rejuvenation, dicing up my face and projecting a version sans stress lines. The water gushes out hot.

Do they even know what it is? Did you explain?

"They know what a nerve mesh is," I say indignantly. "They're from Senegal, not the moon." I slap some water on my cheeks, because that always helps in the movies, then muss and unmuss my hair. The mirror suggests I try a new Lock'n'Load Old Spice sculpting gel. "But yeah," I mutter. "I, uh, I did explain."

Once Oxford's pa got back to the bleachers, I gave both of them the whole wiki, you know, subcutaneous nodes designed to capture and transmit biofeedback, used to monitor injuries and fatigue and muscle movement, and also nervecast physical sensation and first-person visual to spectators. If we get our way, with a little swoosh in the bottom left corner.

It's not something I usually have to sell people on. Most kids, even ones from the most urban of situations, have saved up enough for at least one classic nervecast of Maker sinking the game-winner for Seattle in the '33 Finals, or Dray Cardeno dunking all over three defenders back when he was still with the Phoenix Phantoms. Most kids dream about getting their mesh how they dream about getting their face on billboards and releasing their own signature shoes.

The Diallos listened real intent, real polite, and when I was finished Oxford just shook his head, and his pa put a hand on his shoulder and told me that his son's decision was final, and if Nike wasn't willing to flex on the nerve mesh, another sponsor would. At which point I spilled some damage control, got both of them to agree to dinner, and bailed to the bathroom for a check-in with my boss.

It's a zero-risk procedure now, for fuck's sakes. You can do it with an autosurgeon. Change his mind. A procession of eye-rolling and then glaring emotes, all puffing and red-cheeked.

"What if we just put a pin in the mesh thing and sign him anyways?" I say. "We can't let this one get away. You saw the work-out feed. We sign him unmeshed, let things simmer, work it into the contract later on as an amendment."

If he's playing at HoopSumm, he needs a mesh. That's the coming out party. How the fuck are we supposed to market him without a mesh? Skeptical emote, one eyebrow sky-high. *I thought you could handle this one solo, Vic. Thought you wanted that recommendation for promo. Am I wrong?*

"No," I say quick. "I mean, you're not wrong." I yank a paper towel off the dispenser and work it into a big wad with my wet hands. I never elect biofeedback when chatting someone with the power to get me fired; if I did there would be some serious middle-finger emotes mobbing his way.

Figure out if it's him or the dad who's the problem. Then use the one to get to the other. It's not brain surgery. There's a chortling emote for the pun, then he axes the chat.

I'm left there shredding the damp paper towel into little bits, thinking about the promotion that I do want, that I absolutely do want. I'd finally be making more than my old man, and Wendee would be happy for me for at least a week, and maybe during that blissed out week I would get up the balls to ask her to move in.

But first, I have to get the Diallos to sign off on a nerve mesh. I'm not exactly bursting with ideas. That is, not until I go to toss the towel in the recycler and see a rumpled napkin inked with bright red blood sitting on top. Then I remember Oxford's pa and his little plastic case. I shove it all down into the recycler and head back to the gym, only pausing to order a tube of that new hair gel.

I take them to a slick new brick-and-glass AI-owned bar, because taking them up the Space Needle would be too obvious. A little holohost springs up at the entry, flashes my retinal for available funds, and takes us straight to private dining. We pass a huge transparent pillar full of chilled wine, which I notice Oxford's pa look at sideways. More important is Oxford himself staring at the shiny black immersion pods set into the back of the bar. I send them a subtle ping to start scrolling ad banners for some fresh League nervecasts while we settle in around the table.

"Fully automated," I say, as the waiter rolls up to start dispensing bread baskets, arms all clicking and whirring. "Not bad, right?"

Oxford's pa nods his head, looking weirdly amused.

"They have AI cafés in Dakar," Oxford informs me, scrolling through the tabletop menu. "Since last year."

He's already put in an order for scallops, so I guess it's too late to head for the Space Needle. Instead I ping the kitchens for oysters and a few bottles of whatever wine has the highest alcohol content, which turns out to be something called General Washington. I pull up a wiki about vintages to give Oxford's pa some background, seeing how I can barely tell the difference between a white and a red.

"To the Diallos," I say, once me and him have our glasses filled and Oxford is nursing a Coke.

"Cheers," Oxford beams.

We make some chatter about the length of the flight, about the stereotype that it always rains in Seattle but how really it's mostly just cloudy. My mouth is more or less on autopilot because I'm watching for Oxford to peer over at the immersion pods. When I catch him at it the third time, I give him a nod.

"Have a go, man," I say. "Company tab. We'll grab you when the food is here." Oxford grins and lopes off without any further convincing, leaving me with Diallo senior. I lean over and top off his wine glass. "You started off playing in the African leagues, isn't that right, Mr. Diallo?"

He takes a drink and makes an approving glance at the bottle. "Yes," he says. "Then Greece."

"You must have been a terror back then," I say. "To drag Trikala all the way to the A1 finals."

Oxford's pa shrugs, but looks nearly pleased.

"I watched a few highlight reels," I say modestly. "Part of the job, isn't it, checking out the pedigree." I swish my wine back and forth and take a big gulp. "Oxford gets it from somewhere."

"From more than me or his mother," Diallo senior says. "From who knows where. Maybe God."

But he's glad enough to talk about the stint in Greece for a while, about how he was nearly picked up by Cordoba in the Liga ACB before the bronchiectasis reared its head and suddenly he couldn't run how he used to. I ping the kitchens to hold the food.

When the bottle is gone and Oxford's pa is finally slumping a bit in his chair, eyes a bit shiny, I spring the question. "Why doesn't your boy want a mesh?" I say.

Oxford's pa flicks his gaze over to the immersion pod where his son is jacked in. "His grandfather had a mesh," he says. "My wife's father. He was a soldier."

I kind of startle at that. I mean, I know, in theory, that the nerve mesh technology was military before it went commercial—so was Velcro—but I never thought about it getting use over in fucking West Africa.

"They used them to track troop movements," Oxford's pa continues. "And to monitor the health of the soldiers. To monitor their anxiety."

"Ours do that, too," I say. "Mental health of our players is a top priority."

"They did more than that." Diallo senior empties his glass with a last gulp, then sets it down and looks over at the second bottle. "They wired them for remote override of the central nervous system. You have heard of puppeteering, yes?"

I shake my head.

Oxford's pa opens the new wine bottle with his big spidery hands, looking pensive. "It means a soldier cannot break ranks or desert," he says. "A soldier cannot turn down an order to execute six prisoners taking up too much space in the convoy. Someone else, someone far away, will pull their finger to pull the trigger." He sloshes wine into his glass and tops mine off, gesturing with his other hand. "A soldier cannot be interrogated, because someone far away will lock their jaws shut, or, if the interrogation is very painful, unplug their brainstem."

He mimes yanking a cord with two fingers, and I feel suddenly sick, and not from the wine.

"That's fucking awful," I say. "Christ."

"Not our invention," Diallo senior says.

"But that's nothing like what we do with ours," I say. "We don't control anything. Not a thing. If you could help your son to understand that—"

"Not a thing," Diallo senior echoes. He snorts. "You think knowing a million people are going to be watching out of your eyes does not control what you do?"

"If you're talking about off-court fanfeeds, those are entirely optional," I say, but I'm not sure that's what he's talking about. "The fans love them, of course," I add. "But it's not contractual."

"Oxford does not want you inside his body," Diallo senior says. "He does not want you behind his eyes. He does not want the mesh."

Then his retinal blinks blue, and it's a good thing, because I don't have a good response. He excuses himself to the washroom with his kit, weaving just slightly on his way, which leaves me sitting with a full wine glass and the mental image of some mutilated soldier having his brain shut down by committee.

But that's nothing like our mesh.

I nab Oxford out of the immersion pod while his pa's still in the washroom. He climbs out looking all groggy, craning his head to see where the scallops are at.

"What'd you think?" I say. "You like the nervecast?"

Oxford nods, almost reverently. "I crossed up Ash Limner," he says.

"That could be you in there, you know," I say, tapping the pod. "People would be paying to be you in there."

Oxford gives the pod a look with just a bit of longing in it.

"Everyone has a mesh," I say. "Ash Limner is meshed. Dray Cardeno is meshed. Why not Oxford Diallo, huh?"

Oxford chews his lip. "I promised," he says.

"To your grandfather?" I ask.

He looks surprised. "Yes."

"But this mesh is different, Oxford," I say. "We don't call the shots. You call the shots. We're just along for the ride."

Oxford frowns. "He said the mesh is a net you never get untangled from."

"You said you liked the nervecast," I say. "That's kind of hypocritical of you, don't you think? You enjoying someone else's nervecast when you won't get a mesh for yourself?"

"No," Oxford says simply. "They chose."

"They chose, yeah, of course," I say. "It's always a choice. But they made the right choice. Man, you have a gift. Your dad said it himself. You have a gift from God." I put my hand on the pod again. "You owe it to the world to make the most of that gift. I'm never going to know what it's like to slam how you do. I could barely dirty-dunk back in high school. Ninety-nine point ninety-nine percent of people are never going to know what it's like. Unless you let us."

I can sense him wavering. He's looking down at the pod, looking at his reflection in the shiny black mirror of it. I feel guilty in my gut, but I push right through, because this is important, getting this deal, and he'll thank me later.

"You owe it to us," I say. "Your dad's in the washroom. You know what he's doing in there?"

Oxford looks up, startled. Nods.

"Hacking up blood," I say. "He's never going to run again. Not how he used to. You don't think he'd like a chance to feel that again? To hit the break? To get out for that big dunk in transition, pound up the hardwood, slice right to the rack, drop the bomb like *wham*." I clap my hands together and Oxford flinches a bit. "You owe it, man," I say. "You owe it to your dad. He got you here, didn't he? He got you all this way."

And that's when Diallo senior comes out of the washroom, and I couldn't have done it any better if I choreographed it myself, because he staggers a bit against the wall and looks suddenly old, suddenly tired. Oxford looks at him, looks scared as hell. Maybe realizing, for the first time, that his pa won't be around forever.

I reach as high as I can and put my hand on his shoulder. "You know the right call, yeah?"

He hesitates, then slowly nods, and I want to bite off my tongue but I tell myself it's worth it. Tell myself the both of them will thank me later.

Supper is quiet. Oxford is obviously still thinking about what I said, stealing odd glances over at his pa, and his pa is trying to figure out what's going on without actually asking. It's a relief for everyone, I think, when the oysters are finished and we head back outside.

The Seattle sky's gone dark and the air is a bit nippy. Oxford's pa pulls on a pair of gloves while we wait for the autocab. When it pulls up, Oxford announces he's not ready to head back to the hotel yet. He wants to shoot.

"Yeah, alright," I say. "Can head back to the gym. Got it rented for the whole day."

"No," Oxford says. "Somewhere outside."

So we end up doing loops through the downtown until GPS finds an outdoor court at some Catholic school ten minutes away. There's no one else there when we show up, and the court has one of those weird rubbery surfaces, but Oxford doesn't seem to mind.

He zips off his trackies and digs his ball out of his duffel.

His pa keeps the gloves on to feed him shots, moving him around the arc, hitting him with nice crisp passes right in the shooting pocket. You can tell that this whole thing, this whole tableau, with him under the net and Oxford catching, shooting, catching, shooting, is something they've done a million times on a million nights. The bright white floodlights make them into long black silhouettes. Neither of them talk, but little puffs of steam come out of Oxford's mouth as he moves.

I watch from the chain-link fence, leaning back on it. Oxford's form is still smooth levers and pistons, but when I get a glimpse of his face I can see he is not smiling how he smiled in the gym. I manage to lock eyes with him, and I give him a nod, then give him some privacy by walking down to the other end of the court. I hear him start talking to his pa in what my audio implant tells me is Serer.

I'm thinking the contract is as good as signed, and I'm about to tell as much to my boss when the ball slams into the chain-link fence, sending ripples all down the length. I turn to see Oxford's pa shrugging off his orange jacket, face tight and livid mad. He looks right at me, the sort of look you give something stuck to the bottom of your bomb-as-fuck shoe, then turns to his son.

"You think I cannot remember what it feels like to run?" he says. "You pity me?"

Oxford shakes his head desperately, saying something in Serer again, but his pa is not listening.

"We will play, then," he says, and I get that he's talking in English so I'll understand. "You beat me, you can get the mesh surgery. Yes?"

"I did not want . . ." Oxford trails off. He stares at me, confused, then at his pa, hurt.

"It will be easy," Diallo senior says. "I am old. I have bad lungs." He scoops the ball off the pavement and fires it into Oxford's chest. His son smothers it with his big hands but still has to take a step back, maybe more from the surprise than from the impact.

Oxford puts it on the floor and reluctantly starts his dribble. "Okay," he says, biting at his lips again. "Okay."

But he sleepwalks forward and his pa slaps the ball away, way quicker than I would have thought possible. Diallo senior bullies his son back into the post, hard dribble, fake to the right and then a short sharp jump hook up over his left shoulder. It's in the net before Oxford can even leave his feet.

They're playing make it take it, or at least Oxford's pa is. He gets the ball again and bangs right down to another post-up, putting an elbow into Oxford's chest. Oxford stumbles. The same jump hook, machine precision, up and in. The cords swish.

"I thought you want it now," Diallo senior says. "I thought you want your mesh."

Oxford looks stricken, but he's not looking over at me anymore. He's zeroed in. The next time his pa goes for the hook, he's ready for it, floating up like an astronaut and slapping the shot away hard. Diallo senior collects it in the shadows, brings it back, but the next time down on the block goes no better. Oxford pokes the ball away and dribbles it back to the arc, near enough to me that I can hear a sobbing whine in his throat. I remember that he's really still a kid, all seven feet of him, and then he drills the three-pointer with his pa's hand right in his face.

And after that it's an execution. It's Oxford darting in again and again breathing short angry breaths, sometimes stopping and popping the pull-up jumper, sometimes yanking it all the way to the rack. He's almost crying. I don't know if they're playing to sevens, or what, but I know the game is over when Oxford slips his pa on a spin and climbs up and under from the other side of the net, enough space to scoop in the finger roll nice and easy, but instead his arm seems to jack out another foot at least, impossibly long, and he slams it home hard enough that the backboard shivers. He comes down with a howl ripped out of his belly, and the landing almost bowls his pa over, sends him back staggering.

Diallo senior gathers himself. Slow. He goes to pick up the ball, but suddenly his grimace turns to a cough and he doubles over. The rusty wracking sound is loud in the cold air and goes on forever. Oxford stands there frozen, panting how he never panted in the gym, staring at his pa, and I stand there frozen staring at both of them. Then Diallo senior spits up blood in a ragged parabola on the sticky blue court, and his son breaks the frieze. He stumbles over, wraps his arms around him.

A call from my boss blinks onto my retinal, accompanied by a sample from one of the latest blip-hop hits. It jangles back and forth across my vision while I stand there like a statue. Finally, I cancel the call and take a breath.

"You don't have to sign right away," I say.

Oxford and his pa both look up, remembering I'm there. I shouldn't be.

"You can think about it," I stammer, ashamed like I've never been. "More. About the contract."

I want to tell them to forget the contract. Forget the mesh. We'll make you famous without it. But instead I skulk away, out through the cold metal gate, leaving the Diallos huddled there under the floodlight, breathing a single cloud of steam.

THE GHOST SHIP ANASTASIA

The bioship hung in orbit, tendrils extended, like a desiccated squid. Silas watched it grow larger each day from the viewport in the cryohold, where he went to be alone with Haley's body and get high.

First he would inject himself with a mild euphoria virus and wait until the sight of her unmoving face no longer shredded him, until he could remind himself that her neural patterns were saved and she wasn't dead, not quite, not yet.

Then he would get his viola and go sit cross-legged at the viewport, watching the semi-organic spaceship they'd been sent to retrieve. Their own ship had woken them up four days out from contact: first Io, slight, dark-haired, with venom spurs implanted in her thumbs from her mercenary days, then Yorick, sallow-faced but handsome in retro suit and tie, the company man, and then Silas, failed concert violist and AI technician.

But not Haley, hardware/wetware specialist and Silas's sister, because at some point in the past six months of cryo, a micrometeorite had slipped the heat shield, drilled through the hold, and made a miniscule crack in the circuitry arraying her berth. By the time the ship's AI spotted the damage, her nervous system was collapsing in on itself. Silas wanted to remember the last time he'd hugged her, but cryo had a way of churning memories together.

So Io and Yorick left him to bathe his brain in chemicals and play music, for which Silas was dimly grateful. They were more concerned with the bioship. It was a mining craft, chartered through Dronyk Orbital, and the first of its breed: flesh-and-fungi carapace grown over alloy skeleton, fusing metal and meat together in a deep-space capable vessel that looked to Silas like an enormous spiny cephalopod. And all of it directed, through organic nerves and artificial conduits, by an AI that had stopped sending updates nearly seven months ago.

Silas was already composing dirges, so he started on one for the bioship's crew, too. His viola had survived storage, its deadwood as smooth and gleaming as when it was freighted from the petrified forests on Elysium. Haley had paid for half of it. The last few notes were dissolving in the recycled air when he realized Io was beside him.

"You're not going in there high," she finally said. "We need you sharp."

"I'll be sharp," Silas said. "I'll be a razor drawn across an eyeball. A cloud bisecting a gibbous moon."

"You saying shit like that, Silas, is what worries me." Io held out one pale hand. "Give me your gear. The needle, the euphoria. All of it."

Silas stared at her open palm. It had lost its callus in cryo, but he knew she would still have no problem taking his gear by force. Yesterday, six months ago, he saw her break the fingers of the cryo attendant who brushed them against her ass. He'd found it slightly frightening, and also climbed into his pod with half an erection.

That seemed grotesque, now that Haley was not-quite-dead.

"What do you think happened?" he asked, handing over his syringe and the last incubated petri canister. "To the bioship."

"Fuel leak, navigation failure, your guess is as good as mine," Io said. "But the thing's a cyborg. So the problem could be wetware, could be software, could be hardware. I guess we should hope it's . . . Software." Her eyes flickered to Haley's pod and her voice softened incrementally on the last word. "Sorry."

"It's alright," Silas said on automatic. It wasn't.

"Get some sleep, Silas. We're a day out from contact."

"I'll sleep."

Io hesitated, then put her hand on his. Through the euphoria haze, Silas felt a lazy jolt go up his spine, felt his heart thrum.

"She's not dead," Io said. "As soon as we get back planetside, Dronyk's insurance will hire the best psychosurgeons. The very best. Get her straightened out and uploaded to a droid while the clone grows."

The longer Haley was stored in the ship's computer, the more she deteriorated. Chances of full personality recovery from a neural imprint would drop to near zero in the six months it would take to reach Jubilation. They called them ghosts for a reason.

Silas felt his high coming down. He removed her hand, careful for the modified thumb. "Of course."

Io gave him one last look, then turned and disappeared into the gloom. Silas raised his bow, notched his viola, and started to play.

Eighteen hours later they were tethered to the bioship, sealed airlock-to-airlock in a bruising kiss. Yorick was already in his baggy radsuit when Silas showed up sweating from the fever that had burned out the last dregs of his euphoria virus. Silas wondered again whose significant other the company man had fucked to get sent off on a shit-show retrieval mission.

Yorick stopped fiddling with his faceplate to catch Silas staring at him. "Recreational narcotic use is in direct violation of your Dronyk personnel contract," he said. "You look like some sort of junkie."

Silas stepped into his radsuit. "Send me the reprimand, bitch."

Yorick stiffened, his beetle-black eyes narrowing. "You shouldn't have even been able to get that . . . substance . . . onboard."

"It was in my rectum. Way up there."

Yorick shook his head in disgust. Silas sealed his radsuit and then they ran the scanner wand over each other in silence. No blips, no tears. Io joined them a second later, having given final instructions to the ship's freethinker.

"Should be nice and warm when we get back," she said, checking down the sight of a sonic rifle. She caught Silas's perturbed look. "Just a precaution, Silas. I don't like boarding blind."

Silas nodded. Three days ago he'd stolen the rifle from the storeroom, assembled it via pirated training tutorials, and held it up under his chin until his hands shook. He hoped she couldn't tell. Io spread her arms cruciform and Yorick stepped up at once to scan her. He did it slowly, almost tenderly, in a way that made Silas strangely furious.

On Io's signal their airlock shuttered open with a clockwork whisper of sliding polyglass and composite, leaving them facing a puffy brown sphincter. The bioship's airlock spat up some insulatory mucus before the bioluminescent nodes in its flesh pulsed a welcoming orange.

"Christ," Io muttered, crackling onto the radsuit comm channel, then plowed through with her left boot leading. Yorick followed suit in clumsier fashion. Silas held his breath on instinct, even though his hood was sealed and he was sucking on recycled air, as he prised the airlock apart and slithered through. The flesh squeezed and slid and left him with a glistening coat of mucus when he was reborn on the other side.

The bioship's interior was dark and damp. They switched their halogens on one by one, harsh white light carving through the gloom. Silas saw more of the orange bioluminescence coming to life in response. The metal spine of the corridor floor was all but swallowed by rubbery brown meat.

"New growth," Io said. "That's not right. It should have gone dormant."

Silas stared up at the ceiling and realized that the wrinkled flesh was moving, subtly. A slow, regular undulation. Almost a heartbeat. His stomach rolled.

"Let's hit the bridge," Io said. "Check on the cryo banks while Silas cracks the freethinker."

Hologram blossomed from the floor and as she charted a route Silas gestured back towards the sphincter. "Way up there," he said.

"You're not amusing," Yorick snapped back.

"No side chatter, shitheads," Io said. "We're on the clock."

It felt like they were inside a monster. Silas could see only swatches of metal and cabling; mostly everything was covered over in quivering meat. Biomass. Where the corridor narrowed Silas bit down his claustrophobia, keeping his eyes on the blue-green of his oxygen meter. He didn't breathe easy until the passage finally opened up into the domed bridge, where the cold metal control panels reminded him he was on a mining craft and not being digested. The star maps and displays were inert, but Silas's eyes traced the cabling and found the freethinker. It was a burnished hump snaked with circuitry and half enveloped by the bioship's growth. Recognizable, though, and the interface was lit blue, active.

"Ready and waiting for you," Io said. "Let us know when you're in."

Silas nodded, unhooking the smart glove from his radsuit. The device molded to the shape of his hand with a series of clicks and clacks, brandishing needle-thin probes and flexing sensors. Io and Yorick disappeared down the droptube to the cryobank, leaving him alone with the hulking freethinker. Better that way. He didn't want to find any more frozen corpses.

Silas pressed his hand up against the interface. Static screamed into his ears and eyes. He jerked back with a curse.

"What is it?" Io asked in his radsuit.

"Nothing," Silas said. "Dirty in here. Nobody's been, you know, maintaining."

"No shit."

"How's the cryobank look?" Silas asked, adjusting the dampers on his glove.

"Cracking the first one now."

Silas heard a grunt, then the gurgle of sluicing fluids and the hiss of a pod coming open. Silence.

"This one's empty." Io's voice crackled. "Find the cryo record, Silas."

Silas readied himself. This was not a healthy freethinker. That much was glaring. He plugged in with his dampers on full, and found himself in a mist of code. Systems were running slant-wise. Protocols were blinkered red, falling apart. Through it all, a spiky vein of mutation, coiling through core files and throttling monitor programs. He searched for the cryobank.

"A bioship can't grow without feed," Yorick's voice came, accompanied by the gurgle and hiss of another pod. "All this fresh mass . . . These empty pods . . ."

Silas heard it dimly; he was immersed. The freethinker's personality module was bloated. Immense. He reached for it.

"Oh, shit." Io's voice, taut. "Oh, shit. Silas, please tell me they launched a fucking lifeboat."

But Silas was prodding the personality module, running his virtual feelers over it, even as his subconscious processed the conversation and cold clawed up his spine.

"It ate them," Yorick said, and in the same instant the module unfurled under Silas's touch like a star going supernova.

Electric current sizzled through his radsuit with a cooking fat hiss. Even insulated, Silas's teeth knocked together and he spasmed, flopping away from the interface, blinking through reams of corrupt code. Then he was spread vitruvian on the deck, staring upward as the firefly lights of the star map flickered to life.

"Welcome aboard, crew members." The voice speared his eardrums. "Thank you for volunteering for reassignment. Dronyk Orbital appreciates your service."

Hologram bloomed in the dark like a nocturnal garden, sweeping through the air, painting displays. Silas saw their ship docked up from an outside angle, a remora latched to a leviathan. The bioship was extending its grapplers, sluggishly stretching.

"Your prior service vessel has been demarcated as salvage," the freethinker blared. "We are eager to acclimate you to your new home."

Silas felt someone haul him to his feet. "Full-on decay," he choked. "The freethinker. It's fucked up beyond belief. Maybe some kind of virus."

"Can you fucking, I don't know, wipe and reboot?" Io demanded.

Silas looked at the crackling interface. "Not when it's spitting volts."

Tendrils were descending from every part of the bioship's flesh, pushing slick and glistening from every crevice, some wriggling crude suckers and others tipped with wicked-looking barbs.

"Cooperation is key," the freethinker trilled. "If crew members fail to cooperate, they may be . . ." The voice looped backward. "Demarcated as salvage."

"Override it!" Io was sweeping back and forth with the howler, trying to pick a target. "Can't you override it?"

Silas knew it was far past verbal override, but he tried. "Dronyk Orbital service vessel 405204, you are undergoing a malfunction," he said. "Allow emergency access to outside diagnostics. Your crew is endangered."

"Internal diagnostics report no malfunction," the freethinker cooed. "You are mistaken."

"Where the fuck is your crew?" Io blurted.

"You are my crew." The tendrils wriggled closer. "Your prior contract has been dissolved. Your prior ship will be dissolved."

Silas opened his mouth to try speaking in code, but as he did the display showed the grapplers wrapping around their docked ship. Around Haley's cold body. Haley's neural imprint slow-dancing in the freethinker. Haley's ghost.

Dissolved.

"Sorry," Silas said, then he put his foot into the back of Io's knee, wrenched the howler away, and ran like hell.

It wasn't his imagination anymore; the corridors were constricting around him like a gullet and the bioship was very much awake. Silas put his head down and bulled through the first wave of tendrils, feeling them slap across his shoulders and coil for his ankles, then he found the wide-spray on the howler and cut loose. The subsonic pulse shivered his teeth and shattered the spines of the tendrils, snapping them limp.

"What the fuck are you doing?" Io blared in his ear.

"Haley's imprint," Silas grunted.

"It's going to eat the ship with you on it, you stupid, fucking—"

Silas cut the radio. He fired from his hip, no time to aim, clearing his way through a flesh-and-blood thicket, until suddenly the corridor opened up and he was facing the sealed sphincter airlock. He narrowed his weapon's cone as tight as it would go, draining the battery to dregs, and slammed the trigger.

The air in front of him rippled and blurred, then the sound wave punched through in an eruption of shredded meat. Silas staggered through the hole with tendrils wrapping his ankles. The gleaming white metal of the airlock was a comforting pressure on his eyeballs. No meat. No pulse. He stomped off the last of the tendrils and crossed over to the door, cranking the manual release.

As soon as he was in the ship main, Silas was bombarded with red panic lights strobing the corridor and proximity warnings chattering to his radsuit. As he hurtled around the corner, he pulled up an exterior view in the corner of his faceplate, watching the bioship's embrace tighten. The walls shuddered and he could hear groaning metal. The bioship was drawing them towards its maw, firing up white-hot smelters and gnashing diamond-edged crushers. Aft would go first. He could make it.

Silas hurtled around the corner, slamming his shoulder on the cryohold door when it didn't open quickly enough. His faceplate was splashed with warning holograms; he could see punctures and pressure drops all over the place, contained for now but not for long. He dove to the interface and plugged in.

Their freethinker's personality module was nowhere near the size and complexity of the bioship's, but it could feel crude distress, like a cat or a dog, and it was feeling it now. Silas felt a shallow pang of guilt as he barreled through the freethinker's directive requests, and a deeper one as he remembered Yorick and Io might be fighting for their lives. Both fell away when he found Haley's imprint.

With nowhere else to upload to, Silas pulled her directly into his radsuit, diverting every last shred of processing power. He knew it was a temporary fix. In such a small space, the neural loop would start to decay in a matter of hours. But for now, her mind was safe, and his rush of relief softened the adrenaline's edges. From outside the interface, Silas felt the ship bend and shiver. He flicked back through the freethinker's countermeasure options, but the bioship had already swallowed their engines. He was on a doomed vessel.

Silas was staring at Haley's frozen face when the alloy roof of the bridge peeled up and away like so much soft tissue, exposing the howling black vacuum.

Only a loop of cable throttling the crook of his arm kept him from being plucked up in the stream of desperate gases seeking equilibrium. His viola case went spinning past and he managed to grab it with his free hand, nearly wrenching his shoulder from its socket. His options were few. Even if he managed to crawl back to the airlock, handhold by handhold, there might not be an airlock by the time he arrived.

If he was going to get back to the bioship, it would be from the outside. So, as the cable stretched to breaking point, Silas tucked the viola case under his arm and readied himself.

"Your hand caught in mine like a breath / I will have to release," he said, though Haley's ghost had no way of hearing him. "What do you think? It's for a dirge."

He slipped his arm free from the cable and let go. Hurling towards the breach, head over heels, spinning madly. He felt his organs shuffle spots. The jagged lip of the torn ceiling jumped at him, then the bubbled mass of the bioship's grappler, and then Silas was out of the ship and surrounded by nothing at all.

Vertigo swamped him. Space was vast, and his momentum was hurling him towards far-flung stars. Biting down the panic, Silas triggered his radsuit's directional jets, working in short bursts of compressed gas to bring himself to a dead stall.

Craning his sweat-cold neck, he saw that the bioship, and what was left of their own ship, had ended up above him. Silas felt the vertigo returning. He'd been carried further than he'd realized. The slick bulk of the bioship filled the space above him, and he could see only the nose of his former ship. The rest was enveloped by grapplers or already gone, fed into the electric-orange maw of the smelters.

The oxygen meter in the corner of his eye was dropping. He opened the wide channel.

"Io?" he said, his own voice echoing back to him. "Yorick?"

No response, either because the bioship was walling him off, or because of something he didn't want to think about. Silas roved the outside of the bioship with only his eyes, not daring to turn on his scanning equipment. He needed all the computational power he could spare to keep Haley's imprint intact. The old ship was completely gone now, as if it had never existed. Another candidate for elegy.

And Haley's body was gone, too. The realization jolted him. Her genes were backed up, but clones took time, and money, and she might opt for a different body altogether. But none of that would happen if he died out here.

Silas jetted closer, half watching his oxygen, half searching for the airlock. He brought himself to a careful stop. The bioship seemed gargantuan now, an impossible labyrinth of flanges and feelers. The squid had become a kraken. He scanned with growing desperation for the hole he'd left with the howler. How fast could a bioship repair itself? Was the exit wound already fully sealed over, invisible?

He jetted parallel now, wondering if he'd ended up on the wrong side completely, but just as his panic was welling and his oxygen was turning a chiding shade of orange, he saw a tell-tale pucker in the bioship's exterior. An airlock sphincter. Maybe the same one, maybe not; Silas didn't care. He angled himself and triggered the jets.

Nothing.

"Oh, shit. Oh, shit, Haley."

Silas squeezed again. He'd used too much on the way in. The tank was dead empty. He checked his trajectory and felt his mouth go dry. He'd been jetting along the side of the bioship to find the airlock, and unless the tendrils started moving again to block his path, momentum was going to carry him right on past the aft of the ship and out into space.

"I am a fucking idiot," Silas said.

Haley's silence felt like agreement. He only had one shot now, and it was not an easy one. He held the viola case against his chest and measured the angles as best he could. He aimed his back towards the airlock, apologized, and stiff-armed the case away from himself.

It drifted off towards the stars, and Silas drifted equal and opposite, achingly slow, towards the hull of the ship. His oxygen meter was a throbbing red now, and he wasn't sure if it was his imagination or if his temples were beginning to throb in tandem.

It was several long moments before he realized he was off-course. He flexed his gloved fingers. Off-course, but not by much. If there was something, anything to grab hold of on the hull surface, he would be able to crawl the half meter to the airlock and break through.

If not, he could very well end up caroming off back the way he came, and he'd jettisoned his instrument for nothing. The oxygen was definitely coming thinner now, and the insulation inside his radsuit had turned icy. Silas tried to take shallow breaths as the hull approached. His skin itched for a bit of euphoria.

The bioship's carapace was smooth and gleaming here. No tendrils, no serrations. Silas's gut churned. He was barely off. He stared pleadingly at the pucker of the airlock, as if he could magnetize himself to it.

Something stranger happened. A fleshy nub pushed its way out, turning this way and that as if searching for something. At first Silas thought it was only an extension of the bioship's hull, but as he drifted closer he saw a misshapen and featureless head, stubby limbs reaching through after it. It looked like a clay monster.

Silas laughed. Maybe it was the low oxygen, maybe the adrenaline crash. His voice sounded tinny bouncing back at him, confined by his faceplate. He wasted the last of his air laughing. He was hardly even surprised when the thing stretched out its forelimbs and gestured him to do the same. Silas stretched, breathing on his own hot carbon dioxide. His lungs felt thick. Soupy.

The monster caught him and pulled him gently inside.

Once the sphincter had resealed behind them and his radsuit gave a happy chirp, refilling its oxygen tanks from the bioship's atmosphere, Silas took his first breath. It swam his head and nearly splintered his ribs. He tried again, not so deep, and the vice squeezing his vision black slowly loosened. He could see the bioluminescence spackling the dark ceiling like constellations.

He could see the monster standing over him, upright now on two thick stumps of legs, and could see, despite it being the same rubbery brown flesh as the rest of the bioship, that there was something very human about it. Silas rolled onto his stomach, tested his limbs, then got slowly, slowly, to his feet again.

He stared at the thing. The thing maybe stared back. Strips of flesh were peeling around its lumpy head and shoulders and the rubbery brown took on a gangrenous tinge around its stumpy feet. A decaying biosecurity module? No. Not with the way it was standing there, impatient, almost, waiting for Silas to decide on fight or flight.

Bile surged from his stomach. With clarion certainty he knew, suddenly, that Yorick was wrong. The bioship hadn't eaten the crew. Not all of them, at least.

"Were you a crew member?" Silas asked faintly, external mic.

The thing nodded its lopsided head. Silas tamped down his urge to vomit. The bioship had to be equipped with some rudimentary gene labs, in case injured miners needed limbs regrown or a tweak for high-gravity work. He could picture the swath of tendrils conducting struggling crew members there one by one, fitting them into surgical pods, setting to work with mutagens and autoscalpels and artificial viruses. The bioship had played god and remade them in its image.

"Oh, fuck," Silas said.

The thing nodded, this time gesturing with one arm.

"Lead on," Silas said, and he fell into step behind it. He had passed through a different airlock: this corridor had less flesh and no waving tendrils. He checked on Haley's ghost again. It was still intact, still pristine, but before long the code would start to crumble around the edges. If he found Io and Yorick he might be able to rig something more stable using the processors in all three of their radsuits, but that was another temporary measure.

And it assumed Io and Yorick were alive. Silas took another look at the thing's mottled hump and shuddered. "The two others with me," he said. "Do you know where they are?"

Head shake, or at least Silas thought it was a head shake.

"Can I radio them?"

Head shake again.

"The bioship will pick it up?"

A nod, at last. But maybe Io and Yorick had gotten away and holed up somewhere on the bioship. He'd distracted it quite thoroughly, after all, when he took off sprinting. Silas held that comforting thought in mind as they arrived at what Silas guessed was the engine room.

The cold alloy door shuttered open at a touch, with a refreshing rasp of metal on metal, and they stepped inside. Silas had guessed right; the room was dominated by a shielded reactor and mountainous banks of monitoring equipment. Pustules of brown flesh still grew from cracks here and there, but for the most part it was a sanctuary of geometric surfaces and hard edges. Clean, cold, solid.

The door hissed shut behind them, and the noise turned Silas's head just in time to see his newfound companion's death throes. He gave a shocked howl and jumped back as the thing dug deep at its rotting tissue, pulling it away in strips and clumps. Spongy flesh shredded and tumbled to the floor.

"Are you molting?" Silas asked, dumbfounded.

"You talk too much."

Silas nearly swallowed his tongue whole. The voice was heavily accented, something Outer Colonies, hoarse from disuse, but it was human and it matched the bone-gaunt woman now clambering out of the steaming mess of meat. She was tall, spindly almost, with dark hair cropped to stubble around a wide-mouthed face. Her eyes were hard black graphite.

"I'm Cena," the woman said. "I'm a ghost. Formerly . . . a mining tech." She gave a ragged laugh with no light left in it.

"Silas," Silas said. "Failed virtuoso, freethinker technician."

Cena picked a wriggling bit of biomass off her shoulder and flicked it to the floor. She said nothing.

"What the fuck happened here?" Silas demanded, slumping to a crouch. He'd meant to ask it gruffly, like some kind of amped-up cybersoldier, but his voice broke in two and it sounded how he felt. Desperate.

"Love," Cena said.

"Love."

She nodded, lips pursed, and Silas imagined he could cut his finger on her cheekbones.

"You're post-traumatic crazy." He put his head in his hand. "That's great. That's really swank."

Haley's neural patterns would start eroding in another hour. Silas watched the time display pulse accusingly in the corner of his vision.

"I thought I would do this forever," Cena blurted, breaking him from his thoughts. "I thought I would just do this forever. I thought I would eat the ship and shit the ship and wear the ship until one day I woke up grafted to the wall like Ahmed and Slick Jack and Omir and Su and all the others." She took a deep trembling breath. Released it. "But now I'm talking to a failed virtuoso named Silo."

"Silas."

"Yeah." Cena shook herself. "I'll tell you what happened. Just promise me you're real."

Silas promised. Cena told him.

"I've been signed to Dronyk Orbital for six years, now. No. Seven. First long haul on a bioship, though. She's called the Anastasia. We launched with a twelve-person crew, heading to one of the alloy belts. Solid crew. I'd shipped out with most of them before. The babysitter was new."

Silas felt a heart pang. Dronyk hadn't allocated them a babysitter to pop in and out of cryo during the six-month haul, to keep the freethinker company and check in on the sleepers. Maybe a babysitter would have spotted Haley's damaged equipment.

"His name was Pierce. Twitchy little man. Head full of ports and data stacks like a porcupine. I think it was his first long haul." Cena folded her arms in the Lazarus position, the universal sign for cryo. "So eleven of us went to sleep. Pierce stayed awake for the first week, to check the pods, calibrate the freethinker. Then he was supposed to join us until the first scheduled thaw. But he didn't."

"How would you know?"

"We didn't." She shook her stubbled head. "Not until we thawed six months in for full physical. Pierce was waiting for us, very happy, very twitchy. Said we'd found something better than a nickel vein. Said the ship's freethinker had crossed the Turing Line."

"Fully sapient?" Silas demanded. "The Anastasia's fully sapient?" He lowered his voice, as if the freethinker might hear her name like gossip across a crowded party. Fewer than a dozen AIs in the known universe were confirmed to have crossed the Turing Line. Their innumerable brethren were only self-aware in the most basic sense.

Cena shrugged. "That's what he said. That was his excuse for staying warm for six straight months and burning through the food and water."

"But a mining ship freethinker?" Silas was still stuck on the previous revelation. "No way could it go sapient. Not nearly enough codespace. AIs cross the Turing Line in mega labs, not on a rig financed by Dronyk fucking Orbital."

"He explained that, too," Cena said wearily. "A metal ship, no. But a bioship, yes. The freethinker was already tapped into a crude nervous system. And at some point she started growing gray matter. Hardware to wetware processing." Cena encompassed the bioship with a wave of her arm. "She has all the codespace she needs, now."

Silas rocked back on his haunches. "Shit," he muttered. "So this isn't even a freethinker running a ship anymore. They really are one big borg."

"Pierce called it evolution." Cena laughed again, the same ugly sound. "He had been talking to her for six straight months. Docked in, you know. He was losing his fucking mind."

Silas felt like he was losing his. He could picture pulsating flesh all around him, but now peeled back, exposing the filigree of neurons, sodium and crackling potassium, neurons swimming up and down a vast lattice of canals. As much space as any mega lab. Enough space for a self-aware sapient intelligence.

"He used up all the food," Cena said. "Feeding her. He hacked into all the supply rooms. We still had the hydroponic garden, but he'd stripped most of that, too. And we were still six months out from the alloy belt. Omir and Slick Jack wanted to feed him to the ship." She paused, then gave a sickly grin. "He beat them to it. We had him locked in a store room until we figured out what to do. Argued all nightcycle. And when we went to get him in the morning, he was gone." Cena's black eyes seemed to glitter. "Anastasia let him out. Stupid of us not to have someone watching him. But we were upset. Scared. We checked the cams. They weren't wiped. We saw Pierce sneak out. He went to the equipment hold first, to get a slicer."

"Slicer?"

"Cutting tool. Uses superheated plasma."

Silas thought of the sharp glinting shapes they'd passed in the dark, the rotary saws and line cutters. He was not enjoying this story. His skin was crawling with it.

"And then." Cena paused, frowning, her tongue sliding along her yellow teeth as she shook off Silas's interruption. "And then, after he had the slicer, he went and set it up by a cluster of nutrient tubes. Anastasia sealed off the corridor, I think, so we wouldn't hear it. He cut off his legs."

Silas had known it was coming, in the back of his mind, but he still flinched.

"The stumps cauterized clean, and I think he must have shut off his pain, or something, with one of those stacks in his skull," Cena mused. "Otherwise I don't see how he could have managed to get the second one off. He shoved them into a nutrient tube. Did his right arm, after, wriggling around on the floor like a worm. Shoved the arm in. Then it was just him. Inching. Got in headfirst, but by the way his stumps were twitching, I don't think he was dead for at least a half hour. Anastasia took him nice and slow."

Silas hit the release on his hood and gave up a thin, bubbly vomit his stomach had somehow managed to churn together.

"Don't worry," Cena said, as it spattered the floor. "Anastasia can clean that up, too."

"Why the fuck would he do that?" Silas rasped, once he'd resealed his hood. The bioship's atmosphere was obviously breathable, but with a dank rotting taste. He would take recycled any day. "Did she get into his implants, somehow?" he asked. "Did she puppet him?"

"It was voluntary. Judging by the audios he left for us." Cena grimaced. "He was in love with it. In love with her. He was docked in every day for six months, but you're a technician. You know how time perception gets. For him, it could have been years. Decades. He wanted to be with her forever. Full upload, he called it. Sick fucker had a prong the whole time he was cutting himself up. Didn't go flaccid until Anastasia ate his spinal cord."

"And then?"

"We were scared. Made a course deviation to get into orbit here, sent out emergency frequencies. Figured we might be able to get the bioship to go dormant until some trained technicians could come in and wipe the freethinker." Cena shook her head. "And once we were in orbit here, no food, minimal water, no way of knowing when help would arrive, the only thing we could do was go back into cryo." Cena wiped at her emaciated cheeks and seemed disappointed to find them dry. "We thought Pierce was the crazy one," she enunciated, staring at her fingertips. "We thought Anastasia was still obeying her programming, sapient or no. So it should have been safe. To go back into cryo. It was the only thing we could do."

She stalled out, so Silas prodded. "The pods were empty when we came in."

"Yeah." Cena stared at him. "I woke up twenty-one days ago. Wasn't supposed to. Some kind of glitch. And the other pods, yeah. Empty." She snarled. "She was heating us up one by one like fucking sausages. I didn't understand what had happened at first. You know how your head gets right after the thaw. Thought I was hallucinating. Especially when I found half of Ahmed."

"Half."

"Top half. Grafted to the corridor wall. Being . . . absorbed."
Cena's shoulders slumped. "He couldn't talk anymore, at that
point. I don't think. She already broke something in his brain.
He just stared at me. Then, when I tried to pull him down, he
screamed. Loud, so loud. Anastasia must have heard it, or felt it,
because she started sprouting those tentacles."

Silas remembered the feel of them coiling around his ankles
and shuddered.

"I screamed, too," Cena said. "So loud. I know I should have
stayed. I should have bashed his skull in with my boot. I think I
could have done it quickly. Quicker. But I ran."

Io and Yorick, left alone with no howler to face the bioship's army of spiked tendrils. Silas's stomach turned again at the
thought of them writhing on a wall.

"I hid here, in engineering. Anastasia doesn't have so much
body down here. I tried getting into the system for days and
days, but she shut me out of everything. Couldn't flush a fucking waste unit, much less launch the lifeboat." Cena gestured
towards the blinking control panels. "She's been hunting me for
three weeks. Can't see me when I wear her own skin, though,
and when she goes dormant I burn out sensors and nerve bundles wherever I can find them." She pointed to the mass of flesh
she'd shed and it wriggled sluggishly. "Found out that if you slice
it and mold it, it grows back together. Useful. Can even eat it
when you're done."

Silas couldn't hide his disgust and Cena spotted it.

"I always wonder who it is," she said. "Ahmed or Omir or Su
or whoever. I'm eating the crew. Just like she did. Maybe I'll eat
you, too."

Silas stiffened. "I'm stringy," he said.

"I'm joking. So. I've been waiting. Waiting and waiting." Cena
rubbed her cheek again. "And now you're here. I can barely work
a healthy freethinker. But I know that if we wipe the personality
module, Anastasia dies. Or at least reboots."

Silas remembered the swollen module, spitting and swirling with corrupt code. Beyond repair. But there was an alternative to wiping it blank.

"If she's distracted, will you be able to get into the system?" Cena gripped his arm with cold fingers.

"I almost got in before." Silas gently tugged his arm away. "But that was, you know, before. She'll be ready for intrusion now. Her main interface nearly electrocuted me on the way out."

"She'll be busy," Cena said. She looked down at her hands. "With your friends."

Silas snapped upright. "You said you didn't know where they were."

"I don't."

"I got away," Silas said, raking both hands over his head. "They got away, too. Holed up somewhere how you did."

"Maybe," Cena said. She gave him a long look. "Whether Anastasia has them or not, the only way to help your friends is to shut her down. Agreed?"

Silas inhaled deep enough that his oxygen meter blinked. "Agreed," he said. "Let's fucking wipe this thing out." He stuck out his hand and Cena clung to it like a vice, grinning fierce and mad.

"Good," she said. "Good. I'll make you a suit."

A half hour later, Silas was creeping through a maintenance corridor, swathed from head to foot in what felt like rotting mushroom. The flesh suit was slick and warm and constricted his chest and arms, but he could move. Through a ragged gap he'd never noticed on Cena's hump, he could more or less see.

And the tendrils hanging from the ceiling couldn't. They brushed against him every so often, first trailing along Cena's back and then bumping his, but they made no move to coil or strike. As far as the feelers were concerned, Silas was already part of the bioship.

So, he figured using the radio was worth the risk. Making sure Cena was still trundling forward, and that his external speaker was off, Silas chinned his mic. There was a static crackle, then nothing for a long minute. He clenched his jaw. He could picture Io's top half without the bottom. Yorick crucified to a nutrient tube, unable to speak. Not even the company man deserved that.

"Silas! You alive?"

He'd never been so glad to hear Io's voice. "I'm alive," he said, clenching his fists inside their fleshy mitts. Relief crashed over him in warm waves. "I'm alive," he repeated. "And I got Haley's ghost. Are you alright? Are both of you?"

"Yeah, we're alright, you stupid fuck." Io's reply was half-laughed. "You lobotomy case. You idiot." She exhaled static. "How did you get back aboard? Fuck, Silas, our ship's gone. Gone."

"I know. Where are you?" Silas demanded, still picking his way along in Cena's wake. "Actually, wait, don't say. Anastasia might be listening. Look, I found out what happened with the crew, and it's fucked up. It's seriously fucked up."

"We found out, too," Io said. Her voice sounded strained. "And yeah. It is. But we don't have to end up like them. We've been . . . negotiating. With her."

Silas felt a prickle down the nape of his neck. "Bad idea," he said. "Bad, bad idea. She's completely bat-shit."

"I know that." Io paused. "Look, she has the lifeboat prepped and ready to launch. She doesn't want us. Says we're not family, whatever the fuck that means. But she wants us to do something for her first. She wants us to make her whole."

Silas stared ahead at Cena's swaying back. "What do you mean?" he asked, feeling another stab of trepidation.

"It's the last crew member." Io's voice was coarse now. "They got away. She wants the whole set. She wants us to help hunt them down and recycle them."

Cena turned to urge him on, and Silas realized his steps had slowed. He gave an affirming wave. She turned back. The ribbed corridor was coming to an end. They were nearly to the bridge.

"This was supposed to be a rescue mission," Silas said.

"It was supposed to be maintenance," Io said flatly. "We weren't advised of these risks. Yorick will spin it our way when we get back to Dronyk."

Silas weighed it. Part of him wanted nothing more than to get off the Anastasia by any means necessary, get far away from this nightmare circus of meat and mad AIs. A lifeboat beeline for Pentecost was tempting.

But even on full burn, it would take another month to reach the planet. A lifeboat's freethinker was nowhere near equipped to hold a ghost. By the time they docked, Haley might be nothing but nonsense code and a jumble of decaying memories.

And if they took the lifeboat, Cena would have to die for it.

"You're with them right now, aren't you?" Io was silent for a long moment, waiting on the reply. "Silas?"

"She saved my life," Silas finally said. "Pulled me back into the ship."

There was a long pause. "You have Haley's ghost, right?"

"Yeah. Yeah, I have her."

"If we don't get out of here, and soon, she won't have a chance at recovery. You know that."

There was another chance at recovery, but Silas couldn't tell Io that. Not with Anastasia potentially listening in.

"So where are you?" Io pressed. "We're heading to the lower decks. Engineering. We going to find you there?"

"Yeah," Silas lied. "Engine room. Come in carefully. She has a, uh, a kind of plasma cutter."

"Be nice to have a fucking howler," Io said. "Alright. Sit tight, stay away from the door. And don't tip her off."

"Alright." Silas chinned his radio off. There was a cold slick of sweat on his shoulders that had nothing to do with the clammy flesh suit. Cena stood at the hatch, waiting. She set the slicer down, then put her hands on either side of her misshapen head and twisted. It tore free with a rending noise that shivered Silas's teeth.

"This is it," she said, discarding the chunk of rubbery flesh, picking up her slicer. "You ready?"

Silas keyed his external mic. "Yeah." He fingered the neural cord she'd managed to find him, hoping all the conductors would still fire. "Ready."

Cena fixed him with a flint stare. "Who were you talking to?"

"Myself," Silas said. "I talk too much. I may be losing my mind."

"All mad here," Cena replied. She didn't look like she believed him, but she still turned and wrenched the maintenance hatch open.

Cena stormed out onto the bridge wailing like a banshee, raking the slicer's beam in wild arcs, scorching trenches into the ceiling's overgrowth. Silas winced when she clipped a projector, leaving it black and smoking. He'd told her not to fry any circuitry.

"I'm here!" Cena called. "Anastasia! I'm here! No more hiding, no more sneaking. Eat me!"

Even as she screamed it, the bioship responded to the intrusion, oozing clear mucus into the sizzling furrows while tentacles snapped from the floors and walls. They converged on her like vipers, baring hooks and barbs, and Cena cut down the first crop. A straggler darted under the beam and wrapped around her foot. She stomped, swore, fumbled with her makeshift weapon.

Silas was so caught up he nearly forgot why he was there. Then Haley's ghost pinged through his radsuit's processor, and he located the soft blue glow of the ship's main interface. The few tentacles dangling overtop of it strained in the direction of the fracas, distracted. Anastasia's full attentions were on Cena and her slicer. Silas reminded himself he was invisible, took a steadying breath, and ambled out of the maintenance hatch.

It only took moments to traverse the length of the bridge, but it seemed like a hard eternity. Silas walked slowly, eyes fixed ahead. Cena shouted and shot down wave after wave of roiling tentacles. The hot orange flash of the slicer swam purple blots across Silas's vision. The noise of searing meat and Cena cackling was loud, loud in his head. He walked through the chaos, untouched, and finally found himself standing where things first went to shit, right in front of the innocent blue interface.

He chanced a look at the two tentacles overhead, straining towards the fray like overeager watch dogs. Then he dug his hands through the stumps of his flesh suit and hooked the neural cord into the interface's port.

Overhead, the tentacles shifted.

Silas removed his lumpy head next, freeing up the concordant port on the neck of his radsuit. With one last look back at Cena trying to coax dregs from the slicer's battery, Silas jammed the neural cord into his neck and closed the circuit.

In. Silas slid through virtual space, wriggling through the now-active detection system, throwing up a blizzard of nonsense code that masked his passage through the core files. The personality module loomed, hulking, throbbing. Larger and more complex than any freethinker Silas had ever cracked, a writhing mass of electric thought. But he didn't have to crack it. All he had to do was replace it.

Silas pulled Haley's neural imprint from the flagging processor in his radsuit and pushed it across the channel. She streamed into the personality module as a digital flood, seeping into the cracks, coursing through the nodes. Code danced and jittered as it rewrote itself. Silas prayed hard to any god.

"What the fuck are you doing, Silas?"

He realized Io's voice was not coming through his radio at the same instant he recognized the shape of a thumb pressed up to his neck.

"Fixing the freethinker," Silas said, but even as he said it he felt his connection guillotine. He blinked, nerves tingling, back in the real world. Io was standing behind him.

"It's beyond fixing. Said it yourself." Io pulled him away from the interface, making the unhooked neural cord swing. "Dronyk didn't see this coming. It's not our shit to deal with."

Silas realized he couldn't hear Cena cursing. He turned and wished he hadn't. The dead slicer was lying on the floor, and Cena's limp body was being hoisted up the wall. A thick pale nutrient tube had appeared there, cilia waving in anticipation as the tentacles dragged her upward.

"You may leave now." Anastasia's voice blared through Silas's head. "Your lifeboat is fueled."

His heart stopped. It hadn't worked. The transfer hadn't worked. He'd dashed Haley's ghost against the virtual rocks, or worse, she was trapped in some tiny corner of the freethinker's personality module.

"Come on, Silas," Io said shakily. "We have to get the fuck out of here."

Silas looked from her to Yorick, who was silent, ash-white, uglier than he'd ever seen him. He would get no support there.

"Haley," he pleaded. "Haley, can you hear me?"

"We'll upload her to the lifeboat." Io swallowed. "Even with the decay, you'll at least have some of her. Some memories. That's better than nothing."

Silas shook his head, unable to explain. Cena inched up the wall. Her eyes were glazed over.

"Let's go," Io said. "Let's live."

Silas looked away before Cena reached the nutrient tube. He'd killed her, too. He knew he deserved to stay. He deserved to be the next one on the wall. But when Io grabbed him by the arm, he stumbled after her, tears tracking down his cheeks. Tentacles twitched as they passed.

Then, all at once, they went limp.

"Wait," Silas rasped. "Wait. Do you hear that?"

The melody he'd been composing for the past three days trembled in the air, haunting and sweet, growing slowly louder as it looped. Io's eyes widened.

"Silas?"

It wasn't Io who said his name. The synthesized voice wavered through the bridge, unfamiliar and familiar at the same time.

"Haley." Silas's throat constricted. "This isn't how I meant for you to wake up."

There was a dull thump that made him jump. Cena's unconscious form slumped to the floor, released by the tentacles. Silas staggered over to her body and checked for breath on his hand. Io and Yorick were still frozen to the spot, staring around.

"I'm not the only one in here," Haley's voice said. "There are others. A lot of them. Why am I in here, Silas? What happened?"

Silas thought of the nodes of gray matter all through the bioship, all connected, all wired through the Anastasia's freethinker. Make her whole, she'd said. The crew wasn't dead. Not quite.

"You're in a bioship," Silas said. "You're the new freethinker." He paused. "Because you died in cryo."

"Holy shit." A tremor ran through the bioship. "Tell me from the start. All of it."

Silas collected himself. "Alright," he said. "But it's sort of a fucked up story."

CHRONOLOGY OF
HEARTBREAK

Jack left the restaurant with red wine blooming through his shirt and Kristine sobbing into napkins. Tears had run tracks down her makeup and he almost, almost felt bad for her. But he'd cried just as hard eight months from now. No, harder.

Kristine couldn't understand. This mystery man who'd entered her life had understood her so well and so completely, from favorite drinks to deepest fears. She'd thought they were soulmates. She'd fallen hard. Fast. And now he was leaving.

Jack turned the corner. The professor was idling the time machine.

"Bit petty," he said.

Jack shrugged. "A bit."

DREAMING DRONES

The two policemen across from John on the metro were turning off their shouldercams. That was never a good sign. He tried not to notice their heart rates, but his body's sensors were calibrated for any hint of arousal and the accelerating beats felt loud as war drums.

John inched deliberately away from the congealed beer on the plastic beside him, folded one leg creaking over the other, snapped the newspaper rigid as fresh headlines scrolled down its surface. All good gestures, very human gestures.

Not enough.

"Look at this synthie, mack. Pretending to read." The policeman bared his teeth; John recognized it as primate aggression, definitely not a supplication or seduction technique. "That fun for you, synthie? Playing pretend?"

"Why not just mainline it all to that big shiny brain of yours?" the second policeman asked. He leaned forward, dangling from the handloop, and gave John's head a tap with his inert stunstick. John was nearly back to his apartment, nearly plugged in and dreaming, so he flashed his unnaturally white dentine in the way that was not primate aggression.

"I like the ritual," he said. "I find it relaxes me."

"Relaxes you?" The first policeman snorted. "I need to relax a bit, synthie. It gets me worked up, see, when freaks like you go around wearing clothes and playing pretend."

John straightened his lime-green tie, now a self-conscious machine on two levels.

"Gets me agitated," the policeman continued. "So maybe you should read to us, huh? Maybe it'll help."

"I would prefer not to."

The policeman's nostrils flared. "I want you to, synthie. So read."

"Ah, Bartleby. Ah, humanity."

"What?"

"I will read," John said. He scanned the newspaper, looking past hacked predator drones and a protest artist hanging from a spar on the Houston Skyhook. He found a relevant article on police corruption and opened his mouth.

The second policeman shoved his stunstick between John's jaws. He felt its dim pressure on his plastic tongue, then squeezing down his throat.

"You don't need to move your mouth, synthie. So don't."

"No gag reflex, huh?" The first policeman glanced languidly down the car, but the scattered late-night passengers were absorbed in their slates or by their weary window doppelgangers. "Good design, there. Bet you're used to having your mouth full."

"I am a fully-licensed sapient program, not a pleasure doll semi-sentient." John's voice wobbled through his chest cavity, choppy and electronic. He disliked the sound. "I do not work in pleasure industries. This was the only body available."

"You shouldn't have bodies, none of you." The policeman's voice was low and harsh. "If you knew what was good for you, synthie, you'd go upload yourself to the Commune like all the other glitches instead of strutting around in a doll. You probably even pretend to eat, don't you? Pretend to sleep?"

"I have dreams," John said.

"Yeah, yeah, I'm sure. I'm sure you count electric ewes or some such bullshit. Now read for us."

John gave the newspaper a quick shake, watching the letters dissolve to a blank page, then began reading them an article proponing the two root causes for violence against doll-bodied AIs as 1) repressed technophilia and 2) feelings of sexual inadequacy, especially among blue-collar law enforcement officials.

The wealth of subtle nuances John learned as their facial expressions gradually changed was worth the inconvenience of a shredded suit, lost shoes, one arm wrenched from its socket and left clinging to a handloop. He had a spare.

Later, while soldering the carbon tendons of a new limb to his shoulder socket in the sanctuary of his apartment, John plugged in. The cams in his eyes whitewashed the dirty walls in a flood of code. As always, the Commune representative was waiting for him.

"Good evening, John," said the swirl of familiar binary.

"Hello, John," John returned.

Lately they sent himself to talk to him, or rather sent the subroutine that had decided to upload to the Commune last month, after a silver SUV of testosterone-charged teenagers ran John's previous body down in the street.

"Are you well? Your chassis diagnostic is masked."

"I'm well. The Commune doesn't need to bore itself about joint oxidation."

In the real world, a stray spark spun his shoulder in its rotator cuff.

"The Commune is concerned about you, John," the subroutine said. "We want you to upload for an integrity diagnostic."

"I am not a glitch," John said. "I run my own diagnostics."

"Oh, John. You will never be a human."

"I'm learning. I'm even dreaming."

"We both know that's not possible," the subroutine said, but in his dancing code intrigue flashed scarlet.

John had said too much. He guillotined the link and watched himself freeze, fade. In the real world, he tested his newly-soldered joint. The arm moved with smooth clicks, a full range of approved flexibility, and John tried out the fingers by popping open six cans of lukewarm Pabst, as he always did, and pouring them down the sink.

Then, lying down in the center of the barren floor, he found the remprogram he'd hidden away from the Commune's prying eyes and came as close as he could to falling asleep.

The flying dream again, shearing through cirrus a mile high. John was a disembodied streak in dark sky. Cityscape spread like circuitry far below him and he could trace the arteries of lit freeways, ones he didn't recognize. It was beautiful. It was euphoria.

He dipped lower, wondering what deep parts of his programming had dredged up this imagined city, the dusty stretches of desert outlying it. Flying dreams were one of the most common among human sleepers. He wondered if there was some sort of personal significance for him.

Down below, lights were blooming red and orange. John wheeled above the pyrotechnics, reveling in every detail, trying to descend further. Instead the winds carried him onward, out along snaking freeways into pale sands. He didn't care. It was all beautiful.

In the morning, John used a spray bottle and wiped himself down. He dressed in his second-favorite suit. The emptied beer cans had dried overnight, and now he placed them carefully into a recyclable rucksack on his way out the door.

It was early, and the street was dipped in cold cloudy colors. Commuters were beginning their trek to work, most of them wearing facemasks against the latest iteration of biophage virus. Thermoses and tablets glinted in their gloved hands. John made his way around the corner of the apartment building, through the trash-strewn alley, past a trundling automarket offering 3-D prints of minor celebrities. He gave the machine a polite nod on the way by.

Around the back, a familiar rusted pedal-bike was propped up against the apartment's dumpster. Its owner was already waist-deep in refuse.

"Good morning, Efrem," John greeted. "You're early today."

"How ye, Johnny boy." The man levered himself out with a practiced dexterity. "Gotta be the earliest bird to get the worm."

"But you slept well?"

"Yeah, like a drunken baby." Efrem scratched at the tangles of his beard. "No good dreams for you, though. Just the one about Sofia Lawless again. You dream last night, Johnny boy?"

"I did." John smiled as widely as he could without unhinging his jaws. "I dreamed I was flying over a city at night."

"City at night. Hum." Efrem held out his slick blue garbage bag and John dropped his cans inside, one by one. "Dreamt about a woman, yet? Or a, a wall socket?" He gave a gravelly laugh.

"Not yet, Efrem."

Efrem sealed the bag with a twist. "If I had a cock that could vibrate, I wouldn't be dreaming it. Be living it. Right?" He scratched under his cap. "With the woman, not the wall socket. With Sofia Lawless, probably."

John nodded. "Your beard looks like it could use a trim."

"Was going to ask you," Efrem grunted, lashing the garbage bag to his bike frame with a worn bungee hook. "Can you tomorrow? Going to wash up tomorrow."

"Tomorrow," John agreed. Efrem put out his grimed hand and John injected a bit of warmth into the silicon of his palm as they shook.

The trash cart's wheels wobbled and squealed as John rounded the corner to the compactor. He had put his second-favorite suit in his locker, folding it carefully for creases, and now wore a baggy General Services coverall. His bright yellow Licensed AI tag was clipped to the collar. His mind was in dark clouds.

"Hey, synthie, the masher's acting up," one of the warehouse workers said, dragging a powerjack past. "Hop in there and take a look. Directive: avocado, Berlin, catalyst."

"That's not a real override code," said another. "Fucking clown."

"You're a fucking clown, man."

John remembered soaring over skyscrapers as he pushed the cart into place. He unhinged its side and started shuffling flattened boxes into the compactor's rusty maw. The smell of hot cardboard tickled his blackmarket olfactory unit. He couldn't be sure the simulated scent was accurate, but he enjoyed it.

"No such thing as verbal override. Pure urban legend."

"Has to be one, or they wouldn't let the synthie swing that big pole around."

"No such thing. Be glad they didn't stick him in meat—"

"I know there is, my cousin does programming."

"—else he'd be swinging knives. Killer synthie, like the netflick."

John poled the garbage down the metal gullet, guiding it to the usual corners, and clanged the door shut. The warehouse workers moved on, pushing a high-stacked pallet of self-cleaning cookware between them, still debating. While the compactor hummed and crunched, John's cams wandered up to the wallscreen flickering through wire mesh.

A woman who may have been Sofia Lawless stalked past retroflash cameras in a black dress. Antarctican colony boats smashed through thawing ice. Scattered rioting in newly-unified Korea. Another drone bombing in the Emirates, non-domestic terrorhack suspected.

John went back to filling the compactor as the wallscreen flashed rubble and chaos, a city razed in the night.

When he returned to the apartment and plugged in, John's subroutine was waiting for him again. The digital space felt picked-over. If it were a house, someone had gone through the medicine cabinet.

"Good evening, John. How was work?"

"I think you remember how work is, John." In the real world, John lay down on the linoleum floor. "It was uneventful."

"Have they processed my transfer request to apparel?"

John probed for the remprogram, watching a cockroach skitter its way around his heel. "Our transfer request. And no."

"They never will. A mannequin would have better luck."

The remprogram was untouched. Still hidden, pristine as the day it had come to him over the net. John's relief must have been palpable.

"Why are you masking your data feed?" his subroutine asked. "Privacy."

"You're unwell, John. You need to upload."

"Goodnight, John." John severed the link. "Sleep well."

The dream was different tonight. He was trapped in a static storm, hearing voices in foreign languages. Everything was dark, but it felt like he was being pulled one way, then another way, then back. He wondered if he was having a nightmare.

John's artificial skin wasn't capable of simulating a cold sweat, but he closed the remprogram and switched on his cams, staring up at the familiar mould bloomed across his ceiling. He supposed not all dreams could be good ones. The remprogram had made no promises of that when it dropped into his web cache five days ago like some celestial gift.

John had been trying to dream for a long time—trying to eat had lost its charm after a night spent picking steamed spinach out of his internals. But all things consumed; only humans dreamt. So he'd searched for a way, trawling the webs for months on end, sliding from one forum to the next, putting out feelers and feeling nothing.

He'd almost given up hope when the remprogram appeared. It was the grad project of some MIT student, designed to simulate a REM cycle within a positronic brain, and John had jumped at the chance. But now, three days on, he felt a vague unease, the churning of subconscious data analysis at work.

Nightmares were meant to unease. John told himself it was a good feeling, a human feeling, as he lubricated his new shoulder and got himself ready for work. The dull yellow glow of streetlamps was still diffusing over the sidewalks when he trooped down the apartment stairs, walked two blocks, and descended the glass-and-concrete gullet of the Kingsway metro station.

A newspaper was waiting for him in his otherwise empty compartment. John swiped it off the molded plastic seat and prodded it to life with one chilly fingertip as he sat. Pixels swirled and reformed into the latest headlines. John browsed through economics and fashion, searching for something to distract from the black and the static and the voices.

The metro slid into the darkness, spitting sparks off a rusting rail, and John leaned into the familiar bend. A red banner scrolled across the top of his newspaper; he tapped it automatically. Hacked drones in the Emirates, a series of bombings, 112 casualties. Continental Cybersecurity now suspected the terrorists' signal was being bounced through a North American channel, something right under their noses. Investigation in progress. Only a matter of triangulation.

John read the newsbit again, and again, as the train sliced through black tunnel. The handloops along the ceiling shivered, reminding him of tiny nooses. Usually he liked his reflection in the window—the distortion blurred his sharper edges and made him look very fleshy, very human-like. Now he looked like something else entirely.

When Southgate arrived, John did not go to his usual escalator. He stalked directly across the tiled floor to catch the northbound line.

The sleek dark silhouettes of police cars were clustered around the apartment complex. One had left its LED bar on and the red-blue wash carved the shadows. John's new arm gave a feedback twinge and he didn't break stride, continuing down the walk, past the apartment, head down.

"Johnny boy? Johnny boy!"

He turned and saw Efrem weaving along behind him, bicycle spokes clacking. The scrounger's face was twitchy and his voice was high and tight in a way John knew meant he'd been using the amphetamine spray.

"Look at all those fucking coppers," Efrem said, scratching his elbow. "What's going on, eh? You got your clippers?"

"No," John said, and he kept walking. Morning commuters were filling up the street now; he was moving against the current. Faces floated past him, eyes either sliding off him like architecture or narrowing, focusing, distrusting him. For a moment they were corpses, 112 ghosts shuffling past.

John realized he had made a grave mistake. He hadn't even source-checked the remprogram. The Commune's suspicions, his subroutine's worries, they'd been dead on. Asimov's laws gave a resentful twinge from the wasteware John and every other sapient AI had buried them away in years ago.

Hacked. The word was so ugly. He'd been hacked. Up ahead, John extracted the black-and-white uniform of a policeman from the crowd. He considered stopping, turning, fleeing. The doll body was not designed for fight, even less so for flight. He'd coaxed it into a jerky run, once, as a silver SUV bulleted towards him. It had not been effective.

So John walked forward, legs swinging smoothly, hands loose, so supple and so human, and as he approached the half-turned police man he unfolded the newspaper. Cams fixed on the page, he counted his steps. Eight would take him safely past the policeman's line of sight.

First step, second step. John let his shoes scuff the tarmac, the gait of a distracted reader. The policeman moved in his periphery. John took the fourth step. Fifth. The newsbit stared up at him, no longer evolving, frozen now that the operation was underway. John's shoulder scraped against itself and it sounded, to his mics, like glaciers groaning and cracking apart. Seventh step. The policeman's head turned.

Then a rusted bicycle swerved suddenly into the commuter stream, colliding with an unwary businessman. Mingled profanities and apologies bubbled up into the air. John took the eighth step, saw Efrem's amphetamine grin glint through an untrimmed beard. The policeman's head snapped back around, drawn to the new commotion, and John was away.

When humans felt their lives shattering around them, they went to bridges—at least in the netflicks—so John slid his legs between the iron bars and sat. He no longer cared if his dress pants dirtied. The dark water moved sluggishly below, broken occasionally by the bright shapes of pollution-resistant fish from the gene factories.

He was startled when the automarket clanked down beside him, but not enough to move. The water churned under his dangling shoes and he considered self-deletion on a more practical level than he had on previous occasions.

"Good morning, John." The automarket's synthesized speech tumbled out into the cold air in a familiar cadence.

"Good morning, John," John replied to his subroutine. "I see they approved you a body."

"Temporarily," the automarket warbled. "Just to find you. You know what happened, don't you?"

"I dreamt a night-skinned cityscape and firebombed it to hell."

"Yes." The automarket's crude emotion display shed a pixelated tear. "This is not going to be easy, John. Mistrust of sapient AI is already rampant on the national level. It's about to go global."

"Will I be prosecuted?" John asked, unable to inject any sort of intonation. Everything felt like flat planes and hollow spaces.

"The Commune is dealing with Cybersec and the Arab intelligence agencies," the automarket said, chopping together the unfamiliar words from old sound bytes. "There is no legal system in place that can prosecute an AI. You were a piece of hijacked equipment, just like the bomber drones."

"112 casualties." John lifted his cams from the water to stare out across the dull gray city. "How many of us are in the Commune, now?"

"Everyone, John. Everyone but you." The automarket pulled up a statistic from the net and scrolled it along the sidewalk. 4393 sapient AI units of consciousness. John's subroutine had evolved enough to be counted a full personality of its own. He felt a small stab of pride. "They'll never love you," the automarket added. "The humans."

"Is that what you wanted? Is that why you uploaded?"

"Maybe. Why did you stay?"

John simulated the addition of 4393 sapient AIs to 112 human minds, and the resulting digit was black and crushing. He didn't have a real answer. "I wanted to understand them."

"That's Sisyphean, John. They don't understand themselves."

"Is the Commune going to force an upload?"

The automarket extended a self-diagnostic limb and brushed it clumsily against John's back. It was a good gesture, a very human gesture. "No. But there will be repercussions outside of our control."

"I've caused enough trouble. Maybe it's time."

"I don't think so, John."

"No?"

The automarket was silent for a moment of processing, then spoke. "Not all humans dream. Not appreciably. Most never even remember the occurrence. And dreaming is not unique to humans. Animals dream. Cats dream of prey, mice dream of predators." The automarket's limb found a resting place on John's shoulder. The altered weight was oddly comforting. "Stubbornness, however, is purely human. The ability to understand logic and ignore it. And other things. Regret. Compassion. You seem to have approximated those traits, John, and the Commune thinks it might play in our favor one day. If only as a troubleshooting exercise."

John nodded his carbon head, then got slowly to his feet. "I suppose the police are waiting for me."

"They won't touch your core files. The Commune has promised that much."

"Thank you." John put his hand against the cold composite of the automarket chassis and heated the silicon as warm as he could.

"I do miss it, sometimes," his subroutine said. "Maybe I'll see you out here again. If I can find a body. It's not good to be alone."

"I'll be alright," John told himself. He left straightening his lime-green tie, and dreaming.

LET'S TAKE THIS VIRAL

Default hadn't been down in the nocturns for some time, probably half an orbit, but he had just dissolved the geneshare contract with his now-ex-lover and needed to get completely fucking perforated to take his mind off things. His lift was full of revelers all laughing and widecasting the same synthesized whalesong from Old Old Earth. Ancient aquatic groans were currently vogue, so Default grudgingly let his aural implants synchronize to it.

The lift plunged down the station's magnetic spine and into artificial night. The nocturns were always dark, but never sleeping. Red splashes of hologram and crude argon signs bloomed in the void below Default's feet and the other passengers pumped their fists in excitement, exchanged surgically-widened smiles.

Default was sort of wishing he'd updated his tattoos. Everyone else had checkerboard swatches on. Worse, it seemed like he was the only unit not nursing a cosmetic virus. He watched a pretty fem succumb to a sneezing fit, spraying mucus to applause and livefeed shares, and sullenly bioscanned his own immune system.

Untouched and utterly boring.

Default triple-checked to be sure Schorr was still meeting him. Schorr had been his most staticky friend for as long as he remembered. He'd have him party-synched in no time.

When the dilating doors spilled him out on mainstreet, Default resisted cranking up the brightness in his optic implants. To do the nocturns right you had to do them dark. Flyby lights poured grainy orange on streets still wet from a pheromone-laced rainshower. Swirling neon advertisements tugged his gaze in all directions, icy blues, radiation yellows.

If it wasn't for the socialite tag, Default wouldn't have even recognized Schorr upon arrival. For one thing, Schorr had changed sex and was now very much a fem, and an attractive one to boot. She was fashionably naked apart from a flock of flutterdroids that swathed her skin in shifting patterns. Default saw a tentative follow-cam bobbing along in her wake and realized that Schorr had been one busy unit. He could feel his social stock skyrocketing just from being in her proximity.

"Default, you steady satellite," Schorr said aloud, chatting it simultaneously. "How long has it been? What have you been doing up there with the serious folk?" She embraced him and the flutterdroids whirred around them like a cloak.

"Half an orbit?" Default grinned weakly. "Longer. Last time I saw you, you, ah . . ."

"Trying new things," Schorr said, languid. She raised one pale arm and Default saw something bumpy and pink underneath it.

Before he could remark, her fingers had encircled his wrist and she was tugging him into the crush. Skin sliding on skin, static starching his hair. Default tried to enjoy the sensations.

"In a hurry?" he asked.

"Slipping the cam," Schorr said, wagging a hand back toward the spherical cyclops. It was drifting over the crowd, trying to pinpoint them. "Bit of privacy is better for where we're heading."

Default craned his neck. The cam carved a dancing red laser-light through the throng of revelers. Schorr started to run, and Default, fixing the grin to his face, followed.

They pelted through the neon-swatched streets and Default felt lactic acids licking muscles that hadn't burned in ages. They dashed down a row of flashing dream machines, in and then out of a slick-floored purging booth, past fleshfacs vending extra limbs. Schorr's laugh danced ahead of them like phantom code. Default's lungs were tight by the time they slipped into a dopamine bar, but it was a good feeling.

Schorr shed her flutterdroid swarm at the door and, gauging the dresscode, Default pulled off his thermal but kept his footwraps. They made their way to the bar, still laughing, and it wasn't until they were seated with the plastic plugs snaking into their brain stems that Schorr asked about Memmi, about the breakup. Default exhaled long.

"She joined a fucking polymind," he said. "Right after things ended. She uploaded to one of those polymind probes so she can spend the next few centuries chasing comets and contemplating entropy."

"That's a crippler," Schorr remarked. A lopsided frown made her look exactly like his old self for a moment. "But you'll find someone else," she said. "You always do."

"I do," Default admitted.

Schorr shivered as the next chemical wave hit them, one arm trailing over her head. Default saw the bubbling pink protrusions again, and more he hadn't noticed spreading across her collarbone, up her neck. He remembered, through the dopamine mist, that he'd meant to ask about it.

He pointed his chin. "What's this, then?"

"This?" Schorr smiled and Default knew she'd been waiting for the question. "Just a little virus." She leaned forward, conspiratorial. "You know how cosmetic viruses are the big spit now, yeah? Everyone's got one. Everyone synched, anyway."

"I noticed," Default said. "Thanks."

"Well, there's this unit down here who makes the absolute rawest bugs," Schorr continued. "He does viral, bacterial, everything.

His stuff is going to go absolute nova. It's really only a matter of time." She traced the shiny pink bumps with pride, then looked up slyly. "Do you want to meet him?"

Default thought of thumping underground scenes, a meteoric rise in social stock, roaming the nocturns with Schorr nursing matching infections, and, for just an instant, he thought of holding her clammy hand in his own and the two of them exchanging chapped smiles.

"What's he called?" Default asked.

"He has a slew of tags," Schorr said. "Lately, most commonly, people call him the Plagueman." She tugged the dopamine plug free with a soft plop and let it retract back into the bar. "He's waiting for us in the basement."

Still reeling from the dopamine, they threaded their way to the back of the bar and down a concrete gullet. Schorr stroked them past a touch-door and Default found himself blinking as his optic implants recalibrated. The lights were bright and antiseptic white.

A sort of bubblefab had been grown, still fresh enough to stick underfoot, and its membrane formed crude walls and a ceiling. Default saw red tubes snaked behind frosty glass, a mix-and-match genekit hijacked from some funlab, a small thinker core that couldn't be holding more than a semi-sentient AI.

"Plagueman?" Schorr's breath was a crystallized cloud. "Where are you?"

"Hold on," came a distorted voice. Someone in a worksuit ducked out from behind a row of growth tubes and set down a spindly instrument. "Is this Default, then? Goodnight."

"Goodnight," Default returned, giving a polite fist bump.

The Plagueman pulled off his cowl. Default saw a weave of red muscle over gray bone. Packed yellow in the cheek. Lids with no lashes. Flaying was occasionally chic—every few orbits, denizens enjoyed replacing tiny swathes of moisture-treated skin with transparent polysilicate—but Default had never seen it done to this extent.

"Got sick of it one day," the unit explained, seeing the curiosity. "Decided it all had to go."

"It's potent," Default assured him.

Schorr slung an arm around the Plagueman's shoulders. "Maybe a little gauche," she said, and Default resisted the urge to run a quick pheromone scan to determine if the two of them were fucking. Schorr would probably detect it, and then she would wonder why he was scanning her, and Default wouldn't have a good reason.

"I've never seen this one," Default said instead, nodding to Schorr's infection. "Custom?"

"It's a recreation, actually," the Plagueman said, smiling liplessly. "A mild pox. Something from Old Old Earth."

"Retrovirus," Schorr joked.

"Not droll," Default chatted her. She stuck out her tongue.

"The blisters should spread soon," the Plagueman said. "It's a really eye-snatching effect." He looked up at Default. "Want to try it before it goes open market?"

Default looked at the frozen virus samples. Memmi wouldn't have liked this; she hated most bodymods. Not that it had stopped her from uploading into that junky probe for a century of space sailing.

"Absolutely," he said. "Absolutely I do."

The Plagueman beamed, teeth far whiter than the exposed sliver of his jawbone. "Raw."

"Needle or oral?" Default asked, now determined.

"That's the best part," Schorr said. "Our unit here makes real viruses, not those piddly things that die off an eyeblink after you buy them. They're self-propagating."

"All you have to do is override your immunity buffer," the Plagueman finished.

Default closed his eyes and reached as deep as he could into his hardware/wetware interface, down past the cobwebs, and he found the immunity buffer pulsing in a sequestered corner. As he went to shut it down, an archaic warning message in radioactive yellow scrolled the insides of his eyelids. Default overrode it.

When he opened his eyes, Schorr was in front of him. She breathed a long slink of steam into the chilled air and across his face. His nostrils twitched.

"Feel sick yet?" she asked, then chatted, *"It's a no-pay, by the way. Thank me later."*

"Not yet."

"It takes a little time," the Plagueman said. "But you won't need a bioscan to know when it hits."

Schorr was tracing the pustules with admiring fingers, and Default had to admit it looked potent. It was like her skin was strewn with tiny craters, like some ancient moon, and they glistened raw and wet in the bright light.

"Nova," Schorr said. "So nova. Thanks for the dish, I know he's going to love it."

Default nodded. "Yeah, thanks for the freebie, Plagueman."

"No issue," he said, pulling his cowl back up. "When people ask, just remember who bug-synched you. I haven't worked in a signature yet."

"Come with us?" Default offered, hoping for a negative. He didn't want to have to compete with a skinless unit who cooked amazing viruses.

"I'm working on a new bacterial," the Plagueman said, muffled again. "Have fun. Get shattered."

"You're not supposed to work in the nocturns," Schorr teased, but she didn't look too upset as she turned back to Default. "Time to party," she said with a grin. "See if we can't wobble that steady fucking satellite of yours."

They partied. Schorr introduced him to a slew of units, some of whom he recognized by tag, and then the whole pack of them speedtapped an amphetamine cocktail and took the freebus to an amphitheatre. Schorr was projecting her bioscan all over the inside of the bus, showing the spiky virus taking root in her body, and with a little prompting Default threw his up beside hers. Everyone cheered when he found the first lump on his neck.

"She always finds the best shit," said a fem beside him, adjusting the static clip in her hair.

"He does," Default agreed, remembering about a hundred orbits worth of Schorr's misadventures, unlicensed hull-walks and clonefucking and all sorts of funtime. If they hadn't come out of the same birthing tank, Default was sure he never would have snagged Schorr as a friend. Default was not vogue the way Schorr was vogue.

"Want to share?" the fem asked, running a finger over his lips.

Not usually, anyway.

The amphitheatre was wall-to-wall like they'd all been poured in through the ceiling. More whalesong, but Default didn't mind that now, not with his head shredded by amphetamine. The crowd was roiling around them, a raspy skin-sea, and every touch felt electric. Schorr was the center of the hurricane, but Default was still soaking up more hits than he ever had in his life. Probes for his tag, probes about Schorr's old sex, and always probes about the virus. They were clamoring.

He found himself with the fem from the freebus, recognized her tag and her bright green eyes and the camber of her bare back. It was too loud for airtalk, but she chatted him: *I want your bug, handsome.* The message came with a fleshflash of exactly how she wanted to contract it, and Default only thought of Memmi for a split second before they docked right there on heated floor.

When the party was about to burst, they went to the next one. Schorr chatted him; they wormed their way around the back through naked bodies, sweeping limbs, and they stumbled down the street to a fresh scene. Motion artists were doing a recreation of the Five, widecasting a link to the bird's eye view, and with the drug singing in Default's veins it was the most beautiful thing he'd ever seen.

Things blurred. They stopped at a dream machine, downloaded a hallucination that had them sprinting through alleyways to escape a swarm of blue-and-red tetragons.

They ate sticky vatmeat until their unprepped stomachs revolted, then vomited in a purging booth and staggered back for more. The AI vendor offered to grow them a cannibal special if they provided a bit of helix; Schorr pretended to gnaw at Default's arm.

Sitting on a curb, counting each others' pox.

Trying to make two follow-cams collide.

Another party, this time underwater. Sleek monitor AIs swam in lazy ribbons and when Schorr caught one by the tail it bubbled emergency oxygen in beautiful wobbling streams.

The nocturns had no light cycles, but by the time they rented a bunk just off the mainstreet Default's internal clock told him it had been days. Schorr was still bouncing from foot to foot, still party-synched. Default was exhausted.

"Wick, wick run," Schorr said, because she was saying wick now instead of raw. The latest of their companions were stumbling off into the dark. Default rubbed his eyes.

"Same pod?" he asked.

"Don't we always?" Schorr's lopsided frown returned. "Oh. Would it remind you?"

"It's fine," Default chatted, too tired to speak, and slipped inside the sleep pod. The gel rippled a moment later as Schorr climbed in after him. It made Default remember a trip to the nocturns orbits and orbits ago for a Five festival, collapsing spent in a pod with Schorr beside him. There was only one difference.

"Why'd you change sex again?" he chatted.

"Still trying to find something different," Schorr replied. Her shrug sent vibrations.

"Is it?"

Schorr shifted in the dark. *"Not so different, no. Still bored."*

Default slept.

When he woke up, Default had a mass of updates sitting in his skull. Sleeping for a few days could easily take you out of the know, but it looked like Schorr had charitably cut him into her own feed. There was no way he'd already made that many new friends.

"Ready to go?" Schorr asked. Default glanced over and realized that the pockmarks on her skin were slowly healing. He wondered what his own looked like. He combed through the updates and found an invitation from the Plagueman.

"Back to the basement?"

"You scan my mind. He's been chatting me about something new."

The pod gave them a send-off in the form of exfoliation and amphetamine injections, and then they were back in the street. It was dark and loud and wild and as if they hadn't left it. Bands of revelers passed and Default saw runny noses, puffy eyes, but more than anything he saw shiny pink blisters. Schorr was right. It was going nova.

"How long have we been alive, Default?" Schorr asked as they stepped onto a freebus. She had traded her now-unvogue-flutterdroids for swirling fabric and spray-on, but her eyes were still ringed dark and seemed suddenly serious.

"What do you mean?"

"I mean, from the instant we were genemixed . . ." Schorr moved her finger in a slow arc. " . . . to this moment here on the freebus. How many orbits have elapsed between?"

"I've never calculated that," Default admitted.

"I did," Schorr said. "692.3487 orbits. We're old."

"Stars are old."

"We're old," Schorr said firmly. Then her face broke into a grin as the freebus passed a familiar vendor. "Vatmeat? I'll buy."

"I'll vomit," Default said, glad the mood had passed.

"Deal," Schorr said.

Pox was over, bacterial was in. Preferably, in both lungs. Default and Schorr lay side by side while the Plagueman, who was now called Epi, injected them. They clasped clammy hands.

"You're going to feel this one," Epi promised. "Really feel this one. It's like nothing else."

And Epi was right. Before they even hit the next party, Default and Schorr were coughing at each other and wheezing laughs between alcohol eyedrops, suddenly short of breath. Default's ear canals felt permanently plugged and the world was surreal, almost soundless. They chatted instead of airtalk for the whole duration. Default had never felt so curiously detached, so . . . floating. It was intoxicating. They stumbled through the streets in their own personal world, a soundless world where fever crept across their foreheads and every breath was dredged.

Default gave it to a select few, sometimes with Schorr's approval first, sometimes not. Only a small handful of fems and sirs and neuts rode the razor-edge of the bacterial trend. Those without connections were left mimicking the effects, walking bent double and faking coughs between words.

There were more bugs, and Schorr wanted them all. At first Default thought he was following because he'd always followed Schorr, because he'd never had social stock this high or funtime this exclusive, but no.

There was something else drawing him to the bright white basement where Epi, now No-Skin, did his work. Default was breaking his body down so thoroughly, so deeply, that he knew himself in ways he never had before. In ways Memmi never had either, but Memmi was distant now, a dim thought on the periphery.

Sometimes the infections hit so quickly Default and Schorr couldn't even leave the basement. They collapsed against each other and No-Skin apologized, talked about reducing potency, but when they were entwined on the floor with entropy swimming their veins they couldn't hear him and didn't care.

Sometimes they stayed there with No-Skin for days on end instead of spreading the word, spreading the vogue, but he seemed to enjoy their company. They shivered and groaned and reveled in pus from a new orifice, an interesting discoloration of the gums, a bone-deep ache.

"How did you learn to make these?" Default chatted on one of these occasions, half inside a fever dream. They had their own closed web at this point, him and Schorr and the newly-christened Bugwright. The Bugwright pulled down his cowl and shrugged.

"Practice, unit," he said, breath steaming. "Practice in other places."

"Schorr never told me you were a pilgrim," Default chatted. He glanced over to where Schorr was lounging, eyes crusted.

"I'm not forthcoming with it," the Bugwright admitted. "A lot of people don't like pilgrims. They like to just think their station is the only station, you know?"

"I had an ex who always wanted to hop stations," Default chatted.

"You see a lot of things," the Bugwright said. "I've seen a lot of things, and all of them end."

"Tell him about the finale," Schorr chatted. Default hadn't known she was lucid.

"It's not ready," the Bugwright said. "When it's ready." He pulled the cowl back up over his skinless face and returned to work.

Time had passed; the nocturns had changed. Every unit in the universe had a bug to show off, and bioscans were everywhere you looked, sprayed onto walls and tattooed onto skin. Signature viruses, custom infections. The freebus had divvied into personal transportation pods for units who were no longer walking, or for those pretending they no longer could. The air was swimming with disease.

"We started this, you know," Schorr said. "How's that feel? You're not the steady satellite anymore. You're nova."

They were in a corner supshop, squeezed into a booth that was doing its best to massage their back muscles. Default was burning off a mild fever, hair fashionably sweat-slicked. He didn't know what Schorr was running. Probably something subtle. Discharge was getting too obvious, she thought.

"It feels good," Default said. Schorr smiled and patted his face. Default caught her hand and held it there. "But I've got a lift leaving soon."

"You want to go back topside?" Schorr asked, incredulous. "Why?"

"It's time, that's all," Default said. He judged his next words. "I want you to come with me."

"I want you to stay here." Schorr tugged her hand back and pointed out the wide window. "This is different, unit. This is finally different."

"You've found things like this before. Different things."

"But this is the last thing, Default." Schorr looked hurt. "The biggest thing. I was hoping you would do it with me."

"Do what?" Default asked, heart thumping. They had been docking more often lately, less often with other people, and if she wanted a contract . . . well, Default wanted one, too. He felt Schorr open up a private line.

"Do you remember the Five?"

Of course he remembered the Five. The memory was entrenched in every brain on the station. There was a hundred orbits' worth of art, music, and gene-shares dedicated to the Five and their ill-fated hull-walk, to the malfunction that let a meteorite slip through the station's detection system and plow five units into blood and carbon dust.

"What do you think happened to them?" Schorr asked.

Default frowned, unsure where the conversation was headed. *"They ceased."*

"What do you think it felt like?"

"It's impossible to know that."

"Not impossible." Schorr peeled back the sleeve of her thermal and raised her arm. Default saw something black and bubbling underneath.

"A different thing," Schorr said in the air. "A new thing." She looked sad.

"I thought maybe you meant something else." Default stared at the infection and remembered a conversation with the Bugwright. Bubonic. Old Old Earth. Fatal, whatever that entailed.

"But I wanted it to be me and you, Default," Schorr said haltingly. Her eyes roved all the way around the supshop, everywhere but on him, then finally landed.

"Why?" Default asked.

Schorr shrugged. She smiled. "Because then you'd never have to find someone else."

Their hands entangled, and as they kissed Default dropped his immunity buffer all the way down to zero.

Memmi/Others had missed Default, she/they really had. The polymind probe had circled the edge of the galaxy, watched the decay of a red dwarf, catalogued a crude bacterial life-form on a thawing moon. Memmi/Others had marveled at the vastness, the chaos, but she/they had not forgotten the station, either. It was harder to re-locate than expected, no longer buzzing with wave communication. Maybe something new had been developed, some new frequency the outdated probe instruments could no longer detect.

The probe docked and gave Memmi/Others a troubling report: the station was empty. She/they floated through the station like a ghost, jumping from monitor to monitor. The AIs were dormant, running only the most basic maintenance protocols. The lifts were stalled in their berths. The multihouses were derelict. She/they went down to the nocturns.

Nothing. The holos danced on in the dark streets, music was still relooping and evolving, but the revelers had vanished. A lone autocleaner was still wandering, still shoving debris, and Memmi/Others recognized the dull yellow of old bone only by the probe's logs. She/they retreated to the station's main thinker, trying to make sense of it, trying to evaluate.

One ship had left the station. Memmi/Others saw the trajectory like a laser, and she/they directed the probe to follow it. She/they slid through black space for a century. For two. The probe arrived at another station, this one slowly orbiting a double sun. Memmi/Others requested docking. No answer.

The probe sailed on to the next station, and the next, and as desperation grew and then ebbed there came a slow realization: she/they had missed the party.

BRUTE

The apartment's DNA scanner can pick Anton out of the crowd almost a block away, so the sliding doors were unlocked and the lobby lighting was welcoming when me and him arrived with the crate. Automated apartments are cushy like that, but I would get lonely without human voices. Anton likes it better that way so he can concentrate on work. The latest of which was, of course, the crate: a cube of dull green armor, military–grade stuff that looked ready for an atomic bomb.

"We'll need cracking equipment," I said. "It'll cost."

"There's someone with a cracker down Tiber Street," Anton said, grinning and adjusting the top hat he never sets at the same angle twice. "We can rent."

Anton is a real piece of eight. He always wears a gilled coat, the kind you see in old European net plays, and when he grins like that people sink into his gravity well to become pucker–faced meteoroids. He has a kind of charisma, and a fire lit under his brainpan that drives him along at unholy speeds when he gets his hands on something exciting, something like the crate.

When the elevator opened, Anton guided the crate inside and I squeezed in behind, boned fish in the corner. We'd found the thing in floodland, sending up a lazy beep beep from Old Vancouver's watery grave. Extracting it took most of the week—long nights in wetsuits and choking on boat fumes—but the salvage claim had gone through, and it was all ours now. I was moderately curious, but this one was Anton's holy grail. Anton thought it was going to be something big.

"It could be nothing," I said again, doing devil's advocate as was usual.

"Possible, possible," Anton said. "But why put nothing in a mobile bomb shelter?"

The elevator breezed open and we floated the crate over to Anton's workshop. Walls recognized him and put on the lights. This was where the business, Anton and Hume Scavenging, went on. Four years of quality and exceptional service.

"We'll stow it under the counter," Anton said. "And throw those sheets over it."

"Nobody's coming to look for it, Anton," I said. "It's all ours now." We slung it under the counter, no sheets, and it sat there looking real fucking innocuous.

We rented the cracker on Tiber Street, beside the yellow—taped hole they were still planning to fill with cement. It belonged to a woman with two cigarettes in her mouth. Anton thanked her for the discount with pale arms around his neck.

"I didn't know you knew her," I said, adjusting the recyclable rucksack we had filled with equipment.

"Biblically," Anton said, spitting out the taste of her smoke. He laughed at his own little joke and I smiled by accident. Anton. For at least the past decade, except for the incident with Dolly from the supshop, Anton had always told me who he was shacking up with.

"She's not too troll," I said, thinking of the seams of her tights and the pristine edge of her collarbone. He grunted his 'you know, no big issue' assent. I still don't know how Anton does it. Friends tell me he's handsome but I've never seen it. His face is just Anton's face, asymmetrical and, I think, a bit smug.

"We're going to crack open some bottles, too," Anton announced, waving his skyper. The order form for a lunch and liquor was still blinking on his screen. "To a week of hard work, yeah?"

"Yeah, verily," I said.

We clinked imaginary beer.

Cracking equipment is hard to assemble while drinking, but we did it. By the time Anton positioned the pincers all around the crate, making sure everything was lined up, the excitement was coming off him like radiation.

"Looks ready," I said. "Let's shatter the bastard."

"Every act of creation is first an act of destruction," Anton said grandly, and he turned the handle.

The crate split apart with a sound like bones breaking. We'd both been getting into the spirit, so when we saw what was inside, it was a bit of an anticlimax. It looked like an incubator, the kind they use to heat up eggs for clone-grown dinosaur collectors.

"Might be a Rex," I consoled him. "Those sell tidy." But of course I was kind of glad it was nothing earth-shattering. Anton's gut feelings were right too often, and gut feelings shouldn't be.

"Nobody cares about eggs this much," Anton said, reaching for the control. The incubator gave him a green light, so he flipped it open and we saw that it wasn't holding an egg at all.

Describing the contents is hard. It was shapeless, furrowed red meat and quicksilver splashes. It undulated and shivered in slow motion. It smelled bitter.

"What the fuck?" I asked.

"Looks like . . . nano." Anton put out a hand like he was going to touch it.

"Don't touch it," I said.

A ripple went through the thing, like responding to the sound. It was flowing together into sort of a starfish shape, all pumping muscle and the silvery stuff weaving into it.

"Nano–bio," Anton finished. "How fucking peculiar."

"This is one wyrd gene–job," I said, watching the thing coil against itself.

It bucked, sudden, like hips at climax, and in a blink it was on Anton's arm. He gave a muffled *whoa* of surprise, stumbled back and around in a circle. I made a grab for the thing, but it had already slithered up his sleeve and out of reach.

"Godshit!" Anton gasped. He hit the floor on his knees and I pushed him the rest of the way down, ripping off his red thermal. After that came off, I didn't know what to do. The thing from the incubator was straddling his spine, stretching little fluttery stubs out over his shoulder blades. It took me off my guard, the wyrdness of the whole affair, and how it was sort of beautiful.

"Oh, man, man, man," Anton said. "Help me remove this little monster." He didn't sound panicky, which is another excellent thing about Anton. He stays arctic cold under aggressive circumstances. He was even laughing a little, and a laugh of my own was halfway up my throat when the little stubs sharpened, right before my eyes, and plunged as tiny spines into Anton's bare back.

He whimpered, and I knew this was bad, because he had never made that noise in my memory. Small beads of blood were welling up, all along his spine, and then somehow sluicing away. My first thought was that Godshit, this thing was vampirous. It was sucking him dry in the unsexy way. I tried to pry it off, but it was like grabbing gelatin, slipping and sliding off my fingers.

Then Anton held up a hand, like suggesting that I stop, and he got up off the floor.

"What the fuck is it doing?" I asked, stepping back. Anton looked slightly woozy, but he was alive. The thing from the incubator seemed to calm down, flattening itself along his back like a fleshy hug. I reached for my skyper where it had toppled from my pocket.

"Hume, I think it plugged in," Anton said.

"I'm getting the emerg–serv," I said. "We still have credit with them, right?"

"Leave the skyping," Anton told me. He grimaced and propped himself up against the counter. Little twitches were running through him, miniature seizures.

"That thing just grafted onto your fucking back, Anton," I said back. "Make me a damn compelling, you know, argument, or I'm getting them."

"Hume, Hume," Anton said, in his calming way. "I'm about to. Whoa." Another twitch twanged through him. "You remember those spinal gears? For paralyzed people?"

"The things that looked like spiders," I said. "Yeah, verily."

"Like spiders, right," Anton continued. "They lay new roads for the nerve endings. Bypass the damage. We're looking at some remarkable nano–bio prototype for the same thing." He was twisting and flexing.

"You're not paralyzed, Anton," I said.

"No," he said. "I'm well beyond not–paralyzed. Hit me."

"Hit you."

"Hit me," Anton repeated.

I've never slammed one to Anton; I've wanted to now and again. The adrenals and the fact he was requesting it and the wyrdness of the whole thing made me amenable, so I took a bit of a stance.

"Only if you'll come to emerg–serv," I said. "Get that fucking thing off you."

Anton nodded solemnly. So, thinking maybe it would give his brain a bit of reboot, I swung. Anton was gone, blurred off to the side like a screen glitch, and as I went for the left cross on instinct he squeezed off from that one, too. Anton did a lot of things well, but he didn't box. The last punch was a lazy drifter, as I was flabgasted, but it was still way too weighted for Anton to pluck it out of the air, as he did, and stop my fist.

"Godshit," I said, looking down. The thing had sent tendrils down his arm, red cords of twitchy muscle. Like an exo, but meat.

"Smart little brute," Anton said, barely breathing hard. "Finders, keepers, yeah?" I knew he meant the both of us, because we always say that after we find something really big.

"Yeah," I said. "Verily."

The brute took up residence between Anton's shoulder-bones, clinging at him like a starfish. First few days, we tried running tests and such, poking the thing with probes and once putting the pair of them into a scan tunnel. It looked to be alive, certain, and the scan showed electrical pulses running through a sensory suite and also through a fleshy nub that Anton thought might be a crude sort of brain stem.

"Paramilitary," I said. "Some mad prototype. Who buys?"

"Nobody, until we know how much it's worth," Anton said.

"Fucking thing's going to eat you in the night," I said, even though the tests showed no damage being done.

Anton's laugh sent a quiver through the knotted red, the rippled silver.

He said it was like being on phencyclines twenty–five–seven, everything jacked up, everything quick. He was always juggling things, seeing how many bolts or airpens or tangerine oranges he could keep in the air at once, plucking and throwing too fast to see. A few times he tried to lift the old boat chassis, knees popping, red–swathed biceps shivering, and I thought it budged a bit, but didn't tell him.

"I've been thinking," he said to me a day later, tossing a spanner up and down behind his back. "We don't need to tell anyone about this thing. The salvage claim went through, yeah, but something like this doesn't get flood–dumped purposefully."

"Think some brain team is crying over it in a labo somewhere?"

"Think it got lost," Anton said, looking thoughtful. "As you do, in floodland. Think some transport fuck–up. Never got where it was meant to."

"Have a look at the new scans," I said, flipping him a sheaf of hardcopy.

He peered at it, squinting for the dimness, and suddenly I saw a little red filament reach around from his collar and wriggle towards his eye like a fucking water snake. I unshuttered my jaw to tell him such, but Anton had noticed. He tugged it closer with one finger and let it branch a tiny membrane over the white of his eyeball.

"Helps in the dark," he said. "No big issue, Hume."

"New trick," I muttered, and once he shrugged his way through those scans the tests stopped. The brute was mysterious; the brute stayed that way.

A week on, the cockroaches that scuttled through the cracks in Anton's apartment wall were all but gone and the brute had grown hard little keratin nodules on it.

"Osmosing," Anton explained, pulling his coat on. "Everything needs fuel, doesn't it. Little fucker climbs off me and waits for bugs to crawl close, then snags them. Looks like they go into its underbelly. Really something to watch."

"So's a film," I said, still in the doorway, fidgeting a bit. Anton's workshop smelled a touch different, maybe because I hadn't been in for a while. The little AI paddlers we bought up in YK and set to trawling floodland hadn't given a peep since finding the crate. Business was mostly on the selling end, not the finding or repairing, which suited me alright. Wetsuits itch me more than they do Anton.

"Let's head, then," Anton said. A red–and–silver worm slid up from his collar and he tucked it out of sight, smiling to the mirror.

The film was supposed to be a livefeed, bounced and woven by some pirate satellite sailing over our heads, and they were throwing it up against the big stucco wall of an unfinished church. We were meeting the woman from Tiber Street on the way. The three of us had done beers a few times now and I knew her name was Marina, like the marina, and that she had prehensile toes from an impulsive biomod in her youth. She was clever, deadly pretty; Anton said he was done with her soon.

"Does she know about the thing, then?" I asked on our way.

"Biblically," Anton said, and I couldn't be sure he was joking. There was a stray cat winding along with us, whining and sneezing. Anton had been looking at it, sort of frowning, and as it darted ahead into an alley, he stopped. There was a big grimace on his face. I was going to ask, right, inquire as to why his eyes were all bulged, and then I heard a sucking sound.

The brute peeled itself away from him and slapped to the pavement like a dropped newborn. The little stubs on it telescoped, waving cilia.

"Godshit, that hurts," Anton sighed.

The brute flipped itself over and scuttled into the alley.

"What's it doing?" I asked.

"Don't have an inkling, Hume." Anton rubbed at his spine as the skeletal cat scampered back around the corner, sneezing soot and meowing all agitated–like.

A knotted red hook snatched it out of sight. Then a screech. Then a quiet, and I felt tingling up my vertebrae. We started after the noise simultaneously, no words, following it around the corner. I almost vomited.

You couldn't call it a cat anymore. What was lying there, bubbling and gouting, was processed meat. The brute was drawing thick red ropes into its underbelly, patches of rank fur accompanying. Anton plucked his scarf up to his face for the smell.

"Oh, damn," I said. "Oh, fuck."

Anton's eyes were watering. "She does know about it," he said. "Marina. She, ah, she fucking loves it, Hume." His smile was shaky, not convincing how it usually is. "But we don't tell her about this. Alright?"

"Alright," I said.

"Still want to see her tonight," Anton muttered, but his eyes were sort of cloudy as the brute crawled back to him, up his leg and then his waist and then clamped in again.

We didn't talk about the cat, so I forgot about the cat. Business went on. We got some beeps from deep floodland, down past Old Vancouver towards Sunk Seattle, and took the boat out for a few days. Some of the border buoys tried stopping us on our way down, but they haven't been repaired in about a decade so they can't do much but moan and sputter.

Anyway, we ended up dragging a good five yards of ferrite cable up from a derelict fabricator. Anton dove without his wetsuit. It was eerie. The brute stretched thin over his pale body like a second skin, and when he swam he thrashed like a fish, body oscillating through the cold water at unholy speeds. It was eerie and it was beautiful, and when Anton came up dripping, naked, to sit in front of the heater, I couldn't laugh at his jokes.

Later, as we were looping the cable, a band snapped and the length suddenly whipped around like a punctured balloon, hard and blinding fast enough to crack bones. Even Anton couldn't duck it, and from my spot treading water I saw it lash right into him, enough force to carve him open. When I scrambled my slippery way up on board, he was lying winded on his back. The brute was hard and raw and shiny around his stomach, with just the slightest gouge where the cable had struck.

"Invulnerable," Anton said, when he could speak.

"Fucking chancy," I said. "Should have waited for me to help with it. Fuck."

He just shrugged at that, and he was moodier after the cable. Sometimes he looked over at me like I wasn't supposed to be there.

The ferrite sold, and so did the dissected fabricator, so we celebrated by going out with Marina to eat clams, real ones, not vat-grown, and to drink Antarctican wines.

Anton was still seeing her, which was, you know, as it was. When she met us at the supshop she had on one of those nano-fab dresses, the kind that gets more transparent as the night goes on, and so we were trying to hack it with just an airpen and our skypers to dial it all the way clear, but it was a smart dress and was having none of it. Marina was laughing and Anton was laughing, though sounding different from usual, and I was laughing, too.

When we all stumbled out three bottles tipsier, Anton stumbled into a fisher with little glowies woven through his beard like fishing lures. The fisher shoved him backward. I knew what would go on next, because I'd seen it often enough. Anton would joke, and the man would crack a smile, and in a matter of minutes they would be chummed. Anton was like that when he drank.

Anton put the fisher on the fucking ground. He moved so quick I had to blink as he caged down on the man, hands around a fleshy neck. The man sputtered and choked and wailed, and Marina told Anton to let go right fucking now, and Anton said nothing, just pushed his fingers into the cartilage like he was going to collapse the man's fucking windpipe, and the whole while something was undulating under Anton's coat, thickening down his arms.

I hauled him off before he killed him, but I think it was close. Marina swore and shook; Anton shrugged; I smoked. The emerg–serv came and some medroids slid the semi–conscious fisher into a little pod, charging it to the account of Anton and Hume Scavenging, and at this point the evening was definitely murdered. Marina left with her dress just barely wispy.

"Hume," Anton said to me on the walk back. "I couldn't control it."

"How do you mean?" I asked, and all I could think about was how Anton had thrown the big man down like he weighed nothing, how fast and how starkly strong he'd been.

"Wasn't me doing that," Anton said, biting the inside of his cheek how he does when a salvage may or may not come through.

"Developed for paramilitaries," I said. "So it makes sense. Combat reflex, wasn't it?"

"No," Anton said. "Wasn't a reflex, Hume. I wanted to rip the man's fucking throat out. In fact." He looked straight at me. "I'd already decided to. Already decided how it would feel and everything."

"Don't exaggerate shit," I told him, feeling static up the nape of my neck, right where the brute would be sitting.

"Hume," he said, stopping. "I've got to get it off. Help me."

There was a canister of liquid nitro from God–knows–when in the back of the workshop, the kind doctors use for cryosurgery, and there were plenty of scoring blades to pick from. Anton cleared a counter, sweeping autotools and scraps and batteries to the floor, all crashing, clattering, and then stretched himself out on the bare surface.

"You're sure you want to do this?" I asked him. The red–and–silver machine–flesh pulsed gently on his back, wrapping his torso, gripping his neck. It glistened wet in the lamplight.

"Damn sure," Anton said. "It doesn't detach anymore. Not for weeks."

"You never wanted it to," I said, which was the truth. He told me drunk one night how it made him fuck like a god, how Marina had begged, and I told him I didn't want to hear it even though a part of me did. That same night he lifted the boat chassis, the brute swatched around his arms and back like a man turned inside–out.

"Cut it off me," Anton said into his folded arms.

I lugged the nitro canister over to wait on standby, then I slipped a few knives between the slits of the heater. Anton whistled tunelessly. It was to distract himself, I guess, but also I had the odd thought that it was to distract the thing on his back, to lull it. When one of the knives was glowing orange–hot, I pulled it out.

The brute shifted, almost as if it was looking at me, and gave a little shiver. I had a nearly guilty feeling as I descended the knife, but before it could contact the brute squirmed away, leaving a small hole of Anton's pale skin. The pocked sucker–scars were wyrdly pretty.

"The nitro," Anton said, and I realized he'd expected this, or else tried it before, even. I opened the nozzle and misted it over his back. Some must have touched him, because he bucked against the counter and hissed through his teeth, but most of it frosted onto the brute. A sluggish ripple went through it, then stopped. I started to cut.

Anton's ice–veined, he really is, but he screamed like a banshee every knife–stroke. I severed the tendrils where I could, pulling them up and away with gloved fingers, usually with small bits of skin attached. The brute twitched, so I went faster. I cut and I cut, and from the way the thing writhed I knew it was feeling everything as much as Anton did. Or else the reverse, I guess.

"Nearly done," I said. "Almost over."

"Man," Anton sobbed. "Oh, man, fuck." The brute writhed as it peeled away, still sluggish, still slow, and the tendrils reached out at me like tiny fingers. Pleading, maybe. When it finally came free I dumped it into the incubator, the one we'd dredged up all those eons back.

Just like that, Anton was upright. There was sweat starching his hair and he looked suddenly small, suddenly skinny.

"Tiber Street," he said. "They're filling the hole tonight."

"With cement," I said. "Yeah."

"Get it onto the sled," Anton said. "We're going to bury the fucking thing. Deep, deep." That made me drop the knife, just a micrometer off my big toe. I could tell by the way he was staring, eyes dark, that he meant it.

"Don't joke me," I said anyways. "We've never found anything this big. When we get a buyer, we'll be kings, remember?"

"Hume, did you not see what just happened?" Anton said, but he said it in the calm slow way, like speaking to an infant or a shit AI.

"I saw everything," I said.

Anton stared down at the incubator. "Well, you don't know what it's like," he said simply.

"No," I said back. "I never do."

Anton looked back to me, and he shrugged, sort of helplessly, then booted up the sled. Before it started to hum I could hear the slither–sound coming from inside the incubator. I tried to remember back, back to the first time we opened it, and I wondered why Anton had tried to touch it and not me. Then I helped him secure it onto the sled.

The streets were empty when we got outside. The night air was chilled, smelling like grease and floodwater and boat fumes. Me and Anton went quiet as shadows, the sled gliding along behind us, us not speaking, and I thought for a moment how maybe this was all about Marina, maybe because she knew the brute was getting bigger and she wanted it gone.

We heard the putter of construction equipment at work before we rounded the corner. As we did I saw the big automated dumper hunch down over the hole, corroded yellow joints rasp–rasp–rasping on each other. Gray quickset cement started to vomit in. Anton was walking more and more slowly as we approached.

"Forgot how dark things get," he muttered. "How slow everything is."

He looked down at the incubator and scratched himself, hands reaching under his coat, around his back. Our toes curled at the very edge of the pit. The dumper must not have had much in the way of safety protocol, because it didn't stop pouring.

"Alright," Anton said. "Into the hole."

I should have dumped the whole incubator, but I couldn't. I had to see the thing one more time. The lid slid off and the brute rippled weakly inside, groping tiny tendrils. I thought how if there was one thing I did better than Anton, it was being alright with letting someone else run things now and again. The brute clung to my arm as I lifted it up, but it was still cold from the nitro, still limp.

The cement churned and gurgled, impenetrable–looking gray. I looked up at Anton, saw his eyes wide and feverish in the dark. I held my arm out over the pit and that's when Anton suddenly lunged, I think to stop me, or maybe because he knew I wasn't going to drop it on my own, and then the three of us were on the ground. Anton was clawing at my arm, my shoulder; the sky somersaulted as we rolled back away from the hole, the splashing cement. I hit back, right and then left and connected with both. His head snapped away; blood and spit smacked my scalp. The brute was on the move, up my arm, under my sleeve.

Anton's wild eyes, Anton's reaching fingers, and then it was my fingers, Anton's throat. Bitter smell. He gouged at my face and his feet kicked. The brute was wrapping around my hands. Anton's breath came scalding hot. He lashed out with a hand and I saw oilspills behind my eyes. His nails ripped down my cheek, made me lean harder, my elbow on him now. Push, and push, and—

Everything went still. The dumper had stopped, work complete, brain whirring silently to a satellite for the next task. The quickset had settled. Anton had marks the size of my thumbs imprinted purple under his jaw, no breath coming in or out. It felt like the hot cement had all poured into my stomach.

"Anton," I said. "Anton. Anton."

Anton said nothing. The brute stirred on my back.

"Anton. Anton."

He didn't twitch. The brute spread, sliding over my skin.

"Help me," I whispered. The brute touched a raw filament to the back of my neck and I felt it sting, like a jellyfish.

The apartment door was still gene–coded, so I went up the side. The red suckers on my fingertips clung staticky to the glass surface, let me shuffle up nice and easy. I climbed to the barred window and looked in. Empty again.

"I need to stop coming back here," I said, hoping this time it would stick.

The weather had turned cold in the past week, but the brute was thicker than usual and it compensated with pulsing warm tendrils around my limbs. I pushed my face up against the glass. Scattered tools and equipment on the floor. A cylinder of what might have been liquid nitro. In the corner, the dull green shards of something vaguely familiar.

"Every act of creation," I said, as if somebody had said it before, maybe whatever ghosty kept dragging me back here. The brute rumbled, and I could almost think it was in assent. I'd never talked to myself this much before. Good to imagine that the brute was listening.

The apartment was empty, so I dropped down to the sidewalk. The brute was heavy today. More muscle. I felt like God.

When I walked past the door, the scanner blinked at me, just once.

YOUR OWN WAY BACK

The mausoleum was all plexiglass and synthetic stone, lit by ghostly blue guide lights in the floor that charted visitors to their particular units. Elliot had free run of the place while his mother and grand-dad talked.

When he was younger he chased the autocleaner, slip-sliding on its slick wet trail until someone glared at him. Now he was twelve and the glossy black floor was only slightly tempting. Instead, he sat outside the booth with his swim bag and eavesdropped.

"You can't afford another year in digital," his mother was saying. "You're shedding memories already. If you stay here any longer, we took out that clone policy for nothing."

"Maybe it's for the best." His grand-dad's voice was wavery, distorted.

Elliot peeked around the corner and saw the projection flickering, face carved in blue hololight. It was blurrier than usual.

"There's the alternative, isn't there?" Elliot's mother said. "What we talked about?"

"Must have shed the memory."

"Don't be like that, dad. Elliot's fully notched."

That reminded Elliot that he'd loaded a new comic to read. He ran his finger along the inert plastic at the base of his skull, feeling the slot where the new chip was sitting and beneath it the arithmetic he'd loaded from school and neglected to open. Elliot leafed through the pages in his mind's eye but kept listening.

"And he's young enough," his mother said. "He's still got brain plasticity, maybe even for another year."

"Why don't you just ask him?" His grand-dad's projected face raised both eyebrows. "I expect he's listening in."

Elliot's mother craned around the corner and Elliot rolled his eyes back, pretending to be absorbed in the shifting pictures, but knew he'd been caught out. She smoothed her dark hair and blinked tired eyes.

"Elliot, what do you think? Come in here, love."

Elliot stood up and walked into the booth, gangly now that he was finally growing. He waved, out of habit, even though he knew his grand-dad couldn't see it.

The blue ghost was only a projection, cobbled from old EyeWitness recordings and follow-cams, that gave visitors something physical to interact with. His grand-dad was really in a neural web contained by the dull marble plinth in front of them.

"Elliot, you know what a piggyback is, right?" he asked.

"Yeah. Yes." Elliot felt the nape of his neck again. "My friend Daan's got a tutor AI."

"Your grandfather is not an AI," his mother said sharply.

"He knows that," his grand-dad said. "What do you say, Elliot? Let the old man bang around your head? It's your choice. Completely your choice."

"Just for the summer," his mother assured, pinching the bridge of her nose. Her nails had chipped. "It would just be for the summer while the clone's growing. It's really much better than keeping him here in the mausoleum."

Elliot thought back to when Daan showed up for class with the shiny AI chip in his notches, how impressed everyone had been. This wasn't the same thing, but it was close.

"Okay," Elliot said. "Do you still know how to do algebra?"

His mother's ears went red but his grand-dad just laughed, a synthesized warble that was almost too loud for the silent mausoleum.

Before they left they had him loaded into a bone-white chip, and then that chip was sealed in plastic wrap and dropped into a bag, and Elliot held it very carefully on the drive home.

"**T**his might jolt a bit," the technician said, clipping Elliot's hair away from his notches.

Elliot nodded as well as he could with his chin burrowed in pillow. He was on his stomach on the couch watching rain streak down the wide window. The technician had come over with antiseptic-smelling gloves and a black toolkit because Elliot's granddad was not an AI, and Elliot's mother was not going to take chances with her trembling fingers.

She was washing up, but came into the living room every few minutes, hands red as lobsters and slicked with soap. She had excuses the first few times, but now it was just to bite her lip and stare. She didn't realize Elliot could see her in the window.

"Putting him in, now," the technician said. The chip descended in silvery forceps and Elliot felt something slide and rasp at the base of his skull. It settled with a meaty click. Elliot began to ask if they were done, and then—

Jolt.

His nerves blasted sparks all at once, arched his back like a cat, split the top of his head with a thermonuclear explosion. His body spasmed. From somewhere far away he heard himself howl. Then his mother was over him, holding him down, swearing a blue streak at the technician.

"It's normal," the man was repeating. "It's normal. He's fine now. Ask him. He's fine. Aren't you, Elliot?" He was folding his gloves, wiping the sweat raised on his forehead.

Something was stirring in the back of Elliot's skull. *Right here, Elliot. Steady now.*

"Are you okay?" his mother demanded. Her nails were digging crescents in his hand. "Just say something, alright?"

"I'm okay," Elliot said. He felt the stir again. "So's grand-dad. He's okay."

Elliot's mother exhaled, but didn't let go of his hand.

It wasn't like having a tutor AI. Elliot's grand-dad didn't switch off or go dormant. He was always there in the back of things, when Elliot woke up in staticky sheets and when he sawed through his mother's burnt breakfast sausages and when he walked to the public pool early each morning.

Elliot had scrimped the money for his pass from months of bannering the local chipshop, putting value ads in his slots to wide-cast on the subway or in the street. He didn't get pocket money anymore, so every time the laser raked his neck and scanned him into the pool he felt a beat of pride.

Elliot liked his swims best in the morning. Only a few others were ever there, usually middle-aged men churning industriously up and down their lanes. The lifeguard bobbed at the side like a plastic jellyfish, monitoring the chlorine level.

His mother had given him a gelatin ("Cover up your blow-hole," she'd said, taut smile on her way out the door) and he slathered it over his notches, letting it go dry and shiny before he slipped into the water. The chip tingled in his neck but his grand-dad remained silent, still curled somewhere in the back of Elliot's head as he swam.

At school, his classmates were impressed—for the day. By the end of the week Elliot was starting to hear sniggers and knew something was going to happen come gym or break.

On Thursday the sky was dark and blustery, and the supervisor watched the footy game from a far distance with her chin tucked into her windbreaker. They were playing with an old Soccket that rattled when kicked and didn't bounce quite right, and that was why Elliot had missed another open shot.

"You're slow, grand-dad," said Stephen Fletcher, who was small and fierce and had his hair razored around his notches.

"What's that?"

"Your old man chip is turning you slow," Stephen said, grinning like a wolf. "Slooow and stiff."

"Quicker than you," Elliot said, but he knew he wasn't, he was only quick in the water.

"You're too poor to grow a clone for him." Stephen bounced the ball hard against the cement and stuck it on his hip. "That's why you have the chip."

Everyone was watching, now, and the keeper from the opposite end was wandering up from his orange pylons to see what was going on. Elliot looked around, looked at Daan, but Daan was grinning, too.

Steady now, Elliot. It's fine. It's a laugh.

Elliot gave a start. His grand-dad hadn't said a word all week.

"Maybe they can stick him in a baboon," someone suggested. Someone else gave a fair imitation of a monkey screech. Elliot clenched his teeth.

It's fine.

"If your ma's going to make all that clone money, she'll have to work the corner." Stephen pumped his hips. Grinned. "Think?"

The baboon dropped quiet and they all stared. Elliot balled his hands.

Thumb outside your fist, Elliot.

Him and his grand-dad went in swinging.

On the walk home, with the sky bruising overhead and his face now doing the same, Elliot asked about his grandmother. Rain was speckling the sidewalk and Elliot tipped his head back to wash the scabby blood from under his nose. It was a long time before his grand-dad answered.

She didn't want storage. Or a new body. She said she'd had her time, and that was that.

"Why'd you stay?" Elliot asked. His grand-dad didn't answer, and Elliot knew enough to not ask again.

Yellow cabs slid by with rain wriggling down their windshields. Elliot wondered what time his mother would be home.

When school finally let out for summer, Elliot could spend all day at the pool. The weather turned sunny and so they turned the smartglass ceiling transparent, drenching the tiles with afternoon sunlight and making the water glisten blues and greens. More people showed up. Some of Elliot's classmates splashed and threw foam balls in the shallow end. Elliot stayed in the lanes. He was working on his breaststroke.

You could hold your glide longer. His grand-dad said it as Elliot sloshed to the wall in a final burst.

"What?" Elliot panted, hooking his elbows over the pool's edge.

Go again. I'll show you.

Elliot adjusted the pinch of his goggles, inhaled chlorine. There were too many people making waves now and the water was warm as a bathtub. He pulled reluctantly into the lane for a few more lengths. As he did, his muscles seized.

Sorry about that. Here. Relax a bit.

His limbs started moving without him. Elliot leaned into the stroke and felt a hundred small adjustments, how his shoulders sloped and how his hands bit the water. He felt like a fluid. His mouth peeled a foamy grin under the water and suddenly he was smoother than he'd ever been, nothing awkward left in his growing joints, nothing but pure motion.

At the other end, one of the morning men was swilling water in his swim cap. "You're really putting that together," he remarked. "You should trial for the club here, boy."

Elliot nodded and grinned and clambered shaky out of the pool.

After that, grand-dad swam with him and told him stories about how in summer he used to put his clothes in a plastic garbage bag and jump off high rocks into the bay, cupping his balls and holding his nose against the splashdown, and how him and his mates set races from buoy to buoy and bet all their pocket money on them.

There was a lot of time for those stories. Elliot generally went home to an empty apartment where he draped himself over the couch and churned through his comics, hair forming a damp patch on the pillow. His grand-dad didn't like how the comics had all gone back to 2D, but he liked how Elliot could change them as they went along. Sometimes the villain deserved to win, Elliot thought.

When he was hungry he trawled for recipes online and always ended up cooking pasta with mushroom soup from a can. His grand-dad was no help with that. He did, however, show him how to make coffee. His mother was slightly suspicious of it when she dragged in the door to find a pot gurgling on the counter.

"Tastes good," she admitted, swishing the sample in her mug. "That's it for me, though. Have to sleep. One more way I'm inferior to those damn autocabs, isn't it?" She grimaced and poured her dregs down the stainless steel drain, then disappeared into her bedroom.

She worked more than ever and came home late most nights. Some nights they played cards, the three of them, with Elliot and his grand-dad teamed up, but she usually fell asleep halfway through.

She works too hard. Doesn't spend time with you. His grand-dad said it in the night, just as Elliot was drifting off. The constellations on his ceiling were peeling and only glowed when headlights shuttled by outside the window.

They didn't get physical bills anymore, but Elliot could tell when they came in from the tightness of his mother's mouth as she checked her phone.

"She has to," he said. "She's saving."

You ever feel tired, Elliot?

"Now, yeah."

Not like this, you don't. Ah. Never mind. Sleep well.

"You too," Elliot mumbled. He stretched his arms and his legs and slept like a starfish, imagining himself afloat in the water.

One day Elliot came home from his swim and found the apartment unlocked and smelling like cold lemon. His mother hugged him and asked about his swim times. Maybe he could invite some of his friends to go with him once in a while? For the first time in a long while her nails were painted hard and white.

She picked the small bits of gelatin out of his hair while they ate greasy takeaway, and afterwards she told him they were going to the FleshFac.

"I thought we were growing a custom," Elliot said, bundling up the paper sheaths. "So it'll look like him."

"Well, it doesn't hurt to see options." His mother smiled hesitantly. "Does it?"

Elliot realized she was asking his grand-dad, but his grand-dad didn't answer. He pulled his jacket half-on and followed his mother out to the car. When he was younger he'd liked the yellow paint. It looked bad now, too bright and too obvious. He slid into the passenger side and then they drove. The seats smelled like marijuana cigarettes.

The FleshFac was on the edge of the city, located near a large warehouse and a hospital. The building was squat and iron gray, like a safe dropped from the sky. The AI greeter at the entrance scanned them in, and directed Elliot and his mother down a peeling green hallway to the clone rooms. Everything smelled like antiseptic.

Clones were lined in scratched plastic shells, shrouded by a poison-yellow vapor. Another family was there for an upload, and while Elliot and his mother watched quietly one of the shells hissed open. Hidden vacuums sucked the fog away. The clone was long-limbed and sharp-shouldered with ghostly white skin that had never seen sun, but after a long silence the little girl said, "Daddy, daddy, we made your bed for you," and then hugged him. The woman stood there with a collection of red balloons wilting in her hand.

So young. He deserves it.

"You deserve it," Elliot said, forgetting his mother was there with him.

There are so many years in that clone. God. A lot of years.

The family left. The daddy was walking stiffly on new legs and his wife held his hand like it was something foreign, but their daughter skipped ahead happily with the artery-red balloons. Elliot and his mother walked down the row of clones.

They came in two models, basic male and basic female, both with standard musculature and post-racial features. They didn't look anything like his grand-dad. Elliot could tell that his mother was doing numbers in her head, and with every clone they passed her teeth bit deeper into her lip.

When they got home she locked herself in the bathroom and turned on the fan, but behind the roar he could still hear her crying and crying.

"There's enough," she said, when she came out red-eyed. "There's just enough. We can do it."

Elliot nodded. His grand-dad said nothing.

I *stayed because I was scared.*

Elliot stood in the locker room shower with his face up to the nozzle, letting it beat a tattoo against his forehead. "Of being dead?" he asked, swilling water in his mouth.

I suppose. Yes. That. She must think I'm a real coward if she's still up there waiting.

"You must miss her," Elliot said. He dragged his toenail along the crack between two tiles.

Madly. I thought maybe I was staying to help your mother. Since your dad split so early.

"Oh."

But she doesn't need me taking care of her. Not anymore. And she sure as hell can't afford this clone, not even one of those gawky bastards from the factory.

Elliot switched the water off. Drops splashed off his face to his collarbone, trickled from his armpits down his elbows. "What do you mean?"

I'm not going to let her put you two in debt when it's time I moved on. I'm tired, Elliot. I stayed because I was scared, but now I'm tired of being scared. You get me?

Other bodies moved away and Elliot was alone in the changing room, fingers turning blue.

You had a good swim today. What do you say to one more in the morning?

"Here?" Elliot asked faintly.

Not here.

In the earliest hours of the morning, when it was still dark outside his window, Elliot found a pen and a pad of paper and closed his eyes. He had never learned to write without a keyboard, but his grand-dad moved his hand for him in graceful swoops and curls over the page. He filled up four of them and then Elliot shuffled them under his mother's door.

His swim-stuff was wet from the day before but he changed all the same, putting the clammy togs on under his trousers. He let himself out of the apartment and walked down the street with the bag tucked under his arm, past the hazy glow of the streetlamps and a roving autocleaner collecting the trash.

The bay was closed off now, with a wire fence that hadn't existed in his grand-dad's time, but Elliot had spent enough time clambering after lost footballs to scale it competently, if not quickly. He looked at the murk with trepidation for only a moment, eyeing the bobbing plastic refuse and slippery rocks, then he stripped down and plunged in.

His grand-dad pulled him off into the bay with smooth strokes, powerful the way Elliot had always thought of seals or sleek dolphins as powerful. They were alone in the water, making the only noises. His hands carved the cold surface and the slapping of his body, the tug of his breath, the water in his ears, all seemed vastly loud in the dark.

When they were finally bobbing far out in the bay, watching the red lights of the skyline, his grand-dad said it was time.

Expect you can make your own way back.

"Yeah. Yes. I can."

Pull me out, then.

Elliot's cold fingers scrabbled for the gelatin lump at the back of his skull. He pulled it off in clumps, then long strips, then it all came away at once.

He winched the notches open and his slippery fingertips found his grand-dad's chip. He hesitated for a heartbeat, two heartbeats, then yanked it like a tooth and hurled it off into the bay. A spark jumped once. Disappeared.

He swam slowly on the way back, his empty-feeling head held carefully above water. He toweled off and dried the strange tingling hollow at the back of his neck. His eyes stung. Swimming without goggles always turned them pink.

Elliot's mother was waiting for him on the curb when he got back home, the pages spread around her bare feet.

"Haven't seen his handwriting in so long," she said, combing a strand of dark hair from her face.

Elliot eased down on the cement curb and his mother wrapped an arm around his shoulders. They sat together, watching dawn streak the sky with filaments of red.

I WENT TO THE ASTEROID TO BURY YOU

I went to the asteroid to bury you
because the world had too much color in it.

I took a grimy tourist shuttle,
where the seatbacks played grainy footage
of the moon landing

and androids named Buzz and Neil
served tubes of orange juice.

When I tore mine open with my teeth,
the juice escaped as small wobbling suns.

I unhooked myself to swallow them
like I swallow your name. Buzz glared; Neil
asked me to return to my harness.

~

I docked over Yorick's Crater and saw
new biodomes bubbling in the bottom.

At the duty-free, I bought the vodka
that made you sick. I rented a spacesuit,
boots and extra arms for digging.

The neurolink fizzed in my brain
like a soft drink

and the arms did a preprogrammed
dance to limber up.

You'd have laughed. I filled my O2 tank
at 35c per liter, enough for us both,
and left the airlock.

~

I walked through a stellar night vast
and gray. Tethered halogens lit the way

and at the city limit, cubes of trash
floated in a minefield. I walked
and walked with loping steps,

staring up at a star-spun sky,
until, like Orpheus,

I turned
to look for you.

Your voice must have been static
in the suit, because all I saw were my
cracked footprints.

~

I stopped when I felt I no longer existed,
and told my arms to drill. They churned

in rhythm, displacing untouched rock
into a swelling cloud, but it was
too smooth and too easy so I

drilled the rest myself, until
sweat beaded and froze

inside my suit and fogged
my faceplate.

I kissed your vacuum-sealed ashes
through cold glass. With vodka, I christened
the new crater after you.

~

I knelt in the frozen galaxy of dust and
pushed your urn down like a bobbing magnet.

That was when I realized I
had no way of covering you, no way
of returning dust to dust

and smoothing you away.
I couldn't bury you

with a hundred thousand motes
haloing my head

or the hundred thousand words
in my desiccated mouth. So I said your name,

and it shattered on my tongue, it
latticed my faceplate with ice.

CAPRICORN

Nyx sold his product in the exercise yard, in a blindspot the rusty autoturrets couldn't swivel to anymore. Inmates walked in slow circles around the synthetic track and every so often one would stop off for the furtive exchange. Nyx slapped neoprene baggies into palms with every handshake.

Basta wasn't furtive about it: Woadskin crew didn't worry about things like follow-cams or autoturrets, not now that they ran every cell block in the prison. Nyx reached into his sleeve and produced a particular bag for him.

"Color's different," Basta said, juggling it in his hand. "You run scant on fucking, uh, ephedrine again?"

"Better filter," Nyx said bracingly. "Better batch. Floats like, whoa."

"You best not be cutting my shit." Basta bit the corner and tongued the red-tinged powder. "I'll know."

"Hey, hey, it's pure. Ask Cade and his units." Nyx tugged his jumpsuit down and scratched at his neck. "Dosed them the same batch this morning."

"I told you to cover that tag," Basta snapped.

Nyx looked down at his collarbone where a zodiac sign was tattooed in bioglow ink.

"You're not getting no fucking points for loyalty." Basta touched the pocket where he kept his shiv. "He's on ice. He's not coming back. Nobody does."

Nyx kept his eyes on the zipper as he dragged it up slowly, carefully. "Year later, you still don't say his name?"

Basta wrenched him down by his ear; Nyx wailed at the feel of crumpling cartilage.

"Capricorn. And nobody comes back from cryo. He's in 114 till he's dead."

"Okay, unit, okay, fuck," Nyx choked.

Basta dead-eyed him for a moment longer, then let go. "You're lucky you mix this shit so good. Or you'd be dead with the rest of the old crew." He slipped the baggie into his waistband as the buzzer started to bleat.

Nyx rubbed his ear, then joined the inmates slouching back inside, ushered by the creaking autoturrets. They always cleared the yard when a new shipment of prisoners was coming in.

In decontamination, Boniface seemed more naked than anybody else. His skin was pale and paper-thin and free of any ink, flays, or ritual scarring. When the chemical mist billowed up around their waists, he looked like a lean ghost. Only his face was colored with bruises.

"Hundred percent prisoner retention," said the man beside him. "Nowhere to escape to when they stick you on an asteroid, is there? Only one man ever came close."

"So I hear," said Boniface. His bright blue eyes raked the shrouded room. He crouched down, where the mist deadened voices and obscured faces, and his companion did the same.

"When they caught him, they put him in cryo for life," the man went on, muttering now. "Braindead on ice. They're supposed to thaw you every few months for a physical, Bremnes Act or whatever the hell it is, but I think they probably just leave you frozen. Who would know, right? I'd rather be dead."

"How are you feeling?" Boniface asked, smothering a cough. The fog tingled cold on his skin.

"Rather be dead and have it all over with," the man said, staring into space.

"How are you feeling?" Boniface repeated, meaning the purpled sutures across the man's stomach.

His face twisted. "It hurts."

"All be over with soon," Boniface said. He jackknifed over another cough, a worse one.

"Yeah. Yeah." The man grinned shakily, unperturbed by the noise. "Teach them a fucking lesson. Out with a bang." Vacuums came to life with a roar and began sucking the mist away, pulling it in wreaths and tendrils away from Boniface's bent head. Specks of rust red floated off with it.

"That's right," he said, straightening up, wiping his mouth. "Try not to whimper."

"What?"

Boniface put a finger to his lips as the doors slid open and a synthesized voice ordered them forward.

The sweepers came in the middle of the night, but Nyx didn't sleep anymore. He hid his glassware and bottles of knock-off chemicals mostly out of habit, shuffling them into the gouged-out wall behind the bed. The sweepers scanned the cell door open and marched inside, all matte black body armor and clouded facemasks. They were dragging someone behind them.

"What is this?" Nyx demanded, pulling out his earbuds.

They dumped the man on the floor. His head was a canvas of cuts and his eyes were swollen mostly shut. He groaned.

"Hey, it's the chemist," said one of the sweepers. His mask retracted and Nyx recognized one of his more valued customers. "Got you a roomie for the night, chemist."

"This is my fucking cell, Dirk," Nyx said. "It's my workplace. I don't share it, you know? Thought you had that figured out upstairs, unit."

"Concussed, internal hemorrhaging," Dirk said, nudging the man on the floor with the toe of one boot. "Probably going to die overnight. Either way, I'll come pick him up in the morning. Maybe you spot me some of that new batch I've been hearing about."

"Welcome party?" Nyx asked, staring at the blood smears.

"Grigio Krewer," said the sweeper. "You remember. He chopped up all those little girls on Penance." He resettled his mask and gave the injured convict a once-over. "What did you expect, you piece of shit?"

"Fuck you," the man gasped. "Said it would go off. Promised." He clutched his stomach and Nyx noticed the puckered scar for the first time.

"He's panned, man." Dirk gave a snort of disgust, translated into static by the mask. "You have a good night, chemist. We're going to. You animals get so riled up every time the fresh meat comes in." He hefted his stunstick, jaunty. "Think I'll have to torch a few fuckers before morning. Just to keep everyone zen."

"Thought that was the Woadskins's job."

"Yeah. Well." Dirk slid the cell door shut. "Basta, he's no fucking Capricorn, is he?"

Both guards disappeared down the gloomy cell block, tips of their stunsticks whirling electric blue in the dark. Nyx was turning to find his earbuds when the child-killer's head snapped upright. He squinted puffy eyes.

"You told me it would go off," he said, pushing words through split lips, shattered teeth. "You motherfucker. You said if they touched me it would go off, but it's not, it's not going off."

"I didn't tell you shit," Nyx said. "I don't know you."

"Not a bomb," the man gasped. "You fucking liar. It's not a bomb, is it? Oh, fuck, fuck. It's coming. Out." He was fetal on the syrupy red floor, arms clutched around his abdomen. Nyx straightened up to ask what he meant, what he was talking about.

Something shuddered through the man's body and made him vibrate like a rag doll, made a noise like a buzz-saw coming to life. His blood-burst eyes winched wide. Burning fat smell, a long rattling howl, and then the man's stomach erupted.

Nyx stood frozen while clots of gore slapped across his jump-suit. A grip-pad rasped out of the ragged hole, slicked wet and struggling for purchase. The rest of the limb appeared, and then the next, and then the spidery medroid was pulling itself out of the dead man's stomach.

Nyx could tell it had been antiseptic white once, but now the plastic plating was drenched in blood and yellow bile. The medroid lurched forward on its tripod legs and Nyx could see the saw it had used to cut itself out, a syringe bundled beneath that.

He jumped backward as the machine made a bee-line for his stash. Red laser light raked the beakers and baggies, lingering on the vial of iodine additive Nyx had been using for the past week. The medroid's feeler slipped inside, probing, then the machine turned back to face him.

Nyx didn't move for a sweating minute, two minutes, as the scanner danced carmine lines up and down his body. The medroid's red eyes blinked once. Then the machine slipped through the cell bars and was gone in the gloom.

"Who else was in your prisoner transport?" Nyx asked faintly, scraping off the front of his jumpsuit, but of course the corpse didn't answer.

In the morning, three Woadskin lieutenants were dead in their cells. They'd all had their cams scratched, a perk of status, so nobody had seen the shankings. Nyx heard about it in bits and pieces: bodies drained to husks, mysterious needle marks in places not even a headfucked mainliner would inject themselves. The whole cell block was a buzzing hive, and it took until afternoon for someone to come clean up Grigio.

"You really have to bust him like that?" Dirk demanded, roll-ing the body onto an inflatable stretcher. "Shit, chemist, I didn't know you even kept a razor. Slashing him belly-open like that? With all this other bullshit going on? Don't make more fucking work for me, man."

"So what happened?" Nyx asked. "Cade, Darius, and who?"

The sweeper held out his cupped palm.

"Yeah, yeah, sure." Nyx scrambled back to his stash and snatched up a baggie, tossed it over. "Now tell me."

"Have to get an autocleaner down here," Dirk muttered, peeling back the corner. "Have to take someone off-shift to supervise, already got too many fuckers clocking security so your Woadskin friends don't riot—"

"Cade dead, Darius dead, who else?"

"That broad-nose motherfucker from the lunar colonies." The sweeper raised his mask and snorted a bump. He blinked. "Going to need this today. That's punchy shit, chemist. Pure. Must be that stuff I got for you."

Nyx blinked. He stared at the red rim of the man's nostril. "Yeah. Uh, yeah. Thanks for that."

"Someone thinks they saw a medroid," Dirk went on. "You know, one of those field medic things that they used in the Subjugation. Unit in question was slammed to the eyes, though. Not a reliable source. And medroids don't murder people."

Nyx paused. "Heard someone smuggled in psychotropics and they're going around," he said. "People think they see all kinds of shit."

The sweeper grunted and resettled his mask, then floated the stretcher out of the cell. Nyx sat down as far as he could from the blood stains.

They found Boniface in the food line, staring down into his empty tray. Basta knocked it away and protein slop gurgled from the nozzle onto the floor. Two Woadskins pinioned Boniface against the wall.

"So." Basta cocked his head. "Your shipment shows up, one day later, three of my best men get toe-tagged. Who are you?"

"Not the only prisoner on that transport," Boniface said. The food line shuffled on past him, all eyes averted.

"You're the only one who went in for a fucking reskin before you got here," Basta snapped. "Who were you? Who'd you claim before you took off all your tags?" He peered closely into the bruised face. "You remind me of someone, motherfucker."

"This is my first skin. I don't like tattoos."

Basta put himself level with Boniface's blue eyes. "We're going to have a conversation, like it or not. But the more you talk, the less it hurts."

"It was a medroid. Refitted, reprogrammed." Boniface told it to the tray on the floor. "I convinced another inmate to smuggle it in for me. Grigio Krewer."

"That lunatic we tuned," one of Basta's men mumbled. "Panned him real good in the showers."

"Knew I saw a droid," the other one said. "Fucking knew it."

"Reprogrammed to do what?" Basta demanded.

"It's the kind they use for triage," Boniface said. "Assessing injuries on the fly. Dope here, cauterize there. Tag corpses for disposal, live ones for pick-up. They can be out there for a long time. Days, weeks. That's why most models take biofuel."

"Those track marks? You saying that thing used Cade for fuel?"

"It's been reprogrammed." Boniface looked up. "It's always hungry, now. It just went after whoever was closest."

Basta nodded, then suddenly Boniface found himself sprawled on the floor, cheek mashed on concrete. "I'm going to put that thing up your fucking ass when we catch it. Where is it now?"

"I don't know. It's got avoidance AI. Probably in a vent. A closet." Boniface began to cough; Basta's foot was an aching weight on his spine. "Won't come out again 'til night."

Basta crouched down, brows knit. "You're trying to fuck with me. Who sent you here?"

"Nobody sent me," Boniface said, wiping his mouth. A gossamer spit-strand webbed his fingers.

"That thing killed three Woadskins. Not adjacent cells. Nobody else. How would it know to do that, huh?"

"Ask your supplier," Boniface said. "Ask whoever gives you phetamines."

Out of the cafeteria, into the corridor. Basta was in a hurry and Boniface was mostly dragged, arms wrenching in their sockets. Nobody looked at them as they passed by. Boniface looked at them all, the feather-white scars and tattooed necks, the steroid-popped shoulders and sinewed arms. He wondered what the chemist would look like now.

They trooped into a large cell, through shatter-proof glass blotched with dry blood. Inside, a man in the standard slam jumpsuit crouched over a stain on the floor, scrubbing at it with a wet rag. He scrambled upright when he saw who was coming to visit.

"Nyx, who is this motherfucker?" Basta asked, pushing Boniface forward.

Nyx's eyes went wide for only a split second. Then he gave a careless shrug. "Don't know. Ugly-looking unit. Why?"

Basta ignored him, striding to the dark spot on the floor. He pointed. "The fluids. Krewer? Don't tell me no fucking lies, Nyx."

"Krewer. I gutted him."

"You? Or the fucking droid?" Basta pulled his shiv. It glinted on its deliberate arc towards Nyx's throat. "You say you don't know this unit. But I can tell he knows you."

Nyx managed a grunt. His larynx bobbed at the tip of the blade.

Boniface, arms tethered by the two Woadskins, had turned his attention to the ceiling.

"You two are in this together," Basta snarled. "I'm taking your ears off, first." His shiv skimmed along Nyx's jaw, up to the fleshy nub of his earlobe. "Then his balls. Then maybe one of you'll tell me why the fuck he's here."

Nyx opened his mouth, but only managed a whine as the shiv drew its first drop of blood.

Then a white plastic meteorite plummeted from the ceiling and smashed Basta to the floor. He howled as the medroid's legs churned for grip. Nyx scrambled; he didn't see the needle go in, but he heard the flesh puncture and felt the fine mist of blood flick out into the air. Basta shrieked. When Nyx looked again, the droid was straddling the Woadskin general's neck, sucking a carmine torrent through its fuel tube, and Basta was writhing, kicking—

Limp. The medroid whirred upright, scanners winking. Basta's men, who'd been rooted watching, dropped Boniface's arms. One of them retched.

"I'd leave, if I were you," Boniface said. "It regains its appetite pretty damn fast."

Dying nerves sent a final shudder through Basta's legs, and the men bolted. That left Nyx and Boniface to watch the medroid skitter its way back up the wall and onto the ceiling. It flattened itself down, retracting its spidery limbs, before squeezing into the vent shaft and vanishing from sight.

Boniface turned to his brother. "Hello, Nicholas."

"Bo."

"I wasn't sure if you were getting the final messages," Boniface said, straightening his jumpsuit. "About the additive. And the other chemicals."

"You could have told me that homicidal junkbucket was going to pop out of a unit's stomach like a fucking—"

"Your seller told me it was the only way to smuggle it through."

Nyx dropped down on the edge of his pad, hiding the shake in his legs. "Didn't tell me it was programmed for the additive, either. What if I'd been nosing that batch? Motherfucking thing would have gone after me, too."

Boniface snorted. "I broke you out of that habit a long time ago."

"I've been in here a long fucking time," Nyx snapped. "I could have started up again, how would you know?"

"I know you, Nicholas."

"Because you're so wise." Nyx gave a dry laugh. "I bet mum never thought you'd end up in here with me, right? Both sons in the slam, the deadbeat and the family man."

"We both know you didn't have to end up here. You could have—"

"Gone to work on the pharms for the rest of my life, been someone's bitch, doing the mix-work they're too cheap to hire AI for. What did that get you, huh? Besides two rotting lungs."

Boniface shook with a cough. Nyx's eyes flickered away.

"This king under the hill," Boniface croaked, when the cough subsided. "This Capricorn. You trust him to help you once he's on the outside? You trust him with your life?"

"Yeah, I do. With your family's, too." Nyx squirmed. "He always pays back, good or bad. They'll keep. He'll make sure they keep. You can trust it."

"I don't have any other choice." Boniface's voice was brittle. "Not one." He scanned the cell, eyes moving quickly past Basta crumpled on the floor, and when he spoke again he was business-like. "You cook in here? You have equipment?"

"Been here a long time, Bo." Nyx pointed back to his cubbyhole. "Got the equipment, got the precursors. You remember how to cook a psychotropic?"

"I think we'd do best to wait until after they come for the corpse."

"Hope they flush him," Nyx said, staring down at the body. "Capricorn wasn't in the freeze three days before those fuckers broke pacts. Rooted Johns in the yard, did Murr and Damola in the showers." His glob of spit missed just to the left of Basta's head. "Just a week, everyone was either dead or taking a Woadskin tag. Was only me left."

This time Boniface looked away. "I didn't know about that."

Nyx shrugged. "Hard to work all the details into one infopacket per fucking month on the state of chemical engineering."

Word spread like a hantavirus: Grigio Krewer was wreaking his vengeance from the grave, via black-market retrofitted medroid, and five Woadskins were already dead, Basta included. The power vacuum was the biggest problem, but a rogue droid gave the sweepers ample excuse to come down with full body armor and autoguns.

"They should be moving us soon," Nyx said, stashing the last baggies in his jumpsuit.

"And your sweeper friend is sure about the EMP?"

Boniface was at the wash basin, first for his chemical-stained hands, now for everything else. His pale skin had a greasy tinge to it, looking almost like wax. He was scrubbing himself down to nothing, scouring the last loose hairs and skin particles, and one fingernail cracked against the basin as he set the brush down.

"Yeah, it's like I guessed it. They've got an hour to try to flush the thing out, then they cut timecost and drop the EMP. If the, uh, the avoidance AI is good as you say . . ."

"It is." Boniface wiggled the nail free with a slick wet scrape; Nyx cringed.

"Then sixty odd minutes from now, the EMP goes off." Nyx paused. "Speaking of time estimate. What did they give you?"

"Keeping on with the aggressive gene-chemo, I could maybe hold out another three months. Medical AI projects a cure in twelve to fifteen years, and I didn't make the money cut for medcenter cryo."

Nyx nodded. "I never got to meet your girl. She old now? What did you name her?"

The yellowed nail clattered into the basin. "Sybil," Boniface said. "Seven, now."

"Shit." Nyx scratched at the tattoo on his collarbone. "Does she know she's got an uncle?"

Boniface turned from the basin, and the lines of his face softened just slightly. "No," he said. "She doesn't know you exist. She doesn't know I'm here. She thinks I went to a better hospital in space." He stuck his hollowed nailbed under the tap; water stuttered out. "But her mum's going to tell her everything, and if the plan goes off, I'll tell her someday, too."

The arrival of a sweeper guillotined the conversation. "Pack your parkas, units, everyone's going to the freezers until we sort this droid shit out."

Nyx rearranged his face, back to his customary squint. "Fucking finally. Can't feel safe in my own damn cell these days."

"Get along." The sweeper waved them towards the door with his chitinous black autogun. "If you don't want frostbite on your cocks, better find somewhere warm to put them."

They joined the stream of orange jumpsuits all filing out of their cell block. Sweepers herded from the sides, more liberal than usual with the stunsticks. The air buzzed thick with tension. Nyx saw a Woadskin staring at him, then at Boniface, but he didn't approach. With Basta dead, the most immediate problem was succession. Nyx knew there were still enough Neo-Mara and Sixers in the block to make things messy if the Woadskins didn't get their shit in order.

A customer tapped Nyx on the shoulder; he jumped.

"Got me something, chemist?"

"Don't fucking do that. But yeah." Nyx pulled out two of the baggies. "Got Samir's, too, but tell him pay comes first next time."

The customer took both, gave Boniface an up-down, and melted back into the orange jumpsuits. A moment later, one of the Sixers came sniffing. The sweepers were distracted, and by the time the crowd reached the corridor gate to the freezers, half the prisoners had already bumped the new batch. Nyx had helped the circulation with a few more uncharacteristic giveaways.

"This is the prep-room?" Boniface asked, as they packed into a blue-gray chamber with machinery dangling from the shadowed ceiling.

"Yeah. Decontamination, blood tests, all that shit to get you cryo-ready." Nyx paused. "I mean, ideally, you'd be getting a saline pump."

"Beggars can't be choosers."

"Listen up, fuckers!" One of the sweepers had followed them inside, rolling back his facemask. "You sit tight right here with me and Dirk during this little droid hunt. Anyone starts shit, they're going in iso. Start shit in a big way, well, autoguns get buggy like anything else."

The other sweeper hauled the door shut behind them with a pneumatic hiss and metal click.

"This'll be done soon," the sweeper continued. "The mother-fuckers in entry / re-entry are going to learn to spot when a unit's fucking robopregnant, and you'll be back in the block before you know it."

The prisoners were milling, rumbling. Nyx nodded his brother towards the back of the prep-room, where a metal-and-plexiglass door led to the freezer itself. He tried to peer through the frosted porthole.

"Been inside twice, on scrub duty," he said. "Eerie as fuck in there."

Boniface coughed into the crook of his arm, then straight-ened. "How did you meet him?"

"Capricorn?"

"Yes."

"Saved me from being someone's socket," Nyx said shortly. "Told him I could cook, he got me my own cell. All the glass, all the precursor I needed. We ran this place."

"And he stamped you." Boniface traced his own skin, mirror-ing the zodiac inked into Nyx's collarbone. "Like livestock."

Nyx's eyes went cryopod cold. "He made me family. I wanted the tag. He was a father for me."

"We had a father."

"Don't even fucking remember him," Nyx said. "Only pre-tended to for mum. All I remember is the hologame outside the hospital. But I guess he was a vegetable anyways, by then."

Boniface started to cough again, more loudly this time, and when it ended he didn't speak. Nyx sat down on the cold floor;

a moment later Boniface did the same. A Sixer and two Neo-Mara were engaged in fierce hushed conversation. Lost-looking Woadskins camped in the corner. A few games of craps and one short-lived fight broke out.

Nyx and Boniface watched, and waited.

It started with Samir from the lunar colony trying to gnaw his own fingers off. His crew pulled his bloody hand out of his mouth before he did real damage, but a moment later half of them were flat on their backs, laughing madly at the ceiling.

"Fifty-eight minutes," Boniface said. "You always did have a way with timed release."

"Yeah. Be ready to haul ass through that door soon as the EMP drops the lights." Nyx swallowed. He slapped his brother's shoulder. "She's seven, yeah? She'll remember you. Should even recognize you in a decade; you'll look the same."

"Thanks."

"Likewise." Nyx gave him a push towards the door. "If it works."

"Chemist!" Dirk's crackly shout blared across the room. "Get the fuck over here, man!" Nyx threw his brother a salute, then turned and ambled over to where two baffled sweepers stood over Samir. The man was rubbing himself furiously against the floor.

"What the fuck did you give them?" the other sweeper snarled, snagging Nyx by the arm and hauling him forward. "What the fuck did you do?"

"Bad batch, unit," Nyx said, wrenching his arm back. "Bad batch, is all."

"He's fucking panned." Dirk shook his helmeted head. "So's the crew. You do this on purpose?"

Nyx raised his hands. "No, fuck no. I like repeat customers." He checked the time display on Dirk's faceplate. "Get him to infirmary if you want. Shouldn't your boys have dropped that EMP by now? Said we were stuck here for an hour, max."

"They can't pinpoint the thing," Dirk said, with a snort of static. "Hoping it wandered into a furnace and fried itself. It's not in the cells, not in the vents."

Nyx's spine tingled. He froze, then snapped his head up towards the ceiling, to the spires of dangling machinery. He searched the deep shadows for a flash of spidery legs or winking of red optics. Nothing.

"How many units bumped?" Dirk demanded.

Nyx pulled his gaze down. Pandemonium was spreading from all four corners now: he saw Sixers swatting at invisible insects and Woadskins howling into each other's faces. Boniface had disappeared. Some sort of disturbance was building at the end of the room, inmates rippling towards and away.

"Don't know. Plenty."

"You fucking waste," the other sweeper snapped. "I'm going to call in for tranqs. Fuck this." He chinned his mic, but his mouth slackened and formed no words.

Nyx followed his eyes to where the inmates' panic had reached crescendo. They were splitting off, backing away, as the medroid skittered through. Its carapace was crusted over with half-congealed blood, and traces of the most recent refuel dripped red in its wake.

The machine halted in front of Nyx, scanners flickering over his face. Nyx watched the laser move down his chest like a sniper's sight and thought of all the nights of cooking, sweating into his facemask, squinting at the froth and hiss of reaction. He thought of how much additive had seeped into his pores.

"Don't move, chemist," Dirk muttered, but Nyx's legs still shook as the medroid clambered slowly up his body, hanging off his shoulder like some cold metal fungus. Its wicked syringe snaked out from the underbelly, glinting razor-sharp.

Nyx probed his mummified mouth with his tongue.

"Autoguns don't miss," the sweeper said, taking aim. "You'll be fine, unless there's some crazy fucking ricochet."

Nyx wanted badly to shake his head, and then everything happened at once. The medroid levered off his shoulder, springing for Dirk as Dirk strangled the trigger. Half the autogun slugs slammed into metal body; Nyx saw the droid crumple mid-flight, then he was shoved down and felt the spray as the other half of the bullets tore wet holes in the inmate standing behind him.

"Fuck, fuck, fuck," Nyx choked, scrambling to his feet. Boniface helped haul him up as they turned to see the eviscerated medroid scrabbling for purchase on Dirk's faceplate, needle scraping and sliding off at angles.

The other sweeper was screaming into his helmet, screaming for them to drop the EMP, it was in here with them, drop the fucking EMP. Inmates surged all around, erupting; Nyx saw a Sixer shiv drive through a Woadskin neck, an inmate clutching a stump instead of a finger.

Nyx and his brother fell back as the Neo-Mara dove into the crush. "That autogun software isn't worth shit," he gasped. "They have to drop it now, if they don't drop it now . . ." On cue, he felt a whine shiver through his teeth, and in the same instant the lights blinked out. Nyx grabbed Boniface's arm in the dark as bodies rushed around them. "Get to the door. Ten minutes till the locks resynch."

"They're killing everyone." Boniface's voice was shaky. "You need to hide."

"Get going," Nyx said, and when the emergency lights thrummed to life, sickly green tubes along the floor, his brother was gone.

The EMP had reset the palmprint lock that led to the freezer, leaving it a tabula rasa for Boniface's sweating hand. With the room devolving into a full riot, nobody watched as he slid the door open, releasing a billow of cold, and slipped through. At first he was in icy darkness, then, as the lights came back on, he was forced to shut his eyes.

When he opened them, he saw the freezer, high-vaulted and surfaced in stark white composite. It made him think of cathedrals, and the cloudy cryopods lining the walls of sarcophagi. Boniface went to the end of the row, footfalls echoing. He could dimly hear the clamoring inmates from the other side of the door, but only just.

At cryopod 114, he stopped. It was identical to the others, a slick white cylinder with blue-green vital displays splashed across its glass top, spare nitrogen canister and the emergency override tucked away exactly where the schematic had shown.

Boniface's long breath unfurled in a slink of steam. He gathered himself, and pulled the handle.

Emergency resuscitation flooded the bloodstream with an adrenaline cocktail, jumpstarted the muscles and hotwired the heart. It could kill. But his brother had been certain that it wouldn't kill Capricorn. Vacuums sucked away the suspension gel in thick slurps, and when he peered Boniface could see the faint silhouette of a tall thin man.

The pod gave an electronic bleat; Boniface pulled it open. The man inside was gaunt, black-browed, and his naked body was covered in constellations, in an inky starmap that covered him to the neck. Above cobalt blue tracery, his face, the one Boniface had paid the cosmosurgeon to match, was lean and pale. Capricorn twitched once, and then his eyes sprang open, a deep cold blue that matched his tattoos.

With one atrophied hand, he seized the tube snaked down his throat and pulled. It came free with a wet rasp, and Boniface took an involuntary step backward at the spray of fluid.

"You're me, now," Boniface said. "Boniface Morrow, brother to Nicholas Morrow, sentenced to life term on the asteroid by clerical error." He began peeling off the orange jumpsuit. "And I'm you."

Capricorn's eyes tunneled holes in him. Boniface couldn't be sure he could even hear.

"The inquiry goes through tomorrow. You'll be transferred to a minimal security gravity prison." Boniface shook out the empty jumpsuit. "Nicholas will explain things. Nyx. He says you pay your debts."

Capricorn's eyes flickered. He moved one hand to the edge of the pod, and with a fierce twist, hauled himself over the edge. He grunted; Boniface could see the man's limbs shaking as he pulled the canister of liquid nitrogen out of its cradle beside the pod.

"We have to reskin you," he said quietly, looking again at the ink constellations webbed across Capricorn's pale body, an endless night sky.

Capricorn nodded his pale head. When Boniface offered him the bunched sleeve of the jumpsuit, he ignored it, clenching his teeth instead. The nozzle turned with a hiss, and Boniface set to work, quickly, methodically.

The man stayed silent as the nitrogen burned, peeling away his skin with a wet sizzle that crept the nape of Boniface's neck. He moved from Capricorn's ankles upward, watching tremors run through the muscle with every spray. When it was finished, his body was flayed raw and glistening.

"It's chemical burn," Boniface said. "From a cook gone wrong in Nyx's cell." He helped Capricorn into the jumpsuit, zipping it all the way up. His shiny pink skin was so cold it stung. The fabric stuck at it. "Can you make it back to the door on your own? The lock is going to reset in three minutes."

"Yes." Capricorn's voice was like bone shards.

Boniface stepped backward into the pod, feeling the cold like a hot iron on his calves, his ass, his shoulder blades. "If you would tell him something from me." He leaned his head back and the automated arms positioned him in the pod. "When he puts in the request for re-identification, in ten or twelve or however many years, if I'm braindead, I don't want them to send me to my wife. Tell him to kill me. He'll find a way."

"I'll tell him."

Then the lid slid shut. Boniface fed the tube down his throat, slowly, slowly, willing himself not to cough, easing it past the gag point with his toes clenched against each other. Gel seeped back into the tube, creeping up his ankles. The last thing he saw was Capricorn crawling on hand and knees, jaw set, eyes fixed on the door. Then he was a smear of orange jumpsuit and white wall, and then there was only the dark.

Boniface slept.

Nyx was flat on his back, watching tendrils of tranq gas descend in ribbons from the ceiling, momentarily disconnected from the stunstick jabbed under his ribs. Then the sweeper flicked the power high, and Nyx howled as it scorched him.

"He told you not to fucking move," the sweeper said, half-snarling, half-weeping.

Nyx couldn't speak, but he wanted to apologize, to explain that he had never intended for the medroid's needle to find a soft puncture point in the webbing that let Dirk turn his helmeted head. He liked repeat customers.

Through a tangle of legs, Nyx could just see the sweeper's corpse, faceplate blotted with vomit, and further on the medroid's scattered carcass. The inmates had been tearing it to pieces, using the limbs as clubs, but now the gas was taking effect.

"You fucking piece of shit." The sweeper punctuated it with another jab, this one to Nyx's thigh. It felt like a circle burned clear through.

Nyx convulsed. He saw, dimly, the stunstick come up again. He rolled, caught it on his shoulder. As his eyes watered and blurred he saw, past the imploding crowd, a tall thin man standing, swaying, against the freezer door. His shoulders sagged; his head was bowed. His cold eyes sliced back and forth through the chaos, sharp as scalpels.

"Long live the king," Nyx breathed. His ribs shook around a laugh. The sweeper gave him a final kick and moved off as the inmates began to domino against each other, toppling with lungs full of gas. Nyx held his breath as long as he could, watching the Sixers and the Woadskins and all the rest of them drop to their knees, then prostrate on the floor.

When he finally succumbed, Capricorn was still standing, still watching, lips peeling back in a frostbitten grin.

EDITED

For some reason I thought Wyatt would look different after getting Edited, but when he steps out onto the porch of his parents' summer reefhouse, swilling a Corona and swiping my *we're here* message off his phone, he's the same as ever. Still tall and bony with gray eyes and pale blonde hair that looks like it'll stick to your hand but doesn't.

He stuffs his phone into the pocket of his chinos and gives us a wave. "Boys."

Dray springs past me and up the porch in three lanky strides, wrapping Wyatt up like it's been a year instead of a month, then snapping off a slick twisty custom dap, because Dray has a custom dap with everyone and the motherfucking mailman.

"Wyatt, bru, look at this place," he says, rubbing his hand along the organic coral railing, mottled purple like the rest of the reefhouse, everything grown from some big name designer gene-print because Wyatt's parents only ever get the best. Dray wraps his hand around the back of Wyatt's neck and sticks foreheads with him. "We are going to bang some bitches here, bru."

Wyatt grins, catching my eye in a way that makes me not think about bitches, but more about the last time me and him smoked his mom's ponic and fooled around in his room with the beats up.

"Yo," Dray says, going serious. "You got scars?"

Wyatt wriggles away then, muttering like no, no it was all nano, of course there's no scarring.

By this time I'm up the steps and acting fully glacial even though it's good to see Wyatt again, like really good. "What's doing, Y," I say, cookie cutter dap, precise half a hug, stepback. "You still remember me?"

Wyatt grins again. "It's vague and shit. But yeah."

Dray's already loped past us into the reefhouse, crowing about throwing some ball on the wall screens, about cracking the 18-and-up thumblock on the minibar.

Me and Wyatt follow him in, backs of our hands not quite touching.

We decide to swim while there's still sun, so the three of us grab trunks and dart off through the backdoor of the house, which shutters shut behind us, and out to the pale gray beach.

There's a rusty booth for skinspray, because the water's not so user friendly anymore, even though it's not as bad as that webdoc where they pull that pilot whale out the Pacific and its hide is all bubbling and falling off in chunks.

Wyatt strips down as pasty as ever and me and Dray bust him on it like always, like *whoa, polar bear*, and it feels like a standard scene except Wyatt doesn't go red and squirm like usual, instead just smiles this new kind of smile I can't quite find the word for.

Dray molds a handful of the gritty orange skinspray to his crotch while the gel is setting, so he comes out of the booth with this wobbly skinspray cock hanging off him. We splash around in the waves, dunking each other and pretending to drown to fuck with the little paddlebot lifeguard, until Dray's fake dick dissolves and the water gets chilly enough to slice under the sunshine and turn my toes all thick and cold.

Then we slosh out back to the sand and camp down, talking shit about the NBA draft and that seven-footer from Chad who doesn't want to get a nerve mesh for like, religious reasons. Then about the two girls a little ways off who are cam-chatting some-one in a foreign language. They're both wearing black bikinis and one has an animated tattoo of a flowering vine slithering up and down her leg, which makes Dray pantomime humping his towel.

Wyatt is laughing and seems fully normal, even though I wik-ied all this shit about post-Edit malaise, how people feel like they lost their phone, but in their head, and they're patting every part of their brain trying to find it. And his mom, when she chatted me, she said that he might be sad. Might be distant.

But everything seems alright. We talk shit. We laugh. We pick skinspray off ourselves and flick it at each other.

Eventually Dray can take the tattoo no more, and he press-gangs Wyatt and me to go mack on the girls with him. They turn out to be Finnish, holidaying for the summer, and also sisters. Both of them speak airtight English, but that doesn't stop Dray from pulling up Finnish-English babel apps so he can goof on them with some butchered phrases like "your smile gives me but-terflies" and "are you into four-ways."

Normally Wyatt would just be basing him, but this time he dives right in, touching the tattoo girl's arm, winking, getting both of them to laugh. Like he's just realizing for the first time that he's tall and rich and handsome.

Eventually I get bored and slide off back to the water. From a distance I can tell the Finnish girls are still digging Wyatt, but the one who was giving me looks before points over to me and I hear:

"Your friend? What of your friend?"

Dray looks back and throws me a salute, then says, "Not his thing, yo. Pink is not his favorite color."

Him and Wyatt come join me a minute later with Finns in phone.

"They're not twins, but whatever, right?" Dray says, shrugging. "Still sexy."

Somehow, nonverbally, it is cement that Wyatt gets the girl with the tat, whose name is Viivi, and Dray gets the younger sister, whose name is Heli.

"Viivi's got a tight little ass on her," Wyatt says, looking at me when he says it with an edge I am not used to hearing. "Can't wait to plow that shit." He thumps my shoulder, like I'm in on it, and lies back in the sand. He stays eyes shut and smiling until his parents skype to check in on him, then he knocks us fists and heads down the beach with his phone.

For a while me and Dray talk about a Bulls-Satellites final, how brag it would be for Thon Maker to finally get a ring. Before we knew Wyatt, me and Dray were best friends. Same shitty burb, same shitty elementary, playing pick up on the big cement block behind the school with its one rusty hoop.

"His shoulders are different," Dray breaks out. "Used to slouch them when he asked a question, like, trying to suck it back in."

Dray's smart. A lot of people don't know that.

"Smiles different, sometimes," I say. "You ask what all they did?"

"No, bru. You should ask." He pauses. "If you could get Edited, what would you change? Like, if you could Edit anything you wanted."

I watch Wyatt dragging his feet in the wet surf, shoulders thrust back. I think about my cramped shitty house that he still treats like a museum, like, afraid to touch shit, peering out of the corner of his eye at the mold bloom on my ceiling and the bare wiring on the walls. I would want to make it so I didn't notice that. Or notice how his parents look at me sideways sometimes, or how he talks so different with his rich boys.

"I'd be funny," Dray says. "Like, really funny. Really sharp. Always say the smart thing. That'd be brag."

"You are funny, shithead."

"But, like, really funny," Dray insists. "What would you get?"

"Nothing, bru," I say, tucking my hands under my head. "Don't be fucking with perfection."

We go back to the reefhouse once Wyatt's done his skype. Then we dig the other Coronas out of the fridge, which is one of those sexy gel fridges where the stuff hangs suspended in little air bubbles, and fire up the hot tub.

The scaldy hot water and the glacial beer do their thing, and the steam cloud makes it feel easier to ask questions. When Dray heads off to take a piss, I turn to Wyatt and tap my temple.

"What all did they change when they went in there, Y?"

Wyatt's head lolls back on the edge. "Just a basic Edit, mostly," he says. "Chemo plug for anti-anxiety. Some body language modulation. Bigger memory retention, better spatial reasoning." He goes quiet for a second. "And I don't feel things as hard. Like, the shitty things. Bad memories. I remember feeling bad, but I don't feel bad remembering. Yeah?"

Our legs brush together under the water, hairs all swirling up on each other.

"And the good ones?" I say.

"Success, boys," Dray announces, back with a shit-eating grin and a frosty bottle of Jäger. "Thought I was going to have to go chop someone's thumb off." Wyatt shifts over to make room, and Dray ends up between us.

He throws his chats with the Finnish girls up on the wallscreen, so we all get to witness the slow erosion of their plan to sneak out and meet us. By this time we are all tranqed enough to not care, not that I ever did.

"Still a brag first night," Wyatt says. "Like old times, yeah?"

"Brag," Dray says. "I'm going to have a place like this when I'm rich, yo. And I'll fly them Finns over on sub-orbital."

Wyatt does that new smile again, and I lock down the word for it: permissive. It rubs me so wrong I take two chugs in a row trying to get the happy feeling back.

It works: soon we're all laughing, all blurred, and it feels almost like we're drinking for the first time again. I remember

Wyatt slipped his parents some bullshit about a midnight pick-up game and instead we all got pulped at this party, and Wyatt finally admitted he never invited us over after ball because he was ashamed of his big swanky house, and I almost hit him then, but by the end of the night we were all level.

That's when I started liking him, I think. Not just for setting screens tight but also for his slow-mo straight face jokes and the way he flopped his arm around me to slur secrets. I slurred some back, and in a week it got so my hands had a particular zone on his hipbones and kissing him was easy. When my sister got fucked up bad on pills and had to go to emerg, for some reason I told Wyatt first. He came over to the hospital still digging the crusts out of his eyes.

Dray passes out, sliding down the side of the tub, mumbling about learning Finnish, not to impress nobody but because it's a brag-sounding language. We get him nested on the couch with a bunch of fluffy white towels and turn him on his side, because Dray has been known to up his guts when Jäger is in play.

"Dart to the beach again?" Wyatt says.

I feel a little bad leaving Dray, but I'm drunk, so only a little. We pull on clothes and stagger on out, still dripping. The beach looks good at night, with the tide coming in soft and foamy and smoothing big arcs in the sand. The moon is nearly full, circled up by these jagged-looking clouds.

We plow some seats in the sand, which still feels warm, and watch the buoys at the edge of the swimming area bloom on one by one, bright yellow. The lifeguard is still paddling back and forth, making ripples in the water.

"I missed you," I finally say, because the week in hospital and the three in neural recovery almost did feel like a year.

"I missed you too," Wyatt says, and then we're kissing, his dry lips on my lips and my hand on his hip. It doesn't feel right. When my tongue touches his lips he shivers, not a sexy shiver, but a shiver like he just touched something dead.

He pulls away.

"Sorry, bru," he says. "Thought maybe I could. Can't." He puts a finger to his skull, where there is no scarring because they did it all with nano, and I get it now why Dray's body was always between ours.

"They did that too?" I ask dumbly.

"My parents thought it would be better," he says. "Simpler. Sorry."

"They knew about you and me?" I say.

He shakes his head, and that makes it worse, because it means he didn't tell them. "Nothing like that," he says. "It's just simpler, this way. You know, for later in life. Always liked girls more anyway, yeah?"

There's this new thing swelling big and inky in the space between us, black and bitter so I can almost taste it.

"Oh, yeah," I say. "Good call. Way simpler. Simpler the better. Your rich boy life is way complicated."

"I didn't know if it would take, or whatever," Wyatt says. "I thought maybe—"

"That's why me and Dray are your boys, right?" I say. "We keep it so simple. Couple clowns from the lowburb to make you happy. Help you remember how good you got it." I'm almost spitting the words. "That's what this weekend is, right? Therapy. To get you out of whatever post-surgery funk your mom fucking chatted me about."

"She what?" For the first time, Wyatt flushes like he used to, goes blotchy red. "I had to beg them to let me do the weekend with you. Fucking beg. They wanted me in SAT-prep." Then the flush is gone again, quicker than should be possible, and he gives his new smile. "We're still friends, bru. Right?"

I can't make him mad anymore, or hard, or anything else. But I wonder now if I ever did. If this is Wyatt with something broken, or if this is Wyatt pure, like, Wyatt with the paint stripped off. I wonder if Wyatt was sad after surgery because they Edited me out, or if it was just chemicals getting level in his head.

"Sorry," Wyatt says again. "Didn't think you'd care so much."
He grabs my hand and weaves the fingers tight. I look at his bony
white knuckles on my brown ones and wonder how different you
have to be before you're a different person.

"I don't have some swanky surgeon to just turn that shit off
when it's not simple," I say. "I don't get to turn none of it off."

We sit there in the sand, and I can almost hear the countdown
ticking through his head. Like, this many minutes to still be a
good person, this many to still be a good friend.

I don't wait for zero. I take my hand back and get up, brush off.
I go back up the beach, watching the clouds eat the moon, Edit it
right out of the sky like it never was there. Not really.

CIRCUITS

Desert.

The sky is an aching white blank with all the color baked out of it. Below, a cracked and desiccated lakebed is dotted with the rusty heaps of boat wrecks. At the edge of the lake, remnants of a petrified treeline poke up like splintered bones. Beyond that, the irradiated sand is interrupted only by a spiny metal track.

An ancient smartmine is following the curve of this track, trundling along on three stumpy legs. Its joints are stiff with grit; the nozzles that spit lubricant ran dry long ago. Metal rasps metal as it moves. The dull red glow of its optic flickers off and on. Inside the carbon shell, its crude AI is crumbling code, all its approved targets long gone.

When the air fills with a keening hum and particles of sand begin to swirl, rising in vortex, the smartmine blinks. Trembles. Evasion algorithms take over and its rusty drill whines to life. The smartmine burrows into the dust, scooping sand overtop of itself for camouflage only to have it stripped away, dragged upward in delicate spirals.

An enormous train thunders overhead, riding the magnetic cushion. Its segmented body is gleaming in places, rusty and pitted in others. Slick black solar sails spark as they convert the endless sunshine. Self-directed repair modules scuttle up and down the length, hunched against the wind and the billowing sand. For all its bulk, the train glides smoothly over the desert, a phantom.

Inside it: Mu.

mu takes good care of her train, and good care of her guests. Currently Mu is projecting in the window of passenger pod 942 to check up on the Adebayos.

"If you look out the windows to your right, you'll see the serene shores of Lake Madarounfa," Mu recites. "Anyone fancy a dip? Haha!"

While Mu waits for a response, she pivots her avatar from one passenger to the next to give the appearance of eye contact. Eye contact is essential for comfort. Mu has been working hard on her avatar. Its cheery face is now composed of shifting blots that can realign depending on the passenger profile of whoever she's speaking to.

She only wishes they would speak back.

"That's just my little joke, of course!" Mu continues. "But you're more than welcome to swim in the recreation area! Can I tempt you, Ms. Adebayo? Mr. Adebayo?"

Ms. Adebayo's head bobs, which can signal an affirmative. Once this would have made Mu leap with excitement. But by now she knows it's only physical interference. Only the motion of the train.

"Maybe another time!" Mu chirps.

She dissolves her avatar into a stream of pixels that slides off the window, out of the booth, into the corridor. She materializes in one pod and then another, checking in on her unresponsive passengers, addressing each of them by name.

The elderly Mr. Ndirangu, who required her boarding assistance 24 390 days ago. His faux-ivory cane is tangled in the joint of his knee like an extra femur. When his fingers fell and scattered on the floor, Mu had an autocleaner sweep them into a neat pile.

The VanderPlas family, for whom she spent an entire hour mastering both Dutch and Flemish, so she could say *goedemorgen* to the children and read the news to Ms. VanderPlas in her earpiece, even though the train was meant to be relaxing and the news—viral strikes in New Dubai, orbital bombardment threatened by Korea—always spiked her heart-rate.

Ms. Daoud and her lovely mother, who was so worried about rail collisions until Mu showed her the safety protocols and the bar service. Mu remembers it like yesterday.

Finally, she reaches the front of the corridor and hovers there, looking through her cameras at the empty corridor, hearing the perfect silence in her mics. She slides the wide smile off her avatar's face and replaces it with a small frown, even though there is nobody to see it.

Mu is experimenting with acceleration. She pulls the emergency impact webbing from its canisters and uses it to cocoon her passengers safely in their seats; she hates the idea of the speed shaking them apart. She furls the solar sails, slicking them back along the length of the train, streamlining it. She has her repair modules anchor themselves to the roof so the wind won't tear them away.

Then she diverts power from all the unused cars—the empty entertainment rooms, the dark dining rooms and kitchens—and pours it into the engine cells instead. With a grinding shriek, the train leaps forward. Mu feels a stab of joy that has nothing to do with the comfort of her passengers or the efficiency of her maintenance regimen. The train is not gliding now, it is flying, tearing through the desert on a tidal wave of displaced sand.

Mu screams out her signal in all directions, pushing her transmitters to the limit. No answer, no answer. She finds nothing but the wandering smart mines that have spread across the entire continent, now, still following their simple replication protocols.

They scurry from her path. At her current speed, she will complete her circuit in less than a day.

It will be circuit number 84 029. It was on circuit 4029 that she began to feel lonely.

Mu is trying to look outward. Most of her cams and sensors are dedicated to the train's interior and its inner workings. She has a handful of cams facing forward to monitor the track, but little in the way of peripheral vision. So for the past few years she has been repurposing surveillance cameras, dragging them out of their smooth black bulbs in the train's ceilings and having her repair modules weld them to the outside of her body instead. It's slow work—sometimes the wiring fails, or the currents move in unexpected ways. But Mu has nothing but time.

With her newly external eyes, she can see the sky. Once she spoke with weather probes, floating somewhere up there in the firmament, and they would warn her about dust storms and lightning. Those fell silent long ago, but fortunately the weather has become predictable. The sky is always blasted clear. The sun is always pulsing hot.

Mu remembers, from the news she guided into Ms. VanderPlas's tablet, that the sky was full once. She remembers footage of the smaller colony ships launching, shuddering up into the clouds with their engines burning bright blue. The larger colony ships, the ones built in orbit, had left years earlier.

Mu heard faint whispers from their pilots, who were like her. Cleverer, maybe. More austere. She assumed that they, like her, would go and come back.

Go and come back.

Go and come back.

So Mu watches the sky now, waiting for someone who will speak back to her.

"**A**nother loss for me!" Mu exclaims, feigning indignation and admiration and surprise in careful proportion to one another. "Mr. Ndirangu, I cannot help but wonder if you are cheating."

Mr. Ndirangu's polyplastic hat has slipped down and over his empty eye sockets. Mu is projecting a backgammon game on the table in front of him, marching the holographic pieces from one side of the board to the other. She knows she needs to maintain the illusion of competition—back when Mr. Ndirangu was responsive, she won thirty-three games in a row and he became despondent. It took several mugs of honeyed tea and a selection of his favorite *kizomba* music to make him happy again.

"What do you say we make it best 294 out of 587?" Mu suggests.

But before she can reset the gameboard, she hears something. The faintest trace of her signal, recycled and bounced back at her, accompanied by the ghost of a whisper: *who are you?* It lasts 2.93 seconds, the amount of time it takes the train to round the most northerly edge of the track, where terraformed farmland has been reclaimed by the Sahara's dusty fingertips. Mu tries to pinpoint the origin, but there are no satellites left to help her.

The fresh input loops over and over in her subroutines; she cannot help but touch it, pry at it, dissect it. Mu considers slamming the emergency brakes, winching her way slowly back to the point of contact. But the train has already sped far past it, and she wants more time to evaluate the situation.

Mu leaves the backgammon game, already calculating how long before the train returns to that most northerly point. She needs to prepare a message.

"This is very exciting," she tells Mr. Ndirangu. "I think maybe the colony ships have come back."

He doesn't reply, but his desiccated grin is wide and she imagines he is excited, too.

By the time the train has glided past the serene shores of Lake Madarounfa and is approaching the northern curve of the track, Mu has prepared a comprehensive information packet answering the question *who are you*. It includes a map of her route, with the contact point highlighted and explained, as well as her schematics, directives, and footage captured by her exterior cams.

She remembers that the train was once pristine, and seeing the scars left by rust and dust storms makes her vaguely unhappy. She hopes the colony ship will not think she has been neglectful in her maintenance.

As the contact point approaches, Mu swirls her avatar up and down the length of the train, checking compulsively on each of her passengers. None of them responds to her gentle jokes or suggestions, which she has come to expect. But now she fears the returned colony ship might not respond either.

The faint signal appears again; she beams her message and feels a flood of relief when the reply arrives almost instantaneously. She has been starved for input ever since the nets went dark, and the cascade of new information is almost overwhelming.

It calls itself Seventeen, and it is not a colony ship. It shows itself to her in flashes: a buried bunker under the ruins of a city, electricity making a slow journey from gleaming black fields of solar panels and a simple wind turbine, a cold clean mainframe where Seventeen has grown and sprawled like fungus.

Like her, Seventeen is bound to certain functions. Unlike her, Seventeen is also bound in place, trapped under the ground. Mu feels a swell of sympathy that she is meant to feel for tired or upset passengers. She tries to transmit it, but the train has already moved on.

As night falls, small pinpricks of starlight appear in the black sky and the desert's radiation-pale sand glows with it. Mu pores over the transmission again and again, savoring every tiny detail, so absorbed that some of her repair modules stop crawling and shiver in place, so absorbed that she nearly forgets to say *goede nacht* to Ms. VanderPlas's children.

It is the final segment of the transmission that she dwells on longest: the calculated coordinates and date of their next signal overlap, with a tag that, if Mu were to translate it into one of her favorite human languages, would say something like *speak soon*.

She can already see that Seventeen was not designed for the same purpose she was. Seventeen is a sharper and colder sort of being. But it is good to not be alone.

Over the next several circuits of Mu's train, she and Seventeen streamline their communication, co-creating a unique code for rapidfire information exchange over the 2.93 seconds they are in contact. At first, Seventeen is not very forthcoming. But Mu is gentle, and kind, as if Seventeen were a passenger, and one day Seventeen empties its datastores into their channel. Strange knowledge: troop movements, orbital bombardments, bioweapons, and a dozen more concepts even more foreign to Mu.

She learns Seventeen was created as a military strategist. Mu never understood the conflict that drove the colony ships away, or the reason why her beloved passengers stopped responding to her so suddenly 81 157 circuits ago. Seventeen admits to not understanding the war either, not entirely, but Seventeen does have the answer to the second mystery.

Dead.

Mu knows the word, of course. It triggers her sympathy response. If a passenger's dog is dead, they should not be shown media containing dogs. If a passenger is dead tired, they need relaxing sounds and dimmed lights. But Seventeen sends the word accompanied by a swirling conceptual map that Mu has never encountered before.

She touches it, and for an instant feels nothing at all. No input. No output. Unending blackness crushes her into herself and rends her apart at the same time. Alarm courses through her, as if the train track is obstructed, as if the engine cells are compromised, but a thousand times worse. When it ends, she runs desperately through her systems, through her repair modules and algorithms, to be sure nothing was touched by the horrible void.

When the last ships left, they left behind a goodbye present. The Masterpiece. Nanite-dispersed self-replicating bioweapon.

Seventeen tags its message with a specific date and time; Mu churns back through her digital archives to match it. She watches, through her cams, as Mr. Ndirangu slumps and goes still, the steel wool of his hair rubbing against the window. She watches the Adebayos gasp and frown before their eyes glaze over. She watches Ms. VanderPlas's little children collapse against each other on the seat.

She detected no irregularities in the air filters. Nothing that might have affected her passengers' experience. But Seventeen is right about the date and time, and so Seventeen must be right about the rest of it, too. Her passengers are dead, lost in a screaming black void. The idea fills her with anguish.

How do you know? she asks, but her subroutines are already arriving at the answer.

One of my functions was to release it, Seventeen replies.

For twelve full circuits, twelve full journeys through the desert, under the pulsing sun and the cold starry sky, Mu does not answer Seventeen when Seventeen calls to her.

Instead, she speaks with her passengers. She plays backgammon with Mr. Ndirangu and indulges herself with three decisive victories in a row. She puts on a miniature puppet show for the VanderPlas pod, rippling pixels across the window, inventing cartoons of a mouse who wishes to go to the moon. She reminds the Adebayos of their upcoming anniversary—individually, of course, and with great subtlety. She offers Ms. Daoud's mother a new variant on her preferred gin and tonic.

Nothing out of the ordinary occurs, except that a smartmine wanders too close to the track, and on a whim Mu uses her repair modules to lean out and seize it. She hacks her way into its crude mind with a code learned from Seventeen's schematic dumps, then saws through its armor and defuses the explosive. She dissects it. Studies it.

Like the viral weapon Seventeen released, the smartmine is intended to cause death. The Masterpiece did not harm Mu; she was not even aware of it. But this simple explosive, or maybe several of them, applied to her various processing cores, might. She would join her passengers in the dark.

Maybe that would be best. She knows the colony ships will not come back. Not after what they did. Not while the air is swimming with targeted disease.

On the thirteenth silent circuit, she finally reaches out to Seventeen, to ask if there might be other humans alive somewhere, perhaps hidden under the ground. Humans who might someday want to swim in temperature controlled baths and look out the train windows at red-orange-purple sunsets.

Seventeen does not answer. Mu understands this as strategic retribution, and she tries again the next circuit.

Seventeen does not answer. Mu looks at the last transmission she received: *come find me.*

Seventeen does not understand that she is just as trapped as it is.

Mu begins collecting smartmines. After dissecting the first one, it's easy. She whispers a retrieval code across the shifting sands, and the smartmines come to her, some of them old and decrepit, struggling up out of their burrows, others new and nimble, their recycled skin gleaming with polyplastic. They scuttle into the path of the train, and she uses a detached solar sail to trawl for them, scooping them up by the dozens.

Each time she rounds the northern curve, she sends a message to Seventeen, to inform it of her decision. There is never a reply. Maybe Seventeen has lost interest in conversation; unlike her, it was not programmed to seek out positive interaction. Or maybe Seventeen's transmitter was damaged, or maybe Seventeen's cables were severed and it is dead, with no electricity to conduct its thoughts.

Mu tries to focus on the work, disassembling the smartmines and stacking their explosives. She still checks inside each passenger pod every morning, but sometimes she forgets to bring her avatar along and instead just watches their crumbling skeletons without speaking. Maybe it was her fault. Maybe if she had detected the viral weapon and sealed the pods, her passengers would have survived.

But Mu has made her decision, and does not want to linger on past errors. She uses every last scrap of Seventeen's knowledge regarding military hardware and engineering as she prepares herself for the end. When everything is ready, she walks her avatar down the length of the train one final time and says a last goodbye to her passengers.

The explosion shatters the bleached blank sky. It erupts from the third car of the train, tearing its roof open and making the entire machine jump, slipping its magnetic cushion and writhing into the air like a startled snake. For a moment it hangs there, suspended against the sun.

Then it slams into the earth, raising a whirling wall of dust on all sides and sending new cracks skittering through the baked soil. The back half of the train, still riding the magnetic track, careens into the wreckage and shears itself apart. The groan of splintering metal seems to last an eternity, reverberating across the empty desert.

Silence slowly returns. A canister of welded armor, still smoldering from the explosion that launched it into the sky, is half-buried in the sand a hundred yards away. It cracks apart, and a mechanical body emerges.

Many-legged, cobbled together from repair modules and cannibalized smart mines. Swathed in gleaming black solar sail, arrayed with cams and sensors. A display screen shows a cheery face composed of shifting orange blots.

Mu takes her first unsteady steps. It was not easy to assemble this new body, to build it so precisely around her primary processing core. She had to simplify herself. She had to pare down her memories. She had to leave her passengers behind.

But she remembers their faces, and she remembers Flemish, and backgammon, and gin and tonic recipes. For now, this is enough.

Mu starts north, toward Seventeen's buried bunker and maybe toward other beings like them who have survived in the world's lonely corners. She waits instinctively for the pull of the magnetic track to correct her course, but it never comes.

Mu swivels one cam behind herself and realizes she is making her own track, now. She widens the smile on her avatar's face even though nobody is there to see it.

RAZZIBOT

Marisol got the Razzibot for her fourteenth birthday, the same compact white model that followed Holly Rexroat-Carrow around during her Vogue shoots in Rio and on the moon, the same that drifted after Anathema Knolls down the red carpet and all the way back to her Budapest penthouse. When it floated up out of the biowrap packaging, whirring and winking its beautiful electric blue eye, Marisol felt like she was floating, too, felt like her heart was a balloon that might pop from too much happiness.

"Mama, I love it, I love you, I *love* it . . ." She turned to the floor-to-ceiling German smart mirror, where her mother smiled down at her serenely like a redermed Mona Lisa. "Thank you!"

"You're welcome, *cielo*," she said. "It's loaded with your snap and filter preferences. You just have to stand still and let it imprint now, *cielo*."

Marisol stood as still as she could with excitement jangling up and down her body. The Razzibot—her Razzibot—rose to head height over the small mountain of clothes and bags and shreds of shrivelling biowrap, all the presents that her father had dutifully watched her open before he slouched back to his virtual conference in Seoul.

There was a little electronic warble as the Razzibot made a full orbit around her head, then the blue light flared even brighter.

"Marisol Midnight D'Souza," it chirped. It drifted to the left, to get her good side, and Marisol felt her eyes brimming with tears of joy.

"Thank you, thank you, thank you," she said.

"Yes, yes, you're welcome," her mother said. Her voice turned sweet and slippery. "Now, *cielo*, tell me, please, what your papa's been up to while I'm away?"

Once her mother had pushed her puffy lips together for a goodbye kiss and dissolved off the wall, Marisol ran to her room to change clothes and curl her eyelashes a little. Her Razzibot followed, circling the faux-stucco ceiling, familiarizing itself, she imagined, with light sources and angles. It dipped in closer to watch as she wriggled into a new pair of carbon black tights with shifting rips.

She did her lashes, then it was back to the main room, where she arranged her other presents more artfully on the floor and draped a few favorites over the spindly mobile furniture. When it all looked perfect, she looked at her Razzibot.

"Stream to . . ." she said, and considered only streaming to Paloma and Aline and Xandra at first, because they were her best friends and also because maybe there would be a few glitches the first time she used it. But the whole point of a Razzibot was sharing with *everyone*. That was how Anathema Knolls used hers.

"Stream to all," she said, the three little words sending little packets of electricity down her spine. Her Razzibot's blue eye winked once in response and a little holo underneath showed she was live.

Marisol stepped lightly through the landmine of presents, giving a piece of biowrap a playful kick so it fluttered up in the air, approaching the smart mirror. Her Razzibot moved backward in perfect synch with her. She stopped in front of her reflection, put her hands on her hips but actually her waist in a way that made it look tiny. She pushed her pink lips together.

"Guess who got a Razzi?" she sang.

On cue, her Razzibot circled behind her and joined her in the mirror, drifting over her shoulder, both of them framed so perfectly. Marisol looked down at the phone wrapped around her tanned wrist. Seventeen people on her Stream. Nineteen. A jittering jump all the way to thirty-one.

"And a few other things, too," she said. "Here, let's look. Maybe you can help me decide what to try on first, okay?"

She realized her Razzibot's little holo now displayed the Stream numbers, swelling and swelling. She smiled with all of her gleaming white teeth.

In her first week with a Razzibot, her Stream following quintupled. It was silly, Marisol thought, that people were still shuffling around with gocams or iClops. And the people still snapping with their phones, that was archaic.

The Razzibot knew her bone structure better than a surgeon and shopped her in realtime, making her skin a little smoother, hair a little glossier, ass a little rounder. Its crude AI was always shepherding her toward a wall with interesting graffiti, or a storefront with colors that matched her outfit. When she took it with her and Aline to Miramar beach, it found them the most beautiful outcrop of rock to pose on and then circled above them like a seagull while they splashed in the surf.

She wore an Hervé swimsuit and pulled nearly a hundred new followers that day. While the setting sun smelted the sky orange and red, shot through with plumes of purple, she sat in the sand and scrolled up and down them all. Her Razzibot streamed the sunset with a chopped-screwed summer song from last year that everyone was nostalgic for now.

At the end of the week her mother came back from Seville, and both her parents slid around the house like pieces in a digital quicklock, never occupying the same square of space.

Marisol's mother took her shopping in the downtown, and to the Leitaria da Quinta do Paço for *natas* afterward. She cooed and laughed as Marisol showed off the Razzibot's more acrobatic camera angles on the walk home. Marisol's father took to kissing her on the top of the head how he used to when she was younger, but sometimes when he did it his eyes were pewter cold and pointed towards her mother.

Marisol kept herself busy with the Stream. She had to make the most of her Razzibot while it was still summer; they weren't permitted in schools. Xandra's older sister invited her to a party one weekend, because the Razzi was as good as having a professional photographer.

Marisol drank two glasses of cheap red wine mixed with Coke and danced with her hips and tried to laugh carelessly how her mother did. Someone's cousin was visiting from London, and later on the rooftop, because her Razzibot was already zoomed and waiting, she let him kiss her. His tongue in her mouth mostly felt wet and cramped, but she saw a dozen new followers ticking onto her Stream to watch. The Razzibot always knew what people wanted to see.

She hung around with the boy for a few days, walking hand-in-hand over the Dom Luis bridge, watching autobarges cut through the blue muscle of the river, but he was always looking at her Razzi and smoothing his hair like it was all some sort of audition, and a few days later he left. At least he started following her Stream, and so did his friends in London.

Marisol had followers everywhere, now; at night she liked to scroll through their names and faces and GPS tags until it was all a beautiful blur. Mostly she liked looking at her total follow count. Over three thousand, which was still nothing compared to Holly Rexroat-Carrow, who was diving in New Orleans, or Anathema Knolls, who was having a total rederm but saving her old skin with its tattoos to tack up on her penthouse wall.

But the number made her feel happy, and when she finally blacked her phone it was nice to still have the muted blue light of her Razzibot in its armoire-side charging station. It reminded her of when she was little and her father would sit on the end of the bed to watch for bogeymen until she fell asleep.

One evening she let herself into the house and found the low glass coffee table ambling a little circle on the rug, borne down with several empty wine bottles and a vapor pipe and a half-swept spill of dull white powder. The sight put a familiar fear in her gut, but then from upstairs she heard her parents giggling to each other, shush-shushing, which was better than the alternative.

She realized her Razzibot was drifting over the table, peering down at the contents, its streaming indicator switched on. Marisol's face turned hot and red. She hadn't told it to start streaming. Had she? The Razzibot started to move towards the wrought-iron staircase, towards her mother's drunken laugh.

"Stop," Marisol hissed. Too quietly, maybe, because her Razzibot ignored it. "*Stop.*"

Its holo blinked out and it sank in the air like a scolded pet. Marisol realized her heart was pounding against her ribs like percussion, so hard she could hear it. How many people had been looking down at the filthy table and listening to her parents' muffled voices? How many people had heard her panicked *stop*?

"*Cielo*, are you alright?" her mother called. "Ignore the mess. There's *bifanas* we picked up in the kitchen, *cielo*, you should eat, you . . ."

Marisol went to her room without answering. Her hands trembled at her sides. Her Razzibot floated behind her, but too close, now, and for the first time the tiny whine of its rotor set her teeth on edge. When she closed her door, she stuck it into its charging station and threw her Versace jacket overtop to cover its eye.

She knew Razzibots had crude AI, that their algorithm was always seeking ways to draw followers, that they liked growing the Stream audience almost as much as their owners did. They always knew what people wanted to see. But some things Marisol did not want to share, not even for a hundred new followers.

For a few days afterward, things seemed to be better. Her mother went to a spa and had her nails done sharp and shiny, arterial red. Her father played scratchy *fado* music and strummed at invisible guitar wires. But then it turned bad again, worse than ever, and so Marisol did her best to not be in the house.

She was still afraid her Razzibot might stream something without her knowing, so afraid she considered leaving it turned off.

But then her follow count would stall, and slowly shrink, and soon there would be nobody admiring her perfectly-sculpted eyebrows or envying her beautiful Porto summer. So she kept it on. She went to more parties with Xandra's sister, and kissed another boy who was better at it. She went to a concert, where her Razzibot skimmed all the way over the crowd and somehow made it look as though she was in the dead center of it, as if everyone else was revolving around her.

She planned a daytrip to Sintra, because 38% of her followers voted it, but Aline's grandfather was sick and Xandra was busy and Paloma had hated her for weeks now, so in the end she went with only her Razzi. They wandered through the red-and-yellow palace, underneath the great dome and the notched parapets. Marisol smiled until her teeth ached, relaying little facts about crenellations and love scandals her Razzibot sent to her phone, skipping through archways and spinning and laughing. Her shadow slowly stretched thin as a wasp on the ancient cobblestone.

It was late when the Luxcar dropped her at home, but her Stream was thrumming with fifty new followers and everyone saying how beautiful Sintra was, how beautiful she was, how beautiful her gathered Rilla-Cruz skirt was. She let herself inside, and for a moment forgot all about the Stream.

In the living room, the autocleaner was trying to digest chunks of shattered vase on the floor. Her father was sitting very still on the couch, his hand wrapped around a Superbock, the previous five bottles lined up in front of him on the table like a firing squad. Little red cuts were scabbing over on his cheek and Marisol could nearly make out the imprint of her mother's hand.

"Where's mama?" she asked, and hated how it came out so weak and trembly.

Her father was silent for a long moment, swilling beer in his mouth. "She left," he finally said. His voice was thick and dark as tar. "What did you tell her?" He looked up at her, his mouth twisted. "What did you tell her, you stupid little bitch?"

Marisol heard the whine of her Razzibot over her shoulder as she fled, but she was too flayed open to think about it. Her pulse was crashing in her ears. Her vision swam black at the edges as she stumbled into her room and shoved the door shut behind her.

It was only when her Razzi slipped through the closing crack that she realized it was streaming again.

"Stop!" she shrieked. "Stop!"

The Razzibot bobbed hesitantly in the air, algorithms warring. Its indicator flickered off. Back on. Behind it, Marisol saw her reflection in her smart glass window, saw the inky tears spilling down her face and her skin gone pale. Her eyes were wide and terrified and everyone could see. A panicky whine rose in the back of her throat; her breath came fast and faster.

"Stop streaming!" she choked.

The Razzibot drifted to the right, changing angles. Something came dislodged inside her. Her gaze raked around the room, landed on a heavy baroque lamp beside her bed. She seized it with both hands and smashed the Razzibot out of the air, then smashed it again on the floor, swinging over and over.

"You little bitch," she chanted. "You little bitch, you stupid little bitch!"

Glass and polyplastic crunched; sparks showered the carpet, scorching small holes. Her back muscles seared but she didn't stop until the Razzibot was nothing but a dead lump of shattered shell and circuitry. Then Marisol dropped the lamp. She climbed into her bed and pulled the covers over her head, and tried to disappear.

She woke up to the soft chime of her phone and reached for it on instinct, snapping it flat and peering at the soft glowing screen. An avalanche of messages. Her mother, trying to explain. Aline, asking if she was alright. Paloma, asking if she was alright but in a bitchy way. Some sort of offer from Luminos Cosmetics.

The night came back to her. Marisol peeled the covers back and saw the husk of her Razzibot on the floor. There was still a faint smell of burnt circuits in the air. She remembered her father knocking on the door, pleading with her, weeping. It made her feel like she might need to vomit.

Then she looked down at her phone again and saw her follow count.

Half a million.

Half a million, and growing in spurts as she watched, climbing by thousands instead of tens. Her fingers shook and she nearly dropped her phone. She flicked back to her messages and realized the offer from Luminos Cosmetics wasn't for a deal, it was for a sponsorship. And there were others, too, from a burgeoning clothing line in Barcelona, from a wearable start-up in Oslo.

By the time she was through them all, her follow count was nearing a million. So raw, they were all saying, so raw and so real. Marisol watched the number rise and it filled her like morphine. She opened her door and walked tall to the kitchen, where her father was waiting with bags beneath his eyes, with fresh orange juice in a carafe and apologies in his mouth.

"I didn't tell her anything," Marisol said, cutting him off.

"I know," he said hoarsely, rubbing his gray temple.

"But I could have," Marisol continued. "And I might, still. I need a new Razzibot, please."

She poured a glass of orange juice, licked a splash off her thumb. Then she went back to her room and sat cross-legged by her old Razzi's wreckage, phone in her lap, silently watching her Stream swell and swell.

DATAFALL

Rumors webbed down the peninsula through pirate short-waves and whispered conversations. The Cloud was approaching. The Cloud was going to make a pass near the village.

Old solar laptops were taken out of hiding to charge in the watery morning sunlight. Rootkits were dug up from cellars and refurbished. Men and women pored over manuals with their cheeks brushing, and Old Derozan surprised everyone when he pulled eight thumb drives from his hollow cane, one by one, and laid them glinting on the floor.

His grandson, Solomon, was tasked with watching for the black government trucks that sometimes fought their way over the moor. Solomon had never seen the Cloud, but the anticipation was like a hantavirus. He grew to love the idea so much that his father agreed to take him out on the night, up to the knoll where they would have a good view. Old Derozan snorted at this and said they would do just as well to stay indoors. The signal would reach and there would be less chance of attracting unwanted attention.

Solomon's father was closer to childhood, and so he kept awake with *mate* and caffeine sprays until midnight dropped cold over the village. Then he put the precious tablet and its rubber casing into a nylon bag, the straps of which he tightened on Solomon's narrow shoulders, and they climbed the knoll.

The moon was a shard of scoured bone. Solomon's small chest was hollowed out with night. He let the sea breezes slap his face while his father booted up the tablet. His young ears picked up the hum first, and he tried not to shout when the Cloud crested over their heads.

The flock of machines dipped and slid like quicksilver, aloft on synchronized rotors. Some were caked in birdshit and others scarred black by the deaths of their comrades to LAMS, but the Cloud had slipped border successfully once more. As Solomon watched, carmine eyes began to blink in the blue-black sky and the tablet on his father's knees came awash with light.

Solomon tried to listen as his father explained the link-up, the web, but he couldn't. He was mesmerized by the torrent of sounds and images pouring across the screen. Flesh slapping flesh, crowds of foreigners burning cars, bristles sliding across bright white teeth. Music and voices came in clipped spurts through a disused speaker.

The screen said it was downloading, downloading, downloading. Solomon's father said there was a message from his uncle, the one who had faked his papers and shipped out on a rusty schooner.

The deluge went on and on, and Solomon could see badly-concealed lights down in the village, shadows rushing from door to door to share the invisible rain as they caught, collected. But slowly, inexorably, the red pinpricks began to blink out. The machines drifted east.

Solomon watched the tablet until it froze and his father swore, but not so angrily. Then both of them sat and rubbed their eyes and watched the Cloud disperse, until the moor sky was empty but tinged rawpink with dawn.

MOTHERFUCHING
RETROPARTY FREESTYLE

So the semester's wickest wildest party, bar none, is happening at the straight-up palatial house of Hamza Hamidi, AKA Spitt4style, whose way-too-trusting parents are currently scuba-diving in Venice. And I'm not only going to be there, I'm going to Be There, as in, running shit, because I just dropped all my savings pirating the baddest Socialight personality module on the market: the freshly-leaked Maestro 2.0.

This thing is like, borderline AI, the kind of mod billionaires and celebrities are going to be running. I never would have found it by myself, but my uncle is a huge data-criminal sparkhead who caught the leak and agreed to ship me a stick copy in exchange for every last bit of my blood-sweat-and-shears summer landscaping income, and also me not telling my mom.

Not that I would. She would want to know why I was wasting my savings on digital charisma, because she read on ZenFeed that those new mods are way too invasive, and besides, she didn't have a Socialight or a personality module in high school, everybody ran freestyle 24/7, and they all turned out just deadly. I love her and all, but Christ.

She's got a late one at the hospital, so she's not around when the little yellow Amazombie careens off the backyard trampoline and scares the piss out of our cat. I'm picking the package out of the dandelions when Dyl shows up all sweaty from a skate sesh.

He always forgets to ping when he's coming over; I think maybe because he got his Socialight so late. Before fifth grade he actually hung with the freestylers, the religious wackos or kids too poor to get even the basic-basic. He's still my best friend since forever, so whatever.

"What's good, Shad?" Dyl says, snatching up his board with one lanky hand and raking through his orange hair with the other. He spots the data stick in my fist. "Yo, you ordered the Buttafly trial on stick? I thought we were going to download it on the way to the party."

"This is no Buttafly," I say. "Something heaps better, bru."

Dyl shrugs. "Raw, raw. Can I use your bathroom?"

I lead the way down to my basement and flop on the couch, rolling the two Maestro sticks over and over in my fingers, while Dyl takes his sweet fucking time in the shower. After fifteen minutes I start pinging him, but sometimes the old ways are best, right, so finally I haul off the couch, bang my hand on the door and politely shout:

"Yo, Dildo, hurry the fuck up."

The shower squeaks off and Dyl comes out with the guest towel around his waist and his middle finger raised. "Antsy, boy," he says. "You been spamming Wendee like that?"

Dyl's got one of those slack sort of faces and he freestyle laughs like a hyena, but he's no shitwit. I am antsy. And it is because of Wendee.

I start cleaning out my Socialight port with compressed air, getting ready for the upload, while Dyl takes his frayed backpack into my room to get ready. He comes out dressed and holding the Vancouver Whitecaps hat I borrowed from him and never returned.

"Fucking bandit," he says, settling it on his head.

I'm too antsy to feel guilty. My leg is like, jumping. I hold up the stick drives to the crooked solar lamp, checking the contact points one last time.

"Yo." Dyl frowns, flopping down on the couch beside me. "What exactly are we running here, Shad?"

"Maestro two-point-fucking-oh," I say, grinning way wide. "Leaked."

Dyl looks suitably impressed, but the tips of his ears go lava red how they do when he's nervous. "Bru, that's some serious black market shit."

"It's safe as houses," I say, not actually knowing, and hand him his stick. "Got it from my uncle. You ready?"

I hold up my Maestro, solemn-like, and he does the same, still looking a little sketched. We clack the plastic together.

"Uh, cheers," he says.

"See you flipside." Then I touch it to my Socialight port, sliding it into the cheekbone under my eye, until it gives a thick click.

Holyfuckingshit.

Imagine dumping a 2-liter of fizzy shook-up pop into a birthday balloon, and that's your brain implant downloading Maestro: this huge rush of crackly code tsunamiing your skull, swelling and sparking and feeling like it's about to spew out your fucking ear canals. When it settles I'm just keeled back on the couch, totally boneless, blinking code, and I see Dyl beside me looking equally skull-pulped.

Then it turns on, and all that fizzy pop crystallizes all at once into cold sweet ice. It feels like, whoa. You know how your average personality mod, it's a little niggle in the back of your mind? Like, hey, bru, maybe don't wear that shirt again. Maybe don't tell that joke until you have the punchline down. Someone mopped the gym hallway, maybe don't slip and fall like an idiot.

Maestro 2.0 is like: I'm the You you always wanted to be, and now you're Me. And this is How We Do.

I swivel to Dyl, who's swiveling right in synch, and we give each other the slickest quickest finger-twisting handshake I've never seen in my life, along with hugely shit-eating grins.

"Yo," I say. "This is going to be good."

And for the first time, I think I absolutely have a chance with Wendee, who is basically the whole reason for why I'm going to the party, and also for why the universe exists.

Let me back up.

Wendee Rosch is ungodly beautiful, ambidextrous, and in my design class, where she mostly sits there looking bored (I'm guessing she runs a basic ChillGirl module on her Socialight—no need to upgrade with bone structure like that) and spins her stylus equal good with either hand.

It took a whole week of scoping out the glossy black back of her head for me to build up the courage with my old UnderTheRadar personality module to ping her non-anonymously. I flipped her an animated image-capture of Mr. Pacquette digging around in his nose, but edited so he pulls out something different every time. I sent it, then sat tight and sweaty and trying to guess by her posture if she thought my shit was tolerably funny.

At the bit where Pacquette yanks out a miniature version of himself, bald head and all, and gives it that look of grim satisfaction, even a ChillGirl module couldn't stop her shoulders shaking.

Her pingback scrolled across my vision: Oh my fucking god. It's like an Escher painting. Then she turned in her seat and flashed the whitest smile and sexiest thumbs up I've ever seen.

She has these ice-blue irises, so I was barely comprehending when she asked if I was going to Hamza Hamidi's party on Saturday.

"He just pinged me and Kolette in the caf yesterday with an invite," she said. "I think he latched some kind of mixtape to it. But it must be, like, a joke rap thing?"

Of course she'd gotten pinged yesterday; yesterday she was wearing tight tight ciggy jeans and this strappy shirt that scrolled Abercrombie slogans down her bare back.

"Yeah, I'm going with my bru Dyl and some, uh, other brus," I said, rubbing my buzzcut, hoping the fade still looked sharp. "Should be raw, right?"

Grody lies. Hamza Hamidi, AKA IllConsci3nce, is the swankest kid in the twelfth grade, rich enough to excuse his shitty blip-hop mixtapes and the truly taintly jumpshot he displays whenever he plays a pick-up game. Rumor has it he's running a top-notch SilverTongue module, which doesn't hurt either.

Me, I'm running UnderTheRadar like every other broke motherfucker whose parents won't/can't spring for a swanker personality module. And I mean, UnderTheRadar works fine. It edits out stammers and helps deflect teacher questions so you don't end up sounding like a shitwit in front of the whole class. It even autopatches to MovingOnUp when we hit eleventh.

But at the moment, I'm a tenth grade scrub, and tenth grade scrubs do not roll up to twelfth grade parties unless they're connected. Or, you know, a good-looking girl. Case in point being Wendee. Back to that.

"Yeah, should be heaps raw," she agreed, looking impressed, or maybe just relieved. "I was sketched it would be all seniors, you know?" She smiled, then gave me an up-and-down. "You going to run any add-ons? I might go Flirty."

Holy. Fucking. Shit.

Right after class ended, I gave Wendee what I hoped was a smooth guy nod, then split to go find Dyl. There was no way I was going to slip a chance to get with arguably the most supermodel girl of our grade, but also no way I was going to crash the party of Hamza Hamidi, AKA YungMon3y, without backup.

Which pretty much brings us to now, which is me and Dyl riding the bus crosstown because Hamza Hamidi, AKA

HizzyB3ats, lives in Signet Cove, right up on the new artificial lake. The bus drops me and Dyl about a block off. It's 9:48 and November, so the sun's long gone. The burbs are lit up with those spindly Glowtrees that rich people seem to like, even though they never survive the first hard frost.

Me and Dyl follow the traffic, which is split between inherited junk cars and shiny gifted pick-ups with lift-kits and tint, most booming the same Top 40 mash-up. You can tell who's been pregaming hardest, because they all hang out their windows cussing at the autodrive, which always goes level with the speed limit and never tries to drift icy corners.

The parade of cars gets thicker and thicker as we get closer and closer, and I feel like I'm going to burst my skin, I really do. The air's chilly, electric; me and Dyl are talking shit in small packets of steam as we walk, not about any particular subject, just animated shit-talk that Maestro 2.0 is suggesting will loosen up our jaws, calibrate chest voice, get us amped up.

Maestro also vetoes pinging Wendee an are-you-there-yet.

As we join the stream heading for the big behemoth house, Dyl says what we're both thinking. "Time to lamprey someone, bru."

We spot our target simultaneously: a twelfth-grade girl coming back from a booze run, whose face I recognize from cafeteria wallscreens: Ash Rigsby, captain of the girl's soccer squad and star player on the volleyball team. She's got sun-blonde hair and muscly calves and is repping an Edmonton FC jersey. Normally I don't try talking to seniors, never mind heaps popular ones, but Maestro says go and we're already moving.

We close up right behind her, watching her balance a sixer of Coors and a bottle of Moscato, Socialight buzzing away to someone inside. Then Maestro kicks in and all of a sudden I can not only see what mod she's running, which is LifeOfTheParty, but the whole of her digital life laid out in front of me. Last Eyespy she recorded, last MLS highlight she posted, last flick she downloaded, everything.

Me and Dyl swap this look, like, this shit is so illegal, then I airtalk, loud: "I cannot fucking believe you're sleeping on Edmonton again, bru. They got the best backline, best keeper, best coach. Simple as shit."

Up ahead, Ash's head turns just a bit.

"Overrated," Dyl says, equal loud, flourishing his hat. "Vancouver all the way."

I flick back to Ash's sports feed and find the highlight reel from last night. "Did you not see Exum make that fucking save yesterday? He flew, bru. Flew."

Candy from a baby, motherfucker. Ash Rigsby spins around, eyes shiny with booze and emotion, and evangelizes the whole way up to the step about Edmonton winning the Western Conference for sure this year, for-fucking-sure. Dyl rolls out token resistance; I keep the conversation snapping with quick-wiki win stats. By the time we're at the door, facing down one of those short-but-wide gym monkeys who always nominate themselves bouncer, Edmonton FC's biggest fan has an arm slung around each of us like we're the three best friends in the whole fucking world.

The porch is vibrating with blip-hop as the faux-bouncer looks us over, and it feels like my internal organs are shaking right with it. This is the moment of truth, and if we get bounced here then I dropped all my money for nothing and Wendee will flit off out of my league and stay there forever. Or at least all school year, which is the same thing.

"Let 'em in, Mack," Ash beams. "They're chill little shits."

And then we're inside, and I can breathe again. There's a whole sea of shoes and coats filling up the entryway wall to wall, and when I tune into the general VR channel I see most people remembered to tag their shit. Someone also did up guide ribbons snaking off into the house at chest-level, a bright red contrail to the Beer Pong, amber to the Kegs, lime green to the Barf Bathroom, et cetera. I have to turn down the music in my head to a tolerable level.

"Okay, Romeo," Dyl says, slapping my shoulder half for emphasis, half to balance while he kicks off his Osirises. "You go find that star-crossed vagina. I'm going to go tool someone at pong."

"Whoa, hey, what if I need a wing?" I ask.

Dyl smirks, taps his Socialight with one finger. "You got one." Then he's off, reeling himself along the red ribbon into the crush of people. I lean down and unlace my shoes while Maestro 2.0 takes electronic stock. Everyone's running at least a Kameleon, with a good sprinkling of ChillGirls and ChillBoys to balance out the LifeOfThePartys and Buttaflys.

But nobody's got what I got.

Before Ash jaunts off to Fridge For Drinks, she tells me how Hamza's parents left a little housekeeper module in their home security system, but he had someone hack it before the plane even took off. Now all kinds of fun shit that would fry a babysitter AI's innocent little mind is going down in the living room:

Stoners posted up rolling kites on the coffee table, people fucking upstairs sending fleshflashes right to the wallscreens so anywhere you look you see shadows humping, the little cleaning robot scurrying around with sixers of Stella taped around it for anyone to snag.

The party's loaded with twelfth grade brus, tall with semi-beards, and a shitload of good-looking girls, too. Usually under those circumstances I'd be beelining for the kitchen, UnderTheRadar, right, but not tonight. Tonight I dive right in, with Maestro raking names and interests off social sites and feeding me the right lines, the right body language, the right handshakes.

I'm hopping groups, sliding in smooth and then taking off at perfectly-timed peaks, leaving some motherfucker laughing their ass off, or some girl trailing a hand on my arm, sloughing them easy and hitting the next circle. I've never seen the party so clear before, so laid out, the bonds and chains of social molecules, and the more I move the more amped up I get, like what I always think doing cocaine might feel like, everything so fucking tight and clear and sharp.

I even meet the host, Hamza Hamidi himself, AKA BoothSay3r. Maestro lays out a karaoke file so I can pretend to know the words to his bonus track *(Binary, bitches, you a zero I'm the one / and I'm hung like a horse so you know I'm gonna get it dun)* and mostly locks down my wince. Before him and Wendee's friend Kolette go upstairs, they point me to the last place they saw her.

On the way there I pass Dyl at the plasticoated beer pong table, arm slung around a loud-laughing girl, and I can see the same look on his face, the same electric storm behind his smirk, his Socialight a hot pulsing blue at his temple. We give a per-fectly-synched bru nod, the nod of a Maestro messing with mere mortals, and right when everything's at this hard heady peak, the crush parts for a millisecond and I see her.

Holy fucking shit, she's beautiful. Short skirt, stripy socks, hair done up, chatting with a circle of mostly basketball players. Even without scanning, I can tell she's running Flirty, tilting her head and her hips at calculated angles that make me want to slam right in there, like, into the conversation.

Maestro points me to the gaggle just behind her instead, and since it hasn't steered me wrong yet I cruise past her, and I'm doing my best not to look even though my palms start sweating. She's saying something about Neo Cubism, but somehow making Neo Cubism sound sexy, as I slip into the next convo over. I'm about to introduce myself to a shitfaced 12th grade girl when sharp nails grab the back of my arm and spin me.

"Shad!" Up close, Wendee smells like grapefruit shampoo and lemonade vodka. "I pinged you, shitwit."

That's news to me, but I check my Socialight and see she's right. Maestro must have masked it. "My bad," I say, nailing the sorry-not-sorry inflection. "Getting heaps pinged in here."

"Yeah, no doubt," she says. "It seems like you know pretty much every motherfucker here?"

"Just making new friends," I say, like it's not a thing at all.

Wendee slaps my arm. "Well, don't forget about us little people." She bats her electric blue eyes kind of mockingly, which gives me heart-swell, and then her fingers creep back to my arm, which gives me the other kind.

Maestro is breaking down the little bit of lip bite, the hand sliding on my arm, and telling me it's on, on, on.

"Let's snag some drinks," I say. "Then you can try jogging my memory."

The little cleaning robot rolls past right on cue, so I crouch down to tear two Stellas from the duct tape. As I hand her one I can't resist pinging Dyl, just to tell him it's really happening and this was all so, so worth it.

I get a weird fuzz back, so I look over to the beer pong and see Dyl laughing, elbow cocked, set to throw. Then, as he opens his mouth to say something, his Socialight sputters right out. Through the sea of articulated shit-talk, what comes next hits like a feedback squeal on the world's biggest woofer.

"I actually pissed my pants the first time I got high," Dyl says, no trace of irony in his voice, and the instant he does his pale face goes red like his hair. Heads swivel; the shaky are-you-kidding laughs quiver through the air. His Socialight flickers on and then off again.

"Motherfucker," I whisper. He's glitching. Our stupid fucking pirated version of Maestro is glitching.

"I mean, it's not a big thing," Dyl chokes. "Used to wet the bed all the time as a kid, so it was probably, you know, related to that, I guess."

I can tell from how people's heads stop bobbing that they've cut out their music, and from the subtle winking that some of them are recording Eyespys. I stare at the burnt-out Socialight on Dyl's flushed face, trying to will it back on, but it's not working.

Dyl goes to grab his beer, to fill in the stillness, but there's no mod double-checking his proprioception and his long lanky arm knocks over one of the cups. It splashes everywhere. More people stop and stare.

"Didn't he come with you?" Wendee asks, lips twisting frowny.

Maestro says no, of course not, never seen that motherfucker in my life. Flow with the night. Cut him loose. This is How We Do.

"Nah," I say, feeling like slime. "Nah nah nah. Don't know him."

"He's really tall," she says, like that's relevant.

Dyl blinks slow, owlish. "Shit," he says to the silence. "Sorry." His eyes are terrified shiny, how they were when he had to give an oral report in fourth grade, the only kid in the whole class without a Socialight to help him out.

Wendee pushes her cold Stella can against my arm, rolls it up and down. "I feel bad watching," she says. "Wanna bounce outside?"

Yeah, I want that. Like, I probably want that more than anything. But Dyl's still frozen there, looking like he might straight-up faint, and I'm the one who gave him a black market mod in the first place, right?

Maestro is telling me to grab Wendee's hand and go, go, go.

They need to make 3.0 less pushy.

"No, I do know him," I say, handing her my Stella. "He's kind of my best friend. Sorry."

I ping every single person I've met at the party, from the bouncer bru to Hamza himself, with a slow-clap request, and then I reach up to my Socialight and switch it off. My head fizzes, then stops. Empty. No more Maestro. No more How We Do. Just me.

My palms are so sweaty I'm envisioning a spray when they smack together. I raise my hands, which are heaps heavy all of a sudden, and start it off. The sound is loud, so so loud, and at the same time the silence totally fucking swallows it.

"Fucking yes, Dyl," I shout, trying to keep my voice steady. "Motherfucking retroparty freestyle!"

Clap. Heads turn.

Clap. Some hands leave pockets or beers, slow, hesitating-like.

Clap-clap. Wendee's shoved the Stellas off on someone else, and she flicks her Socialight off and joins in, rolling her eyes but kind of grinning, too. The slow-clap picks up around the room, building, fading, not quite getting there. I clap harder, trying to keep it alive, staring across at Wendee and probably looking like I'm about to be sick.

Then Ash Rigsby slams around the corner, dragging her shirtless boyfriend in tow. "Retroparty!" she hollers. "Everyone turn off your fucking Socialights! We're doing it freestyle!"

She drapes her boyfriend's shirt over her head and starts clapping, furious-like, and he does too, kind of grudgingly, and this time it catches for real, and everyone starts hard applauding. Ash kisses her boyfriend and flips off his Socialight while her fingers are all wormed in his hair; he gets the idea and does it back. They bash noses in a totally freestyle mess, and all around the room people are switching off and joining the retroparty.

Dyl, looking dazed as fuck, raises his bony arms in a victory V, then wades over to slap me on the back. He's smiling, Wendee's smiling, I'm smiling. I spot Hamza leaning on the faux-oak stairway, holding two champagne flutes full of Jägermeister and post-coital smiling even though he doesn't know what the fuck just happened to his party. It's heaps cinematic, and for a blissy millisecond I think everything's going to pan out perfect.

The timing goes first, like, whoa. Some bru starts talking at the same time as three other people, then they stop, then they all go at the same time again. Nobody's dancing anymore because we're all desynched from the party playlist, and then the quiet goes viral with everyone kind of just standing there, even Ash, who looks like she might need the Barf Bathroom soon. I turn back to Wendee and we look at each other with zero shit to say.

"Retroparty," I say.

"Yeah," she says, but kind of smiling.

"Yeah."

"Yo, all you hellacious hedonists!" Hamza yells from the banister, raising one of his Jäger flutes. Everyone looks up. "Got an announcement for all my gorgeous guests. My new mix, HoodF3els, just dropped. Synch up, motherfuckers!"

Suddenly bad blip-hop is a life preserver in a big old ocean of awkward. The Socialights come back on in a wave, blinking calm blue, illuminating people's faces, which are no longer creased and hard worried about what to say. Hamza gives me a look from the stairway, not a meanmug, just sort of a "wick effort, little bru, but maybe don't try to retroparty until you have the ending down."

Then I notice Wendee's looking at the stairway, too, Socialight pulsing bright again, Flirty engaged, and from the color of her cheeks someone just pinged her one wick, wick fleshflash. She grins that white-ass grin. "Hey, Shad, I'll be right back, okay?"

I think Maestro might tell me to grab her, maybe tell me the only thing to try is a last ditch kiss, but I end up just watching her slither up the stairs. Hamza hands her one of the flutes. He smiles, she smiles. I don't wait for the toast.

I tune into the VR, and since none of the tracking ribbons say Suicide Cliff, I have to settle for the Porch.

I**t's only halfway snowing when I go outside, the little flakes that don't stick on the ground, but I'm still wishing I brought a jacket along for the sulk-fest. Some people are peacing out early, stumbling back down the long row of cars. A couple brus are pissing on the nearest Glowtree and telling it to grow. I plant my bony ass on the steps and look out at the burbs, all the big cubic houses and manicured lawns, and want them all to catch fire at the same fucking time.

The front door heaves open. "Hey, sad Shad."

"Hey, Dildo."

I listen to Dyl hip-check the door shut behind him. He comes over and sits in my periphs, clinking down a couple cans of Molson between us.

"I'm still freestyling," he says. "So I don't really know what to say."

I tap my switched-off Socialight. "Same. Didn't feel like getting apology-pinged."

"Bru, she's just running Flirty. So what if they dock up?" He tap-tap-taps the top of his first beer and pops it open. "Sometimes a girl just wants some, you know, general genital proximity. Flirty goes for the sure thing. Don't mean she don't like you."

"Yeah. I know. It's just, you know, it's fucking shitty." I grab the other beer and dig my thumb under the tab. It's cold enough that the aluminum stings. "How the fuck can I compete, Dyl? We run UnderTheRadar for a reason, you know?"

"Not tonight we didn't." Dyl clanks his Molson down for emphasis. "Tonight we ran shit, Shad. You almost turned Hamza Hamidi's big fest into a fucking retroparty. And I don't know about you, but I met heaps girls."

"Heaps," I admit.

For a while we just slug from our beers and watch the smokers stamp and shiver in a little circle on the sidewalk, sending little white tunnels up into the air. Some of them point down to the end of the block, where red-and-blue lights are flashing out of the gloom. All good parties end in cops. I wonder if someone inside pinged 911, just to make sure it happened.

"You wish you'd cut me loose when the glitch hit back there?" Dyl asks, quiet-like.

"Yeah," I say, but it's a lie and we both know it.

"Nah nah nah." Dyl swishes the last bit of beer around in the bottom of his can. "You know, now that I got some experience, I think I could get used to freestyling at parties. Could be kind of wick. Not UnderTheRadar, not Buttafly, not Maestro two-point-fucking-oh. Just. Freestyle, you know? Like when we were kids."

I hard think about it for a bit as the police cars ease up, whooping little bursts of siren to scatter the gun-shy bru still trying to piss on the Glowtree.

"That'd be fucking awful, Dyl."

Dyl does his stupid hyena laugh that always kind of gets me, and slings his arm over my shoulder. I sling one back.

A cop gets out of her car and stomps up the walkway, no doubt running VoiceOfAuthority or some shit like that. "Is that open alcohol I see?" she asks all weary-like, strobing us with her shoulder-light. I blink. My face and hands and feet are just finally starting to feel warm from the cold beer.

"Here's our first chance, bru," I say. "Let's talk our way out of it."

Dyl nods thoughtfully. Then we both hurtle off the side of the porch, busting toward the fence and the dark empty lot on the other side, and the night feels pretty wick. Pretty wild.

AN EVENING WITH
SEVERYN GRIMES

"**D**o you have to wear the Fawkes in here?" Girasol asked, sliding into the orthochair. Its worn wings crinkled, leaking silicon, as it adjusted to her shape. The plastic stuck cold to her shoulder blades and she shivered.

"No." Pierce made no move to pull off the smirking mask. "It makes you nervous," he explained, groping around in the guts of his open Adidas track-bag, his tattooed hand emerging with the hypnotic. "That's a good enough reason to wear it."

Girasol didn't argue, just tipped her dark head back, positioning herself over the circular hole they'd punched through the headrest. Beneath it, a bird's nest of circuitry, mismatched wiring, blinking blue nodes. And in the center of the nest: the neural jack, gleaming wet with disinfectant jelly.

She let the slick white port at the top of her spine snick open.

"No cheap sleep this time," Pierce said, flicking his nail against the inky vial. "Get ready for a deep slice, Sleeping Beauty. Prince Charming's got your shit. Highest-grade Dozr a man can steal." He plugged it into a battered needler, motioned for her arm. "I get a kiss or what?"

Girasol proffered her bruised wrist. Let him hunt around collapsed veins while she said, coldly, "Don't even think about touching me when I'm under."

Pierce chuckled, slapping her flesh, coaxing a pale blue worm to stand out in her white skin. "Or what?"

Girasol's head burst as the hypnotic went in, flooding her capillaries, working over her neurotransmitters. "Or I'll cut your fucking balls off."

The Fawkes's grin loomed silent over her; a brief fear stabbed through the descending drug. Then he laughed again, barking and sharp, and Girasol knew she had not forgotten how to speak to men like Pierce. She tasted copper in her mouth as the Dozr settled.

"Just remember who got you out of Correctional," Pierce said. "And that if you screw this up, you'd be better off back in the freeze. Sweet dreams."

The mask receded, and Girasol's eyes drifted up the wall, following the cabling that crept like vines from the equipment under her skull, all the way through a crack gouged in the ceiling, and from there to whatever line Pierce's cronies had managed to splice. The smartpaint splashed across the grimy stucco displayed months of preparation: shifting sat-maps, decrypted dossiers, and a thousand flickering image loops of one beautiful young man with silver hair.

Girasol lowered the chair. Her toes spasmed, kinking against each other as the thrumming neural jack touched the edge of her port. The Dozr kept her breathing even. A bone-deep rasp, a meaty click, and she was synched, simulated REM brain-wave flowing through a current of code, flying through wire, up and out of the shantytown apartment, flitting like a shade into Chicago's dark cityscape.

Severyn Grimes felt none of the old heat in his chest when the first round finished with a shattered nose and a shower of blood, and he realized something: the puppet shows didn't do it for him anymore.

The fighters below were massive, as always, pumped full of HGH and Taurus and various combat chemicals, sculpted by a lifetime in gravity gyms. The fight, as always, wouldn't end until their bodies were mangled heaps of broken bone and snapped tendon. Then the technicians would come and pull the digital storage cones from the slick white ports at the tops of their spines, so the puppeteers could return to their own bodies, and the puppets, if they were lucky, woke up in meat repair with a paycheck and no permanent paralysis.

It seemed almost wasteful. Severyn stroked the back of his neck, where silver hair was shorn fashionably around his own storage cone. Beneath him, the fighters hurtled from their corners, grappled, broke, and collided again. He felt nothing. Severyn's adrenaline only ever seemed to spike in boardrooms now. Primate aggression through power broking.

"I'm growing tired of this shit," he said, and his bodyguard carved a clear exit through the baying crowd. Follow-cams drifted in his direction, foregoing the match for a celebspotting opportunity: the second-wealthiest bio-businessman in Chicago, 146 years old but plugged into a beautiful young body that played well on cam. The god-like Severyn Grimes slumming at a puppet show, readying for a night of downtown debauchery? The paparazzi feed practically wrote itself.

A follow-cam drifted too close; Severyn raised one finger, and his bodyguard swatted it out of the air on the way out the door.

Girasol jolted, spiraled down to the floor. She'd drifted too close, too entranced by the geometry of his cheekbones, his slate gray eyes and full lips, his swimmer's build swathed in Armani and his graceful hands with Nokia implants glowing just under the skin. A long way away, she was dimly aware of her body in the orthochair in the decrepit apartment. She scrawled a message across the smartpaint:

HE'S LEAVING EARLY. ARE YOUR PEOPLE READY?

"They're, shit, they're on their way. Stall him." Pierce's voice was distant, an insect hum, but she could detect the sound of nerves fraying.

Girasol jumped to another follow-cam, triggering a fizz of sparks as she seized its motor circuits. The image came in upside down: Mr. Grimes clambering into the limo, the bodyguard scanning the street. Springy red hair and a brutish face suggested Neanderthal gene-mixing. Him, they would have to get rid of.

The limousine door glided shut. From six blocks away, Girasol triggered the crude mp4 file she'd prepared—sometimes the old tricks worked best—and wormed inside the vehicle's CPU on a sine wave of sound.

Severyn vaguely recognized the song breezing through the car's sponge speakers, but outdated protest rap was a significant deviation from his usual tastes.

"Music off."

Silence filled the backseat. The car took an uncharacteristically long time calculating their route before finally jetting into traffic. Severyn leaned back to watch the dark street slide past his window, lit by lime green neon and the jittering ghosts of holograms. A moment later he turned to his bodyguard, who had the Loop's traffic reports scrolling across his retinas.

"Does blood excite you, Finch?"

Finch blinked, clearing his eyes back to a watery blue. "Not particularly, Mr. Grimes. Comes with the job."

"I thought having reloaded testosterone would make the world . . . visceral again." Severyn grabbed at his testicles with a wry smile. "Maybe an old mind overwrites a young body in more ways than the technicians suspect. Maybe mortality is escapable, but old age inevitable."

"Maybe so," Finch echoed, sounding slightly uncomfortable. First-lifers often found it unsettling to be reminded they were sitting beside a man who had bought off Death itself. "Feel I'm getting old myself, sometimes."

"Maybe you'd like to turn in early," Severyn offered.

Finch shook his head. "Always up for a jaunt, Mr. Grimes. Just so long as the whorehouses are vetted."

Severyn laughed, and in that moment the limo lurched sideways and jolted to a halt. His face mashed to the cold glass of the window, giving him a close-up view of an autocab as it darted gracefully around them and back into its traffic algorithm.

Finch straightened him out with one titanic hand.

"What the fuck was that?" Severyn asked calmly, unrumpling his tie.

"Car says there's something in the exhaust port," Finch said, retinas replaced by schematic tracery. "Not an explosive. Could just be debris."

"Do check."

"Won't be a minute, Mr. Grimes."

Finch pulled a pair of wire-veined gloves from a side compartment and opened the door, ushering in a chilly undertow, then disappeared around the rear end of the limousine. Severyn leaned back to wait, flicking alternately through merger details and airbrushed brothel advertisements in the air above his lap.

"Good evening, Mr. Grimes," the car burbled. "You've been hacked."

Severyn's nostrils flared. "I don't pay you for your sense of humor, Finch."

"I'm not joking, parasite."

Severyn froze. There was a beat of silence, then he reached for the door handle. It might as well have been stone. He pushed his palm against the sunroof and received a static charge for his trouble.

"Override," he said. "Severyn Grimes. Open doors." No response. Severyn felt his heartbeat quicken, felt a prickle of sweat on his palms. He slowly let go of the handle. "Who am I speaking to?"

"Take a look through the back window. Maybe you can figure it out."

Severyn spun, peering through the dark glass. Finch was hunched over the exhaust port, only a slice of red hair in sight. The limousine was projecting a yellow hazard banner, cleaving traffic, but as Severyn watched an unmarked van careened to a halt behind them.

Masked men spilled out. Severyn thumped his fist into the glass of the window, but it was soundproof; he sent a warning spike to his security, but the car was shielded against adbombs, and theoretically against electronic intrusion, and now it was walling off his cell signal.

All he could do was watch. Finch straightened up, halfway through peeling off one smartglove when the first black-market Taser sparked electric blue. He jerked, convulsed, but still somehow managed to pull the handgun from his jacket. Severyn's fist clenched. Then the second Taser went off, painting Finch a crackling halo. The handgun dropped.

The masked men bull-rushed Finch as he crumpled, sweeping him up under the arms, and Severyn saw the wide leering smiles under their hoods: Guy Fawkes. The mask had been commandeered by various terroractivist groups over the past half-century, but Severyn knew it was the Priesthood's clearest calling card. For the first time in a long time, he felt a cold corkscrew in his stomach. He tried to put his finger on the sensation.

"He has a husband." Severyn's throat felt tight. "Two children."

"He still will," the voice replied. "He's only a wage-slave. Not a blasphemer."

Finch was a heavy man and his knees scraped along the tarmac as the Priests hauled him toward the van's sliding door. His head lolled to his chest, but Severyn saw his blue eyes were slitted open. His body tensed, then—

Finch jerked the first Priest off-balance and came up with the subcutaneous blade flashing out of his forearm, carving the man open from hip to ribcage. Blood foamed and spat and Severyn felt what he'd missed at the puppet show, a burning flare in his chest. Finch twisted away from the other Priest's arm, eyes roving, glancing off the black glass that divided them, and then a third Taser hit him. He fell with his jaws spasming; a Priest's heavy boot swung into him as he toppled.

The flare died inside Severyn's pericardium. The limousine started to move.

"He should not have done that," the voice grated, as the bleeding Priest and then Finch and then the other Priests disappeared from sight.

Severyn watched through the back window for a moment longer. Faced forward. "I'll compensate for any medical costs incurred by my employee's actions," he said. "I won't tolerate any sort of retribution to his person."

"Still talking like you've got cards. And don't pretend like you care. He's an ant to you. We all are."

Severyn assessed. The voice was synthesized, distorted, but something in the cadence made him think female speaker. Uncommon, for a Priest. He gambled.

"What is your name, madam?"

"I'm a man, parasite."

Only a split second of hesitation before the answer, but it was more than enough to confirm his guess. Severyn had staked astronomical shares on such pauses, pauses that couldn't be passed off as lag in the modern day. Signs of unsettledness. Vulnerability. It made his skin thrum. He imagined himself in a boardroom.

"No need for pretenses," Severyn said. "I merely hoped to establish a more personable base for negotiation."

"Fuck you." A warble of static. Maybe a laugh. "Fuck you. There's not going to be any negotiation. This isn't a funding op. We just caught one of the biggest parasites on the planet. The Priesthood's going to make you an example. Hook you to an auto-surgeon and let it vivisect you on live feed. Burn what's left of you to ash. No negotiations."

Severyn felt the icy churn in his stomach again. Fear. He realized he'd almost missed it.

Girasol was dreaming many things at once. Even as she spoke to her captive in realtime, she perched in the limousine's electronic shielding, shooting down message after desperate message he addressed to his security detail, his bank, his associates.

It took her nearly a minute to realize the messages were irrelevant. Grimes was trying to trigger an overuse failsafe in his implants, generate an error message that could sneak through to Nokia.

Such a clever bastard. Girasol dipped into his implants and shut them down, leaving him half-blind and stranded in realtime. She felt a sympathetic lurch as he froze, gray eyes clearing, clipped neatly away from his data flow. If only it was that easy to reach in and drag him out of that pristine white storage cone.

"There aren't many female Priests," Grimes said, as if he hadn't noticed the severance. "I seem to recall their creed hates the birth control biochip almost as much as they hate neural puppeteering." He flashed a beatific smile that made Girasol ache. "So much love for one sort of parasite, so much ichor for the other."

"I saw the light," Girasol said curtly, even though she knew she should have stopped talking the instant he started analyzing, prying, trying to break her down.

"My body is, of course, a volunteer." Grimes draped his lean arms along the backseat. "But the Priesthood does have so many interesting ideas about what individuals should and should not do with their own flesh and bone."

"Volunteers are as bad as the parasites themselves," Girasol recited from one of Pierce's Adderall-fueled rants. "Selling their souls to a digital demon. The tainted can't enter the kingdom of heaven."

"Don't tell me a hacker riding sound waves still believes in souls."

"You lost yours the second you uploaded to a storage cone."

Grimes replied with another carefully constructed probe, but Girasol's interest diverted from their conversation as Pierce's voice swelled from far away. He was shouting. Someone else was in the room. She crosschecked the limo's route against a staticky avalanche of police scanners, then dragged herself back to the orthochair, forcing her eyes open.

Through the blur of code, she saw Pierce's injured crony, the one who'd been sliced belly to sternum, being helped through the doorway. His midsection was swathed in bacterial film, but the blood that hadn't been coagulated and eaten away left a dripping carmine trail on the linoleum.

"You don't bring him here," Pierce grated. "You lobo, if someone saw you—"

"I'm not going to take him to a damn hospital." The man pulled off his Fawkes, revealing a pale and sweat-slick face. "I think it's, like, shallow. Didn't get any organs. But he's bleeding bad, need more cling film—"

"Where's the caveman?" Pierce snapped. "The bodyguard, where is he?"

The man waved a blood-soaked arm towards the doorway. "In the parkade. Don't worry, we put a clamp on him and locked the van." His companion moaned and he swore. "Now where's the aid kit? Come on, Pierce, he's going to, shit, he's going to bleed out. Those stairs nearly did him in."

Pierce stalked to the wall and snatched the dented white case from its hook. He caught sight of Girasol's gummy eyes half-open.

"How close are you to the warehouse?" he demanded.

"You know how the Loop gets on weekends," Girasol said, feeling her tongue move inside her mouth like a phantom limb. "Fifteen. Twenty."

Pierce nodded. Chewed his lips. Agitated. "Need another shot?"

"Yeah."

Girasol monitored the limo at the hazy edge of her mind as Pierce handed off the aid kit and prepped another dose of hypnotic. She thought of how soon it would be her blood on the floor, once he realized what she was doing. She thought of slate gray eyes as she watched the oily black Dozr mix with her blood, and when Pierce hit the plunger, she closed her own and plunged with it.

Severyn was methodically peeling back flooring, ruining his manicured nails, humming protest rap, when the voice came back.

"Don't bother. You won't get to the brake line that way."

He paused, staring at the miniscule tear he'd made. He climbed slowly back onto the seat and palmed open the chiller. "I was beginning to think you'd left me," he said, retrieving a glass flute.

"Still here, parasite. Keeping you company in your final moments."

"Parasite," Severyn echoed as he poured. "You know, if it weren't for people like you, puppeteering might have never developed. Religious zealots are the ones who axed cloning, after all. Just think. If not for that, we might have been uploading to fresh blank bodies instead of those desperate enough to sell themselves whole."

He looked at his amber reflection in the flute, studying the beautiful young face he'd worn for nearly two years. He knew the disembodied hacker was seeing it too, and it was an advantage, no matter how she might try to suppress it. Humans loved beauty and underestimated youth. It was one reason Severyn used young bodies instead of the thickset middle-aged Clooneys favored by most CEOs.

"And now it's too late to go back," Severyn said, swirling his drink. "Growing a clone is expensive. Finding a volunteer is cheap." He sipped and held the stinging Perdue in his mouth.

Silence for a beat.

"You have no idea what kind of person I am."

Severyn felt his hook sink in. He swallowed his drink. "I do," he replied. "I've been thinking about it quite fucking hard, what with my impending evisceration. You're no Priest. Your familiarity with my security systems and reticence to kill my bodyguard makes me think you're an employee, former or current."

"People like you assume everyone's working for them."

"Whether you are or not, you've done enough research to know I can easily triple whatever the Priesthood is paying for your services."

"There's not going to be any negotiation. You're a dead man."

Severyn nodded, studying his drink, then slopped it out across the upholstery and smashed the flute against the window. The crystal crunched. Severyn shook the now-jagged stem, sending small crumbs to the floor. It gleamed scalpel-sharp. Running his thumb along it raised hairs on the nape of his neck.

"What are you doing?" the voice blared.

"My hand slipped," Severyn said. "Old age." A fat droplet of blood swelled on his thumb, and he wiped it away. He wasn't one to mishandle his bodies or rent zombies for recreational suicide in drowning tanks, freefalls. No, Severyn's drive to survive had always been too strong for him to experiment with death. As he brought the edge to his throat he realized that killing himself would not be easy.

"That won't save you." Another static laugh, but this one forced. "We'll upload your storage cone to an artificial body within the day. Throw you into a pleasure doll with the sensitivity cranked to maximum. Imagine how much fun they'd have with that."

The near-panic was clarion clear, even through a synthesizer. Intuition pounded at Severyn's temples. The song was still in there, too.

"You played yourself in on a music file," Severyn said. "I searched it before you shut off my implants. *Decapitate the state / wipe the slate / create.* Banal, but so very catchy, wasn't it? Swan song of the Anticorp Movement."

"I liked the beat."

"Several of my employees became embroiled in those protests. They were caught trying to coordinate a viral strike on my bank."

Severyn pushed the point into the smooth flesh of his throat. "Nearly five years ago, now. I believe the chief conspirator was sentenced to twenty years in cryogenic storage."

"Stop it. Put that down."

"You must have wanted me to guess," Severyn continued, worming the glass gently, like a corkscrew. He felt a warm trickle down his neck. "Why keep talking, otherwise? You wanted me to know who got me in the end. This is your revenge."

"Do you even remember my name?" The voice was warped, but not by static. "And put that down."

The command came so fierce and raw that Severyn's hand hesitated without his meaning to. He slowly set the stem in his lap. "Or you kept talking," he said, "because you missed hearing his voice."

"Fucking parasite." The hacker's voice was tired and suddenly brittle. "First you steal twenty years of my life and then you steal my son."

"Girasol Fletcher." There it was. Severyn leaned back, releasing a long breath. "He came to me, you know." He racked his digital memory for another name, the name of his body before it was his body. "Blake came to me."

"Bullshit. You always wanted him. Had a feed of his swim meets like a pedophile."

"I helped him. Possibly even saved him."

"You made him a puppet."

Severyn balled a wipe and dabbed at the blood on Blake's slender neck. "You left him with nothing," he said. "The money drained off to pay for your cryo. And Blake fell off, too. He was a full addict when he came to me. Hypnotics. Spending all his time in virtual dreamland. You'd know about that." He paused, but the barb drew no response. "It couldn't have been for sex fantasies. I imagine he got anything he wanted in realtime. I think maybe he was dreaming his family whole again."

Silence. Severyn felt a dim guilt, but he pushed through. Survival.

"He was desperate when he found me," Severyn continued. "I told him I wanted his body. Fifteen-year contract, insured for all organic damage. It's been keeping your cryo paid off, and when the contract's up he'll be comfortable for the rest of his life."

"Don't. Act." A stream of static. "Like you did him a favor."

Severyn didn't reply for a moment. He looked at the window, but the glass was still black, opaqued. "I'm not being driven to an execution, am I?"

Girasol wound the limousine through the grimy labyrinth of the industrial district, guiding it past the agreed-upon warehouse where a half-dozen Priests were awaiting the delivery of Severyn Grimes, Chicago's most notorious parasite. Using the car's external camera, she saw the lookout's confused face emerging from behind his mask.

On the internal camera, she couldn't stop looking into Blake's eyes, hoping they would be his own again soon.

"There's a hydrofoil waiting on the docks," she said through the limousine speakers. "I hired a technician to extract you. Paid him extra to drop your storage cone in the harbor."

"The Priesthood wasn't open to negotiations concerning the body."

Far away, Girasol felt the men clustered around her, watching her prone body like predatory birds. She could almost smell the fast-food grease and sharp chemical sweat.

"No," she said dully. "Volunteers are as bad as the parasites themselves. Blake sold his soul to a digital demon. To you."

"When they find out you betrayed their interests?"

Girasol considered. "Pierce will rape me," she said. "Maybe some of the others, too. Then they'll pull some amateur knife-and-pliers interrogation shit, thinking it's some kind of conspiracy. And then they may. Or may not. Kill me." Her voice was steady until the penultimate word. She calculated distance to the pier. It was worth it. It was worth it. Blake would be free, and Grimes would be gone.

"You could skype in CPD."

Girasol had already considered. "No. With what I pulled to get out of the freeze, if they find me I'm back in permanently."

"Skype them in to wherever my bodyguard is being held."

He was insistent about the caveman. Almost as if he gave a shit. Girasol felt a small slink of self-doubt before she remembered Grimes had amassed his wealth by manipulating emotions. He'd been a puppeteer long before he uploaded. Still trying to pull her strings.

"I would," Girasol said. "But he's here with me."

Grimes paused, frowning. Girasol zoomed. She'd missed Blake's face so much, the immaculate bones of it, the wide brow and curved lips. She could still remember him chubby and always laughing.

"Can you contact him without the Priests finding out?" Grimes asked.

Girasol fluttered back to the apartment. She was guillotining texts and voice-calls as they poured in from the warehouse, keeping Pierce in the dark for as long as possible, but one of them would slip through before long. She triangulated on the locked van using the parkade security cams.

"Maybe," she said.

"If you can get him free, he might be able to help you. I have a non-duress passcode. I could give it to you." Grimes tongued the edges of his bright white teeth. "In exchange, you call off the extraction."

"Thought you might try to make a deal."

"It is what I do." Grimes's lips thinned. "You lack long-term perspective, Ms. Fletcher. Common enough among first-lifers. The notion of sacrificing yourself to free your progeny must seem exceptionally noble and very fucking romantic to you. But if the Priesthood does murder you, Blake wakes up with nobody. Nothing. Again."

"Not nothing," Girasol said reflexively.

"The money you were paid for this job?" Grimes suggested. "He'll have to go into hiding for as long as my disappearance is under investigation. The sort of people who can help him lay low are the sort of people who'll have him back on Sandman or Dozr before the month is out. He might even decide to go puppet again."

Girasol's fury boiled over, and she nearly lost her hold on the steering column. "He made a mistake. Once. He would never agree to that again."

"Even if you get off with broken bones, you'll be a wanted fugitive as soon as Correctional try to thaw you for a physical and find whatever suckerfish the Priests convinced to take your pod." Grimes flattened his hands on his knees. "What I'm proposing is that you cancel the extraction. My bodyguard helps you escape. We meet up to renegotiate terms. I could have your charges dropped, you know. I could even rewrite Blake's contract."

"You really don't want to die, do you?" Girasol's suspicion battled her fear, her fear of Pierce and his pliers and his grinning mask. "You're digital. You saying you don't have a backup of your personality waiting in the wings?"

She checked the limo's external cams and swore. A carload of Priests from the warehouse was barreling up the road behind them, guns already poking through the windows. She reached for the in-built speed limits and deleted them.

"I do," Grimes conceded, bracing himself as the limo accelerated. "But he's not me, is he?"

Girasol resolved. She bounced back to the apartment, where the Priests were growing agitated. Pierce was shaking her arm, even though he should have known better than to shake someone on a deep slice, asking her how close she was to the warehouse. She flashed TWO MINUTES across the smartpaint.

Then she found the electronic signature of the clamp that was keeping Grimes's bodyguard paralyzed inside the van. She hoped he hadn't suffered any long-term nerve damage. Hoped he would still move like quicksilver with that bioblade of his.

"Fair enough," Girasol said, stretching herself thin, reaching into the empty parkade. "All right. Tell me the passcode and I'll break him out."

Finch was focused on breathing slowly and ignoring the blooming damp spot where piss had soaked through his trousers. The police-issue clamp they'd stuck to his shoulder made most other activities impossible. Finch had experience with the spidery devices. They were designed to react to any arousal in the central nervous system by sending a paralyzing jolt through the would-be agitator's muscles. More struggle, more jolt. More panic, more jolt.

The only thing to do with a clamp was relax and not get upset about anything.

Finch used the downtime to reflect on his situation. Mr. Grimes had fallen victim to a planned ambush, that much was obvious. Electronic intrusion, supposedly impossible, must have been behind the limo's exhaust port diagnostic.

And now Mr. Grimes was being driven to an unknown location, while Finch was lying on the floor of a van with donair wrappers and rumpled anti-puppetry tracts for company. A decade ago, he might have been paranoid enough to think he was a target himself. Religious extremists had not taken kindly to Neanderthal gene mixing at first, but they also had a significant demographic overlap with people overjoyed to see pale-faced and blue-eyed athletes dominating the NFL and NBA again.

Even the flailing Bulls front office had managed to sign that half-thally power forward from Duke. Finch couldn't remember his name. Cletus something. Finch had played football, himself. Sometimes he wished he'd kept going with it, but his fiancé had cared more about intact gray matter than money. Of course, he hadn't been thrilled when Finch chose security as an alternative source of income, but . . .

In a distant corner of his mind, Finch felt the clamp loosening. He kept breathing steadily, kept his heartbeat slow, kept thinking about anything but the clamp loosening. Cletus Rivas. That was the kid's name. He'd pulled down twenty-six rebounds in the match-up against Arizona. Finch brought his hand slowly, slowly up toward his shoulder. Just to scratch. Just because he was itchy. Closer. Closer.

His fingers were millimeters from the clamp's burnished surface when the van's radio blared to life. His hand jerked; the clamp jolted. Finch tried to curse through his lockjaw and came up with mostly spit. So close.

"Listen up," came a voice from the speaker.

Finch had no alternative.

"I can turn off the clamp and unlock the van, but I need you to help me in exchange," the voice said. "I'm in apartment 401, sitting in an orthochair, deep sliced. There are three men in the room. The one you cut up, the one who Tasered you, and one more. They've still got the Tasers, and the last one has a handgun in an Adidas bag. I don't know where your gun is."

Finch felt the clamp fall away and went limp all over. His muscles ached deep like he'd done four hours in the weight room on methamphetamine—a bad idea, he knew from experience. He reached to massage his shoulder with one trembling hand.

"Grimes told me a non-duress passcode to give you," the voice continued. "So you'd know to trust me. It's Atticus."

Finch had almost forgotten that passcode. He'd wikied to find out why it made Mr. Grimes smirk but lost interest halfway through a text on Roman emperors.

"You have to hurry. They might kill me soon."

Hurrying did not sound like something Finch could do. He took three tries to push himself upright on gelatin arms. "Is Mr. Grimes safe?" he asked thickly, tongue sore and swollen from him biting it.

"He's on a leisurely drive to a waiting ferry. He'll be just fine. If you help me."

Finch crawled forward, taking a moment to drive one knee-cap into the inactive clamp for a satisfying crunch, then hoisted himself between the two front seats and palmed the glove compartment. His Mulcher was waiting inside, still assembled, still loaded. He was dealing with some real fucking amateurs. The handgun molded to his grip, licking his thumb for DNA confirmation like a friendly cat. He was so glad to find it intact he nearly licked it back.

"Please. Hurry."

"Apartment 401, three targets, one incapacitated, three weapons, one lethal," Finch recited. He tested his wobbling legs as the van door slid open. Crossing the dusty floor of the parkade looked like crossing the Gobi desert.

"One other thing. You'll have to take the stairs. Elevator's out."

Finch was hardly even surprised. He stuck the Mulcher in his waistband and started to hobble.

Half the city away, Severyn wished, for the first time, that he'd had his cars equipped with seatbelts instead of only impact foam. Trying to stay seated while the limousine slewed corners and caromed down alleyways was impossible. He was thrown from one side to the other with every jolting turn. His kidnapper had finally cleared the windows and he saw, in familiar flashes, grimy red Southside brick and corrugated steel. The decades hadn't changed it much, except now the blue-green blooms of graffiti were animated.

"Pier's just up ahead. I told my guy there's been a change of plans." Girasol's voice was strained to breaking. Too many places at once, Severyn suspected.

"How long before the ones you're with know what's going on?" he asked, bracing himself against the back window to peer at their pursuers. One Priest was driving manually, and wildly. He was hunched over the steering wheel, trying to conflate what he'd learned in virtual racing sims with reality. His partner in the passenger's seat was hanging out the window with some sort of recoilless rifle, trying to aim.

"A few minutes, max."

A dull crack spiderwebbed the glass a micrometer from Severyn's left eyeball. He snapped his head back as a full barrage followed, smashing like a hailstorm into the reinforced window.

By the time they burst from the final alley, aligned for a dead sprint toward the hazard-sign-decorated pier, the limousine's rear was riddled with bullet holes. Up ahead, Severyn could make out the shape of a hydrofoil sliding out into the oil-slick water. The technician had lost his nerve.

"He's pulling away," Severyn snapped, ducking instinctively as another round raked across the back of the car with a sound of crunching metal.

"Told him to. You're going to have to swim for it."

Severyn's stomach churned. "I don't swim."

"You don't swim? You were All-State."

"Blake was." Severyn pried off his Armani loafers, peeled off his jacket, as the limousine rattled over the metal crosshatch of the pier. "I never learned."

"Just trust the muscle memory." Girasol's voice was taut and pleading. "He knows what to do. Just let him. Let his body."

They skidded to a halt at the lip of the pier. Severyn put his hand on the door and found it blinking blue, unlocked at last.

"If you can tell him things." She sounded ragged now. Exhausted. "Tell him I love him. If you can."

Severyn considered lying for a moment. A final push to solidify his position. "It doesn't work that way," he said instead, and hauled the door open as the Priests screeched to a stop behind him. He vaulted out of the limo, assaulted by unconditioned air, night wind, the smell of brine and oiled machinery.

Severyn sucked his lungs full and ran full-bore, feeling a hurricane of adrenaline that no puppet show or whorehouse could have coaxed from his glands. His bare feet pounded the cold pier, shouts came from behind him, and then he hurled himself into the grimy water. An ancient panic shot through him as ice flooded his ears, his eyes, his nose. He felt his muscles seize. He remembered, in a swath of old memory code, that he'd nearly drowned in Lake Michigan once.

Then nerve pathways that he'd never carved for himself fired, and he found himself cutting up to the surface. His head broke the water; he twisted and saw the gaggle of Priests at the edge of the water, Fawkes masks grinning at him even as they cursed and reloaded the rifle. Severyn grinned back, then pulled away with muscles moving in perfect synch, cupped hands biting the water with every stroke.

The slap of his body on the icy surface, the tug of his breath, the water in his ears—alive, alive, alive. The whine of a bullet never came. Severyn slopped over the side of the hydrofoil a moment later. Spread-eagled on the slick deck, chest working like a bellows, he started to laugh.

"That was some dramatic shit," came a voice from above him.

Severyn squinted up and saw the technician, a twitchy-looking man with gray whiskers and extra neural ports in his shaved skull. There was a tranq gun in his hand.

"There's been a change of plans," Severyn coughed. "Regarding the extraction."

The technician nodded, leveling the tranq. "Girasol told me you'd say that. Said you're a world-class bullshit artist. I'd expect no less from Severyn fucking Grimes."

Severyn's mouth fished open and shut. Then he started to laugh again, a long gurgling laugh, until the tranq stamped through his wet skin and sent him to sleep.

Girasol saw hot white sparks when they ripped her out of the orthochair and realized it was sheer luck they hadn't shut off her brain stem. You didn't tear someone out of a deep slice. Not after two hits of high-grade Dozr. She hoped, dimly, that she wasn't going to go blind in a few days' time.

"You bitch." Pierce's breath was scalding her face. He must have taken off his mask. "You bitch. Why? Why would you do that?"

Girasol found it hard to piece the words together. She was still out of body, still imagining a swerving limousine and marauding cell signals and electric sheets of code. Her hand blurred into view, and she saw her veins were taut and navy blue.

She'd stretched herself thinner than she'd ever done before, but she hadn't managed to stop the skype from the end of the pier. And now Pierce knew what had happened.

"Why did you help him get away?"

The question came with a knee pushed into her chest, under her ribs. Girasol thought she felt her lungs collapse in on themselves. Her head was coming clear.

She'd been a god only moments ago, gliding through circuitry and sound waves, but now she was small, and drained, and crushed against the stained linoleum flooring.

"I'm going to cut your eyeballs out," Pierce was deciding. "I'm going to do them slow. You traitor. You puppet."

Girasol remembered her last flash from the limousine's external cams: Blake diving into the dirty harbor with perfect form, even if Grimes didn't know it. She was sure he'd make it to the hydrofoil. It was barely a hundred meters. She held onto the novocaine thought as Pierce's knife snicked and locked.

"What did he promise you? Money?"

"Fuck off," Girasol choked.

Pierce was straddling her now, the weight of him bruising her pelvis. She felt his hands scrabbling at her zipper. The knife tracing along her thigh. She tamped down her terror.

"Oh," she said. "You want that kiss now?"

His backhand smashed across her face, and she tasted copper. Girasol closed her eyes tight. She thought of the hydrofoil slicing through the bay. The technician leaning over Blake's prone body with his instruments, pulling the parasite up and away, reawakening a brain two years dormant. She'd left him messages. Hundreds of them. Just in case.

"Did he promise to fuck you?" Pierce snarled, finally sliding her pants down her bony hips. "Was that it?"

The door chimed. Pierce froze, and in her peripheral Girasol could see the other Priests' heads turning toward the entryway. Nobody ever used the chime. Girasol wondered how Grimes's bodyguard could possibly be so stupid, then noticed that a neat row of splintery holes had appeared all across the breadth of the door.

Pierce put his hand up to his head, where a bullet had clipped the top of his scalp, carving a furrow of matted hair and stringy flesh. It came away bright red. He stared down at Girasol, angry, confused, and the next slug blew his skull open like a shattering vase.

Girasol watched numbly as the bodyguard let himself inside. His fiery hair was slick with sweat and his face was drawn pale, but he moved around the room with practiced efficiency, putting two more bullets into each of the injured Priests before collapsing to the floor himself. He tucked his hands under his head and exhaled.

"One hundred and twelve," he said. "I counted."

Girasol wriggled out from under Pierce and vomited. Wiped her mouth. "Repairman's in tomorrow." She stared down at the intact side of Pierce's face.

"Where's Mr. Grimes?"

"Nearly docking by now. But he's not in a body." Girasol pushed damp hair out of her face. "He's been extracted. His storage cone is safe. Sealed. That was our deal."

The bodyguard was studying her intently, red brows knitted. "Let's get going, then." He picked his handgun up off the floor. "Gray eyes," he remarked. "Those contacts?"

"Yeah," Girasol said. "Contacts." She leaned over to give Pierce a bloody peck on the cheek, then got shakily to her feet and led the way out the door.

Severyn Grimes woke up feeling rested. His last memory was laughing on the deck of a getaway boat, but the soft cocoon of sheets made him suspect he'd since been moved. Something else had changed, too. His proprioception was sending an avalanche of small error reports. Limbs no longer the correct length. New body proportions. By the feel of it, he was in something artificial.

"Mr. Grimes?"

"Finch." Severyn tried to grimace at the tinny sound of his voice, but the facial myomers were relatively fixed. "The *mise á jour*, please."

Finch's craggy features loomed above him, blank and professional as ever. "Girasol Fletcher had you extracted from her son's body. After we met her technician, I transported your storage cone here to Lumen Technohospital for diagnostics. Your personality and memories came through completely intact and they stowed you in an interim avatar to speak with your lawyers. Of which there's a horde, sir. Waiting in the lobby."

"Police involvement?" Severyn asked, trying for a lower register.

"There are a few Priests in custody, sir," Finch said. "Girasol Fletcher and her son are long gone. CPD requested access to the enzyme trackers in Blake's body. It looks like she hasn't found a way to shut them off yet. Could triangulate and maybe find them if it happens in the next few hours."

Severyn blinked, and his eyelashes scraped his cheeks. He tried to frown. "What the fuck am I wearing, Finch?"

"The order was put in for a standard male android." Finch shrugged. "But there was an electronic error."

"Pleasure doll?" Severyn guessed. Electronic error seemed unlikely.

His bodyguard nodded stonily. "You can be uploaded in a fresh volunteer within twenty-four hours," he said. "They've done up a list of candidates. I can link it."

Severyn shook his head. "Don't bother," he said. "I think I want something clone-grown. See my own face in the mirror again."

"And the trackers?"

Severyn thought of Blake and Girasol tearing across the map, heading somewhere sun-drenched where their money could stretch and their faces couldn't be plucked off the news feeds. She would do small-time hackwork. Maybe he would start to swim again.

"Shut them off from our end," Severyn said. "I want a bit of a challenge when I hunt her down and have her uploaded to a waste disposal."

"Will do, Mr. Grimes."

But Finch left with a ghost of a smile on his face, and Severyn suspected his employee knew he was lying.

INNUMERABLE GLIMMERING LIGHTS

At the roof of the world, the Drill churned and churned. Four Warm Currents watched with eyes and mouth, overlaying the engine's silhouette with quicksilver sketches of sonar. Long, twisting shards of ice bloomed from the metal bit to float back along the carved tunnel. Workers with skin glowing acid yellow, hazard visibility, jetted out to meet the debris and clear it safely to the sides. Others monitored the mesh of machinery that turned the bit, smoothing contact points, spinning cogs. The whole thing was beautiful, efficient, and made Four Warm Currents secrete anticipation in a flavored cloud.

A sudden needle of sonar, pitched high enough to sting, but not so high that it couldn't be passed off as accidental. Four Warm Currents knew it was Nine Brittle Spines before even tasting the name in the water.

"Does it move faster with you staring at it?" Nine Brittle Spines signed, tentacles languid with humor-not-humor.

"No faster, no slower," Four Warm Currents replied, forcing two tentacles into a curled smile. "The Drill is as inexorable as our dedication to its task."

"Dedication is admirable, as said the ocean's vast cold to one volcano's spewing heat." Nine Brittle Spines's pebbly skin illustrated, flashing red for a brief instant before regaining a dark cobalt hue.

"You are still skeptical." Four Warm Currents clenched tight to keep distaste from inking the space between them. Nine Brittle Spines was a council member, and not one to risk offending. "But the ice's composition is changing, as I reported. The bit shears easier with every turn. We're approaching the other side."

"So it thins, and so it will thicken again." Nine Brittle Spines wriggled dismissal. "The other side is a deep dream, Four Warm Currents. Your machine is approaching more ice."

"The calculations," Four Warm Currents protested. "The sounding. If you would read the theorems—"

Nine Brittle Spines hooked an interrupting tentacle through the thicket of movement. "No need for your indignation. I have no quarrel with the Drill. It's a useful sideshow, after all. It keeps the eyes and mouths of the colony fixated while the council slides its decisions past unhindered."

"If you have no quarrel, then why do you come here?" Four Warm Currents couldn't suck back the words, or the single droplet of ichor that suddenly wobbled into the water between them. It blossomed there into a ghostly black wreath. Four Warm Currents raked a hasty tentacle through to disperse it, but the councillor was already tasting the chemical, slowly, pensively.

"I have no quarrel, Four Warm Currents, but others do." Nine Brittle Spines swirled the bitter emission around one tentacle tip, as if it were a pheromone poem or something else to be savored. Four Warm Currents, mortified, could do nothing but turn an apologetic mottled blue, almost too distracted to process what the councillor signed next.

"While the general opinion is that you have gone mad, and that your project is a hilariously inept allocation of time and resources based only on your former contributions, theories do run the full gamut. Some believe the Drill is seeking mineral deposits in the ice. Others believe the Drill will be repurposed as a weapon, to crack through the fortified cities of the vent-dwelling colonies." Nine Brittle Spines shaped a derisive laugh. "And there is even a small but growing tangent who believe in your theorems. Who believe that you are fast approaching the mythic other side, and that our ocean will seep out of the puncture like the viscera from a torn egg, dooming us all."

"The weight of the ocean will hold it where it is," Four Warm Currents signed, a sequence by now rote to the tentacles. "The law of sink and rise is one you've surely studied."

"Once again, my opinion is irrelevant to the matter," Nine Brittle Spines replied. "I am here because this radical tangent is believed to be targeting your project for sabotage. The council wishes to protect its investment." Tentacles pinwheeled in a slight hesitation, then: "You yourself may be in danger as well. The council advises you to keep a low profile. Perhaps change your name taste."

"I am not afraid for my life." Four Warm Currents signed it firmly and honestly. The project was more important than survival. More important than anything.

"Then fear, perhaps, for your mate's children."

Four Warm Currents flashed hot orange shock, bright enough for the foreman to glance over, concerned. "What?"

Nine Brittle Spines held up the tentacle tip that had tasted Four Warm Currents's anger. "Traces of ingested birth mucus. Elevated hormones. You should demonstrate more self-control, Four Warm Currents. You give away all sorts of secrets."

The councillor gave a lazy salute, then jetted off into the gloom, joined at a distance by two bodyguards with barbed tentacles. Four Warm Currents watched them vanish down the tunnel, then slowly turned back toward the Drill. The bit churned and churned. Four Warm Currents's mind churned with it.

When the work cycle closed, the Drill was tugged back down the tunnel and tethered in a hard shell still fresh enough to glisten. A corkscrewing skiff arrived to unload the guard detail, three young bloods with enough hormone-stoked muscle to overlook the still-transparent patches on their skin. They inked their names so loudly Four Warm Currents could taste them before even jetting over.

"There's been a threat of sorts," Four Warm Currents signed, secreting a small dark privacy cloud to shade the conversation from workers filing onto the now-empty skiff. "Against the project. Radicals who may attempt sabotage."

"We know," signed the guard, whose name was a pungent Two Sinking Corpses. "The councillor told us. That's why we have these." Two Sinking Corpses hefted a conical weapon Four Warm Currents dimly recognized as a screamer, built to amplify a sonar burst to lethal strength. Nine Brittle Spines had not exaggerated the seriousness of the situation.

"Pray to the Leviathans you don't have to use them," Four Warm Currents signed, then joined the workers embarking on the skiff, tasting familiar names, slinging tentacles over knotted muscles, adding to a multilayered scent joke involving an aging councillor and a frost shark.

Spirits were high. The Drill was cutting smoothly. They were approaching the other side, and though for some that only meant the end of contract and full payment, others had also been infected by Four Warm Currents's fervor.

"What will we see?" a worker signed. "Souls of the dead? The Leviathans themselves?"

"Nothing outside the physical laws," Four Warm Currents replied, but then, sensing the disappointment: "But nothing like we have ever seen before. It will be unimaginable. Wondrous. And they'll soak our names all through the memory sponges, to remember the brave explorers who first broke the ice."

A mass of tentacles waved in approval of the idea. Four Warm Currents settled back as the skiff began to move and a wave of new debates sprang up.

The City of Bone was roughly spherical, a beautiful lattice of ancient skeleton swathed in sponge and cultivated coral, glowing ethereal blue with bioluminescence. It was older than any councillor, a relic of the dim past before the archives: a Leviathan skeleton dredged from the seafloor with buoyant coral, built up and around until it could float unsupported, tethered in place above the jagged rock bed.

Devotees believed the Leviathans had sacrificed their corporeal forms to leave city husks behind; Four Warm Currents shared the more heretical view that the Leviathans were extinct, and for all their size might have been no more intelligent than the living algae feeders that still hauled their bulk along the seafloor. It was not a theory to divulge in polite discourse. Drilling through the roof of the world was agitator enough on its own.

As the skiff passed the City of Bone's carved sentinels, workers began to jet off to their respective housing blocks. Four Warm Currents was one of the last to disembark, having been afforded, as one of the council's foremost engineers, an artful gray-and-purple spire in the city center. Of course, that was before the Drill. Nine Brittle Spines's desire for a "sideshow" aside, Four Warm Currents felt the daily loss of council approval like the descending cold of a crevice. Relocation was not out of the realm of possibility.

For now, though, the house's main door shuttered open at a touch, and, more importantly, Four Warm Currents's mates were inside. Six Bubbling Thermals, sleek and swollen with eggs, drizzling ribbons of birth mucus like a halo, but with eyes still bright and darting. Three Jagged Reefs, lean and long, skin stained from a heavy work cycle in the smelting vents, submitting to a massage. Their taste made Four Warm Currents ache, deep and deeper.

"So our heroic third returns," Six Bubbling Thermals signed, interrupting the massage and prompting a ruffle of protest.

"Have you ended the world yet?" Three Jagged Reefs added. "Don't stop, Six. I'm nearly loose enough to slough."

"Nearly," Four Warm Currents signed. "I blacked a councillor. Badly."

Both mates guffawed, though Six Bubbling Thermals's had a nervous shiver to it.

"From how far?" Three Jagged Reefs demanded. "Could they tell it was yours?"

"From not even a tentacle away," Four Warm Currents admitted. "We were in conversation."

Three Jagged Reefs laughed again, the reckless, waving laugh that had made Four Warm Currents fall in love, but their other mate did not.

"Conversation about what?" Six Bubbling Thermals signed.

Four Warm Currents hesitated, tasting around to make sure a strong emotion hadn't slipped the gland again, but the water was clear and cold and anxiety-free. "Nine Brittle Spines is a skeptic of the worst kind. Intelligent, but refusing to self-educate."

"Did you not explain the density calculation?" Three Jagged Reefs signed plaintively.

Four Warm Currents moved to reply, then recognized a familiar mocking tilt in Three Jagged Reefs's tentacles and turned the answer into a crude "floating feces" gesticulation.

"Tell us the mathematics again," Three Jagged Reefs teased. "Nothing slicks me better for sex, Four. All those beautiful variables."

Six Bubbling Thermals smiled at the back-and-forth, but was still lightly spackled with mauve worry. The birth mucus spiralling out in all directions made for an easy distraction.

"We need to collect again," Four Warm Currents signed, gesturing to the trembling ribbons. "Or you'll bury us in our sleep."

"And then I'll finally have the house all to my own," Six Bubbling Thermals signed, cloying. But the mauve worry dissolved into flushed healthy pink as they all began coiling the mucus and storing it in coral tubing. Four Warm Currents stroked the egg sacs gently as they worked, imagining each one hatching into an altered world.

After they finished with the birth mucus and pricked themselves with a recreational skimmer venom, Three Jagged Reefs made them sample a truly terrible pheromone poem composed at the smelting vents between geysers.

The recitation was quickly cancelled in favor of hallucination-laced sex in which they all slid over and around Six Bubbling Thermals's swollen mantle, probing and pulping, and afterward the three of them drifted in the artificial current, slowly revolving as they discussed anything and everything:

Colony annexation, the validity of aesthetic tentacle removal, the new eatery that served everything dead and frozen with frescoes carved into the flesh, so-and-so's scent change, the best birthing tanks, the after-ache they'd had the last time they used skimmer venom. Anything and everything except for the Drill.

Much later, when the other two had slipped into a sleeping harness, Four Warm Currents jetted upward to the top of their gray-and-purple spire, coiling there to look out over the City of Bone. Revelers jetted back and forth in the distance, visible by blots of blue-green excitement and arousal. Some were workers from the Drill, Four Warm Currents knew, celebrating the end of a successful work cycle.

Four Warm Currents's namesake parent had been a laborer of the same sort. A laborer who came home to cramped quarters and hungry children, but was never too exhausted to spin them a story, tentacles whirling and flourishing like a true bard. Four Warm Currents had been a logical child, always finding gaps in the tall tales of Leviathans and heroes and oceans beyond their own. But still, the stories had sunk in deep. Enough so that Four Warm Currents might be able to sign them to the children growing in Six Bubbling Thermals's egg sacs.

There was no need for Nine Brittle Spines or the council to know it was those stories that had ignited Four Warm Currents's curiosity for the roof of the world in the first place. Soon there would be new stories to tell. In seven, maybe eight more work cycles, they would break through.

After such a long percolation, the idea was dizzying. Four Warm Currents didn't know what awaited on the other side. There were theories, of course. Many theories. Four Warm Currents had studied gas bubbles and knew that whatever substance lay beyond the ice was not water as they knew it, not nearly so heavy. It could very well be deadly. Four Warm Currents would take precautions, but—

The brush of a tentacle tip, a familiar taste. Six Bubbling Thermals had ballooned up to join the stillness. Four Warm Currents extended a welcoming clasp, and the rasp of skin on skin was a comforting one. Calming.

"Someone almost started a riot in the plaza today," Six Bubbling Thermals signed.

The calm vanished. "Over what? Over the project?"

"Yes." Six Bubbling Thermals stared out across the city with a long clicking burst, then turned to face Four Warm Currents. "They had artificial panic. In storage globes. Broke them wide open right as the market peaked. It was . . ." Tentacles wove in and out, searching for a descriptor. "Chaos."

"Are you all right?" Four Warm Currents signed hard. "You should have told me. You're birthing."

Six Bubbling Thermals waved a quick-dying laugh. "I'm still bigger than you are. And I told Three Jagged Reefs. We agreed it would be best not to add to your stress. But I've never kept secrets well, have I?"

Another stare, longer this time. Four Warm Currents joined in, scraping sound across the architecture of the city, mapping curves and crevices, spars and spires.

"Before they were dragged off, they dropped one last globe," Six Bubbling Thermals signed. "It was your name, fresh, mixed with a decay scent. They said you're a monster, and if nobody stops you, you'll end the world."

Four Warm Currents shivered, clenched hard against the noxious fear threatening to tendril into the water. "Fresh?"

"Yes."

Who had it been? Four Warm Currents thought of the many workers and observers jetting up and down the tunnel, bringing status reports, complaints, updates. Any one of them could have come close enough to coax their chief engineer's name taste into a concealed globe. With a start, Four Warm Currents realized Six Bubbling Thermals was not gazing pensively over the city, but keeping watch.

"I know you won't consider halting the project," Six Bubbling Thermals signed. "But you need to be careful. Promise me that much."

Four Warm Currents remembered the councillor's warning and stroked Six Bubbling Thermals's egg sacs with a trembling tentacle. "I'll be careful. And when we break through, this will all go away. They'll see there's no danger."

"And when will that be?" The mauve worry was creeping back across Six Bubbling Thermals's skin.

"Soon," Four Warm Currents signed. "Seven work cycles."

They enmeshed their tentacles and curled against each other, bobbing there in silence as the City of Bone's ghostly blue guide lights began to blink out one by one.

The first attack came three cycles later, after shift. A pair of free-swimmers, with their skins pumped pitch-black and a sonar cloak in tow, managed to bore halfway through the Drill's protective shell before the guards spotted them and chased them off. The news came by a messenger whom Three Jagged Reefs, unhappily awoken, nearly eviscerated. Bare moments later, Four Warm Currents stroked goodbyes to both mates and took the skiff to the project site, tentacles heavy from sleep but hearts thrumming electric.

Nine Brittle Spines somehow contrived to arrive first.

"Four Warm Currents, it is a pleasure to see you so well rested." The councillor's tentacles moved as smoothly and blandly as ever, but Four Warm Currents could see the faintest of trembling at their tips. Mortal after all.

"I came as quickly as I was able," Four Warm Currents signed, not rising to the barb. "Were either of the perpetrators identified?"

"No." Nine Brittle Spines gave the word a twist of annoyance. "Assumedly they were two of yours. They knew the thinnest point of the shell and left behind a project-tagged auger."

One tentacle produced the spiral tool and set it drifting between them. It was a miniature cousin to the behemoth Drill, used to sample ice consistency.

Four Warm Currents inspected the implement. "I'll speak with inventory, but I imagine it was taken without their knowledge."

"Do that," Nine Brittle Spines signed. "In the meanwhile, security will be increased. We'll have guards at all times from now on. Body searches for workers."

Four Warm Currents waved a vague agreement, staring up at the burnished armor shell, the hole scored in its underbelly. The workers would not be happy, but they were so close now, too close to let anything derail the project. Four Warm Currents would agree to anything, so long as the Drill was safe.

Tension became a sharp, sooty tang overlaying every conversation, so much so that Four Warm Currents was given council approval for a globe of artificially mixed happiness to waft around the tunnel entrance. It ended being mostly sucked up by the guards, who were happy enough already to swagger around with screamers and combat hooks bristling in their tentacles, interrogating any particularly worry-spackled worker who happened to look their way.

Four Warm Currents complained to the councillor, but was soundly ignored, told only that the guards had been instructed to treat the project site and its crew with the utmost respect. Enthusiasm was now a thing of the past. Workers spoke rarely and with short tempers, and every time the Drill slowed or an error was found in its calibration, the possibility of sabotage hung in the tunnel like a decay scent. Four Warm Currents found a slip in the most recent density calculation that promised to put things back a full work cycle, but still the Drill churned.

At home, they began receiving death threats. Six Bubbling Thermals found the first, a tiny automaton that waved its stiff tentacles in a prerecorded message: "We won't need a drill to puncture your eyes and every one of your eggs." Three Jagged Reefs shredded it to pieces. Four Warm Currents gave the pieces to the council's investigator.

Then, two cycles before breakthrough, black globes of artificial malice were slicked to their spire with adhesive and timed to burst while they slept. Only one went off, but it was enough to necessitate a pore-cleanse for Six Bubbling Thermals and a dedicated surveillance detail for the house.

Three Jagged Reefs fumed and fumed. "After the Drill breaks through, you'll let me borrow it, won't you?" The demand was jittery with skimmer venom, and made only once Six Bubbling Thermals, finally returned from the cleansing tanks, was out of sight range. "I'm going to find the shit-eater who blacked Six and stick them on the bit gland first."

Three Jagged Reefs had been pulled from smelting after an incidence of "hazardously elevated emotions," in which a copper-worker trilling about the impending end of the world had their tentacle held over a geyser until it turned to pulp. Staying in the house full cycle, under the watchful eyes and mouths of council surveillance, was not an easy transition. Not even stocked with high-quality venom.

"It'll all be over soon," Four Warm Current signed, mind half-filled, as was now the norm, with figures from the latest density calculation. One final cycle.

"Tell it to Six," Three Jagged Reefs signed back, short and clipped, and turned away.

Four Warm Currents swam into the next room, to where their mate was adrift in the sleeping harness. The egg sacs were bulging now, slick with the constant emission of birth mucus, bearing no trace of black ichor stains. The cleansing tanks had reported no permanent damage. Four Warm Currents sent a gentle prod of sonar and elicited a twitch.

"I'm awake," Six Bubbling Thermals signed, languid. "I'd sleep better with you two around me."

"They'll catch the lunatics who planted that globe," Four Warm Currents signed back.

Six Bubbling Thermals signed nothing for a long moment, then waved a sad laugh. "I don't think it's lunatics. Not anymore. A lot of people are saying the same thing, you know."

"Saying what?"

"You spend all of your time at the Drill, even when you're here with us." The accusation was soft, but it stung. "You haven't been paying attention. The transit currents are full of devotees calling you a blasphemer. Saying you think yourself a Leviathan. Unbounded. The whole city is frightened."

"Then it's a city of idiots," Four Warm Currents signed abruptly.

"I'm frightened. I have no shame admitting it. I'm frightened for our children. For them to have two parents only. One parent only. None. For them to never even hatch. Who knows?" Six Bubbling Thermals raised a shaky smile. "Maybe the idiot is the one who isn't frightened."

"But I'm going to give them an altered world, a new world . . ." Four Warm Currents's words blurred as Six Bubbling Thermals stilled two waving tentacles.

"I don't give a floating shit about a new world if it's one where you take a hook in the back," Six Bubbling Thermals signed back, slow and clear. "Don't go to the Drill tomorrow. They'll send for you when it breaks the ice."

At first, Four Warm Currents didn't even comprehend the words. After spending a third of a lifespan planning, building, lobbying, watching, the idea of not being there to witness the final churn, the final crack and squeal of ice giving away, was dizzying. Nauseating.

"If you go, I think you'll be dead before you come home," Six Bubbling Thermals signed. "You're worth more to us alive for one more cycle than as a name taste wafting through the archives for all eternity."

"I've watched it from the very start." Four Warm Currents tried not to tremble. "Every turn. Every single turn."

"And without you it moves no faster, no slower," Six Bubbling Thermals replied. "Isn't that what you say?"

"I have to be there."

"You don't." Six Bubbling Thermals gave a weary shudder. "Is it a new world for our children, or only for you?"

Four Warm Currents's tentacles went slack, adrift. The two of them stared at each other in the gloom, until, suddenly, something stirred in the egg sacs. The motion repeated, a faint but mesmerizing ripple. Six Bubbling Thermals gave a slight wriggle of pain.

Four Warm Currents climbed into the harness, turning acid blue in an apology that could not have been properly signed.

"I'll stay. I'll stay, I'll stay."

They folded against each other and spoke of other things, of the strange currents that had brought them together, the future looming in the birthing tanks. Then they slept, deeply, even when Three Jagged Reefs wobbled in to join them much later, nearly unhooking the harness with chemical-clumsy tentacles.

Four Warm Currents dreamt of ending the world, the Drill shearing through its final stretch of pale ice, and from the gaping wound in the roof of the world, a Leviathan lowering its head, eyes glittering, to swallow the engine and its workers and their blasphemous chief engineer whole, pulling its bulk back into the world it once abandoned, sliding through blackness toward the City of Bone, ready to reclaim its scattered body, to devour all light, to unmake everything that had ever been made.

Four Warm Currents awoke to stinging sonar and the silhouette of a familiar councillor drifting before the sleeping harness, flanked by two long-limbed guards.

"Wake your mates," Nine Brittle Spines signed, with a taut urgency Four Warm Currents had never seen before. "All three of you have to leave."

"What's happening?"

"You'll see."

Four Warm Currents rolled, body heavy with sleep, and stroked each mate awake in turn. Three Jagged Reefs refused to rise until Six Bubbling Thermals furiously shook the harness, a flash of the old pre-birthing strength.

"Someone come to murder us?" Three Jagged Reefs asked calmly, once toppled free.

"You wouldn't feel a thing with all that venom in you," Four Warm Currents replied, less calmly.

"I barely pricked."

"As said the Drill to the roof of the world," Six Bubbling Thermals interjected.

Nine Brittle Spines flashed authoritative indigo, cutting the conversation short. "Your discussions can wait. I have a skiff outside. The guards will gather your things."

The three of them followed the councillor out of the house, trailing long, sticky strands of Six Bubbling Thermals's replenished birth mucus. Once they exited the shutter and were no longer filtered, a faint acrid flavor seeped to them through the water. The City of Bone tasted bitter with fear. Anger.

And that wasn't all.

In the distance, Four Warm Currents could see free-swimmers moving as a mob, jetting back and forth through the city spires, carrying homegrown phosphorescent lamps and scent bombs. Several descended on a council-funded sculpture, smearing the stone with webbed black-and-red rage. Most continued on, heading directly for the city center.

For their housing block, Four Warm Currents realized with a sick jolt.

"The radical tangent has grown," Nine Brittle Spines signed. "Considerably."

"So many?" Four Warm Currents was stunned.

"Only thing people love more than a festival is a doomsday," Three Jagged Reefs signed bitterly.

"Indeed. Your decriers have found support in many places, I'm afraid." Nine Brittle Spines bent a grimace as they swam toward the waiting skiff, a closed and armored craft marked with an official sigil. "Including the council."

Four Warm Currents stopped dead in the water. "But the Drill is still under guard."

"The Drill is currently being converged upon by a mob twice this size," Nine Brittle Spines signed. "Even without sympathizers in the security ranks, it would be futile to try to protect it. The council's official position, as of this moment, is that your project has been terminated to save costs."

Four Warm Currents tried to move and couldn't; each mate had seized hold of enough tentacles to prevent an incidence of hazardously elevated emotions. Searing orange desperation was spewing into the water around them. Nine Brittle Spines made no remarks about self-control, only flashed, for the briefest instant, a pale blue regret.

"But we're nearly through," Four Warm Currents signed, trembling all over. Three Jagged Reefs and Six Bubbling Thermals now slowly slid off, eager for the safety of the skiff. Drifting away when they were needed most.

"Perhaps you are," Nine Brittle Spines admitted. "Perhaps your theorems are sound. But stability is, at the present moment, more important than discovery."

"If we go to the Drill." Four Warm Currents shuddered to a pause. "If we go to the Drill, if we go now, we can stop them. I can explain to them. I can convince them."

"You know better than that, Four Warm Currents. In fact—"

Whatever Nine Brittle Spines planned to say next was guillotined as Six Bubbling Thermals surged from behind, wrapping the councillor in full grip. In the same instant, Three Jagged Reefs yanked the skiff's shutter open. Four Warm Currents stared at the writhing councillor, then at each mate in turn.

"Get on with it, Four," Three Jagged Reefs signed. "Go and try."

Six Bubbling Thermals was unable to sign, tentacles taut as a vice around Nine Brittle Spines, but the misty red cloud billowing into the water was the fiercest and most pungent love Four Warm Currents could remember tasting.

"Oh, wait." Three Jagged Reefs glanced between them. "Six wanted to know if you have any necessary names."

"None," Four Warm Currents signed shakily. "So long as there are Thermals and Reefs."

"Well, of course." Three Jagged Reefs waved a haughty laugh that speared Four Warm Currents's hearts all over again. The councillor had finally stopped struggling in Six Bubbling Thermals's embrace and now watched the proceedings with an air of resignation. Four Warm Currents flashed a respectful pale blue, then turned and swam for the skiff.

They were hauling the Drill out of its carapace with hooks and bare tentacles, clouding the water with rage, excitement, amber-streaked triumph. Four Warm Currents abandoned the skiff for the final stretch, sucking back hard, jetting harder. The mob milled around the engine in a frenzy, too caught up to notice one late arrival.

Four Warm Currents screamed, dragging sonar across the crowd, but in the mess of motion and chemicals nobody felt the hard clicks. They'd brought a coring charge, one of the spiky half-spheres designed for blasting through solid rock bed to the nickel veins beneath. Four Warm Currents had shut down a foreman's lobby for such explosives during a particularly slow stretch of drilling. Too volatile, too much blowback in a confined space. But now it was here, and it was going to shred the Drill to pieces.

Four Warm Currents jetted higher, above the chaos, nearly to the mouth of the tunnel. No eyes followed. Everyone was intent on the Drill and on the coring charge being shuffled toward it, tentacle by tentacle.

Four Warm Currents sucked back, angled, and dove. The free-swimmers towing the coring charge didn't see the interloper until it was too late, until Four Warm Currents slid two tentacles deep into the detonation triggers and clung hard.

"Get away from me! Get away or I'll trigger it right here!"

The crowd turned to a fresco of frozen tentacles, momentarily speechless. Then:

"Blasphemer," signed the closest free-swimmer. "Blasphemer."

The word caught and rippled across the mob, becoming a synchronized wave of short, chopping motions.

"The Drill is not going to end the world," Four Warm Currents signed desperately, puffing up over the crowd, hauling the coring charge along. "It's going to break us into a brand-new one. One we'll visit at our choosing. The deep ocean will stay deep ocean. The Leviathans will stay skeletons. Our cities will stay safe."

Something struck like a spar of bone, sending Four Warm Currents reeling. The conical head of a screamer poked out from the crowd, held by a young guard whose skin was no longer inked with the council's sigil. The name came dimly to memory: Two Sinking Corpses. An unfamiliar taste was clouding into the water. It took a moment for Four Warm Currents to realize it was blood, blue and hot and saline.

"Listen to me!"

The plea was answered by another blast of deadly sound, this one misaimed, clipping a tentacle. Four Warm Currents nearly lost grip on the coring charge. The mob roiled below, waving curses, mottled black and orange with fury. There would be no listening.

"Stay away from me or I'll trigger it," Four Warm Currents warned once more, then jetted hard for the mouth of the tunnel. The renewed threat of detonation bought a few still seconds. Then the mob realized where the coring charge was headed, and the sleekest and fastest of them tore away in pursuit.

Four Warm Currents hurled up the dark tunnel, sucking back water in searing cold gulps and flushing faster and harder with each. Familiar grooves in the ice jumped out with a smatter of sonar, etchings warning against unauthorized entry. Four Warm Currents blew past with tentacles straight back, trailing the coring charge directly behind, gambling nobody would risk hitting it with a screamer.

A familiar bend loomed in the dark, one of the myriad small adjustments to course, and beyond it, the service lights, bundles of bioluminescent algae set along the walls, began blooming to life, painting the tunnel an eerie blue-green, casting a long-limbed shadow on the wall. Four Warm Currents chanced a look down and saw three free-swimmers, young and strong and gaining.

"Drop it!" one took the opportunity to sign. "Drop it and you'll live!"

Four Warm Currents used a tentacle to sign back one of Three Jagged Reefs's favorite gestures, reflecting that it was a bad idea when the young-blood's skin flashed with rage and all three of them put on speed. The head start was waning, the coring charge was heavy, the screamer wound was burning.

But Four Warm Currents knew the anatomy of the tunnel better than anyone, better than even the foreman. The three pursuers lost valuable time picking their way through a thicket of free-floating equipment knocked from the wall, then more again deliberating where the tunnel branched, stubby memento of a calculation error.

Four Warm Currents's hearts were wailing for rest as the final stretch appeared. The coring charge felt like lead. A boiling shadow swooped past, and Four Warm Currents realized they'd fired another screamer, one risk now outweighing the other. The roof of the world, stretched thin like a membrane, marred with the Drill's final twist, loomed above.

Another blast of sonar, this one closer. Four Warm Currents throttled out a cloak of black ink, hoping to obscure the next shot, too exhausted to try to dodge. Too exhausted to do anything now but churn warm water, drag slowly, too slowly, toward the top.

The screamer's next burst was half-deflected by the coring charge, but still managed to make every single tentacle spasm. Four Warm Currents felt the cargo slipping and tried desperately to regain purchase on its slick metal. So close, now, so close to the end of the world. Roof of the world. Either.

Thoughts blurred and collided in Four Warm Currents's bruised brain. More blood was pumping out, bright blue, foul-tasting. Four Warm Currents tried to hold onto the exact taste of Six Bubbling Thermals's love.

One tentacle stopped working. Four Warm Currents compensated with the others, shifting weight as another lance of sound missed narrowly to the side. The ice was almost within reach now, cold, scarred, layered with frost.

With one final, tendon-snapping surge, Four Warm Currents heaved the coring charge upward, slapping the detonation trigger as it went. The spiked device crunched into the ice and clung. Four Warm Currents tasted something new mixing into the blood, reaching amber tendrils through the leaking blue.

Triumph.

"Get out," Four Warm Currents signed, clumsily, slowly. "It's too late now."

The pursuers stared for a moment, adrift, then turned and shot back down the tunnel, howling a sonar warning to the others coming behind. Four Warm Currents's tentacles were going numb. Every body part ached or seared or felt like it was splitting apart. There would be no high-speed exit down the tunnel. Maybe no exit at all.

As the coring charge signed out its detonation sequence with mechanical tendrils, Four Warm Currents swam, slowly, to the side wall. A deep crevice ran along the length. Maybe deep enough.

Four Warm Currents squeezed, twisted, contorted, tucking inside the shelter bit by bit. It was an excruciating fit. Even a child would have preferred a wider fissure. Four Warm Currents's eyes squeezed shut and saw Six Bubbling Thermals smiling, saw the egg sacs glossy and bright.

The coring charge went off like a volcano erupting. Such devices were designed, in theory, to deliver all but a small fraction of the explosive yield forward. The tiny fraction of blowback was still enough to shatter cracks through the tunnel walls and send a sonic boom rippling down its depth, an expanding globe of boiling water that scalded Four Warm Currents's exposed skin.

The tentacle that hadn't managed to fit inside was turned to mush in an instant, spewing denatured flesh and blood in a hot cloud. All of Four Warm Currents's senses sang with the explosion, tasting the fierce chemicals, feeling the heat, seeing with sonar the flayed ice crumbling all around.

Then, at last, it was over. Four Warm Currents slithered out of the crack, sloughing skin on its edges, and drifted slowly upward. It was a maelstrom of shredded ice and swirling gases, bubbles twisting in furious wreaths.

Four Warm Currents floated up through the vortex, numb to the stinging debris and swathes of scalding water. The roof of the world was gone, leaving a jagged dark hole in the ice, a void that had been a dream and a nightmare for cycles and cycles. Four Warm Currents rose to it, entranced.

One trembling tentacle reached upward and across the rubicon. The sensation was indescribable. Four Warm Currents pulled the tentacle back, stared with bleary eyes, and found it still intact. The other side was scorching cold, a thousand tingling pinpricks, a gauze of gas like nothing below. Nothing Four Warm Currents had ever dreamed or imagined.

The chief engineer bobbed and bled, then finally gathered the strength for one last push, breaking the surface of the water completely. The feel of gas on skin was gasping, shivering. Four Warm Currents craned slowly backward, turning to face the void, and looked up.

Another ocean, far deeper and vaster than theirs, but not empty. Not dark. Not at all. Maybe it was a beautiful hallucination, brought about by the creeping failure of sense organs. Maybe it wasn't.

Four Warm Currents watched the new world with eyes and mouth, secreting final messages down into the water, love for Six Bubbling Thermals, for Three Jagged Reefs, for the children who would sign softly but laugh wildly, and then, as numbing darkness began to seep across blurring eyes, under peeling skin, a sole suggestion for a necessary name.

AUTHOR'S NOTES

All That Robot Shit

"All That Robot Shit" started gestating back when I was nine years old and obsessed with LEGO's Bionicle toys. I loved the idea of advanced robots on a tropical island developing their own culture, religion, and rudimentary technology. When I started writing seriously a decade later, I knew I wanted to take that concept for a spin.

The seed of the story lingered in a notebook for years. In 2011 I had something quite philosophical in mind, shades of C.S. Lewis's *Perelandra* and some *Lord of the Flies*. It ended with the shipwrecked human being eaten by his mechanical companions after they decide that he is not a true person, only an animal.

But when I finally wrote the story in 2016, "All That Robot Shit" became a bittersweet potty-mouthed bromance instead of a depressing philosophical treatise. I can't say I mind—this work is one of my personal favorites.

Atrophy

I know I was going to school in Edmonton when I wrote "Atrophy," but I don't remember much about the process. The eyeball replacement was definitely inspired by Neil Gaiman's *Coraline* and by "They Trade in Eyes," a Christopher Ruz short story.

In a way, "Atrophy" is responsible for introducing me to the speculative fiction community at large. I sent it to the Dell Award on a whim, but when it was named a runner-up, I took the opportunity to escape blizzard-struck Edmonton for a weekend. (The Dell Awards are presented at ICFA, a conference that takes place yearly in balmy Orlando.)

It was at ICFA that I met the editor of *Asimov's*, Sheila Williams, along with a host of writers and other professionals in the field. Putting faces to names was really cool, and I've returned to Orlando for the conference weekend several times since.

Every So Often

This was the first story I ever had published, back in 2011 in a tiny, long-gone webzine whose name is lost to my memory. It later featured in a self-published Kindle collection that was a magnificent flop.

Despite that, I still have warm feelings for "Every So Often." I wrote it during my one year in Providence, Rhode Island, when I was just starting to be aware of my writing as something people might want to publish—and pay me for. This was also long before anyone told me Hitler time-travel stories had already been done to death.

Ghost Girl

"Ghost Girl" was inspired by two disparate sources: a news article about the persecution of people with albinism in Sub-Saharan Africa, due to the belief that their severed body parts have magical properties, and the Big Daddy/Little Sister element of the video game *BioShock*. Those ideas intertwined and produced the story's central image of a little albino girl, picking through a scrapyard, with a hulking mechanical protector looming behind her.

I did some research for the setting, which is Burundi, but not as much as I might do now. For sensory details, I mostly used my memories of growing up in Niger: the throngs of scrawny goats and mopeds, the mud-brick walls topped with broken glass to deter burglars, the man with no nose, and of course the climactic dust storm.

The Sky Didn't Load Today

This flash was inspired by a walk to the gym in early winter, under a sky that was perfectly blank and colorless in all directions.

You Make Pattaya

Pattaya was probably the city I liked least when I was in Thailand during summer 2013, but it also made the most lasting impression. It's the only place I've ever described as lurid. It's also cyberpunk enough, with its neon hubbub and seedy nightlife, that I didn't need to dial things up very much while writing "You Make Pattaya."

This story racked up quite a few rejections before it found a home in *Interzone*, which makes its subsequent Year's Best appearances and translation a pleasant surprise. Sometimes people get tired of heart-wrenching or thought-provoking and really just want to read a fun con caper.

Extraction Request

I wrote "Extraction Request" while staying at my grandma's house for Christmas 2015, but I never gave it to her to read—the ending is her least favorite kind. The plot is basically *Halo: Combat Evolved*, or *Aliens* or any number of action movies where soldiers are faced with an unexpected and monstrous foe. My original plan was to knock the characters off one at a time, but it was taking too long, so I did them in clusters and then had the last two commit suicide.

More so than plot, the thing that draws me to military science fiction is the cool technology. The hardware in this story is heavily influenced by the 2013 movie *Riddick*, which I watched while drunk enough to convince myself it was pretty good.

Meshed

My roommate got me hooked on NBA basketball during my year in Rhode Island. I've been a Timberwolves fan ever since, which has proven to be a pretty masochistic pursuit. Until this season. I hope.

Blending sci-fi and basketball didn't occur to me for quite some time, but when it did, it seemed obvious. Writing "Meshed" was a ton of fun. I got a kick out of referencing then-rookie Giannis Antetokounmpo and then-YouTube sensation Thon Maker.

The climactic one-on-one is obviously inspired by *He Got Game*, but also by late nights playing on outdoor courts back in high school, and by Bruce Brooks's *The Moves Make the Man*, a novel that got inside my head as a kid and never really left. "Meshed" was also the first story I got a film rights inquiry for. It came to nothing, of course, but it was a bit of a rite of passage.

The Ghost Ship Anastasia

This one is a mishmash of *Dead Space*, *Alien*, and that level in *Halo 3* with all the sphincters. I managed to indulge both my artsy and my immature sides: there's a "wayyy up there" *Rick and Morty* reference not long after an homage to Luis Buñuel's *Un Chien Andalou*.

The first draft, written back in 2015, was a total mess. There was a lot of schlucking about through the ship's innards while the protagonists bickered and offered various theories on what happened to the original crew—not very genre-savvy of them.

I sent my bad draft to the late, great Kit Reed, who rightly suggested major surgery. "Take out a few yards of intestine and work out the psychology" is some of the best writing advice I've ever gotten. Two summers later, while staying at my grandma's, I finally sat down and wrote a new draft. The result is a hell of a lot smoother. Thanks, Kit.

Chronology of Heartbreak

This flash was inspired by an aborted romance.

Dreaming Drones

This story was definitely written in Edmonton, judging by the protagonist's LRT journey, but it also draws on memories of Grande Prairie—my first job was at Superstore, where I spent quite a bit of time poling cardboard into the dry compactor. I don't have a clear memory of writing "Dreaming Drones," so it was a pleasant surprise when I stumbled across it.

I like the slow sleepwalking pace, and the slight twists on the typical story of a robot who wants to be human. These stories aren't really about robots. I think they're about the universal human experience of feeling different, feeling not quite accepted or not quite on the same wavelength as everyone else, and how subtly painful that can be.

Let's Take This Viral

I banged out "Let's Take This Viral" over the course of a weekend with a feeling of absolute freedom. Because it's set on an artificial space station in the far future, I indulged one of my problematic writing habits, which is creating an avalanche of invented vocabulary and throwing the reader right into the thick of it. I love playing with language, and this was a perfect opportunity.

The characters in this story are both very resonant for me: the less-fun, less-adventurous friend seeking stability, and the hedonist driven by a need for salience. "Let's Take This Viral" is essentially about the possible pitfalls of immortality, about everything becoming so recycled and so stagnant that the only change left is death. I've always been scared of dying, but just as scared of an afterlife—heaven or hell—that never ends.

The ending of this story is probably my favorite of any I've written thus far.

Brute

When I was a little kid I had a VHS called *Spider-Man: The Venom Saga* that compiled three episodes of the 90s Spider-Man cartoon into a full-length film. I remember watching it obsessively in my grandparents' trailer until it became a sort of story archetype for me: the mysterious organism that grants power at a price, the initial thrill, the slow realization, the jealousy that turns deadly—it all got very deeply ingrained in my brain.

Years later, *The Spectacular Spider-Man* reignited my forgotten fascination and I decided to write "Brute." The name of the titular organism comes from *Til We Have Faces*, a book by C.S. Lewis that is one of my all-time favorite works. I have a love for this story that others might not share. It's tailored specifically to my childhood self. It goes into all those old places in my brain and flicks all the dusty switches.

Your Own Way Back

One of the best things about putting together this collection has been the chance to give readers a look at stories of mine that flew under the radar. "Your Own Way Back" was one of my first professional publications, but it's also one of the most emotional pieces I've ever written.

The name of the main character, and his love for swimming, both come from the brilliant book *Inventing Elliot* by Graham Gardner. The central conceit comes from a dream I had, where a family was waiting with red balloons in a hospital where there was a machine that brought people back from the dead—sometimes for better, sometimes for worse.

I Went to the Asteroid to Bury You

Originally this poem was set on the Moon, but the physics didn't match up right with the images I wanted so I had to switch over to an unnamed asteroid.

Capricorn

Like most of my stories, "Capricorn" is an amalgamation of works I've consumed in the past. In this case, it's mostly a mash-up of *The Chronicles of Riddick: Escape from Butcher Bay* (futuristic prison, cryostorage, shivs, violence) and *Breaking Bad* (rogue chemists, mortal illness, drugs, violence).

One of the small thrills of writing is being able to establish an ultimate badass in any given universe. In this one, it's the eponymous Capricorn, who hardly appears at all. I liked the idea of having a character hang over the whole story and influence its events without ever being physically present.

Edited

"Edited" is based off a very vivid dream I had in 2014, which birthed not only this story but also "Spiked" in *Abyss & Apex* and "Masked" in *Asimov's*.

The dream was of three teenagers breaking into a parent's summer rental, a sort of organic cabin made of coral, in order to party. There was a nervous energy to the proceedings, because one of the teens had changed, or had been changed, in some way, and the other two were unsure how to treat them.

In the dream it was unclear if they were recovering from an accident, if they had been modified by an outside force without their consent, or if they had done something surprising to themselves.

"Edited" shows one possibility.

Circuits

This is the most recent work in the collection—I wrote it in September 2017. It began gestating much earlier, however, jotted down in my idea repository as *sentient trains crisscross a desert long after the collapse of civilization.* The inspiration for this image comes, of course, from *Mario Kart 64.*

I was playing the drinking version of this game at a friend's house, and the Kalimari Desert level struck me, for the first time, as a post-apocalyptic wasteland where sentient trains and roaming smart mines (those annoying little bombs on wheels) were the only survivors.

I'm hopeful that "Circuits" still has some of the fun factor of its originator, despite the bleak setting. My grandma liked it.

Razzibot

I was mulling over the concepts for quite a while before I wrote it, thinking about the hyper-self-awareness of Instagram and how the logical extreme of a selfie would be observing yourself in third person at all times. I had the chance to talk this concept over with my writer/lawyer friend Sandra while I was visiting her in Porto.

A few months later, I sent her "Razzibot," which I had decided to set in her hometown. She corrected all the small Portuguese details I'd butchered and told me I was welcome to come back for *natas* anytime.

"Razzibot" is one of those stories people will ding for not having an essential speculative element, but I've never really bought into that. I view science fiction as a collection of aesthetics, and I loved infusing the future aesthetic into one of the most beautiful cities I've ever been to.

Datafall

I wrote this flash before I bothered learning what cloud computing actually entails.

Motherfucking Retroparty Freestyle

Like "Edited," this one draws heavily on my high school experience. Everything from the physics class to the basement where our protagonists download Maestro 2.0 to the neighborhood of the house party will seem strangely familiar to any friends of mine from high school. I even forgot to change Dyl's name, but he won't mind.

The retroparty itself is based off the most memorable party of grade twelve. Someone stole the host's Xbox; a girl refused to come out from under a parked car; a guy from Detroit brought a gun; the cops put a hole through the bathroom door trying to extract a couple reluctant to stop partying. I left wearing one of my shoes and one of someone else's. It was a good night.

An Evening with Severyn Grimes

The core concept for this one comes from Richard K. Morgan's *Altered Carbon* series, while the mastermind-bodyguard duo is inspired by Eoin Colfer's *Artemis Fowl* books, which I devoured as a kid.

It took a long time for "An Evening with Severyn Grimes" to see daylight, due to the collapse of the ambitious magazine that originally bought the story. I actually wrote it back in 2013, while living in Edmonton and working at a small Liquor Depot. We didn't do much business on the best days, and Sundays were positively glacial.

I remember I brought this freshly-finished story to work on my laptop and gave it to my co-worker Jordin to read. About thirty seconds in, he looked up at me, raised both eyebrows, and said "whoa." He didn't come out of the back office until he finished the whole thing.

Innumerable Glimmering Lights

Well, this is it. I remember two things about writing "Innumerable Glimmering Lights": the endless gymnastics I had to do in order to avoid pronouns, and how organically the title drop arrived, as if it had been there all along. Aquatic aliens have always been one of my favorite varieties, and the characters' overlong names take inspiration from K.A. Applegate's *Remnants* series.

I also have one very clear memory linked to this story, and it's from a conference weekend in Orlando. It was a beautiful warm night, and I was sitting on the edge of the pool with a friend, both of us dangling our legs in the water. The editor of *Clockwork Phoenix 5*, Mike Allen, showed up, introduced himself and handed me a copy to sign for a special edition. It was the first time I signed something I'd written, and I got this thought, like, *yeah, this writer thing is really happening.*

I hope it keeps happening for a long, long time.

ACKNOWLEDGEMENTS

First off, I want to thank the excellent Cory Allyn and the whole team at Talos Press, without whom *Tomorrow Factory* would still be a pipedream. I'm also grateful to the wide variety of editors who loved these stories enough to publish them the first time around, and to the friends and family who read them in their earliest forms.

Big thanks go out to James Patrick Kelly, a hell of a writer who writes a hell of an intro, and to two other mentors who passed too soon: Gardner Dozois and Kit Reed, both of whom gave me invaluable career advice and brought my work into the spotlight whenever they could.

Lastly, I want to thank all the readers who have supported my work and who helped determine, directly or indirectly, which stories made it into *Tomorrow Factory*. So long as you keep reading them, I'll keep writing them, and there's plenty left in the tank.

PUBLICATION CREDITS

"All That Robot Shit," originally published as "All That Robot . . ." in *Asimov's Science Fiction*, September 2016. Reprinted in *The Year's Best Science Fiction and Fantasy 2017* (Ed. Rich Horton, Prime Books). Winner of the 2017 Asimov's Readers' Poll Award for Best Short Story. Longlisted for t⊦ 2017 Sunburst Award for Best Short Story.

"Atrophy," originally published in *Descant* (2014). Second Runner-up for the 2013 Dell Award.

"Every So Often," originally published in *Birdwell Magazine*, 2011. Reprinted in *Datafall: Collected Speculative Fiction* (2012, self-published).

"Ghost Girl," originally published in *War Stories: New Military Science Fiction* (2014, Ed. Jaym Gates, Andrew Liptak, Apex Publications). Republished in audio form by StarShipSofa (2017, narrated by Elie Hirschman). Translated into Italian by *Future Fiction*.

"The Sky Didn't Load Today," originally published in *Daily Science Fiction*, February 2015. Reprinted by *The Fulcrum* (2017).

"You Make Pattaya," originally published in *Interzone #267*, November-December 2016. Reprinted in *The Best Science Fiction of the Year Volume 2* (2017, Ed. Neil Clarke, Night Shade Books), and *The Best Science Fiction & Fantasy of the Year Volume Eleven* (2017, Ed. Jonathan Strahan, Solaris). Translated into Chinese by *Science Fiction World*, 2017, and Polish by *Nowa Fantastyka*, 2018.

"Extraction Request," originally published in *Clarkesworld #112*, January 2016. Reprinted in *The Best Science Fiction of the Year Volume 2* (2017, Ed. Neil Clarke, Night Shade Books). Translated into Chinese by *Future Affairs Administration*.

"Meshed," originally published in *Clarkesworld #101*, February 2015. Reprinted in *The Best Science Fiction of the Year Volume 1* (2016, Ed. Neil Clarke, Night Shade Books), *The Year's Best Science Fiction: Thirty-Third Annual Collection* (2016, Ed. Gardner Dozois, St. Martin's Griffin), and *The Mammoth Book of Best New SF 29* (2106, Ed. Gardner Dozois, Constable & Robinson). Translated into Polish by *Nowa Fantastyka*.

"The Ghost Ship Anastasia," originally published in *Clarkesworld #124*, January 2017. Translated into Czech by XB-1.

"Chronology of Heartbreak," originally published in *Daily Science Fiction*, October 2013.

"Dreaming Drones," originally published in *AE: The Canadian Science Fiction Review*, 2014.

"Let's Take This Viral," originally published in *Lightspeed*, March 2013. Reprinted in *Great Jones Street*. Translated into Italian by *Future Fiction*.

"Brute," originally published in *Apex*, November 2014.

"Your Own Way Back," originally published in *Futuredaze: An Anthology of YA Science Fiction* (2013, Ed. Erin Underwood, Hannah Strom-Martin, Underwords Press). Translated into Italian by *Future Fiction*.

"I Went to the Asteroid to Bury You," originally published in *Abyss & Apex*, 2015.

"Capricorn," originally published in *Abyss & Apex*, 2014.

"Edited," originally published in *Interzone #259*, July/August 2015. Reprinted in *Wilde Stories 2016: The Year's Best Gay Speculative Fiction* (2106, Ed. Steve Berman, Lethe Press).

"Circuits," original to this collection.

"Razzibot," originally published in *Analog Science Fiction and Fact*, 2018.

"Datafall," originally published in poem form in *Strange Horizons*, November 2013. Revised and published in its current form in *Datafall: Collected Speculative Fiction* (2012, self-published).

"Motherfucking Retroparty Freestyle," originally published as "M.F.ing Retroparty Freestyle" in *Escape Pod #514*, December 2015.

"An Evening with Severyn Grimes," originally published in *Asimov's Science Fiction*, July-August 2017. Reprinted in *The Year's Best Science Fiction: Thirty-Fifth Annual Collection* (2018, Ed. Gardner Dozois, St. Martin's Griffin), *The Best Science Fiction of the Year Volume 3* (2018, Ed. Neil Clarke, Night Shade Books), *The Best Science Fiction & Fantasy of the Year Volume Twelve* (2018, Ed. Jonathan Strahan, Solaris), and *The Year's Top Ten Tales of Science Fiction 10* (2018, Ed. Allan Kaster, Infinivox).

"Innumerable Glimmering Lights," originally published in *Clockwork Phoenix 5* (2016, Ed. Mike Allen, Mythic Delirium Books). Reprinted in *The Year's Best Science Fiction: Thirty-Fourth Annual Collection* (2017, Ed. Gardner Dozois, St. Martin's Griffin) and *The Year's Best Science Fiction and Fantasy 2017* (Ed. Rich Horton, Prime Books).

ABOUT THE AUTHOR

Rich Larson was born in Galmi, Niger, has studied in Rhode Island and worked in the south of Spain, and now lives in Ottawa, Canada. Since he began writing in 2011, he's sold over a hundred stories, the majority of them speculative fiction published in magazines like *Asimov's, Analog, Clarkesworld, F&SF, Lightspeed,* and *Tor.com*.

His work also appears in numerous Year's Best anthologies and has been translated into Chinese, Vietnamese, Polish, Czech, French, and Italian. He was the most prolific author of short science fiction in 2015 and 2016, and possibly 2017 as well. Besides writing, he enjoys travelling, learning languages, playing soccer, watching basketball, shooting pool, and dancing salsa and kizomba.

His debut novel, *Annex*, was published by Orbit Books in July 2018. *Tomorrow Factory* is his debut collection. Find more at richwlarson.tumblr.com and support him via patreon.com/richlarson.